The
Dutch

*Also by Les Roberts
in Large Print:*

The Chinese Fire Drill

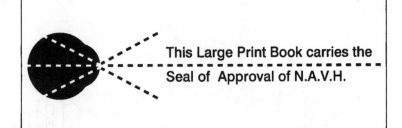

The Dutch

A Milan Jacovich Mystery

Les Roberts

Thorndike Press • Waterville, Maine

Published in 2002 by arrangement with St. Martin's Press, LLC.

Thorndike Press Large Print Americana Series.

The tree indicium is a trademark of Thorndike Press.

The text of this Large Print edition is unabridged.
Other aspects of the book may vary from the original edition.

Set in 16 pt. Plantin.

Printed in the United States on permanent paper.

Library of Congress Cataloging-in-Publication Data

Roberts, Les.
    The Dutch : a Milan Jacovich mystery / Les Roberts.
       p. cm.
    ISBN 0-7862-4096-2 (lg. print : hc : alk. paper)
    1. Jacovich, Milan (Fictitious character) — Fiction.
2. Private investigators — Ohio — Cleveland — Fiction.
3. Slovene Americans — Fiction. 4. Cleveland (Ohio) —
Fiction. 5. Suicide victims — Fiction. 6. Large type books.
I. Title.
PS3568.O23894 D88 2002
  813'.54—dc21   2001059663

For Helga Sandburg Crile

Thanks

The author's deepest gratitude goes out to several good friends whose assistance in the creation of this book was invaluable:

Lieutenant Lucie J. Duvall, Cleveland PD (retired),

Debi Buettner, who has forgotten more about computers than I'll ever know,

Helga Sandburg Crile, the mistress of Unicorn's Lair,

My wellsprings, Dr. Milan Yakovich and Diana Yakovich Montagino, who had no idea what they were getting into fifteen years ago,

My saintly editor, Ruth Cavin,

My incomparable agent, Dominick Abel,

And all of the anonymous chatroomies who provided inspiration.

Chapter One

The dark space under the Lorain-Carnegie Bridge is, I think, a singularly lousy place to die.

The bridge, with its four landmark pylons in the shape of giants, "Titans of Transportation," holding in their huge hands various modes of travel like buses and trucks and streetcars, stretches across the Cuyahoga River and connects the two avenues for which it is named, and is one of the primary arteries between the east and west sides of Cleveland. A few years back it was officially rechristened the Hope Memorial Bridge, after the father of local favorite son Bob Hope; the elder Hope worked as a stonemason during its construction. But no real Clevelander ever calls it that, just as New Yorkers still say "Sixth Avenue" instead of the newer "Avenue of the Americas," even after fifty years.

The bridge is less than a mile from my office on the west bank of the river in the industrial area known as the Flats. I wasn't anywhere near it, though, but home asleep when Ellen Carnine plunged one hundred and forty-some feet over the concrete balustrade, smashing her skull, breaking her neck and fracturing most of the other bones in her body when she landed.

The coroner estimated that the time of death was around four o'clock in the morning, but I didn't know about it until just before nine, when I was driving to work down Cedar Hill from my apartment in Cleveland Heights, sipping a go-cup of the last of my morning coffee and listening to the news and the laughs on the *John Lanigan and Jimmy Malone Show* on WMJI radio.

I winced a little when newsman Chip Kullik read the report — jumping off a bridge had to be one of the worst ways to go — and felt sad for a moment that a woman had taken her own life, but after that I didn't give it much thought. Bad things happen to nice people every day, and while poet John Donne had a valid point when he wrote that each man's death diminishes us, the fact is that the death of a complete stranger doesn't diminish us very *much*. Practically speaking, we can't allow it to. We all have our own lives and our own concerns, and we couldn't even

8

function if we went around feeling diminished every time somebody succumbs to old age or takes a notion to do a half-gainer off a bridge.

Ellen Carnine died on a Tuesday. A cool Tuesday in spring, the first week in May. After a long and dreary winter the Midwest was struggling through its annual rebirth. Lawns and trees were greening again, and the early spring flowers that bordered the houses of suburban Shaker Heights and Lakewood and Rocky River were gaily proclaiming that the season was finally turning and we could at last be almost certain that the snows were gone for the duration.

Of course in Cleveland, you never really know about snow, even in May.

By the time the following week rolled around, the cool Tuesday had given way to a warm Monday, and I had switched from my wools and tweeds to a lightweight linen sports jacket over tan chinos and a dark blue shirt without a tie, and when I parked my car in front of the old warehouse–turned–office building that I had bought several years earlier I took a moment to stroll down to the riverbank and enjoy the view across the water to Tower City and Jacobs Field and the great gray hunchbacked whale that is Gund Arena, to suck some clean spring air into my cigarette smoke–cured lungs, and watch the flock of hungry gulls darken the bright blue sky with their wings as they dipped over the water looking for breakfast.

Almost one hundred years ago this hairpin turn in the Cuyahoga River was christened Collision Bend, and while there hasn't been an aquatic fender-bender between two six-hundred-foot ore boats in some time, there is a certain romance in the name that appeals to me, perhaps because it sometimes seems we are all on collision courses in our lives, bumping into one another head-on or sideways or maybe just scraping each other's sides, acknowledging the dents and dings, and then moving along in spite of them.

I finally went upstairs to my office. It's one very large room and one small storage and utility room that takes up half of the second floor, the other half being occupied by a surgical supply house who, along with me, endures the noise of the wrought-iron company that chuffs and clanks and clangs down on the first floor. It's a constant irritant, but for that view across the river to the city I would have even suffered listening to rap music all day.

Well, maybe not rap music.

Milan Security is my one-man operation, christened out of my own ego after my own first name. It's pronounced MY-lan, by the way, and the only thing that kept me from giving my company my last name is that it's even harder to pronounce properly than Milan. Spelled J-A-C-O-V-I-C-H, pronounced YOCK-o-vitch. And if someone is looking in the Yellow Pages for an industrial security specialist such as myself, they'll probably call the one whose name they feel more comfortable in saying aloud, even though many people manage to screw that up, too, giving it the old-world pronunciation, MEE-lahn, or saying it like the city in Italy, M'-LAHN.

I set to work typing up a report commissioned by an insurance company that was trying to wriggle out from under a workman's-comp payoff. I had spent the better part of a month keeping an undercover watch on a fifty-two-year-old factory employee who had filed a huge claim for a work-related back injury; the insurers were hoping I'd catch him playing tennis, running a 10K marathon, or dancing the lambada so they could deny him his benefits, but during my surveillance I'd seen him do nothing more strenuous than limp pain-

11

fully to and from his car on his way to his physical-therapy sessions.

My clients were going to be annoyed with me, but I couldn't find fraud where there was none. So the insurance folks were going to wind up not only paying the workman's comp claim, but my fee as well.

Too bad for my clients, but in a way it gave me a good feeling to know that the injured worker I'd been surveilling wasn't trying to run a shitty on them. In my business when I find someone who is not crooked or corrupt or playing an angle, it restores my faith in the basic decency of the human animal.

I had just about finished the report when a new client called and requested an appointment for that afternoon. Despite the urgency in his tone, he opted not to give me any details over the phone. That immediately made me suspicious, but most people who seek the services of investigators like me desire discretion and confidentiality, and I figured he could have been someplace where other people might overhear, or be paranoid enough to think his telephone was bugged. Either way, it would only cost half an hour of my time to listen to him and find out, and I could afford that, at least.

He told me his name, which tinkled a very distant bell, and when I asked what firm he was with, he said, "It's a private matter."

That rang a louder bell, all right. A warning bell.

I have a private investigator's license, which means that occasionally I am compelled to take on a job that has nothing to do with industrial security. I don't like those much; they tend to get sordid. Being my own boss, I am able to pick and choose my assignments, and I regularly turn down the ones that involve window-peeping on errant spouses and other such ugliness. If someone's marriage is imploding, I'd just as soon it blew without any involvement on my part. But workman's-comp stakeouts and subcontracting security systems and vetting new employees for large corporations was for the most part pretty dry stuff, and I took on the private clients in between the more mundane assignments either as a favor to someone or simply to get my blood flowing a little faster.

The name of my two-thirty appointment was maddeningly familiar, but I couldn't retrieve it from my subconscious. Sort of like a computer file document lost in cyberspace. And despite my owning and

13

using a computer for the last few years, my knowledge and expertise is woefully inadequate. So I know about losing files.

I saved my insurance report to my hard drive and printed out two copies, one for my client and one for myself, and went out to lunch. I sorely miss the convenient and honest steak sandwiches and deliciously greasy hash browns I used to eat regularly at Jim's Steak House, an old Cleveland landmark and a favorite hangout of mine, only a fifty-yard walk from the office. But it had closed down a few years earlier only to be reincarnated as a nightclub, and now I had to drive someplace every day to eat.

On this particular day I chose a place on Old River Road on the Cuyahoga's east bank, and kept my mind occupied watching the railroad bridge go up and down to accommodate the river traffic heading out to the lake. There were quite a few pleasure craft on the water, which should have been surprising but wasn't. I guess if you can afford a forty-foot powerboat that sleeps six, you can afford to play with it on a Monday afternoon when the rest of the world is at work. Almost every one of the boats had a beautiful woman somewhere on board, dressed skimpily in warm-weather casual wear and usually waving to us landlubbers as they floated by, like the original Queen Elizabeth greeting the peasants from her carriage. Hang around the Flats near where the Cuyahoga enters Lake Erie and you'll get the notion that beautiful women are apparently de rigueur as a boating accessory.

Fortified by a tuna-and-pasta salad, one of my pathetic periodic attempts to cut down on my consumption of red meat, I got back to the office before two o'clock and waited for my appointment.

He arrived on time, at two-thirty.

He was a dapper little man, comfortably weighing about fifteen pounds more than he should have, in a brown tweed jacket that was too heavy for the weather, and a little bow tie that somehow managed not to look ridiculous on him and made me feel sadly underdressed in my open-collared shirt. Only a sparse fringe of tightly-cropped light brown hair ringed his otherwise bald pate, and he had one of those round, sweet, pinkish faces that had gone sour in the middle. I figured him to be in his middle fifties. In one short-fingered hand he clutched a leather folder that looked new.

"Mr. Jacovich, thank you for seeing me," he said when he walked in the door. "I'm William Carnine." He gave it the long *i*, rhyming it with the number nine. We shook hands and he sat down on the edge of one of my client chairs, clearly uneasy at being in the presence of a private investigator.

I get that a lot.

I offered him coffee or a soft drink, but he shook his head at the idea.

"How can I help you, Mr. Carnine?"

"It's Dr. Carnine, by the way," he said in a precise, fussy way. "I'm chairman of the biology department at Bryarly College."

I had heard of it, a small and highly regarded private school on a lovely campus midway between Cleveland and Columbus, more celebrated for its English and writing programs and not so much for biology. His little aging-cherub face turned a trifle more red as he cleared his throat and took a breath that was so deep it became almost a desperate gasp for air.

"My daughter Ellen," he said on the exhale, "is the woman who jumped off the Lorain-Carnegie Bridge last week. Perhaps you read about it?"

That was why his name had sounded familiar. Ellen Carnine. "Yes," I said. "I'm very sorry." The words rang impotent and hollow; it is not in the nature of things for parents to outlive their children, and I

16

knew he must be devastated.

"Thank you," he said, and then fell morosely silent. I didn't have the heart to prod him further, so I just waited until he was ready.

It took a while.

"Mr. Jacovich," he said when he had finally mustered his courage or marshaled his thoughts, "I have no idea why my daughter would take her own life. It's eating me up inside."

I had no doubt that it was, even though he didn't look like anything ever bothered him very much; I intuited that his sour look was perpetual, almost institutionalized. He was the kind of formal, correct man it was inconceivable to imagine wearing a polo shirt, watching a football game, or eating Doritos.

"Was she ill?"

"No, not that I know of. And the medical examiner's report didn't indicate anything like that." He kind of gestured at me with the leather folder, so I deduced that the coroner's report was inside.

"Could it have been because of a love affair gone bad?"

"I hardly think so," he said dismissively, shaking his head and closing his eyes briefly as he did so, and I found it curious

17

enough to make a mental note that he'd said it that way.

"Was she having money problems?"

"No. She wasn't wealthy, but she made a very good living, and she had a small trust fund from her grandmother."

"Career problems, then?"

"She was the senior vice president of a medium-sized Internet company here in Cleveland. Quite a remarkable achievement for a woman not yet thirty." He said it with a sort of ravaged pride.

"Clinical depression, then?"

He shook his head. "I think I would have known."

I wasn't enjoying my role; I'm a private investigator, not a behavioral psychologist, and I was suddenly tired of the guessing game. "Dr. Carnine, there are many reasons people decide, rightly or wrongly, that it's simply too much trouble to go on."

"I'm aware of that," he said. "I live on campus at the college, and Ellen moved up here five years ago, so I have no idea what her life was like. Her day-to-day life. As a father, I need to know. Mrs. Carnine and I need the closure."

He was one of those people who referred to his wife as "Mrs." in conversation, I noted. And I wondered what people used to say before the word "closure" became fashionable about twenty years ago.

"We need to find out why," he continued. "For our own peace of mind."

"I see." I should have heeded the warning bell that rang when I first heard his name; failing to do so was a lot like noticing a red traffic light and barreling through the intersection anyway. But not paying attention to the chiming of warning bells was a personal failing of mine. "And you'd like me to look into it for you?"

He nodded.

"Dr. Carnine, I think you should know that the bulk of my work is industrial. I can give you the name of other investigators here in town who would be much better equipped to . . ."

"I know your reputation, Mr. Jacovich. In the past few years you've engendered a certain amount of — publicity in this city. And we *do* get the Cleveland newspapers down in Bryarly."

I winced at that one. I bend over backwards to avoid getting my name and picture in the newspaper or on television, but things don't always work out the way I'd like them to, and I had been involved in several very high profile cases over the past few years, one involving a

Hollywood movie star.

"Besides," Carnine continued, "you come highly recommended."

"By whom?"

"When Ellen . . . When she died, we were of course in contact with the Cleveland police. The investigating officer — Detective Matusek, is it? — when I mentioned our concerns to him, he suggested that you were highly qualified in discreet inquiries of this kind."

"Matusen," I said. Bob Matusen. The protégé of my best friend, Lieutenant Marko Meglich, who had been killed two years earlier. Who had died in my arms. Trying to keep me alive. "That was kind of Detective Matusen, but I still think you'd be better off with another firm, one who specializes in situations such as yours."

"Are you turning me down?" His voice quavered, and all of a sudden the naked anguish that had been kept festering deep inside him where no one could see appeared on his face and in his sad eyes. I couldn't bear to send him away.

"No, sir," I said. "I just wanted you to be aware that this kind of thing is not my usual area of expertise."

A gush of relief flooded his features, and he offered a sad attempt at a smile that didn't even come close. "Thank you, Mr. Jacovich. I appreciate your candor. But I think you'll do very nicely. If you're willing."

"Well, let's talk for a while and then we can decide." I smiled at him, but of course he did not smile back.

He put the leather folder on my desk between us; it squeaked. It even smelled new. "You'll find everything you need in there. A list of Ellen's friends and acquaintances, her co-workers, her church, the various organizations she belonged to, even where she vacationed for the last three years. And of course the . . ." His bones seemed to collapse beneath the skin of his face. He couldn't bring himself to say it.

So I helped him. "The report from the county coroner's office?"

He swallowed hard. "Yes. And a printout of the suicide note she left for us on her computer screen." It was obviously painful for him to mention it.

"She left a note on the computer screen?"

He nodded miserably.

"And you want me to . . . ?" I let it hang up there in the atmosphere.

"To find out why. Why my daughter committed suicide when she had everything to live for."

21

Chapter Two

I hate taking cases like this, almost as much as I hate spying on cheating spouses. Maybe even more, because in one of those "domestics" there is at least a chance that someone, maybe even three or four someones, will wind up happier than when I began. But trying to ascertain the reasons for Ellen Carnine's voluntarily terminating her life held out no such hope. The possibility for a happy ending was nil before I started. And there was high emotion involved, grief and anger and worry and certainly a gnawing guilt on the part of the parents of a young suicide who wondered what they possibly might have done to prevent the tragedy.

And the bottom line was that whatever I might discover about the life and times of Ellen Carnine was not going to bring her back.

But while I found William Carnine a bit of a prig, I had to respect anyone so obviously accustomed to keeping a tight rein on his well-ordered, scholarly life who was now trying desperately not to let it go spinning off into free fall and chaos. He had maintained courageous control while he was in my office, and while as an emotional Slovenian myself I found that hard to understand, there was something so brave and so poignant about him that I decided to help him.

When he left, his signed service contract was tucked in my top drawer, and his two-thousand-dollar retainer was already endorsed and in a deposit envelope, and as the sun dipped low behind the spires and Byzantine onion domes of the churches of the west side and its hue changed from fiery-proud midafternoon white to a softer, more orange effulgence, I opened the slick leather folder and settled back to read what amounted to Ellen Carnine's life story.

You can't glean the real essence of a person you didn't know from a stack of papers unless they have been chronicled by a skilled writer. Ellen's father was a scientist and pedant, not a wordsmith, and there was precious little literary style to be found in a coroner's report. So if I wanted to learn anything at all about her to help me piece together the reasons her life had ended the way it had, I was going to have to read between the lines.

According to the notes her father had written, Ellen Marie Carnine was twenty-nine years old when she died.

She was born in Nashville, Tennessee, while her father, William Barnes Carnine, was a nontenured associate professor of biology at Vanderbilt. Her mother, Fern Simms Carnine, had been an administrator at the same school. An offer of a full professorship on the tenure track for William moved the family to Bryarly, Ohio, when Ellen was seven years old. She attended Bryarly College, matriculating with twin degrees in business administration and computer science. She worked for a software firm in nearby Akron for several years — I was surprised to read that Ohio is number four among states that are home to software companies — before moving to Cleveland to accept the position she held until her death, that of senior vice president of Wheetek, Inc., an Internet service company based in downtown Cleveland.

The CEO of Wheetek was listed as Barnard Landenberger, and beneath his name was a roster of several other Wheetek employees, along with their corporate positions. From what I could figure out from their titles, Ellen had been the company's number three, reporting to Landenberger and his executive vice president, Red Munch.

Her last three vacation trips had been, from earliest to most recent, to San Francisco, Cozumel, and London.

For the last three and a half years she had shared an apartment in the warehouse district with one Duane Starrett, a stock trader at a nationally known brokerage on East Ninth Street. I circled Starrett's name, and then circled it again. Apparently Ellen had a live-in boyfriend, and her father had strangely neglected to mention it while we were talking, even poohpoohing the idea that her death was the result of a broken heart.

There was a list of her closest friends as well. There were only four of them, their addresses and phone numbers included, and they were all women. Bronwyn Rhys, who lived in Ohio City, just across the river from downtown. Karen Conley, with an address in Lakewood, where so many under-thirty singles settle. Anna Zarafonitos, also in the warehouse district, her address being less than four blocks away from Ellen's. And Sarah Donnem, of Shaker Heights.

I read the coroner's report next.

I had seen other autopsy reports, and

they never failed to chill me. They were detailed and thorough in a clinical way, and yet minimalist — the absolute reduction of a human life to statistics and numbers and dispassionate observations that gave short shrift to any concept of humanity or soul.

When I was through I knew what Ellen Carnine had eaten for dinner the night she died, how much each of her internal organs had weighed, the names of all the bones that had been broken in her fall from the bridge, the fact that she had never been pregnant, and that she had shaved her pudendum within two days of her death.

The dead can keep few secrets, and when the death is sudden and violent, their lives and souls are violated just as much as their bodies are by the coroner's knife.

I knew that the medical examiner had determined that she had come to earth on her head, smashing her skull like a watermelon dropped from a great height, breaking her neck and compressing her spine.

I also discovered that in life she had been five feet four inches tall and had weighed two hundred and thirty-one pounds.

There was a black-and-white picture of

her in the folder as well — one of those stiff, corporate-type studio poses designed for a prospectus that is supposed to impress investors with the absolute lack of humor of the company's officials. I looked at the photograph and felt sad.

Ellen Carnine had not been an attractive woman.

Most of the people in this world are not blessed with movie-star good looks. For every Cary Grant or Elizabeth Taylor there must be a million people like me. I suppose I am no more than pleasant-looking; no one is going to stumble on the street or lose their breath at the sight of me. But while I am probably not everyone's type — six foot three, flirting with two hundred and thirty-five pounds, and fighting the curse of the Slovenes, a thinning hairline — not too many would find me downright ugly. Few people can be honestly categorized as such; even those not blessed with exceptional beauty can find ways to look attractive, if only by their expression.

That could not be said of Ellen Carnine.

She had a round face and head and her father's sour-cherry features, but surrounded as they were by layers of subcutaneous fat, they seemed pinched and unnatural-looking, and a prominent forehead and ramrod-straight eyebrows gave her what must have been a perpetual scowl. Her chin would have been ill-defined at the best of times, but the weight she carried around her jawline had rendered it almost nonexistent. Even in the retouched photo her skin looked overly powdered to hide her curds-and-whey complexion. There was a depression on her upper lip that looked as if it had been made in soft clay by a careless thumb. Her small, Betty Boop cupid's-bow mouth seemed wildly misplaced in the rest of her face. She appeared at least ten years older than she actually was.

A smile, even a noncommittal executive-type smile, might have softened her aspect in the photo, but she wore the dour expression of someone who was about to invade Poland.

Ellen Carnine's looks went beyond plain; she had been a homely woman.

What struck me most about her were her eyes. Small and dark and round like marbles, there was little life behind them, and certainly no joy. With my hands I covered the rest of her face and just regarded her eyes for a long while. They seemed deep and unutterably sorrowful.

There can be many reasons why a

person chooses to end her own life, even in a horrible way. I wondered if Ellen Carnine's reason might have had something to do with the unfortunate way she looked.

Last was a computer printout of what was apparently a suicide note. Written in 16-point type with a font that was ironically called Comic Sans MS, it simply said:

**TOO SAD – SORRY . . .
ELLEN**

I put all the material back into the leather folder, vowing to file it later, and sat back and lit a Winston, staring out the window at the slow-moving current of the river, and the memory of a classmate of mine from the fourth grade sprang unbidden to the forefront of my consciousness. She had looked nothing like Ellen Carnine; as a matter of fact, physically she was Ellen's complete opposite. But they had in common the misfortune of causing revulsion in those who looked at them.

Back then I was never really sure whether Eunice Bostic was suffering from some sort of terrible disease or if she was simply the ugliest little girl ever born. But then I was only nine years old, so what did I know?

She was skinny to the point of emaciation, her calves and ankles about the thickness of the handle of a Little League bat, and beneath the straight, flowered print dresses she always wore that had faded in the wash to mottled gray and smelled vaguely musty, her always-scabby knees were very bowed. Her teeth were severely bucked and crooked, and behind thick steel-rimmed glasses her rye-and-water–colored eyes were alarmingly crossed and squinty, and they blinked and batted incessantly. Her hair was white-blonde, lank, and hung down unevenly because her mother couldn't afford to have it cut by a professional. The elastic on the pink ankle socks she wore nearly every day had years before lost its reason to live, so that the socks puddled around her worn shoes like underpants that had humiliatingly fallen down. Her voice, unlike that of most fourth-graders, was low and rumbly and sounded as if she needed to clear her throat.

As I think back on her as one of the more misty memories of my own childhood that was in no other way remarkable, I don't think she was actually deformed.

She just had the misfortune to have been born poor, slow-witted, ungainly, and unimaginably homely.

To make matters worse, Eunice pronounced her name in a way all the other kids found funny. Not YOU-niss, which would have been funny enough, but You-NEECE, accent on the second syllable. One would think that in the old east-side Cleveland Slovenian-Croatian neighborhood on either side of St. Clair Avenue, where we all had relatively funny names like Bosco, Draco, Stupan, and my own, Milan Jacovich, that the unusual pronunciation of her name would not have given anyone else a second thought. But coupled with her grotesque appearance and the fact that she was what would now be kindly termed "educationally-challenged," the name was simply more gasoline added to the hot fire of the unspeakable cruelty of children.

"Eu-*neece*, Eu-*neece*, give us a piece," the boys would chant, although at nine and ten years old they had only the vaguest idea of what a "piece" was or what on earth they might do with one once they got it. I can never remember any of our classmates speaking directly to her unless it was to deliver some form or another of childish verbal brutality. Even in a room full of her peers Eunice Bostic must have been horribly lonely, wrapped in a remoteness so profound that it made the normal nightmares of isolation and abandonment most kids suffer from time to time seem like a festive birthday party with clowns and a pony ride.

When we would line up to go to recess or an assembly or to leave for the day, if anyone accidentally brushed up against her they would recoil in mock horror, scream, "Aaaaghh! I've got *BOSTIC!*" and wipe their hand over the part of their body that had touched her and then smear it on their neighbor, who would then go into his own exaggerated frenzy to wipe off "Bostic" and pass it on to somebody else.

I say without pride or self-congratulation that I never once joined my chums in ranking on her. If anyone rid themselves of Eunice's cooties by wiping them on me, the cooties stayed there. Of course, no one would come near me for several minutes afterward, but my shunning never lasted very long, only until they had forgotten just exactly where the plague had ended. Besides, I was always big and strong and no fun to torment; in fact, to do so was to court danger.

I am ashamed to confess, however, that my championing of Eunice Bostic was strictly passive. I never told the other kids how I felt about their barbaric insensitivity, and while I occasionally did say hello to her, which was more than any other boy and most of the girls in the class did, it was always furtive and fast, with the unspoken hope that none of the other kids had noticed.

I'm not proud of that. But there's a limit to how much guts you can expect from a nine-year-old.

Eunice had them, though — guts to spare. She would look hurt when she was tormented; the amount of abuse she was regularly subjected to made pain inevitable. Or she would raise her head proudly on her skinny neck and look away, seeming to ignore the barbs and keeping the anguish inside so as not to give her torturers the satisfaction of knowing how deeply and mortally their verbal arrows had pierced. On occasions when someone would taunt, "Hey, Bostic, why don't you take that barrel out from between your legs?" she would attempt to fight back with something like, "Oh, shut up, you filthy thing!" But such ineffective retaliation had little effect on the prepubescent lynch mob

33

that would come after her out of boredom; they had her outmanned, outflanked, and outgunned, and everyone knew it.

But Eunice never cried. Not once. Not when the sadistic chants grew loud and insanely rhythmic, not when the boys would put their faces up next to hers and cross their eyes in mockery, not when they would wipe her touch from their clothing in disgust and inflict it on each other, not even when a twelve-year-old in our class who had been held back to repeat fourth grade for the third time, bigger and taller and scarier than the rest of us, told her loudly and publicly that her cunt smelled like fish.

If she ever did cry, which I'm sure she must have, it was later, when she was away from school, alone where no one could see her.

That might not have been her wisest course. Perhaps if she had cried, if she had let them know how much pain they were inflicting, they would have eventually tired of the torture, or in time they would have matured enough to realize that what they were doing to her was cruel and monstrous. As it was, I think it became a game to see what it would take to break her.

They never found out.

Too sad — sorry — Eunice.

I heard several years later from a fairly unreliable source that Eunice had gotten pregnant by a much older man at the age of thirteen, but in actual fact I never knew what became of her.

Her mother moved away and Eunice transferred to another school after that one year, and I'd like to think that she found peace and a respite from her own personal nightmare. But I doubt it.

Because I learned a very sad fact of life from poor little Eunice Bostic: That while men can get by on strength or luck or brains or pluck or talent no matter what they look like, there is a special corner of hell-on-earth all staked out and reserved for girls who are born ugly.

Chapter Three

The old Third District police headquarters on Payne Avenue at East Twenty-first Street underwent a face-lift a few years ago, and while it no longer resembles a rockpile, the Federal architecture does nothing to camouflage the reality that it is a police station. Just as when I worked there in uniform, the very walls seemed to have absorbed all the sins and sorrows to which they've borne mute witness for over forty years, new paint job and sandblast notwithstanding, giving the place a feeling of quiet, weighty dread.

There was a time, back in the late, lamented days of the high-rollers and major players who had stalked the streets of the Third District — legendary mob names like Danny Green and Shondor Birns and Jake "Greasy Thumb" Guzik — when the area was cheerfully dubbed "the Roaring Third." That was when the downtown Cleveland crooks had class, style, moxie, and panache. Things have changed since then.

I found Detective Bob Matusen at his

desk in the bull pen, surrounded by other shirtsleeved male detectives and several plainly dressed female ones who were working the phones or pushing papers, looking not at all like the handsome or beautiful blow-dried Hollywood police on the weekly TV dramas. Most real cops are blue-collar people in a blue-collar job whose hottest showers can't wash off all the depravity they encounter in the course of a normal duty shift.

Bob's own collar on this particular morning was beige, starched stiff, and cutting into the flesh around his thick neck. Despite the running-around they do, many detectives tend to gain weight because they subsist on fast food eaten in the car — midday or midnight donuts for a quick energy boost, a wolfed-down lunch of tacos or pita sandwiches or klobasa sausages at a little ethnic joint in their patch — and invariably a few after-shift cocktails to wash away some of the ugliness, brutality, corruption, and sorrow that are a policeman's daily portion. Bob Matusen was no different. On this day his tie was brown and gold, aggressively ugly, and probably a Father's Day gift he didn't have the heart not to wear.

A telephone receiver was mashed to his

ear, and when he saw me he waved me into the chair next to his desk.

"I need it by end-of-day, Willie," he was snarling. "This isn't some fucking shop-lifting at a 7-Eleven, it's a homicide, okay?"

He listened, screwing his mouth up.

"I'm asking you nice. If I have Lieutenant McHargue call you, she's not gonna ask so nice like I am, okay? And if she does, oh brother, I wouldn't wanna be you! She's PMSing to the *max* today."

Matusen listened again, nodding, starting to smile, his shoulders relaxing under a shirt that despite the heavy starch was already starting to wrinkle, even at nine o'clock in the morning. Evidently Willie, whoever he was, was sharing a Lieutenant McHargue PMS horror story of his own. Then Bob Matusen laughed and said, "Tell me about it," and hung up.

"Fucking forensic guys," he grumbled. "You ask them to do something, put on a rush for you, they act like they've got all the fucking time in the world, like they're working for IBM or somebody, not a police department." He slapped shut a manila file on his desk. "I figured you'd be around eventually, Milan. What'sisname, the father — Carnine — he come to see you like I told him to?"

"Yes," I said. "Thanks for the recommendation, Bob. It's always nice to get some extra work. I owe you lunch."

He waved the suggestion away. "Hey, we couldn't do nothing for him. Our job is to find out *who*, not *why*. And this one is a slam-dunk. No evidence of anything hinky. The woman did the Dutch, that's all."

The Dutch. Or sometimes "the Dutch act." Longtime street slang for suicide. I wondered where it originally came from.

"Can we talk about it a little, Bob?"

He glanced at his watch. "I don't know what I can tell you about it that you don't know already, but sure. Come on outside with me, though, I could use a cigarette." He shook his crew-cut head sadly. "It's tough being in here all day now that the Loo put the kibosh on smoking."

The Loo, cop-talk for "Lieutenant," here referring to Lieutenant Florence McHargue, she of the apparent PMS, who had taken over running Homicide after Marko Meglich's death. My relationship with her was problematic.

Check me on that; my relationship with her was terrible.

I didn't know whether it was because I was Caucasian to her African American, because I was male, because I was a former

39

cop who had ankled the department to become a private investigator, or whether she simply couldn't stand the sight of me. I had become involved in two of her recent murder investigations, and I think on the last one she had developed a grudging tolerance for me that fell somewhat short of respect, but we were never going to be best buddies and I was glad I didn't have to sit at Matusen's desk and risk having her see me there and demand to know what the hell I wanted.

Matusen put on a lightweight sports jacket to cover the weapon holstered at his hip and I followed him back downstairs and out into the parking lot behind the station house. The breeze was coming in from the lake and we could smell the water. I offered him one of my Winstons and took one for myself, and he lit them both with an old-fashioned Zippo lighter, sucking in the smoke like an underwater swimmer who had just broken the surface and was gasping for air. I wondered how morale was at the Third District now that smoking in the detective bull pen had been outlawed by the new commander. Lieutenant McHargue had more guts than I do.

"So you're taking the old guy on? Carnine?"

"Yeah," I said. "I feel sorry for him. I can imagine what he's going through right now. Confusion, sorrow, guilt."

Matusen's eyes narrowed with sudden interest. "Guilt? What's he got to feel guilty about?"

"The way his daughter died. God forbid if it was your kid, Bob, wouldn't you wonder if maybe somewhere along the line you'd done something differently, it wouldn't have happened?"

"I suppose," he grudged.

"So what makes you so sure it was a suicide?"

"I've got no reason to think it was anything else. She did leave a note, if you count glaring letters on a computer screen as a note. Why? Do you know something I don't?"

"Not at all."

"You sure, Milan?"

"I have no reason to think otherwise, either. I'm just trying to get the whole picture. How did she get there? To the bridge, I mean?"

"She drove. Parked her car in that lot kitty-corner from Jacobs Field on Commercial Avenue just before it goes down the hill, and evidently walked out onto the bridge from there."

"She could have jumped in the river," I said, "but she made pretty sure she was going to hit the ground and not the water."

He nodded. "People sometimes survive jumping in the river, even from that height, and I guess she just wanted to make sure. She landed right on her head on the hard dirt. It was a mess, Milan. I've seen some bad shit in this job. You know. But I've never seen anything like this before, anyone busted-up quite so bad. They could have picked her up with a broom and a dustpan." He wiped a hand across his uneven features. "And a blotter."

An involuntary shudder skidded up my spine from my waist to my neck. "Pretty graphic, Bob."

"That's nothing. Having to look at it — *that* was graphic!" Despite the balmy temperatures of May, he hunched up his shoulders to ward off the unexpected chill wind that blew through his soul.

"Did she land on the east bank or the west?"

"The west. Just west of the train tracks. And she went over the south side of the bridge." He gave me a curious look. "What the hell difference does it make, anyway?"

"I'm not certain it does," I said. "But she lived on the east side of the river, and that's where she parked her car. Why would she walk all the way across the bridge so she'd land on the west bank?"

"How the hell should I know? Maybe she was taking a long walk trying to get her courage up."

"Okay, that makes a certain amount of sense. Anybody see her go off?"

"Who was gonna see her? It was four ay-em. Not a lot of traffic going over the bridge at that hour."

"How was she dressed?"

" 'Dressed'?"

"Yes. When she went over."

"Pajamas and a robe. Barefoot. How are *you* dressed at four o'clock in the morning?"

"She was barefoot? Where were her shoes? Or slippers, at least. Did she leave them in the car?"

"She left them in her apartment."

"So she drove from her apartment to the lot across from the Jake and walked clear across the Lorain-Carnegie Bridge barefoot?"

"Apparently so."

"You didn't find that unusual?"

"Milan, for chrissakes, she was on her way to kill herself! Who knows what was going through her head?"

"I'm getting paid to find out what was going through her head, Bob. Did she have her purse with her?"

"No, just her wallet, in the pocket of the robe. That's how we identified her so quick."

"Was the purse in her car?"

"No, she left it in her apartment."

"And the roommate didn't hear her leave?"

He shook his head gravely. "Out of town when it happened."

"Who discovered the body?"

"There was a freight train going by at about six-thirty, quarter to seven, just when it was starting to get light. Moving at a crawl, apparently. One of the brakemen happened to see her lying there and he called it in." He scratched his chin and it made a rasping noise; even this early in the morning Matusen had a five-o'clock shadow. "Even railroad brakemen have cell phones now."

"And the M.E. set the time of death at about four?"

"Yep. The Loo dragged me out of bed to go take a peek."

We sucked at our cigarettes. "Did it strike you at all odd that she was in her pajamas?"

"Not particularly. Look, she's lying in

44

bed, can't get to sleep, troubled about whatever. She decides she doesn't want to hang around in this world anymore, so she jumps up, types a quick bye-bye on the computer screen, gets in her car, and does a Brodie off the nearest bridge. She wouldn't have gone to all the bother of getting dressed."

"She wouldn't?"

"Probably not," he said. "Maybe she figured that if she took the time to put some clothes on she'd lose her nerve. It was an impulse."

"That kind of knocks hell out of the theory of her walking all the way across to the west side to get her nerve up, though, doesn't it? Besides, it isn't the nearest bridge to her home; the Detroit-Superior Bridge is."

He pinched the hot ash off the end of his cigarette and fieldstripped the butt between his fingers; like me, he had done a hitch in the army. He turned to face me squarely, squinting against the bright sunlight that was now directly in his face. "So what are you saying here?"

"I'm not saying anything, Bob, I'm just asking questions."

"Don't try to make something out of this that isn't there."

"I'm not."

"I don't need my life complicated."

"None of us do."

"The M.E. called it a suicide, the Loo is happy with that, even the father doesn't believe it was anything else, and so that's how it is on the books. Ellen Carnine did the Dutch. Case closed."

"Okay," I said, disposing of my own cigarette butt the same way he had. "But there's something about it that doesn't smell right."

"Deal with it, Milan," he said.

It was past ten-thirty when I finally got to my office. I made coffee, took out William Barnes Carnine's leather folder and read through everything in it once more. Matusen's description of how Ellen had looked when they found her made me try to avoid looking at her photo again, but it was inescapable, and I found myself glancing away quickly, instinctively.

I input the data onto a computer disk, and then printed off the pages listing Ellen's friends and co-workers. I read the autopsy report again, found it vaguely troubling, but could put my finger on nothing solid, so I set it aside.

Then I called Bronwyn Rhys, the first name on the list of Ellen's best friends, according to her father. She had a chilly, patrician voice, and seemed a little taken aback by my request to see her, but finally invited me out to her shop in Rocky River that afternoon.

I didn't have daytime numbers for two of Ellen's other buddies, Sarah Donnem and Anna Zarafonitos, but I did manage to reach the fourth on the list, Karen Conley, who said she would meet me at my office when she got off work. And I contacted Ellen's bosses at Wheetek, Barnard Landenberger and Red Munch, who agreed to see me the following morning at ten.

I knew the way to Rocky River by heart, having memorized it during a recently ended relationship with a woman whose family owned a restaurant there. I regretted the love affair ending, but it had been a while now and that particular pain had come and gone, leaving a tender spot but no real discomfort anymore. Whatever regrets that still hung on had to do with never being able to eat at the White Magnolia again. It was a very good restaurant.

Bronwyn Rhys's Detroit Road women's-wear shop was one of the priciest in town, and I noted when I walked in that the hours posted on the window in discreet gold lettering indicated it was only open

47

from noon to five, Tuesday through Saturday. Christened "BeAttitude" by its owner, it was in a little jewel-box setting in Rocky River's main shopping area, Beachcliff Market Square, which resembles not at all the soulless, carbon-copy malls that embrace Wal-marts and Target stores all over America. This was elegant, intimidating in a low-key way, and fairly reeked of money and élan.

As did Bronwyn Rhys. Tall, cool, and tawny-blonde, probably in her early thirties, she had the body of a ballet dancer, the look of a predator, and eyes as blue and cold as a curacao cocktail over ice. She was a walking mannequin advertising the fine clothes she sold to the well-off young matrons of the west side. Beneath the clinging knit dress, her bottom looked like an upside-down heart. When I handed her my business card, I felt chastened that I wasn't presenting it to her on a silver salver.

"I'm happy to help Ellen's father in any way I can, Mr. Jacovich," she said. Her voice was modulated by years at finishing school in the East and her chin was held high over her exquisitely arched neck. She spoke as if her jaws were wired shut, and with an air that made me feel like a salesman who had come to peddle inexpensive ballpoint pens out of a sample case, letting me know from the get-go that if I had any interest in her beyond my stated business that I was wasting my time.

As it turned out, she needn't have worried. Bronwyn Rhys looked as though she would be icy to the touch.

"But I assure you," she continued, "I am just as puzzled as anyone else about what happened."

Puzzled. Not sad, distraught, confused, shattered. Puzzled. Not enough to allow a frown line to crease her smooth, clear brow, though. That might have sent her running in panic for a collagen injection.

We stood at the small counter of her shop, surrounded by racks of designer clothing that no woman I was ever likely to know could afford. The colors were muted, discreet beiges and grays and lavenders and dark blues. Rhys herself wore a clingy coffee-with-cream–colored dress that I imagined would be more sensual to the fingertips than the skin beneath it. Her perfume was unfamiliar to me, a brand probably so expensive I'd never sniffed it before.

"How did you know Ellen?" I said.

"I met her through her company," she

said. "About two years ago, I decided to go with the flow and utilize the Internet to enhance my business. I design some of the clothes here, and carry other designers as well, and I wanted to expand my operation beyond strictly retail." She added, "It's hard to make ends meet just waiting for walk-in business."

I suppressed the urge to smile, thinking the only time Bronwyn Rhys ever had difficulty making ends meet was in trying to fasten the clasp of her slim gold necklace beneath her hair.

"So you called Wheetek?"

"Yes," she said. "They have a wonderful reputation. And I like to support local businesses; it's good for Cleveland's economy."

I ignored her minor noblesse oblige. "And Ellen helped you design your Web site?"

"She had marvelous ideas, she was very creative when it came to graphics and colors." She handed me her own business card with a Web site address on it: www. beattitude.com. "The Web site is really smashing. Give us a look when you get back to your computer and let me know what you think of it."

"I will," I lied. "So you were pleased

with Ellen's work, and you became friends."

Bronwyn Rhys laughed, a delicate, practiced, and patently insincere little laugh so soft that no one else could have heard. "I don't know if I'd characterize her as a *friend,* exactly. She was extremely gifted in many ways, and one of the most intelligent people I've ever met. So we started having lunch together on a regular basis, or even dinner. I felt I could learn a lot from her."

"About computer graphics?"

"About business in general. She was the driving force behind Wheetek, and her bosses knew it, too."

"And did you? Learn from her?"

"A tremendous amount, yes. She was a hard-driving go-getter. I suppose God compensates people who are physically unattractive in other ways, and he gave Ellen a set of brains."

"But you liked her, too?"

"Oh, yes. I enjoyed the way her mind worked. Very different from the way I think, of course."

" 'Of course'?"

She let the frown in that time, but banished it quickly. "Well, we were two extremely different people."

I nodded.

"My father is a noted cardiologist, Mr. Jacovich, one of the most highly regarded in the world. And frankly I grew up never having to worry about money. I traveled in different circles than Ellen." She ran a pink, perfect tongue over her lip gloss. "It's just a shame she was . . ." She stopped.

"Yes?"

She blinked a few times. "A shame things ended up the way they did for her. It's such a waste of a first-class mind."

"Ellen never spoke to you of being unhappy?" I said, shifting my weight from one foot to the other and wishing in vain there was someplace in the shop to sit.

"Well . . ." She offered a chilly smile.

She wanted to be coaxed, but I wasn't going to play that game; I find I learn more by keeping my mouth shut. So I just looked at her until the smile scuttled back into the ice cave from whence it had come.

"Ellen was — well, she was physically, um . . ." She searched desperately for words to take the sting out. "She wasn't prepossessing-looking." Her search was a dismal failure, despite the sympathetic wave of her bejeweled hand. "I think that bothered her a lot."

"Most people are not beautiful, Ms. Rhys," I said.

She raised one perfect eyebrow to let me know she could not even conceive of such a thing.

"And," I continued, "certainly not too many take their own lives because they aren't."

"No, I suppose not. But I know it troubled her."

"She spoke of it?"

"Well, no . . ."

It was my turn to lift a cynical eyebrow, even though mine were not nearly as perfectly arched as hers.

"I could just — tell," she said.

"How could you tell?"

"I'd rather not say."

"Why?"

"It's a little embarrassing."

"That's all right," I assured her. "I'm a professional." It was a non sequitur, but Bronwyn Rhys didn't notice. And if she had, I don't think she would have understood the definition.

She touched the precise middle of her upper lip delicately with a scarlet acrylic fingernail. "Ellen was always asking me about my life. My social life, the men I date. As fascinated as I was with her mind and her intellect, that's how fascinated she was with . . ." She lowered her eyes, but didn't bother to blush; I probably wasn't worth the effort. "I told you this would be embarrassing."

"Please don't be embarrassed," I said, hoping that she would be anyway, although the aura which emanated from every part of her precluded her even knowing the meaning of the word. I was disliking her a lot. "You're actually being quite helpful."

She dipped her head in acknowledgment. "I really believe that Ellen's attraction to me was the result of a certain kind of voyeurism. Poor Ellen," she said with condescension to spare, "a hundred pounds too heavy and even if she'd lost it she still wouldn't have been very attractive — Ellen Carnine wished that she were me."

Chapter Four

Driving back toward downtown, I reflected on how very different people are. It takes all kinds, they say, and Bronwyn Rhys certainly had her niche. There was no denying she was stunning, eye-catching, decorative, and alluring; yet she was self-involved and self-absorbed to the point where even the suicide of a friend became all about *her*. If indeed Ellen Carnine had counted Rhys among her best friends, I felt sorry for her all over again.

I went back to my office to clean up my phone messages and wait for my six-o'clock appointment. I tried calling Ellen's live-in, Duane Starrett, but I got a recorded message instead, and was startled and discomfited when I realized it was Ellen's voice telling me no one was there to answer my call right now. Even though I had never heard the voice before, her "Hi, this is Ellen," prickled the hairs on the back of my hands. In this brand-new, high-tech century, when electronics and microchips and voice mail and video and audiotape are available to almost everyone, it takes a long time for the dead to really go away.

The outgoing message resonated for me in another way; it was a happy voice, an upbeat voice. Not sexy or sensual, but cheerful and enthusiastic. Not the voice of someone who hated her life enough to end it. I realized the recording could have been made months, even years ago, and wondered what had happened in the interim to render Ellen Carnine's existence intolerable for her.

Maybe her other friends could enlighten me; Bronwyn Rhys certainly hadn't.

At a few minutes after six, Karen Conley climbed the stairs to my office, walked across the hardwood floor like John Wayne going into the Lordsburg saloon in *Stagecoach*, and sat down across the desk from me. My first thought upon seeing her was that Ellen Carnine certainly had eclectic taste in friends.

Karen was the opposite of Bronwyn Rhys in every way. Skinny and shapeless, with unpolished, blunt-cut fingernails and a mannish haircut, wearing khakis, men's loafers, a plaid short-sleeved rayon shirt over a white T-shirt. She had no discernible hips. Until she introduced herself, I had thought she was a sixteen-year-old boy selling magazine subscriptions in order to win two weeks at summer camp.

"I appreciate your taking the time to come over here, Ms. Conley," I said, and I suppose my surprise was evident. One of my own failings in life was my inability to keep my thoughts off my face.

She crossed one ankle over the other knee, exposing thick white athletic socks, and grinned at me. "It's the least I can do for Ellen, after what happened. Call me Karen, okay? And for chrissakes, pick your jaw up off your chest before a moth flies into your mouth."

Karen Conley made up for in aggressive and refreshing directness whatever she lacked in attractiveness. I guess I closed my mouth, if it indeed had been open, but I was stumped for something to say. I opted for a mumbled apology.

"Forget it. I know what I look like. And yes," she added, helping me out, "I am a lesbian, and no, Ellen wasn't, if those were your next questions."

Now it was my turn to grin, more from embarrassment than any sort of amusement. "They were going to be," I admitted, "but I didn't know how to go about asking them."

"My friendship with Ellen had nothing to do with sexual preference, it was a case of two outsiders huddling together for warmth." She spoke matter-of-factly, without bitterness or irony. "Men usually laugh when they look at me — women, sometimes, too. That's okay, it's my choice to dress this way, so I take my lumps and like it. When people saw her, though, they just averted their eyes, which was probably harder to take than laughter or ridicule. But Ellen and I accepted each other, unconditionally, and that's why we were friends."

"Good friends?"

"I think so."

"You talked with her a lot?"

"Sure."

"Were you aware of her being unhappy?"

Karen frowned. "I don't know that I'd say she was unhappy, exactly. Life isn't easy for a lot of women who look like her, especially when they're bright and vital and are trying to make their way in the business world where everyone puts so much stock in appearances. But it was my impression that she had come to terms with her looks a long time ago, and was making up for it in other areas."

"What other areas?"

"Her work, primarily. She was damn good at her job, and her bosses respected her for it, and compensated her accordingly. She worked mostly in the office with them, didn't have much face-time with their clients, so nobody at her firm gave a good goddamn about her appearance." She sat back easily in the chair. "If you look hard enough, there is a comfort zone someplace for everybody, even the outsiders, the freaks like us. And if we're lucky, we manage to find it."

"For the record, I don't think Ellen was a freak," I said, "and I don't think you are, either."

Amused, she waved a hand at me. "Who the hell are you, anyway? Alan Alda, Private Eye? Spare me the Mr. Sensitivity snow job, okay? I've been across the street a few times."

"It's not a snow job," I said. "But okay. Man to man."

Karen Conley threw back her head and laughed, a hearty guffaw that came up from the middle of her gut. "That's more like it."

I laughed, too, finding myself liking her almost as much as I had disliked Bronwyn Rhys. Then I said, "Could Ellen have been despondent over a love affair that went wrong?"

"I didn't know a lot of things about Ellen's private affairs," she said. "She wasn't completely comfortable discussing my sex life with me, and I understood that and respected it, but as a result she didn't talk much about hers, either." And then she added, "If she had one at all."

I frowned. " 'If she . . .'? What about Duane Starrett?"

She looked at me blankly for a moment, and then laughed again, even louder.

"What?" I said.

"Oh my." She wiped her eyes.

I waited.

"It isn't *'Dwain,'* " she said, parroting my pronunciation. "It's *'Dwahn.'* Duane Starrett is a woman."

"Wow," I said, "I'm glad you told me."

"And she was certainly not involved romantically with Ellen. They were just roommates, like ten thousand other single women in this city. People live together for economic reasons sometimes, but neither Ellen or Duane was hurting financially. I think it was for more than that, for someone just to *be* there when they came home from work at night. Even if they aren't particularly close friends — and I don't think Ellen and Duane were — it's comforting to know there is someone else in the house. Even if they are in the other room."

"Do you have someone in your house?" I said.

"I have a partner, yes." She smiled. "Not in the next room, either."

"Was she friends with Ellen, too?"

Karen shook her head. "They never met."

"Oh?"

"You know, Mr. Jacovich, there are a lot of people who keep the various components of their lives in different little compartments, and rarely let them mix. My family doesn't know my friends, my friends are kept separate from my work, my lovers certainly don't much interact with my family. And so forth."

"If I'm going to call you Karen, you have to call me Milan, okay?" I said, and she nodded. "Was Ellen like that? Keeping the various pieces of her life apart?"

"Pretty much, yes."

"So you didn't know her other friends?"

She shook her head. "I ran into her with one of them several months ago in a restaurant. I can't remember her name, but I think it was Greek. She was a stone knockout, by the way, although not really my type. And we just said very brief hellos all around and moved on so as not to cause any questions or embarrassment."

Anna Zarafonitos, I thought. "Isn't it odd that, being such a good friend, Ellen didn't know your — partner?"

"Ellen was my friend. Janet understood that and was okay about it." She took her leg down from her knee and leaned forward over the desk. "But not everyone is as accepting as Ellen was. Let's face it, nobody is going to mistake me for Martha Stewart; it was easier for Ellen not having to explain me to her other friends."

"That was her choice?"

"It was mine. Like I said, I've been there and done that." She took a pack of Camels from her shirt pocket and showed it to me. "Do you mind if I smoke in your office?"

"No, as a matter of fact I think I'll join you," I said, and shook a Winston out of my own pocket pack.

"Thank God," she said. "These days people are more likely to accept my being butch than being a smoker." Her rueful smile was genuine. "The national pastime isn't baseball anymore, it's minding other people's business."

We each lit our own, and for a moment the air above my desk was blue, until a river breeze came through the open window, curled the tobacco smoke around the room, and swept it all out into the atmosphere.

"You talk a lot about acceptance, Karen."

"Well," she said, "when you're different from everybody else, acceptance becomes a real issue. You know, there's a reason why Cleveland, and cities like it, have ethnic neighborhoods. People like to surround themselves with their own kind, with people who will accept them and not judge them for their skin color or country of origin or funny accent or who they share their bed with. It makes it easier to be comfortable in your own skin."

"Was Ellen comfortable in her skin?"

She took another long draw at her Camel and considered the question. "Would she rather have been drop-dead beautiful like those bimbos on *Baywatch*? Sure, who wouldn't? Was she miserable enough about her appearance to do the Dutch act? I doubt that very much."

The slang surprised me. " 'The Dutch act'? Where'd you hear that?"

She gave me a small, sardonic smile. "I'm an E.R. nurse at MetroHealth, Milan. I hear people talk about the Dutch act almost every night."

By the time she left it was past seven-thirty, pretty late for me to be making appointments. But I tried Ellen Carnine's roommate anyway, and was successful in reaching her this time. I said a silent Thanksgiving prayer for Karen Conley's having clued me in on the pronunciation of Duane Starrett's name, and on her gender as well. I know how much it annoys me when people get my name wrong, even though, like "Duane," it's easy to mispronounce.

I told her who I was and what I wanted, and asked whether she had a few minutes to see me.

"You want to come over *now?*" she said.

"I tried you during the day, Ms. Starrett, but you weren't at home."

"Yeah, but calling at the last minute?"

"I'm not calling for a date," I said. "I want to ask you some questions about your late roommate, at her father's request. I don't have your work number so I couldn't very well have called you earlier."

I heard her breathing through her nose while she thought about it. "Give me forty-five minutes," she said.

Let no one say I am inconsiderate; I gave her an hour.

The apartment Duane Starrett had shared with Ellen Carnine occupied the entire fourth and topmost floor of an old, recently remodeled building in the newly trendy Warehouse District just off Public Square, with a hot new restaurant occupying the ground level. The building was at least eighty years old, designed in that wonderfully overstated baroque style that, for me, defines the architecture of the early twentieth-century Midwest, and as I parked across the street I took a moment to study it, admiring its flourishes and furbelows and the stout patterned columns that stood guard on either side of the doors, some thirty feet west of the entrance to the restaurant. The building was within two blocks of the river and three blocks of the lake, but without the sight of either.

I went into the small vestibule where there were only three doorbells and found the one marked *Starrett-Carnine*. I wondered as I pushed it whether Ellen Carnine had been one of those people who always had to settle for second billing, like Katherine Hepburn to Spencer Tracy and Oliver Hardy to Stan Laurel, and how she had felt about it.

An answering buzz unlocked the inner door and I trudged up three flights of uncarpeted steps, my leg muscles protesting on the final incline. Maybe that was why mostly young people lived in the Warehouse District, where elevators were as rare as underpaid basketball players; anyone over forty-five would have a hell of a time regularly making the climb.

Duane Starrett was waiting for me at an open door at the top of the stairs, dressed in white tights that looked like men's long underwear, Nike cross-trainers, and a blue button-down man's shirt the tails of which came down below her hips. She was about thirty, a Clairol-girl redhead, her chin-length hair held away from her face by a rubber band with two decorative marble-sized white balls. She was pretty in an undramatic way, with wrists, thighs, and calves a bit too thick and breasts a bit too full for her five-foot-four-or-so frame. Her makeup was light, but looked freshly applied. She leaned against the doorjamb with one forearm; the other hand was balled into a fist and resting on her hip. She didn't seem particularly pleased that, after a hard day's work, she was being forced to entertain company.

"Mr. Jacovich?" she said, and when I nodded she stood aside so I could enter the apartment.

Once, in its original incarnation as warehouse space, it had been all one large room, similar to my own office but three times the size. The walls were old, natural brick to which not much had been done by way of gentrification. One side of the room was all big windows, looking down on St. Clair Avenue. The ceiling was mostly opaque skylight, crisscrossed with the steel girders that held the building together and some heating ducts big enough for a man to crawl through. Rectangular, neutral-colored sisal area rugs covered the hardwood floors, and much of the furniture was white or beige, accented with aggressively printed throw pillows. Modernistic black metal halogen floor lamps that looked like praying mantises provided spot illumination, and near the window was an art-deco standing lamp whose lilylike glass shade diffused a soft buttery-yellow glow up toward the ceiling.

Against one wall were all the accoutrements of a modern kitchen, stainless-steel range and refrigerator and a double sink, with a butcher's-block table set up for working and a broad array of custom-built walnut-stained cabinets. At either end of the huge long room, temporary movable walls had been erected, and I gathered these were used to define the bedroom areas. I assumed there were bathroom facilities behind each door, too, because I couldn't see any others.

I got myself settled on a nubbly wool sling chair designed for someone half my weight and size, and Duane Starrett made polite noises about refreshments until I declined. Then she sat down on the curved sofa and said, "What do you want to stir up a lot of unhappiness for? It's not going to do any good, you know. Ellen is gone, and that's the end of the story."

"I *don't* want to. But Ellen Carnine's father does, and he's paying me to help him. That's what I do for a living, Ms. Starrett. I help people find things out that they don't know how to discover for themselves."

"I see. Well, look, I can understand how upset Mr. and Mrs. Carnine must be, but I can't imagine what's going to be gained by your poking around like this. Let her rest in peace, for God's sake." Her speech was rapid but precise, her voice firm and well-modulated, and as she talked she leaned forward intently as if she was negotiating the quick transfer of a large block of Microsoft stock.

"What's going to be gained, I think, is

peace of mind for her parents. Don't you think that's worth something?"

"I suppose," she said without conviction. "But they might not like some of the answers they get."

"Oh? Do you know something we don't know?"

She raised her palms in front of her the way she might to fend off an overly amorous suitor. "Whoa! I don't know anything at all. But everyone has areas of their life they don't want anyone to know about, and I imagine Ellen did, too. And I'm not sure I want to be dishing about her after she's dead."

"Even if it will help us to figure out *why* she's dead?"

"I doubt if anything I know will shed much light on that. Ellen was a very private person, and she never discussed her personal life with me. Or much of anything else, frankly. If she went to a movie, she'd usually tell me about it when she got home. And she always took pictures on her vacations and shared them with me, one by one. Otherwise I have no idea what her life was like."

"Someone you lived with for more than three years and you had no idea what her life was like?"

"No, I didn't." She looked grave and sincere, but still delivered her words like automatic-weapons fire. "Don't get me wrong, now. We always got along just fine, but we weren't really friends. Not *friends*-friends. Just roommates. We had different lifestyles, you know?"

"Was she seeing anyone?"

"You mean dating?"

"Yes."

She shook her head firmly. "As far as I know, Ellen went on exactly one date in the three years–plus that we shared this place. That was sometime around Christmas, two years ago, and she was home and in her robe by ten-thirty at night, and wouldn't tell me anything about it. She wasn't into the dating scene." She treated me to a short, bitter little laugh.

"From the way you say that, I take it you thought she should get out more."

"It was none of my business. I date a lot, because I think it's fun and exciting. And I happen to like men. And one of these days I'm going to find one who's a keeper, and trade this bachelor girl's paradise for the picket fence and the crabgrass in the pachysandra. But what floats my boat doesn't necessarily float anyone else's." She shifted her position on the sofa, tucking her legs under her into a sitting position many women favor but most men would find extremely uncomfortable. "Ellen went out with her gal pals sometimes — not very often, though, and when she did, I suppose it was just so she could see something else once in a while besides the inside of her office and the four walls of her bedroom here."

"Where did they go? Do you know?"

"Around here. Fat Fish Blue sometimes, to listen to the music. A dance club in the Flats, or maybe the Spy Bar around the corner. You know, the usual places where single people hang out. But going out was more of a rarity than a lifestyle; it couldn't have been easy for her."

"Why not?"

"Let's face it, Ellen was not attractive to men, and when and if she did go out I doubt many of them paid any attention to her. I suppose after a while she figured that loneliness was a better alternative to rejection."

"So she went to the movies a lot?"

"She used to. I guess she had to make do with the romances of Winona Ryder and Nicole Kidman, because she had none of her own. But about — oh, a year and a half ago, I guess, she got very into her computer, and started spending hours and hours in her room every night. I can't see it myself, but some people really get off on it."

"Her computer? She was working?"

"I don't know what the hell she did in there every night, but I don't think she was working all the time. She spent a lot of hours in the chat rooms."

"Chat rooms?"

"Yes." She looked at me oddly. "Don't you have a computer?"

"Sure I do," I said, "but I've never been in a chat room."

She laughed. "Jump right into the twenty-first century, okay? It's swept the country, Mr. Jacovich. There are millions of people whose entire social life is carried on in the privacy of their rooms, 'chatting' with strangers online."

"How does that work?"

"Well, you log on, you go into a chat area . . ." She snorted impatiently. "Oh, hell, it's easier to show you than try to explain it. Come on."

She stood up and led me into her bedroom.

It was a pretty, feminine room, with a dark pink satin comforter covering a king-sized waterbed, pink pillow covers, a white dust ruffle along the bottom of the bed, and a stuffed panda toy propped up against the pillows. Cheerful makeup clutter on the dresser in front of a large, rectangular mirror. Photographs of her parents, I assumed, a few other women closer to her own age mugging and waving for the camera, one picture of Duane all dressed up in a slinky green dress with a pleasant-looking guy in a dark suit at what appeared to be a party, arms around each other's waists, both smiling broadly.

Next to the room's single window was a computer desk with all the toys: hard drive, monitor, stacked speakers, laser printer. I was beginning to wonder if there was anyone left in the world who didn't own a personal computer.

"I use this mostly for business," Duane Starrett said. "For research. I'm a stock-broker, you know. I'm not much into chatting. But I'll pop into the rooms once in a while if I'm really bored, or want to take a half-hour break."

I wondered whatever happened to reading a book or watching TV. She sat in front of the monitor, which had a *Star Wars* screen-saver on it, booted up the computer and logged on to her

Internet provider.

The welcome screen showed two screen names. One of them was "DUANESTAR;" the other, the one she logged on to, was "BROKERESS."

"You don't want to go into a chat room under your own name," she explained. "There are weirdos out there."

"I see."

"Where do you want to go tonight?"

"Where do I want to go?"

"There are all sorts of chat rooms, for every interest," she said. "Sexy, gay, straight, kinky. Want to fall in love? Want to talk to other people in Cleveland? Or would you rather go someplace where they talk about needlepoint or pets or gourmet cooking or Jesus?"

I laughed. "I haven't the foggiest notion. I didn't know there were that many options."

"Oh, the number of choices would knock your socks off. Okay, what shall we do here?" She tapped her fingernails on the top of the desk, thinking, and then made several clicks with her mouse. The screen changed with each click, and finally we were in a chat room.

"This one is 'MARRIED AND LOOKING,' " she said. "For cheaters and the people who love them. We're not going to chat, we'll just lurk, okay?"

" 'Lurk'?"

"That means hanging out but not joining in. I don't have anything to say to these people."

"Fine with me," I said.

"Of course" — and she pointed to a corner of the screen that listed the room's occupants — "they can see that I'm here, but if I'm lucky, no one will notice. Pull that other chair over here if you want to, and take a look."

I did, sitting right next to her so I could see the screen. As I watched, a spirited conversation appeared on the monitor, line by line.

Online Host: *** You are in "Romance − Married and Looking". ***
LdyMuff: Hey, room? Sup?
Gngrpchee:<~~~~~ cheating husband here
Studcruzr: say something profound . . . these PIG lips only flap BAD stuff
Medolark: wet birds don't fly at night − howz that?
Gngrpchee: LdyMuff, you better say hello to me
LdyMuff: LOL

"What's 'LOL'?" I said.

" 'Laughing out loud.' The chat rooms are full of shorthand."

"Even for laughing?"

She nodded.

LdyMuff: You married, Ginger?

EDSIZRHAND: in the ecological sanctuary of your marital bedroom, is the pussy on the endangered species list?

Katizcute: Ed, my hubby thinks so!

MrLuckee69: boring room . . .

MovieDave: To the ladiez . . . Ever lose a foreign object inside you?

Gngrpchee: I am when I feel like it

Lonestar222: Anyone from Texas?

FISHSTORY: No, Cali here.

Katizcute: no, Dave . . . baby came out once, tho! LMAO

" 'LMAO'?"

" 'Laughing my ass off,' " Duane translated.

"That's even better than LOL?"

"Oh, yeah. It's all a matter of degree."

A little chime rang and a box appeared at the upper left-hand corner of the screen.

"An instant message," she explained.

"One of the sickos has noticed me."

"HI" the text in the box said. *"SENSUAL 37/M, MARRIED, HUNG, WITH HOT PIC. WANNA CHAT?"*

Duane Starrett moved the cursor to the CANCEL button and clicked the box away.

"Aren't you going to answer him?"

"No," she said. "It's rude to I.M. someone you don't know. If I answered him, even to tell him to fuck off, it would just encourage him."

The dialogue in the chat room continued:

MovieDave: A foreign baby??

Nixo127: Ladies, what name do you like for your v?

Medolark: think Ken is doin Barbie?

HorndogUNLV: Ken is a fag I think

Notherwun: Is Ken properly equipped?

Gavi2222: Ken doing Barbie? With WHAT????

Notherwun: how do you think Barbie likes to do it?

EDSIZRHAND: later got to go to work

LdyMuff: bye Ed*********

"Those asterisks are kisses," Duane explained.

> Katix4u: ED***** licccccks till ya cum back
>
> Hummer64: 28/M with pics. Age/sex check?
>
> HorndogUNLV: would you get carpule tunnel from masturbating in the chat rooms?

"Oh my god, this is stupid," I said. "I can't believe anyone would waste even five minutes doing this."

"Some people spend their lives at it." She looked up at me and grinned. "And by the way, chat-room shorthand for 'Oh my god' is 'OMG.' "

"I'll have to remember that," I said. "Doesn't anybody in these rooms even know how to spell?"

"Evidently not. Seen enough?"

"Plenty for now."

"Me too." She exited the chat room, logged off, and we both stood up and went back out into the living room.

"And Ellen spent her evenings doing that?"

"She spent just about every evening on

her computer, even if she'd been out to dinner with friends first. What she did I don't know. But she mentioned to me once that she was corresponding with someone she'd met in a chat room."

"A guy?"

"Yes. Although you never know who you're talking to. I'm sure half the people who chat lie about who they are. How old they are, what they look like, whether they're married."

"It's like fantasy land, then."

"Exactly," she said. "When Ellen was online and anonymous, she could be 36-24-36 and drop-dead gorgeous, and everyone would want her. What's the harm, Mr. Jacovich? *Everyone* needs a little fantasy now and then."

Chapter Five

First thing the next morning, I called William Carnine at Bryarly College. When they put me through to his office, his assistant told me he was having breakfast in the cafeteria, and I asked her to have him call me back immediately, as I was off to an appointment at ten. I lit a cigarette to wait for him.

It took him fifteen minutes.

"You have anything to report?" he said when I answered the phone two cigarettes later.

"Nothing concrete yet. A situation like this is obviously going to take some time."

"As long as it takes, take that long, then."

"I saw Ellen's roommate last night, and we had a rather interesting conversation. I didn't learn much, but it's a start, anyway."

"Oh?"

"I understand you haven't touched anything of Ellen's yet, or moved her effects out of the apartment."

"No," he said. "Frankly, I can't bear the

thought of it right now, nor can Mrs. Carnine. Perhaps in a month or two . . ."

"I understand," I said. "In the meantime, I'd like your permission to search through her room."

He didn't answer right away. When he did, it was halting and hesitant. "That's getting awfully — well, personal, don't you think?"

"This whole thing is awfully personal," I said. "You want reasons for her taking her own life, and we can't possibly discover what those reasons were unless I *get* personal. Don't you agree?"

"Well, yes, but — going through her private effects . . ."

"That's exactly where I might find what I'm looking for."

He was thinking it over; I could almost hear the wheels grinding through the receiver.

"I don't know, Mr. Jacovich," he said at last, "maybe this wasn't such a good idea after all."

"That's up to you, sir. I'll refund your retainer if you like, minus my fee for one day's work."

"Yes. Well." He hummed softly under his breath for a few seconds. I think that deep inside, he was afraid of what he might discover about his daughter if I were to continue. Nothing specific, I didn't think, but the unknown was dissolving his innards like a corrosive.

Finally, "All right, then. I suppose I'll let you go ahead."

"That's fine," I said. "I'll need you to call Duane Starrett and tell her you gave me permission to search. It's her apartment, too, you know."

"You think she'll be all right with that?"

I'd wondered the same thing myself. "I don't know, but we have to ask, don't we? And I'll have to get a key from somewhere so I won't have to be there to bother her when she's home trying to relax and get on with her life."

"That's . . ." He cleared his throat. "I can do that. I'll have Duane give you an extra set."

"The other thing is, I want to access Ellen's computer."

I heard a little intake of breath, like a small and unexpected puff of wind on an otherwise calm afternoon. "Is that absolutely necessary?"

"No," I said. "But it's thorough. You would like me to be thorough, wouldn't you?"

"I suppose," he said, "that if we're going

to do this at all, we might as well be thorough about it."

"Duane told me Ellen spent a lot of time online. Maybe her death had something to do with someone she knew from the chat rooms."

" 'Chat rooms'? What do you mean?"

I had to smile. If I was a chat-room virgin, I was pretty certain that, behind the ivy-covered walls of academe, Dr. Carnine assuredly had never chatted online with anyone who was curious to know what women called their vaginas.

With my own somewhat limited knowledge, I explained chat rooms to him as gently as I could.

"My daughter didn't waste her time and intellect on anything that banal," he proclaimed.

"Her roommate says otherwise."

He sighed, and there was a winter of sadness in the sound. "I am truly shocked to find that out, Mr. Jacovich."

I was afraid there would be a great deal that was going to shock William Carnine before I got through pawing through the detritus of his late daughter's private life, and for a moment before we terminated our conversation I thought strongly about recommending to him again that he take back whatever was left of my retainer, give in to his grief, and allow himself to heal.

But I was not in business to turn down jobs, and I comforted myself that this time, for a change, I was taking on a private case in which I was probably not going to get beaten up, shot at, or otherwise put in physical jeopardy.

What it might do to my head, I had no idea.

I had to face the fact that the three friends of Ellen Carnine's I had met were not particularly devastated by her death. Karen Conley, as an emergency-room nurse, had seen so much suffering and tragedy that she'd become inured to it. Bronwyn Rhys was a textbook example of a cold fish — a user and a brain-picker who really hadn't cared about Ellen personally, one way or the other.

And Duane Starrett — I couldn't figure that one out at all. She said that she and Ellen had been roommates more than friends, but if someone I saw every day of my life had died suddenly and violently, I think I might take it a little harder.

Then again, that's just me.

I got to Public Square about fifteen minutes before ten, rightly estimating that it would take me that long to find a space in one of the many downtown lots or multi-level garages that charge outrageous prices to ignore your car. From there I walked the two blocks to the offices of Wheetek, Inc.

It occupied an entire floor of one of the newer and smaller buildings off the square, and as I noted that the employees there — who were young and energetic and all wearing designer jeans and look-alike items from the Eddie Bauer catalog — seemed to be rushing around busily and going about their daily routines without any outward show of grief, I remembered once again that Ellen Carnine had died more than a week before and that life does and must go on for the rest of us.

I don't know what I was expecting when I walked into Barnard Landenberger's office. The name, pronounced BARN-erd, had conjured up visions of a slightly paunchy, middle-aged establishment rain-maker with a Phi Beta Kappa key, a now-deceased uncle who'd served at the mid-levels of the Reagan administration, and an old-money membership at the Union Club. Instead Landenberger was about thirty-two, wore his hair slicked back and sported a black turtleneck under a black silk jacket, and affected ominous and intimidating gray-tinted wire-rimmed glasses with round lenses the size of half-dollars. I would have bet anything that he played racquetball four times a week. Around his right wrist was a dazzling gold ID bracelet with links as big as those of a padlock chain on a warehouse gate. On the other wrist was a gold Rolex. When he rose to meet me, I saw he was nearly as tall as I am, and when he introduced himself it was all filtered through his adenoids and clenched teeth the way he had been taught at some Eastern prep school. He was very rich, very Waspy, and for some reason was trying hard to look like a wiseguy.

Red Munch, who according to Carnine's notes was number two on the Wheetek depth chart, didn't look the way I'd imagined him to be, either — mainly because he had dark brown, almost black hair, which grew low on his forehead and temples. It wasn't anywhere near red. I discovered that his nickname was simply a diminutive of his given name, which was Redmond, and I was certain the confusion that might cause gave rise to a lot of good-natured chuckling and elbow-nudging in the locker room at his country club. Red spoke in the same lockjawed upper-crust accent as his partner, but was shorter than Landenberger by about five inches, and portly, which is a word you don't hear much anymore. He wasn't fat, exactly; just padded thickly in the middle, with an almost Elizabethan ruff of suet beneath his jawbone, and a neck the size of a bison's. The cream-colored cable-knit sweater he wore added to the illusion of bulk; he looked like a beer truck. It was too early for sunbathing at the beach, but his sunkissed glow seemed real and not induced by a tanning bed, and I decided he was probably a golfer.

My overall impression was of two kids born to privilege who had gotten into the Internet business and become obscenely wealthy.

And none of that brilliant Holmesian deduction told me a damn thing I cared to know.

They were solemn of mien when they said how sorry they were about the death of Ellen Carnine.

"She was absolutely the guts of Wheetek," Landenberger said. "There's no question about that. I don't know what we're going to do without her, and I'm not just making sympathetic noises. Since she came along, our business has tripled. In addition to being a creative and imaginative graphic designer, she was a marketing genius, and she literally place-kicked this company into the twenty-first century. Largely due to her efforts, we were able to go public last year." He allowed himself a smirk. "Our shares are traded on the NASDAQ, and are still healthy."

"Beyond that," Red Munch added, "she was a truly decent and caring human being. Everybody loved her here. We have thirty-six employees in this office, and she was kind of the unofficial den mother to all of them." He shook his head sadly. "Talk about leaving some footprints . . ."

"She was well paid, I gather?"

Landenberger patted his slick-backed hair, making sure everything was in place. "I don't feel free to discuss the specifics of that. But yes, she was very well paid, especially with her stock options."

"She liked her work?"

"She loved it, yes," he said. "Most of it, anyway."

" 'Most of it'?"

"Mr. Jacovich," Munch cut in, "we're an online service company. We design and maintain Web sites, both private and commercial. Some of the Web sites that we deal with are adult-orientated."

Apparently his prep-school education had missed informing him that there is no such word as *orientated*.

"Porno?"

He screwed up his face, then lifted and dropped his broad shoulders. "We prefer the term 'adult entertainment.' "

The old saw about quacking like a duck and walking like a duck came to mind, but I declined to offer it aloud. "And Ellen didn't like that?"

"An awful lot of women don't," Landenberger said. "But there is obviously a need for it, because it's a multibillion-dollar industry. Look, most men enjoy looking at naked women, that's just how it is. And while a lot of them wouldn't walk across the street to see it, to go to a titty bar or a dirty movie, or even to rent a porno tape at their local video store, you'd be surprised how many like to view it in the privacy of their homes on the World Wide Web — in complete, total anonymity. There's a lot of lonely people out there, guys who don't or can't or are afraid to try and score with women. Adult entertainment is their only option."

"And it's safe and risk-free," Munch added.

"How so?"

"You can't get AIDS or the clap from looking at pictures. You don't risk being seen with some porno bimbo by a friend or associate who'll never let you forget it. And there's no emotional commitment, no dinners and flowers and having to remember anniversaries."

"I see."

"You disapprove," Landenberger said, making it more of a statement than a question.

I shook my head and tried without much success to keep the disapproval out of my tone. "Let's just say that if I had a daughter, I wouldn't be crazy about her making a living that way."

Munch shrugged again. "It doesn't serve your purposes to be judgmental about the sex industry, Mr. Jacovich. Fortunately for you, you apparently don't have the need for it, that's all. But a lot of people do, and we simply make *our* living providing it for them. Well, part of our living, anyway. Sixty percent of our business deals with regular, ordinary commercial Web sites promoting products and services that you wouldn't mind showing to the Archbishop of Canterbury."

"And the adult stuff we do have is just good, sexy fun," Landenberger said. "We don't deal with hardcore or underage, we don't do the sick fetishes like S&M or scat or golden showers, even though we could probably double our earnings by handling it. Just pretty men and women in provocative poses, that's all. It's one hundred percent legal, and protected by the First Amendment. We'd be happy to show you some of our sites if you'd like."

"No, thanks. Pornography is a lot like going to a restaurant, ordering a great meal, and then just looking at it."

"That's okay," Landenberger said. "Everyone has different tastes. For instance, basketball bores the crap out of me, but I don't put Cavs fans down. Nobody makes me watch basketball, and nobody makes anyone download our sexy pictures on their hard drive. So, no harm, no foul."

"Gentlemen," I said, using the word with difficulty, "all of this is fascinating, but it interests me a lot less than finding out what it was that caused Ellen Carnine such pain that she took her own life."

Landenberger turned solemn again. "I wish I could tell you," he said, "because I wish I knew, too. I wish I knew if I . . ." He glanced at Munch and gestured inclusively. ". . . if *we* could have done anything to prevent it, to make her happier. I'd rest a lot easier about that."

"I did notice in the last six months or so," Munch said, "that Ellen wasn't quite as upbeat and positive as she used to be. Like something was bothering her. I can't put my finger on it, exactly, but there was a sort of sadness."

"It didn't affect her work, though," the senior partner said.

"No, but I noticed," Munch said. "Barney worked a lot more closely with her than I did. He's the computer genius of this firm, I'm just the guy who makes the sales and crunches the numbers." He grinned. "Frankly, I don't know the first thing about computers, except how to turn one on and pick up my e-mail. But I could tell. I even asked her about it once. You know, 'Is everything okay, is there anything we can do to help?' — that sort of thing. But she insisted that everything was fine, and I didn't want to pry. Ellen was pretty closemouthed about her personal life most of the time."

"You don't think maybe she was laboring under a profound self-disgust at what she was doing with the porno?"

Landenberger fairly lurched forward in his high-backed leather executive chair. "Absolutely not! She was a professional. She looked at it as a business, like any

92

other business. And she understood economic necessities. There are things you do to make a living that you're proud of, and other things connected with the job that you don't like so much. I'm sure you find that in your business, too."

"Sometimes," I admitted.

"Let's say you own a bookstore," Munch said in a reasonable tone. "You're a big reader, you love the classics like Shakespeare and Tolstoy and Hemingway and Fitzgerald, that's why you opened your store in the first place. But you can't just sell the good stuff today, the great literature. You have to carry those stupid pop best-sellers, too, like the *Star Wars* books and the romance-novel crap, or else you can't keep your doors open. You don't have to actually read all the books you stock, but you sure as hell have to peddle them."

"The point is," Landenberger said, "whatever drove poor Ellen to do what she did couldn't possibly have been connected in any way to Wheetek, because she was truly happy here."

"Well, that's comforting to know," I said. "Was there anyone here she was particularly close to? That she hung out with or went to lunch with?"

"Not really," Munch said. "Nobody I can think of, anyway. As we mentioned, Ellen was a very private person."

"She didn't take lunch hours very often," Landenberger added. "Or when she did, she'd just walk the three blocks home. So she could eat her cottage cheese or whatever rabbit food she was always having. She was on a perpetual diet."

I wanted to jot things down in my notebook, but was afraid I'd spook them if I did. "What about clients?"

"What about them?"

"Well, I've already talked to a past client of hers who's become a friend. Bronwyn Rhys."

Landenberger seemed never to have heard the name before, and looked a question at Munch. "We have a client named Bronwyn Rhys?"

"BeAttitude," Munch explained. "The clothing company."

Landenberger swiveled his gaze back to me, penetrating, thinking about whether to be angry. "You're talking to our clients now? That makes me very unhappy, Mr. Jacovich. It might also be actionable. That's sticking a knife right between the shoulder blades of our business."

"I didn't know Bronwyn Rhys was a

client until I met her. Ellen's father told me they were friends, that's all."

"Ah."

"I was wondering," I said, "if there was anyone in particular she was currently working with, that she was in close contact with at the time she died, that I might be able to talk to."

Landenberger said, "Look, Mr. Jacovich, we loved Ellen very much, and we'd like to help her father out. But I can't just go passing out our client list to everybody willy-nilly."

"Not Willy or Nilly," I said. "Just me."

"Obviously," Munch said, "there are some of our clients who don't want to go public about the Web sites they're putting up. They'd take a pretty dim view of our violating their confidentiality, even just to you."

"The other thing is," Landenberger went on, "we don't want our clients being bothered with something as serious and depressing as this. Certainly not coming from us, anyway. It's just not good business."

"I see," I said. "So they don't know that Ellen Carnine killed herself?"

"Sure they know. Or they probably do — it was in the papers and on the news. As a matter of fact a few of them called last week to express condolences. The ones who worked directly with her feel pretty bad about it, I'm sure, but at the end of the day it has nothing to do with them, and I don't want them being bothered."

"We don't know whether it has to do with them or not, Mr. Landenberger. That's why I'm asking questions."

Red Munch said, "Nevertheless, they wouldn't take kindly to our siccing a private detective on them. Even for a good cause."

His senior partner nodded affirmation. "It's just not good business practice."

I stood up. "Well, I guess you've been as helpful as you could be. I appreciate your time."

Landenberger stood up too. "Whatever you find out, Mr. Jacovich, I'd like you to keep me in the information loop, too. I felt very close to Ellen — we all did — and I'd sure like to know what happened to her."

"Mr. Landenberger," I said, "William Carnine is my client. He's paying me a lot of money to get this information for him. It would be a breach of confidentiality and of professional ethics for me to share it with other people." I gave him my most dazzling smile. "It's just not good business practice."

Chapter Six

When I got back to the office I thought about things for a while.

I didn't much like either Landenberger or Munch; they were both snotty, too-rich yuppies, and I don't care for the type. And their holier-than-thou pronouncements about the economics of the Internet did little in my mind to camouflage the fact that they were sleazy porn distributors masquerading as entrepreneurs. But I knew that online sex was big business indeed, and if they were to be believed, what they were peddling wasn't much worse than anything you could see in the pages of *Hustler* at your corner newsstand.

How Ellen Carnine might have felt about it was another story altogether. But she had worked at Wheetek for a long time, had certainly known what they did to make their daily bread before signing on, and it seemed unlikely to me that after several years she would suddenly be overwhelmed by guilt and remorse and jump off the Lorain-Carnegie Bridge.

Everyone who'd spoken to me seemed in agreement that she'd been a very private person, although if she'd been in the throes of a romance, surely she would have mentioned it to *someone*. Then again, people who spend all their spare time shut up in a room toasting in the glow of a computer screen don't have much opportunity to get involved in romantic relationships.

That sent me off in another direction. Perhaps her depression and eventual suicide had roots in her chat-room activities, and all at once it didn't seem that far-fetched. I couldn't imagine it myself, but I'd heard that some marriages had been shattered and others inspired by online contacts, so maybe Ellen Carnine had fallen in love and been jilted and heart-broken without ever leaving her apartment.

Being techno-challenged as I am — if I didn't have one of those automatic VCR programmers I would never have learned how to tape a TV show without being there to push the buttons, in which case I wouldn't have to tape it in the first place — I hadn't a clue as to how I could go about finding out who Ellen's chat-room friends had been. I needed some expert assistance.

I had to wait until lunchtime to see if I could get it.

My elder son, Milan Junior, was finishing up his freshman year in college. Like me, he had opted for Kent State, and also like me he had a partial athletic scholarship for football. Unlike me, he was a wide receiver, while I had toiled at left tackle on the defensive line, which just goes to prove that our kids are a hell of a lot smarter than we were.

As a freshman, he chafed at his lack of actual playing time; he was lucky if he was involved in five plays per game, even luckier if anyone actually threw the ball in his direction. A quiet, serious kid, he was never overly cheerful at the best of times, but he accepted his part-time-player status stoically, the way he might a tight, starched-collar shirt — knowing that eventually he'd be able to loosen the button and move around a little bit.

I had his class schedule memorized, not out of any need to be a controlling and all-knowing father, but because with his sports activities and the table-waiting jobs he worked for some spending money, it was virtually impossible to find much time he could spend with me on weekends, and I tried to get down to Kent every so often during the week for some lunch and the chance to gaze upon the dark, handsome face of my firstborn.

So I knew that he had no classes between noon and two, and chances were excellent that, if he wasn't lunching with me, he'd be at the desk in his dorm room studying while he wolfed down whatever it is that college kids delusionally call sustenance. As an athlete Milan Junior was better about eating healthy than some of his peers, but only marginally so.

Since my taste in food resembles that of an Irish peasant — a lot of meat and potatoes with gravy and, because I am Slovenian to the bone, klobasa sausage and onions and very little that is good for me — Milan's eating habits were another chip off the old block, one about which I had a nagging sense of guilt. But I suppose it's the nature of things: apple trees make apples.

I waited until twelve-fifteen to call.

"Hey!" he said — as always, a man of few words.

"Hey, yourself."

"What's goin' on?"

"Same old same old. How about you?"

"Studying for finals."

"I'll try not to keep you long," I said.

"That's okay. This way when I get a D in

calc, I can blame it on you."

"How much do you know about computers?"

"How to turn them on," he said. "How to get on the Internet. How to use e-mail. What do you need?"

"Somebody with better computer skills than you. Know anyone? I'd be willing to pay him."

He thought for a minute. "She's a her," he said. "And she's got finals too. It's May, you know."

"Right, I know. I'd just need her for an afternoon, though. But pretty soon."

"How much are you paying?"

"A hundred bucks. Not bad for one day's work."

He whistled. "Is there a finder's fee?"

"Since when did you get so mercenary?"

He laughed. "Since I got to college and have to spend a whole evening redoing my budget if I want pepperoni on my pizza."

"You don't eat pizza."

"Jeez, Dad, you're so literal!"

"We'll negotiate it later," I said. "It's kind of important, Milan."

"Oh. Okay," he said, serious again. "We have a class together this afternoon at two o'clock. Let me ask her, and I'll call you back."

"If it's all right with her, why don't you just have her call me back, and eliminate the middle man?"

"Good thinking, old Dad," he said. "Hey."

"What?"

"You know Loftis Jones is graduating?"

"Your starting wide-out?" Loftis Jones was one of the top twenty college wide receivers in the country, marginally good enough to turn pro, and the man whose talent kept my young freshman on the bench. "There was a question about that, wasn't there? His graduating?"

"Yeah, he really tanked on a couple of his midterms. But he did some heavy tutoring sessions where he was weakest, like in science, and it's starting to look like they're actually gonna let him out of here. So that means I move up to number two."

"Great, Milan!"

"Coach says I'll get some playing time in the fall."

"You'll knock 'em for a loop with those soft hands of yours," I said. "And I'll be at every game. Even the road games, if I can."

He paused for a moment. "You were there almost every Saturday this year anyway, even when you knew I wasn't going to do much more than get bench splinters in my ass." He paused again. "I just want you to know it meant a lot."

Unlike his six-years-younger brother Stephen, who flew his emotions like a regimental banner, Milan's expressions of feelings were so rare that this one had caught me unawares. "Good," I said, trying to talk around the tennis ball that had mysteriously appeared in my throat, and I smacked my forehead with the heel of my hand at the sheer banality of my response.

"Uh, so, okay, I'll have Taffy call you."

"Taffy? Oh, the computer gal."

"Wow, you're swift today, Dad," my son said.

After a quick lunch at Frank's sausage stand in the West Side Market, consisting of a couple of bratwurst sandwiches eaten standing up in the aisle and washed down with a lemonade, I went back to the office and spent the rest of the day trying to make contact with Ellen Carnine's other two friends, Sarah Donnem and Anna Zarafonitos. I finally connected with Donnem, and when I told her who I was and what I wanted, she agreed to meet me for a drink at Noggin's in Shaker Heights after work that evening.

At about four-thirty I got a call from

Milan Junior's friend Taffy Kiser. She had a low, mellow voice that sounded like it always had a smile in it.

"Milan told me you wanted someone who was good with computers," she said. "I'm pretty good, but I don't know exactly what you want."

I explained to her about Ellen Carnine, and said that I was hoping to find out what she did and where she went on her computer every night.

"I see," Taffy said. "Well, I don't know if I can help you or not. It depends on whether she bookmarked."

" 'Bookmarked'?"

"Yes. People who visit the same sites all the time often 'bookmark' those places to get into them more quickly, so they don't have to go to all the trouble of typing in keywords."

I laughed. "Taffy, you might as well be talking Lithuanian to me."

She laughed back, a musical, tinkly laugh. "That's okay, Mr. Jacovich, I'll explain it to you as we go along. When did you plan on doing this?"

"Is tomorrow too soon?"

"Just a sec." I heard her flipping pages. "My last class tomorrow is at one o'clock. I could probably be at your office by four.

Would that be soon enough?"

"That would be perfect. But I don't want to interfere with your studying for finals, though."

"Oh, that'll be Milan's problem."

"It will?"

"We're supposed to go out Friday night. Now I'll have to cancel so I can study instead to make up for the time I spend with you, so he's the one who's going to lose out." She sounded merry, teasing. "You and he can work it out together."

"He might never forgive me, you know."

"Sure he will. I'll make it up to him."

I thought about *that* for a long time after I hung up. So this was the young woman Milan Junior was dating. He hadn't mentioned it to me, hadn't mentioned he was seeing anyone at all. That wasn't surprising; my son had kept his own counsel since he was eight or nine years old, and it occurred to me that although I knew many of his high-school friends, I had never met any of the girls he had gone out with. That was only one of the consequences of being a nonresident father, along with the pain of watching my boys grow up at a distance, seeing them every other Sunday as the divorce judge had mandated, sometimes more often when my ex-wife Lila would forget she was mad at me and remember that boys need a father. Their *own* father and not the man she had chosen as her consort, one Joseph Bradac, who had worshiped her dumbly since high school and had waited in the bushes like a carrion-eating hyena until what was Lila and me had finally imploded and died and he could move in for the leavings.

Had Lila dumped me for a Sean Connery look-alike, I suppose I could have borne it more easily. There was no jealousy at the end; we had stopped loving each other long before. But her taking into her bed a skinny, runty wimp like Joe Bradac, whose main attraction for her seemed to be the spinelessness which she could easily dominate, still rankled after lo these many years. Whenever I show up at the house to pick up the boys for our weekend outings — it used to be *my* house, *our* house, but I hardly ever think of it that way anymore — it gives me perverse pleasure that Joe Bradac always seems to be hiding upstairs or in the basement or somewhere else he doesn't have to see me.

He's scared to death of me, even though I've never laid a hand on him. Lord knows I've wanted to, and still fantasize about smashing his wussy little face in. But I never did and, I suppose, never will. Out of respect for the mother of my children.

But it was Joe whom the boys saw nightly as they were growing up. Joe stretched out in front of the television set commenting on the Indians' starting pitching or the happenings in Washington and the world. Joe at the breakfast table. Joe emerging from their mother's bedroom wrapped in his bathrobe. Joe was part of their daily world, a member of the regular cast of the domestic sitcom that was their life — I was a once-in-a-while special guest star.

Maybe it was also Joe to whom they told their secrets. I couldn't say. I never really asked my sons whether or not they liked or approved of him, because I truly did not want to know. Didn't want to know whether he functioned as a third parent to them, or was simply the guy who brought home the paycheck and sometimes drove them to sports practice. I was satisfied he didn't mistreat them, and that was all I really cared about.

And now Milan Junior was eighteen and a college man, and Slovenian-fair and sunny-dispositioned Stephen was thirteen, hormones fizzing like Alka-Seltzer in a glass of water, and I still only saw them every few weeks. They were growing up in spite of my absence, growing to be their own men.

With their own secrets.

How well do any of us know our own kids after they grow up? There are things one simply does not share with one's parents — the dark, secret things that virtually everyone does at one time or another. And if they don't do them, they surely think them, fantasize them, dream them, and perhaps, if they are very secure, they share them with a lover. They do not tell their fathers about them.

And a good thing, too; there are some secrets I would never want to know. Whether Milan Junior was sleeping with Taffy Kiser was one of them.

How many secrets had Ellen Carnine kept from her father, secrets that now she could never tell him? Obviously he was curious, too, or else he wouldn't have hired me to uncover them.

I hauled out the leather binder he'd left with me — his terse, academic's rendering of his daughter's life and the medical examiner's even more bloodless telling of her death, and read it over one more time, and a kind of quiet melancholia settled itself about me like a wool comforter draped around the bony shoulders of a forgotten old man staring his life away on the front porch of a nursing home and dribbling Cream of Wheat down the front of his pajamas. And I wondered whether, in the end, William Carnine would sleep easier knowing Ellen's secrets.

I was vaguely bothered about the contents of the binder. It seemed incomplete, as if there was a piece missing. I knew it in my gut, but I couldn't quite put my finger on what it was. It was a little empty place inside me, like after you've eaten a full, satisfying meal but are still hungry — for *something*.

Well, I thought, that's why I was getting paid — to fill in the blanks.

I put the folder away in a locked drawer and battened down all the rest of the office hatches except for one floor-to-ceiling window, which I left slightly open. Cleveland is afflicted with long winters, and when the weather is fair, as it was this May, I like as much fresh air as possible. I looked forward to coming back to work the next morning and starting my workday smelling the river, and the breeze from Lake Erie a mile or so away. It wasn't supposed to rain that night, and if it did so unexpectedly, the hardwood floor would suffer some, but not much. It was worth it.

I headed east on Carnegie Avenue, but instead of turning up Cedar Hill toward my apartment, I swung right on Carl Stokes Boulevard, renamed a few years ago in honor of the first African American mayor of a major city, and then on up the winding incline of Fairhill Road into Shaker Heights.

Noggin's nestled in the corner of a slight jog of what might be called an upscale strip mall. Good for lunch, nice for dinner, and an impressive wine list. I had gone through a period in my life, years before, when I'd hung out at the bar sometimes, but I hadn't done that in eons.

When I walked in, a woman wearing a gray double-breasted jacket over a white blouse and black slacks rose from the bar to greet me, and every eye in the place of either gender found her. They were not admiring glances, however. For Sarah Donnem was built like an NFL linebacker.

I'm six foot three and she could almost look me straight in the eye. Her shoulders were broad, her wrists were thick and solid, and too-white, too-powdery makeup didn't quite cover an acne-scarred face. Her lusterless black hair was worn thick and frizzy like a Chico Marx wig, her horn-rimmed glasses were of a bygone era, and around her substantial neck was a thin gold chain. I tried not to look startled, smiling at her instead, and wondered for a moment if she were actually a cross-dressing male, or a pre-op transsexual. Upon looking more closely as we talked, I discovered that unfortunately for Sarah Donnem, she was neither. She was simply a tragically unattractive woman.

And I mentally awarded her fifty bonus points because of the way she stood tall and proud and dared anyone to make something out of it.

I took the stool next to her. "Thanks for seeing me, Ms. Donnem."

"Sarah," she corrected me. "Everyone calls me Sarah."

"I'm Milan, then."

She grinned, and when she did so, her blue eyes danced and her whole face changed and became almost pleasing. I judged her to be around thirty-five years old. "You're Milan anyway," she said.

"A semanticist."

"Well, yes, an English teacher."

"College?"

"High school. And I'm very good at it. I discovered a surefire way to get those little bastards all involved with *Romeo and Juliet*; I let them know those two kids were actually *doing* it." She lifted her wineglass and showed it to me. "I recommend the 1995 Cakebread Cellars Chardonnay Reserve."

"I'm not much into wine these days," I said, remembering my recently expired relationship with Connie Haley, whose father owned a restaurant and who had an encyclopedic knowledge of wines. "I prefer beer, actually."

Her smile broadened. "So do I, if the truth be known. But I look enough like a stevedore as it is without sitting here knocking back Rolling Rock. So . . ." She raised the glass again and took a sip of it.

I ordered a Stroh's beer with no glass, my drink of choice from my earliest days of adulthood.

"You want to talk about Ellen," she said.

"Yes. If it won't bother you."

Her big shoulders rose and fell. "The whole thing bothers me, Milan. It was so sudden, so shocking. Ellen was the last person I'd imagine would want to take her own life. She always seemed to me to be a very positive person, despite the way she looked. Most of the time she just didn't let it bother her."

I nodded.

"But I can fully understand why her dad wants to know what went down. I only wish I knew. If I did, I'd tell you."

The bartender put a frosty beer bottle in front of me, and a chilled glass, despite my request. I ignored the glass and drew the bottle closer. "What's your take on it?"

"I don't have a 'take,'" she said. "I can't imagine why Ellen would do something like that."

"She was happy, then?"

"What the hell does that mean? I've found perfect happiness so many times in my life I've learned not to expect much from it. But she wasn't miserable, if that's what you want to know."

"That's one of the things I want to know, yes."

"Well, she wasn't. At least not so anyone could notice." She tinked her glass against my bottle. "Here's looking up your ancestors."

"How often did you see her, Sarah?"

"Maybe every two, three weeks. It used to be more often, but life changes, people get busy and involved in their own stuff."

"Known her long?"

"Two years, give or take. Well, wait — we met via the Internet, so we 'knew' each other, if you could call it that, for about four months before we ever met in real time."

"The Internet," I said. "Chat room?"

"Yes."

"Which one?"

She made herself as large as she could and pointed her chin at me. "It's called the PLAIN JANE/CLEVELAND room."

I blinked.

"Not everybody in the chat rooms lies about how beautiful they are," she said. "Some of us just come out and admit we're plain." She shook her head rapidly as if to discourage a gnat buzzing around her nose. "Aaaghh! That's such a bullshit word. Homely. Not plain, *homely*. There isn't much we can do about it, so we accept it and do what we can with it. In the Plain Jane room there is a level of self-acceptance and sisterhood that can be very comforting sometimes on cold nights." She looked at me levelly. "You understand?"

"I do," I said.

"I suppose that's really all Ellen and I had in common. She was pretty high-powered in the business world, and I couldn't relate to that. But I liked going out for dinner or drinks with her because it was easy, because we both knew what would and wouldn't happen."

I guess I cocked an eyebrow at that.

"You're a man, Milan, and a fairly attractive one, too, so you have no idea what women go through. All women. Granted, a lot of it is in our own heads, but that's because of how we've been socialized, how the world has become."

A noisy group of Attitude Adjustment revelers, from their dress and manner probably parolees from one of the offices in Beachwood on nearby Chagrin Boulevard, came in and took a corner table. Three men, two women, all in their thirties. I watched the body language for a short while and decided there were no "couples" here, just co-workers blowing off some steam before they went home to their frozen dinners and their rented videos and their cats.

Sarah Donnem looked at them too, and if there was envy in the dark blue depths of her eyes, I couldn't discern it.

"Two women go out for a few drinks together," she said. "Not necessarily looking to 'meet' someone, although for singles that particular hope is never far from the surface."

"I'm single," I said. "Divorced. I know what you mean."

"So they're sitting there with their 'girly' drinks, their Fuzzy Navels or Godmothers or Black Russians or something with a little paper umbrella in it, and all of a sudden they look up and there is this guy. Hovering. Looming. Getting ready to deliver his prepackaged opening line."

"Are we really that bad?" I said. "Men?"

"You men are not bad at all, I'm just telling you the way it is," she said. "And because it's a bar or a club, there's no time for the social niceties. He's got to take the ball downcourt, shoot, and score — or toss an airball. Either way, time is of the essence for him."

Inside my jacket, my phone pager vibrated. I resisted taking it out to look at the readout. "So . . ."

"So he zeros in on the one of the two women he's decided that he wants, and just about treats the other one as if she was an empty chair."

I started to say something, but she put up a hand to forestall it. "He doesn't do it to be mean, it's just the way things work, okay?"

"Okay."

"So the other woman, the one he's *not* interested in — she suddenly becomes a nonperson. She shrinks and shrivels like your skin does when you stay in the bathtub too long, and even if she chooses to ignore being ignored, to pretend the slight isn't happening, even if she looks around the room herself as if she's scoping out the action and cutting her own mustang out of the herd, inside she dies the death of a thousand cuts. It doesn't matter whether or not she likes the guy or thinks he's cute or would be interested in him even if he wanted her; she still feels like dogshit. Because we all want to be wanted, to be noticed, to be validated."

"Some women will say they don't need a man to validate them."

"Need it? No, you're damn right they don't. I don't, for instance, because I've learned to live without it. But want it? Ah, that is another story altogether." She took a gulp of her wine as if it were straight whiskey, and grimaced. "And this way is rejection in its purest and cruelest form — indifference."

I nodded. "Men get rejected all the time, though," I said. "Because even in our new and enlightened and raised-consciousness age, we're still the ones who do most of the asking."

"I agree, Milan," she said, and she leaned forward slightly, her face setting and hardening in a way I'm sure she was unaware of. "But there are safeguards in place for men. Rationalizations and denials they can use to save face. A woman shoots a guy down and he can tell himself it's because she's already seeing somebody else, or she's the type that just isn't easy, or she doesn't want the friend she's with to know that she sometimes fucks guys she meets in bars. For some reason it just never occurs to men that a woman might not find them attractive. But it occurs to women, all the time. It's something we accept and live with, like cellulite or getting cramps once a month, but it's there."

"I'm sure it is. But I don't quite see your point."

"My point is," she said, "that when Ellen and I were out together we never had worries like that, because we knew damn well nobody was going to try to bust a move on either one of us. We could just be comfortable and enjoy each other's company and giggle and have our girl talk, knowing that neither one of us was going to go home feeling bad or rejected or left out while the other one was passing out phone numbers or getting laid. Okay?"

"Okay," I said.

"I don't know if that tells you what you

wanted to know."

"Partly," I said. "Because when a young, healthy single woman commits suicide like that, it's not unreasonable to wonder whether there might be a broken romance at the heart of it."

"You'll forgive me if I find that a little condescending," she said without rancor. "Believe it or not there are some people — even some men — who are completely at peace with not having a significant other. Whether they've talked themselves into it because they figure they don't have a chance in hell anyway, or whether they just don't happen to enjoy sex and intimacy, they're okay with being who they are and enjoying their own company. Ellen was like that, I think. I never heard her pulling a Snow White."

"A 'Snow White'?"

She grinned. "Yes, mooning and sighing and fluttering and singing to the bluebirds, wishing aloud that someday her prince will come. That wasn't what she was about."

"Probably not," I said. "But my point stands. Quite often when a young adult takes their own life, there's love or romance involved, and I'd be remiss in my duties not to ask you."

"Well," Sarah Donnem said, "I can't say

119

yes or no on that for sure. I mean, Ellen might have fallen head over heels for someone she was worshiping from afar and decided she didn't have a chance in hell with him and couldn't live without him. But if she was in love, she didn't share it with me. I can tell you one thing, though."

"What's that?"

"That she wasn't *in* a relationship anytime before she died. She once told me she hadn't had sex since she was in college. I'm sure if that situation had changed, I would have heard about it."

"You were that close?"

Her eyes got damp and shiny, and she rotated her head around on her neck as if she had a sudden crick. "We were that close," she said. "I was the only real friend Ellen had."

Chapter Seven

A person dies, someone you don't know and have never seen. You begin to find out about them, getting little nuggets of insight from a variety of different sources, each having his or her own perspective. Each piece of information fits into a different slot, and gradually a recognizable image begins to emerge. It's almost like watching a photograph in a tray of developing fluid. First the general outline appears; details follow, becoming sharper, more precise. You hang it up on the line to dry and step back to look at it, and suddenly what was fuzzy and indistinct coalesces and becomes more comprehensible.

And despite some contradictory bits of information I'd gleaned from her friends and father and co-workers, I was beginning to get a pretty recognizable picture of Ellen Carnine.

Born into comfortable middle class, she had managed herself into scholastic and business achievement by dint of hard work and a first-class mind. She had carved out for herself what she thought was the best life possible, and unlike so many children of the late twentieth century who have raised the "poor me" of victimhood to an art form, Ellen Carnine had refused to wallow in self-pity just because her appearance was not pleasing to most people.

I've played a good bit of poker in my day, and while games sometimes seem frivolous, there is much to be learned from them. My card-table experience has taught me, for instance, that the measure of a successful life is how well a person is able to play whatever cards they've been dealt, whether good or bad. By that standard Ellen had amassed an impressive stack of chips.

And all at once I found myself wanting to know the reason for her suicide almost as much as her father did, hoping — knowing — it had to be some other reason than simply feeling sorry for herself. From what little I knew of her, that just did not seem to be in her character.

Despite glowing news reports of neighbors saving children from burning houses, or military men risking their lives to take out an enemy position, or glandular fortunates who can knock a baseball over the center-field wall at Jacobs Field or sink more than twenty baskets per game, the real heroes in life are the quiet ones whose contributions don't make headlines or lead off the *Six O'Clock News*, who don't even want to know the meaning of self-pity, and can't conceive the concept of blame for others. The ones who unobtrusively keep on keeping on.

Ellen Carnine fit that heroic profile. It did not jibe with her doing the Dutch.

When I left Sarah Donnem at Noggin's and climbed back into my car, I jotted down much of what she'd told me in my little spiral notebook. I must have twenty of them lying around the apartment or the office so there's always one within easy reach to shove into a pocket. But I've found that when I'm dealing with civilians, ordinary people not used to questions and crimes and the ways of private investigators, taking notes in front of them often puts them on edge and makes them guarded. Watching someone write down what you say makes your words seem so permanent, so unretractable. So I've developed a pretty good memory, and rarely miss anything as long as I make my notes immediately after my interviews while they're still fresh and green in my mind. Then I transfer the notes to my hard drive.

I filled three pages.

I took out my phone pager and checked the readout to see who had called while I was sitting at the bar in Noggin's A. ZARAFONITOS, it said, a number with a downtown exchange. The multiple messages I'd left on her voice mail had finally gotten through to her.

I waited till I got home before I called her.

She picked up on the third ring, sounding a bit out of breath, as though she'd been racing to the telephone. In the background I could hear Celine Dion singing that inescapable song from *Titanic* that I'd hoped would finally go away when the movie did. It hasn't.

I explained who I was and why I was calling, even though I had already done so the first time I had talked to her voice mail.

"I was as shocked as anyone about Ellen," she told me, her voice low and smooth and sexy like the purr of a Porsche's engine. "About what she did. And just as much in the dark. It's keeping me awake at night, thinking maybe I could have said something to her, done something . . ."

"To make her jump off the bridge?"

"No, of course not," she said quickly and

a little icily. "I meant maybe I could have said or done something to prevent it."

"I'd like to sit down and talk to you about it," I said.

"I can't imagine what I could tell you that might help."

"I can't, either. We won't know until we talk."

"Well, I'm kind of pressed for time . . ."

"Can I take you to lunch tomorrow, then?" She didn't answer me for a moment. "You have to eat, anyway," I added.

"Mr. Jacovich, are you asking me out?"

"Hardly, Ms. Zarafonitos. I've never laid eyes on you."

Her embarrassed laugh came too quickly, feathery, breathless and flirtatious. "I'm sorry. It's just that I've had that line used on me before. Men think if they say lunch and not dinner, I'll be too dumb to realize they're hitting on me."

I was dying to ask her if it usually worked, but I didn't. "This *is* lunch, not dinner. That way, our meeting won't cut into your workday or your free time, either. What do you say?"

"I guess it would be all right. I work downtown, you know."

"So do I."

"Good. Is Johnny's Downtown all right?"

"Sure," I said. Apparently Anna Zarafonitos had elegant tastes, especially when someone else was footing the bill. "Noon?"

"That's fine, or maybe just a few minutes after. I'll meet you at the bar, all right?"

"Okay. How will I know you?"

"Oh, you'll know me," she purred. "I'm tall, with very long dark hair and I'll have on glasses. I can't be more specific than that because I haven't decided what I'm going to wear tomorrow."

Dark hair and glasses might describe five thousand women who worked downtown, I thought as I hung up. But how many of them would be walking into Johnny's a few minutes after noon and alone? I didn't think identifying her would be a problem.

I couldn't help wondering about her, though. About her self-image. A woman whose best friend has just committed suicide and who automatically assumes the private investigator who wants to talk to her about it is asking her for a date, sight unseen, was someone about whom I couldn't help being curious.

The morning was January-dark, overcast and very warm even for May, the nine A.M. temperature in the low seventies and the dewpoint at 67, which translates to muggy and uncomfortable. There was moisture hanging in the air like recently washed laundry on a line, making deep breathing wet and difficult. My car's air conditioner, which had grown noisy of late — not unusual for a nine-year-old Pontiac Sunbird — almost drowned out WMJI's John Lanigan on the radio, who was merrily eviscerating a local politician with funny, on-target barbs. *Almost* is the operative word here; the air conditioner hasn't been invented yet that can drown out Lanigan when he's on a roll.

I parked in a garage on East Ninth Street and went up to the twenty-sixth floor of the high-rise where Duane Starrett worked in a brokerage. The reception area was all done up in black marble, dark green leather, and white-tiled floor, dominated by an enormous scrap-iron sculptured world globe. The entire effect made the Cuyahoga County Morgue seem downright homey.

I gave my name to the woman at the desk, who picked up her telephone, punched a few buttons on her console, and announced me to Duane Starrett. Then she told me to have a seat. The leather of the armchair I chose crackled when I sat in it.

After five minutes Duane came briskly down a long corridor and out into the reception area, wearing a dark gray no-nonsense business suit. I hauled myself out of the deep chair as she approached me. More crackling.

"I'm still not comfortable with this," she said. "Your searching the apartment. It's kind of a violation, if you know what I mean."

"I'm not searching the apartment, just Ellen's room. I promise I won't even go into your room, Ms. Starrett, and I won't touch anything in the living room, either."

"Well . . ." she said dubiously.

"And I won't take anything as a souvenir."

She allowed herself the distant whisper of a smile. "I wasn't really worried that you would." She handed me a set of keys on a chain with a tiny ceramic baseball with the Chief Wahoo logo on it. "The silver one is for the regular lock and the gold one is for the deadbolt."

"Thanks." I pocketed them.

"Those are Ellen's keys," she said, casting her eyes to the pristine white floor.

"I probably won't get there until about four-thirty this afternoon, if that's all right."

She nodded. "I don't particularly want to be there when you are. It would be creepy. I'll call up a friend and go out for dinner until you're through. Any idea how long you're going to be?"

"A couple of hours," I said. "Probably not more. At least I hope not."

"I'll come back at ten o'clock, then. I have to get *some* sleep. You be gone by then, okay?"

"Fine."

"Keep the keys for as long as you like, in case you have to come back again. Just let me know in advance when you're going to be there. If I come in and find you unexpectedly, I'll probably faint dead away. And if you just walk in unannounced while I'm there, I might shoot you first and ask questions later."

"You have a gun?"

"Of course," she said, as if it were the most natural thing in the world. "It's downtown."

That gave me something else to brood about besides paying seven dollars to park for twenty-five minutes. While downtown Cleveland is safe and well patrolled, especially in the last several years since so many residential units have opened up there, it is not a bucolic suburb. And as I drove through the downtown streets, now buzzing with morning vehicular and pedestrian traffic, I wondered whether Ellen Carnine had been subject to dangers no one had thought of yet.

When I got to my office shortly before eleven, I made my morning coffee, creature of habit that I am, and while it bubbled and dripped I read the autopsy report again, wondering if perhaps Ellen Carnine might have been sexually assaulted and become so unhinged by it to cause her to kill herself. That proved to be a dead end; there was no mention of recent sexual activity in the autopsy findings.

Of course it might have happened days, even weeks earlier, and gnawed on her until she could bear it no longer. But none of her friends had mentioned any radical changes in her behavior and attitude just prior to her death, except for Redmond Munch saying she'd become more withdrawn in the past six months, and I decided I might be building a scenario that was not only fanciful but would lead me down the wrong paths when I might better expend my efforts elsewhere.

Still, the autopsy report troubled me, not so much for what it said, but for what it did not. And I couldn't quite identify exactly what there was about it that left me feeling incomplete.

I transferred the remembrances of my meeting with Sarah Donnem from my spiral notebook to my hard drive, and added some reflections of my own. Impressions. Not just from Sarah, but from everyone I had talked to so far, even William Carnine. I didn't know how valuable they might prove to be, but they were like kaleidoscopic fragments that were falling into patterns that might present a discernible portrait.

I wondered what kind of a picture would ultimately be drawn by a private investigator who wandered around interviewing *my* family and closest associates. My ex-wife. My children. My former girlfriends. My buddies. My clients — the satisfied ones and the ones who didn't like me much. The cops with whom I frequently came in contact. Did they know me any better than Ellen's parents and gal pals and business associates knew her? Would a clear and true image of Milan Jacovich appear in the developing tray, or would there be wildly conflicting viewpoints?

Conflicting, I decided. Because I believe all of us are different depending on who's across the table. I certainly wouldn't treat a potential lover, or my insurance agent, or my downstairs office neighbor, the wrought-iron guy, the same way I would a Catholic priest or my poker buddies or a librarian, or a snitch who lived in a near-west-side rooming house and made it from one short dog to the next on the occasional double sawbuck I slipped him for information.

Everyone requires their own special treatment, a face that, in essence, you show only to them. Each of us has a trunkful of masks and wigs and false noses we don for different occasions. Even you, probably.

So I donned my concerned and dogged private-eye persona, and just before noon I headed back up out of the Flats. Since Johnny's Downtown has no valet parking during the day, I paid another five bucks to stash my car in the lot across the street. The Ellen Carnine case was getting expensive.

The only person at the bar when I walked in was close to sixty, dressed in a fifteen-hundred-dollar Italian suit and smoking a fragrant cigar, and had no hair at all, long and dark or otherwise. He looked vaguely familiar to me, and I thought perhaps he might be a sitting judge, the restaurant being a regular lunchtime watering hole for the nearby courthouse crowd. In any case, he was not the person I'd come there to meet. Nevertheless he nodded pleasantly to me, and blew some cigar smoke my way. He must have figured I was a voter.

In keeping with the understatedly elegant ambiance of the bar, I decided to forgo my Stroh's with no glass and ordered an Absolut Citron on the rocks, kept one eye on the television set for whatever nuggets of interest the Channel Twelve noon news might have to offer, and waited.

At twelve-fifteen Anna Zarafonitos walked in.

She had not misspoken about her height — I estimated her to be about five foot nine — or her long dark hair; it hung six inches below her waist in luxuriantly tumbling curls, and the hem of the skirt to her turquoise-blue suit missed meeting it by less than a foot. The jersey blouse she wore beneath the suit jacket stopped short of concealing the lush swelling of the tops of her breasts. It was business chic, all right, but designed to keep men's minds pretty much off business. Her face was not pretty in the conventional sense, but her large, aggressive features were definitely exotic, and the rimless round glasses she had promised she'd be wearing were lightly tinted a soft gray and magnified her dark green eyes. She was very striking, and would have been much more so if she hadn't known it. I don't think I've ever seen someone so aware and confident of her own sensuality.

She looked from me to my bald friend at the end of the bar, who came very close to falling off his stool when he saw her. She must have decided he just didn't look like a private investigator should and that I fit the bill much better. She then turned on me the full wattage of a dazzling, practiced smile that I could only characterize as desperately flirtatious.

"You must be Milan," she said to me, and held out her hand in such a way that I could choose to shake it or kiss it. I opted for the former.

The hostess led us to a table up front near the window, the facade of the Renaissance Hotel and Terminal Tower rising across Superior Avenue in full view. Even while she flirted with the waiter, Anna

Zarafonitos was very particular about the glass of merlot she ordered, asking so many questions about it that they began falling into the too-much-information category, enough so that when the waiter finally served it, he stood by somewhat nervously while she tasted it and looked relieved when she nodded her satisfaction. She was the kind of person who drank as though she were starring in a television wine commercial and millions of people were watching.

"What do you want from me, Milan?" she said, her soft throaty purr insinuating that nothing I could ask would be too great a sacrifice. "Just what is it you're looking for?"

"As I told you on the phone, Ellen's parents want to know what happened. They want to know why."

She looked at me over the tops of her glasses. "What makes you think I'd be able to tell you?"

"Well, you were her friend . . ."

"Yes," she said, suddenly serious. "And I am devastated. I was practically prostrate for three days after it happened." She took another sip of her merlot, less self-aware than she'd been for the first taste. "Prostrate. It's a terrible thing to lose a friend."

Tell me about it, I thought, and all at once the pain of Marko Meglich's death clamped down on my insides like the sharp teeth of a burrowing rodent. It took me unawares sometimes, the pain, and I wondered whether it would ever really fade away or whether I'd lug it around with me always like one of those suitcases on wheels that flight attendants have trailing along behind them.

"You knew Ellen pretty well," I said.

She reached both hands up to her hair, grabbed two fistfuls, and pushed it behind her ears where it stayed for all of ten seconds. "Well enough. We went out together a few times a month. For dinner. Sometimes to the Spy Bar or the Velvet Tango for a drink afterward. We talked a lot."

"About?"

"Everything. Single women don't just talk sports and sex the way single men do. Ellen and I discussed business quite a bit, because that was her main focus, since she didn't really have any sort of social life." She tried not to make it sound judgmental, and failed.

"You and Ellen seem very different," I said.

She raised her chin and her breasts at the same time, and beamed as if I'd paid

136

her a compliment; I didn't like her much for that. "I guess that was the attraction. I go out with men a lot. I'm always either in a relationship or just getting out of one, and frankly I think Ellen lived vicariously through me, through listening to my stories."

"That explains why she was your friend. Why were you hers?"

She colored slightly and looked away. "She — had a great sense of humor." It took her a few moments to think of that one, I noted; the answer had not come to her easily or quickly. "I laughed a lot when I was with her."

"That was it?"

Her eyes flashed behind the lenses. "What more do you want?"

"I don't know. Maybe something I can get my teeth into."

"Try the meat loaf," she suggested, and picked up her menu. The expectant waiter hovered nearby.

"I was planning to. I love Johnny's meat loaf at lunch. But that isn't exactly what I meant."

"What did you mean, then?"

"Look, Ms. Zarafonitos . . ."

"Anna." A flash of flirtatious smile again; I think it was second nature with her. Perhaps genetic.

"Anna. Every relationship is symbiotic in some way or another, or else it doesn't last. You know what I mean?"

The smile flickered and retreated from whence it had come. "I went to college, Milan, I know what 'symbiotic' means. You just can't imagine why somebody like me, someone who is very social and outgoing and, frankly, attractive, would spend time with someone like Ellen."

"Besides the laughs, yes."

She put her menu down on the table and took off her glasses. She fluttered her eyelashes at me, and the hovering waiter, disappointed, went somewhere else. "I wonder if I can really trust you."

I shrugged. "As much as I can trust you, I guess."

The eyes opened wide. "Don't you trust me?"

"I have no reason not to. Don't you trust *me?*"

"Yes," she said after some deliberation. "Yes, I do. I just don't want you to think badly of me."

It was already too late for that, but I didn't say so. "I won't," I promised, mentally crossing my fingers.

"I hope not." She took a deep breath

which did interesting things to her chest. "To be honest, I liked being out with Ellen because she was absolutely no competition for me when it came to men."

"I wouldn't think you'd have to worry about competition," I said, knowing it was the right thing to say to her; Anna Zarafonitos was the kind of woman who would wither and droop if she wasn't paid a generous number of compliments by men every day.

"It's difficult in the club scene," she explained. "A woman really doesn't like going someplace like the Velvet Tango by herself; we've come a long way, baby, but not far enough that a woman alone in a bar isn't considered loose."

I nodded.

"But yet when there are two attractive women together, very often men won't even come over to talk because they don't want to be in the position of offending one of them by showing more interest in the other."

"Just in case it's the other one who might be interested in them."

She nodded.

"And that didn't happen when you were with Ellen?"

She just laughed. "I don't mean to speak

ill of the dead, Milan, but give me a break, okay?"

The one I'd like to have given her would have been her kneecap. "You mean you'd just leave Ellen sitting there in a bar and go off with some man?"

Her laughter stopped and she sucked it back into her mouth as her features hardened into granite — gray and very cold. "Do I look like some sort of bar slut? Of course I wouldn't go home with anybody ten minutes after I met them." Then the hard look turned playful again. "I'm not averse to giving out my phone number, though. When the right person asks for it."

"And when you were with Ellen you never had to worry that anyone was going to ask for hers instead."

"I suppose it could have happened. But it never did." She shook her head at the unimaginable. "What a blow to the old ego *that* would have been."

"And you didn't much care that it might have made Ellen uncomfortable?"

She tossed her hair. "Everything made Ellen uncomfortable when it came to men. Hey, I couldn't help it that she looked the way she did. I kept telling her to lose weight, to do something with her hair, maybe change her makeup; every time we were together, I told her. And one of her other friends, Bronwyn Rhys, told her too."

"You know Bronwyn?"

"Yes, we've met several times. She seemed to think Ellen was the smartest woman in the world." She lowered her voice. "Bronwyn isn't exactly a rocket scientist, you know. Beautiful, but not much going on upstairs."

"But you and Bronwyn were always after Ellen to lose weight?"

"Not *after* her, exactly. But we always mentioned it to her. It was for her own good, you know. I even gave her the name of the spa where I go. I mean, she was never going to be pretty, but she could have at least been presentable." She sighed deeply again and leaned forward, giving me the full-bore treatment. "So I'm sorry she was so miserable, but I'd be less than honest if I didn't say it was kind of her own fault."

"That she was lonely and unhappy."

"Of course."

"She told you she was?"

Anna's eyes opened wide. "Well, no. Not in so many words, at least. But she just *had* to be."

"Because she wasn't getting laid every night?"

141

She turned brittle again. "Hey, is that some kind of crack? Because if you think I'm some kind of round-heeled bar bimbo, think again, buster! I've been in a steady relationship for the past seven months. That might have been what was driving Ellen so crazy."

"Why would it?"

She picked up the menu once more and studied it as if cramming for an exam. "Maybe because I've been seeing her boss."

"Barnard Landenberger?"

"No," she said disdainfully, without looking up. "He's married. I don't do married men, Milan, there's no future in it." And then she glanced at my left hand to see if I was wearing a wedding ring; I don't think she was interested, but she was the type of woman to whom checking out ring fingers was almost reflexive. And then she said, "I've been seeing Red Munch."

And having at last made her decision about what to eat for lunch, she looked around and imperiously summoned our waiter.

Chapter Eight

Okay, so one of Ellen Carnine's best friends was dating her boss. In light of Ellen's diving off a bridge, was that supposed to be significant? Was she in love with Red Munch herself and despondent that Anna had taken him away from her?

I thought about Red Munch and decided it was unlikely.

Although — everybody loves somebody sometime.

I assumed that by saying she was "seeing him," Anna Zarafonitos meant that she was sleeping with him, which didn't say much for her taste. But she hadn't said she was in love with him. I didn't think she was the type to fall in love anyway. She definitely had an agenda. An attractive woman who had learned to use what she had, flirtatiousness and sensuality came as naturally to her as walking or breathing. And the positive attention of men was obviously very important to her, enough so that she made sure that when she went out trolling she was with someone like Ellen who would pose no competition for her.

Some friend.

I suppose in that regard she wasn't unlike most of the rest of us. It would certainly be nice for me to believe that all women look on me as a hunk, even though I know I'm just average. The difference is that if they don't happen to, I don't get exercised about it. After one brief lunch I knew Anna Zarafonitos well enough to think that she would go postal if she ever met a man she thought didn't get jelly-kneed by just looking at her.

What all that had to do with Ellen's death, I had no idea. The only thing that had struck me about the lunch meeting was that Anna was practically alone among Ellen's friends and associates in thinking that her suicide was not terribly surprising.

When I got back to my office I added Anna to the notes on my computer file. Then, because I had an hour to kill, I pulled out a stack of blank three-by-five cards and inscribed eight of them with the names of all the people I had talked to: Anna, Redmond Munch, Barnard Landenberger, Duane Starrett, Karen Conley, Sarah Donnem, Bronwyn Rhys, and Ellen's father, Dr. William Carnine. Then I put Ellen's name on another one. I laid them out on my desk, Ellen's a constant in the center, and moved the others around it like orbiting satellites, forming different patterns, just to see whether I could make any sense out of the relationships.

It didn't work. Sometimes it does, but in Ellen's case it didn't, and I was frustrated to realize I was no closer to a reason for her death than I had been when I started.

I stacked the cards and put them into Ellen Carnine's folder, had another cup of coffee, and then stood to greet Taffy Kiser as she walked into my office and lit it up like the sun emerging from behind a cloudbank.

My son's girlfriend was beautiful. Not in the classic sense, and certainly not in the *Playboy/Baywatch* mode, but so pretty that it made my teeth ache. She had a smile that radiated genuine warmth, unlike that of Anna Zarafonitos, whom I was certain practiced hers daily in front of a mirror. Taffy Kiser's eyes were blue, her hair was chin-length and soft blonde, and I estimated her height at about five foot eight, just perfect for Milan's six foot one. Long legs appeared beneath khaki shorts, and she wore a gray Kent State T-shirt a lot like one I frequently wore myself, with blue-and-gold lettering. Over it she had slipped a man's blue plaid shirt, worn open all the way, that I thought looked familiar. Then I realized I'd bought it for my son the previous Christmas. She was a year older than Milan, nineteen, and all at once I was a hundred and seven.

"I've heard so much about you," she said, taking my hand in her cool one.

"I wish I could say the same. I didn't even know Milan was seeing anyone until yesterday."

She laughed. "Why doesn't that surprise me? You know Milan. He's the most private person I ever met." Her eyes sparkled a little when she talked about him, softly, like the effervescence in champagne. And I felt the bubbles in my heart, too, knowing Milan had found someone so special.

My son had been a moody, quiet child who had grown into a quiet young man. Athletically gifted, it had always seemed to me that his only true zeal in life was for catching a football and that very little else brought him real happiness. Seeing this lovely, glowing, coltish creature who obviously adored him, gave me hope for him — that perhaps when her head was on his shoulder some shafts of sunlight, or maybe even moonbeams, illuminated the darkness he had inherited from his Serbian mother.

I had to shake myself loose from the reverie that perhaps this woman would be the mother of my first grandchild. She and Milan Junior were still only kids, after all, and both had many miles to travel.

Even so . . .

"I should tell you that even though I'm pretty good with computers, I'm no hacker," she said, jerking me roughly back into reality. "I'm not sure what Milan told you, or what you're hoping I can help you with, but I'm not good enough to break into the White House's secret files or anything."

"Nothing like that," I said, laughing. "This is a personal computer we're talking about. The woman who owned it committed suicide last week. Before that she used to spend all her time on the Internet. I just want to find out where she went and who she was talking to. Possible?"

"It's not *im*possible," Taffy said. "It all depends."

"On?"

She smiled and shrugged. "I won't know until we get there."

"Let's go, then. We can grab something to eat first if you're hungry."

"That's okay," she said. "Milan and I had a late lunch."

I tried not to beam as I locked up the office.

On the short drive over I explained Ellen Carnine a little bit — her history as I knew it, her looks, her job — at least enough so that Taffy could get an idea of what I was looking for on that computer.

When I let us into the Starrett/Carnine apartment, Taffy couldn't contain her admiration. Empty and pristine and free from clutter, it must have looked to Taffy like a bachelor girl's dream pad. I found it without warmth or personality, and perhaps a little sad.

"Wow," she said. "What a neat apartment. And right in the middle of downtown, too."

"You think you'd like living downtown?"

She cocked her head to one side like a bird, listening. "My first impulse is to say yes, but I tend to think it's more fun to think about it than actually do it."

"Is your family from Cleveland?"

"No, I'm just a small-town girl from Mansfield. But I know Cleveland pretty well. We used to come up here for shows and concerts and ball games."

"Let's try it. The computer in question is in here."

We turned to our right and went to the

door at that end of the long, square living room. As I opened it and stood aside for Taffy to enter, I realized I hadn't been inside that room before.

Ellen Carnine's room.

A feminine room, perhaps a little fussy and frilly for someone almost thirty years old, a ruffled sham around the bottom of the double bed, rag dolls on the dresser along with a bottle of Shalimar and another of White Diamonds, framed art-deco posters on one wall. On a second wall was her college diploma, a Bryarly College flag, and several framed photographs of Ellen, some showing her years younger and a few pounds lighter, including one in her cap and gown with her parents and an older man, and several of her with youthful-looking female friends, one of whom wore a Bryarly sweatshirt. Obviously they all had been taken in Ellen's college days, which I supposed had been the happiest times of her life.

The other two walls were nearly all large windows; one looked north toward the lake, and the other facing west toward the Detroit-Superior Bridge with the river swirling beneath it.

The bed was unmade but still neat. One corner of the sheet and blanket were turned down, and there was an indentation on one of the two pillows, as if one person had been sleeping on the side of the bed closest to the window. A reading lamp was clipped onto the headboard. The other side of the bed looked almost untouched, save for the presence of a teddy bear about the size of a year-old baby, dressed in a miniature Bryarly College T-shirt and rally cap, who perched regally cross-eyed on the unused pillow against the headboard, another mute witness to Ellen's nostalgia for her days in the groves of academia.

Next to the bed was a nightstand. Small lamp with a frilly shade, notepad, ballpoint pen, a paperback romance novel by Julie Garwood, with a bookmark about two-thirds of the way to the end.

"It's a PowerSpec," Taffy said.

"What?"

"The computer." She sat down in the chair before the computer desk. "A Power-Spec, that's the brand."

"Okay," I said. I glanced over at it. It was a laptop, about the size of a large notebook. It was closed.

"Shall I boot it up?"

"Sure, go ahead. I'm going to prowl a little."

Taffy opened the laptop and turned it

on, and I heard it beeping and whirring as I walked into Ellen's bathroom. The room told me nothing. It contained cosmetics, toothpaste, deodorant, makeup, cotton balls, and all the usual accoutrements on a small wicker table. Towels were neatly folded on their racks except for one large bath sheet that was hung over the shower rod. I imagined that Ellen had taken a shower on her last night on earth.

I looked in the medicine cabinet. Tylenol, Midol, a large box of tampons, Vicks Formula 44 cough medicine with about half of it gone. I opened the medicine bottle; obviously Ellen Carnine hadn't used it for a long time because the cap stuck until I gave it a good hard twist. No birth-control pills or any other form of contraceptives that I could see.

The drawers under the sink held no surprises, either. Scrubs, mud masques, a hair dryer and curling iron. The space beneath the sink held a tall bottle of mouthwash, a plastic container of talcum powder, a spray bottle of cleanser, a can of Lysol room deodorizer, some sponges, and a tin of Comet cleanser.

I pulled open the shower curtain; the plumbing fixtures looked fairly new, probably because the old building had been remodeled and converted to apartments only very recently. There was a nearly new cake of Dial soap in the soap dish, and two bottles of shampoo, one for dandruff and one for oily hair, and a bottle of conditioner in the shower caddy. A puffy plastic scrubber was looped over the shower head. The tub and the wall tiles were spotless. I was impressed with Ellen's fastidiousness and neatness; it bordered on the compulsive.

I had a small snapshot camera in my pocket, one that I always carry in the glove compartment of my car, and I took it out and photographed the bathroom from every angle, making sure I didn't shoot directly into the mirror, to avoid the glare of the flash.

I went back out into the bedroom.

"Okay, here I am," Taffy said, and when I looked over she had a main menu on the computer screen. "Where do you want to go?"

"Let's take a look at her word-processing program first."

"You've got it." Her fingers flew across the keyboard, and in a few seconds there was another menu displayed, with all Ellen's files listed.

I looked at them. None of them

appeared to contain any sort of journal or diary, and I wondered whether she had kept one by hand rather than on her computer.

"Can you get into any of those files?" I said.

"Unless they're password-protected, sure. Let me try."

I pointed at one that was marked LTRS001.

"You think those might be letters?" I said.

"Probably."

"See if you can get into that one first."

Taffy put her hand on the navigating stick and moved the arrow to that file, then double-clicked.

"No password — we're in luck," she said.

After a few seconds the screen filled up with a business letter, dated January 4, 2001, written to a Volvo dealership on the east side, complaining about some repair work that had not been done to Ellen's satisfaction.

"Next one," I said.

Taffy hit the PAGE DOWN key, and a letter to a Professor Richard Goodman at Bryarly College appeared, dated January 11. It was chatty, newsy, and mostly about her work.

"Can you print out this whole file of letters, Taffy?"

"Sure," she said. "But it's forty-one pages long. It'll take a while." She pointed to the printer next to the computer itself on the desk. "This isn't a high-speed printer."

"Okay, never mind," I said. "I'll do it myself later."

Her eyes twinkled. "You know how?"

"I'm not a complete idiot."

She laughed. "Milan said when it comes to computers, you are."

"Milan doesn't know everything," I said. I jotted down Goodman's name and address in my notebook. "Can you get onto her Internet provider?"

"Sure, but we're probably going to need a password to access it."

"Maybe we can figure one out," I said. "Let's give it a try."

Taffy did some more things with keys and the mouse, and in about a minute the SIGN-ON DIALOGUE box appeared on the screen. More beeps and clicks, and we were given two screen names.

"How come two screen names, Taffy? I just have one, and it's my last name."

"Lots of people do that. Sometimes they have more than two." She pointed to the

first one, which was simply "ECARNINE."
"This one, for instance, which is basically her real name. She probably uses it to log on to the World Wide Web for research or maybe to buy things online, like books and stuff, correspond with friends via e-mail, maybe even for business, if she works at home." She moved her finger downward. "This one is obviously her chat-room name."

I read it and the hair stood up on the backs of my hands.

"CHUBETTE," it said.

"Why would anyone choose such a self-deprecating screen name?"

"Maybe she didn't think it was," Taffy answered. She swiveled around in the chair and looked at me. "Maybe she'd come to an acceptance of her size and her looks where she would think that calling herself a 'chubette' was either kind of cute or something to actually be proud of. You know, there's a magazine called *Big, Beautiful Woman* that actually celebrates being heavy. That old saying about 'inside every fat person is a thin person screaming to get out' is just a lot of crap, you know."

"You think?"

"I know so. My mother is heavy. She's not obese or anything, but she's at least forty pounds overweight, and it doesn't bother her a bit. Not every woman dreams of looking like a centerfold, Mr. Jacovich. And not every man wants her to, either."

"I guess you're right," I said.

"But we've come to something of a road-block on this 'puter. I need a password to go any farther."

I looked around the room. "Would she have written her password down some-where?"

"I doubt it, any more than she'd have written down her own phone number. It's one of those things people tend to remember, especially the ones who spend lots of time online the way you say she did."

"So we're stuck?"

"There are some software programs to figure out passwords," she said. "We have them at school. But this computer doesn't seem to have one."

"Damn!"

"How old was she?"

"Twenty-nine. Why?"

"Some people use a combination of their name and age. Wait, let me try a couple of things."

She typed and clicked, typed and clicked. Eight times. Then she sat back in the chair. "No dice. I tried her first and last names with her age and with the year she was born, but nothing worked."

"Try anything with 'fat' in it," I suggested. " 'Fat girl,' 'fat chick,' 'heavyset,' combinations like that."

"You really think anyone would choose that as a password?" she laughed.

"Her screen name was Chubette. Why not?"

She nodded. "I'll try."

She began clicking again, and I took the time to scope out the room. I moved to Taffy's side and opened the drawers of the desk. A vinyl-bound checkbook from Firstar Bank, phone bills and credit-card receipts, and a small Day Planner were the only things that interested me. I removed them and put them into my briefcase, which I'd put on the bed when we came in. I would look at them at my leisure.

I opened the closet again, ruffling idly through the hanging clothes. They were mostly business attire, suits and tailored dresses. A few outfits that could have been worn for a night on the town, silk blouses, two "little black dresses" in a size 20. The scent of White Diamonds was very strong here. There was a dresser in one corner of the closet, and I pulled open the drawers.

157

Serviceable and not-very-sexy underwear, sweaters, stockings. The usual stuff, with nothing hidden in the back, no secret envelopes taped to the bottom of the drawers. That only happens on television cop shows.

Neatly arranged along the floor of the closet were twenty-three pairs of shoes. Most were black or dark brown business shoes with sensible heels, two pairs of black three-inch heels, and an array of athletic shoes in black, white, blue, and gray. When I checked I found them all to be size 8½ D.

I stared at the shoes for a long while, feeling as if I was missing something. Then I remembered.

I closed the closet door, knelt down on the floor and looked under the bed. An old-fashioned leather suitcase was stored down there, enough dust bunnies to start a rabbit farm, and a pair of pink bedroom slippers, quite near the edge of the bed on the side where Ellen had slept.

I took out the slippers. They had seen some wear. What niggled at me now was why Ellen had not put *them* on, at least, before taking that last drive to the Lorain-Carnegie Bridge.

I slid the suitcase out and flopped it onto

the bed. Taffy Kiser raised her head from her labors and smiled at me over her shoulder. "I hope you're having better luck than I am."

"Not really," I said. "Not yet."

The suitcase was unlocked. I sprung the twin latches and opened it.

The contents could have stocked a Bryarly College museum. It seemed Ellen Carnine had saved practically everything from her academic career — notebooks, personal letters, photographs, theater and concert programs, folders with the Bryarly logo on them. An address book which I paged through quickly, discovering it held entries with the names and numbers of her college friends. Four diaries covered in white leather, one for each year she had spent as a student at Bryarly. Three yearbooks. There was also a gardenia corsage pressed in a clear plastic bag, the petals brown and wilted. I closed the suitcase and set it on the floor near the door; something else to go through later.

Taffy pushed herself away from the computer. "Sorry, Mr. Jacovich, but I'm not getting anything."

"Shit," I said. "Pardon my French." I sat down on the edge of the bed. The teddy bear in the Bryarly shirt and cap stared at me almost mockingly.

"I've tried every variation I could think of on 'fat girl,' 'chubby,' 'plump,' and 'big beautiful woman,' but I keep getting denied access. Unless you have any other ideas."

I made firm eye contact with the bear. "Just one. Ellen graduated from college in 1984 . . ."

"So?"

"So just for grins," I said, "try 'BRYARLY84' as a password and see if anything happens."

Taffy turned back to the computer, and typed the password. She hit enter, and after a couple of clicks and whirls, a new menu appeared on the screen, and a mechanical-sounding voice boomed startlingly through the small speaker embedded in the laptop.

"*Welcome,*" it said.

Chapter Nine

"There's Bryarly College stuff all over this room," Taffy Kiser said. "I should have figured it out myself. That was pretty astute of you, Mr. Jacovich."

"That's why they pay me the big bucks, Taffy." I said it with my tongue firmly planted in my cheek, and Taffy had the breeding and good grace not to laugh. I thought — again, not for the first time since I'd met her — that my son had chosen well.

"Okay, we're in," she said. "Now what?"

"You're asking the wrong guy. What are our choices?"

"The easiest one is to check her e-mail. She has some in her mailbox. Quite a bit, actually. I guess that's because no one has picked them up since . . ." Taffy's whole body quivered. Her world was not my world and she wasn't used to dealing with violent death. Then again, the suicide of a young, healthy woman like Ellen Carnine made me quiver a bit, too.

"Let's go there first, then."

161

"I have to tell you, this is creepy," she said. "It's like eavesdropping. Or being a Peeping Tom or something."

"I know the feeling."

"You do this all the time." It wasn't a question. "For a living."

"I frequently invade people's privacy, yes. And very often it *is* creepy. Most of the time they have good reasons for keeping secrets."

"And you think this Ellen had reasons for her secrets?"

"I don't know. I've gotten no place so far, and what's on this computer might be a key to why she did what she did."

"If you say so."

She called up the MAIL INBOX box screen. Seventeen messages were waiting. The first two, sent the day after Ellen had died, were identical, informing her that she MAY have won a trip to Florida.

"Shall I delete them?" Taffy said.

"No, let's just go on."

The third e-mail was a joke about a woman walking a rottweiler at the head of a funeral procession; Ellen had been one of more than two dozen people to whom it had been sent.

"What's the deal?" I said.

"Internet jokes. There are thousands of

them going around at any given moment. I saw this one last week sometime. Everybody gets them."

"I don't."

"That's because you don't have any online friends."

The picture I suddenly had of myself sitting forlorn and lonely in front of my computer because I didn't have any online friends was both amusing and kind of pathetic — the twenty-first-century version of the terminally dateless waiting for the phone to ring. "Who sent it?"

"The sender's screen name is 'Brownshoe,' " she said.

I saw where her finger pointed, and scribbled *Brownshoe* in my notebook. "People have nothing better to do than to send bad jokes to other people?"

"Some of the jokes are pretty good, though. It all depends."

"Okay," I said. "Next one."

She clicked onto the following message. It advertised an "XXX ALL TEEN PORN-SITE" and promised "NAKED WILLING TEENS."

"Child pornography?" I said.

Taffy shook her head. "No, just young women. I've seen a few of those sites, and I'd hate like hell to hold my breath since some of them were teenagers. But Internet pervs will believe anything."

"Now why do you suppose Ellen is getting mail like that?"

"Everybody who goes into chat rooms gets mail like that," Taffy said. "It's a mass-mailing, and it's called 'spam.' The electronic version of junk mail. Except it's illegal to send pornography through the United States mails and it's perfectly legitimate on here."

"Is spam always porno?"

"No. As a matter of fact, that's only about a quarter of it. You saw those first two about winning a trip to Florida. Most spam is get-rich-quick schemes or investment opportunities. Or else they're trying to sell you some kind of software. It's usually unsolicited, and most people delete it without reading it. I wouldn't think anything of it if I were you."

"The wonders of cyberspace. What's next?"

The next e-mail turned out to be an invitation to order Viagra, without a doctor's prescription, from a pharmacy in Thailand at a cost of about six dollars per pill. The real thing, or sugar-based placebos? I wondered. Or something worse, something harmful? Desperate people often take des-

164

perate measures, I guess.

After that came an offer of a dental insurance plan. And then, as Taffy had warned, an investment "opportunity" to "work at home in your spare time and make more money in a year than you've ever dreamed of." The nature of the work was not specified. We then skipped to a petition which, when signed and passed on, would supposedly raise money for a nine-year-old cancer victim in Oleantha, Kansas.

"That's phony," Taffy told me. "It's been circulating around for years."

"What's the point?"

She shrugged. "What's the point of most of this stuff?"

I was amused by a mass-mailed poem, illustrated with a smiley-face made up of keyboard characters, instructing each recipient to pass it along to five people, which would result in the recipient getting asked on a date; to ten people to fall in love; and to twenty people to find the "person of your dreams."

"Who has time to do all this crap?" I said.

"From the motion picture *Get a Life*," Taffy answered. "More?"

I sighed. "I suppose so."

The screen flickered, changed. There was a letter, this time addressed only to "CHUBETTE." Taffy and I both leaned forward to read it.

Ellen,
   What's up? Haven't heard from you in a while or seen you in chat.
   Hope everything is okay. You know how much I love to chat with you. And I worry about you when you aren't here.
   I miss you.
   You aren't mad at me, are you? :-(
                              Love as always,
                     *********Stan

The sender's screen name was "BREAM-BOAT."

I was struck by the strange little figure after *"You aren't mad at me, are you?"* "What's that, Taffy?"

"That's what you call an emoticon. When people are chatting or e-mailing, they realize the other person can't hear their tone of voice or see their face, so they use one of these to indicate what they're feeling." She pointed to the :-(and said, "This is a sad face. If you tilt your head to one side, you can see it."

166

I cocked my head sideways. Sure enough, I could see the eyes, the nose, the mouth downturned at the corners, the classic theatrical mask of tragedy. "How did Shakespeare and Hemingway and Dostoyevsky ever manage without emoticons?" I said.

"*They* knew how to write."

"I suppose that if you used the other parenthetical mark, it would be a smile, right?"

"You catch on quick."

"What are all those asterisks?"

She blushed prettily. "Kisses."

I felt my stomach do a little flip. "Now we're getting somewhere," I said. "A love affair."

"Probably not much more than an online love affair. I'd be willing to bet they never laid eyes on each other. It happens all the time. People become very attached to chat buddies. Marriages have busted up so one of the partners could run off with someone they've never even seen."

"Maybe. But it's still the first thing I've found that interested me. Can I get a hard copy of this?"

"Sure," she said. She did her digital magic, the printer hummed and buzzed, and after about thirty seconds a sheet of paper slid out onto the top of the desk. I read it over quickly and slipped it into my briefcase.

"Any more e-mails?"

We checked them all, but they turned out to be spam, and I grinned inwardly when I realized I had so quickly adopted the lingo and made it a part of my thinking. No wonder it's widely acknowledged that the Internet is addictive, like drugs or sex or tobacco or gambling.

"Except for Breamboat's letter, none of this tells me much," I said. "There must be someplace else we can go."

"Lots of places, depending on what you're looking for."

"She spent a lot of time in chat rooms. Can we go there?"

"There are thousands of chat rooms," she said. "I don't think it would do us any good just to surf around at random. Maybe she bookmarked some of them."

" 'Bookmarked'?"

Taffy sighed, ever patient. "You can put special places or rooms or sites on your computer and get to them via shortcut, rather than having to type out the entire URL. It speeds up the process quite a bit."

"And where would we find Ellen's special places?"

"In 'HANGOUTS,' " she said. She moved the pointer to an icon on the toolbar that sure enough said "HANGOUTS," and clicked.

Immediately another drop-down menu appeared. There were several lines, each containing a name. Some of them, like "SEARCH THE INTERNET MOVIE DATA-BASE," were self-explanatory. Evidently Ellen, like me, had been an old-movie buff.

Some of Ellen's other "HANGOUTS" had rather mysterious names. They seemed mysterious to me, anyway.

"Some of these are Web sites," Taffy explained. "And some of them look like chat rooms. Where shall we go first?"

"One of her friends said that she spent a lot of time in a chat room called the 'PLAIN JANE/CLEVELAND' room."

She scrolled down Ellen's list of hang-outs. "Yup. Here it is."

With the joystick, Taffy moved the arrow to the "PLAIN JANE" line. One click and we were in cyberspace, in the middle of a conversation.

OnlineHost: ***You are in "Romance – PlainJane Cleveland".***

Glamorama: um, i was paying more attention to my date then the movie, hun.

Endomorf: What type you like?

BigEmma: COME AGAIN?

CRTCLMASS: BOYS ARE GROWED

UP, NO SUPPORT, NO ALIMONEY
OhioCity: Send pic?
Endomorf: i love tequila it's the only
    hard liquor I drink.
CRTCLMASS: ELLEN! HI! WHERE YA
    BEEN?
Glamorama: Hey, Ellen. Missed ya,
    girlfriend

I looked at Taffy. "How do they know?"
She pointed to a box at one side of the screen. "There's a list of people who are in the room here. Should I answer them?"

"Sure. Play it cool, don't say too much."
She nodded and began typing.

Chubette: Hi, everybody
CRTCLMASS: WHAT'S UP, ELLEN?
    LONG TIME NO
Clevemama: {{{{{{{{{{Ellen}}}}}}}}}}

"That's a hug," Taffy said to my querying look.

"A hug?"

"Uh-huh."

"We're under a phony screen name. How do they know it's Ellen?"

"Oh, people who hang out in chat rooms on a regular basis all get to know each other's real first names." She smiled. "It would be kind of rude if everyone called her 'Chub,' wouldn't it?"

"Maybe you'd better answer," I said.

She typed.

Chubette: thnx, Clevemama
RuB2sday: We thought you'd given up on us, Ellen.
Chubette: No, just been busy.
RuB2sday: I bet
CRTCLMASS: IT'S BEEN BETTER THAN A YEAR SINCE I HAD ANY NOOKIE!!!!!
Glamorama: omg, Crtcl, u poor thing
Rex4Sex: go to bed by urself, Crtclmass
CRTCLMASS: I DON'T KNOW HOW MUCH LONGER I CAN LAST THIS WAY!!!
Endomorf: stop yelling, Crtclmass

" 'Yelling'?" I said.

"When you type all in capitals in a chat room, it's like you're yelling. It annoys people."

"It sure annoys me," I said. "Is it always this stupid in chat rooms?"

"Sometimes it's worse," she said.

★ ★ ★

OhioCity: Ellen, R U seeing someone?
Chubette: Well . . . <G>

"What's the '<G>' for?" I said.
" 'Grin.' "
"Good, keep it noncommittal."
Taffy nodded.

RuB2sday: Ellen's not getting any nooky. She's just trying to make us jealous.
Endomorf: You just can't stand the thought of anyone else having a life, RuB.
RuB2sday: You losers call what u have a life??????

"That was kind of hostile, wasn't it?"
"Oh, chats can get very bitchy," Taffy said. "Just like in real life, people take instant likes and dislikes to each other. And there's always one sour apple in any room. In here it looks like Ruby Tuesday."
"Well, I'm sure it's all fascinating, but meantime I'm falling asleep," I said.
"Want to get out?"
"OMG, yes."
She had a tinkly laugh. "Wait. I have to say good-bye."

172

"You do?"

"They'd think it was rude if I didn't." She typed some more.

Chubette: Well, g/2/g everyone, just popped in to say hi.
Glamorama: Bye, Ellen
Granithed: Ellen, c-ya
OhioCity: Don't stay away so long, Ellen, not the same in here without ya.
OhioCity: Maybe we cld go to a movie sometime . . .
RuB2sday: Good to see you back, Ellen. Someday u'll have 2 tell us what u've been up to.
Loxsmith: Buh-bye Ellen
BigEmma: Niters Ellen
Chubette: :::poof:::

Taffy clicked the boxed × in the right hand corner of the screen and we were back at the menu page again.

" 'Poof'?"

"So they'd know I'd actually gone."

"What was 'g/2/g'?"

" 'Got to go.' "

"I can't believe people spend all their leisure time doing this," I said. "And most of them can't even spell. I've never been so

173

bored in my life."

"Well," she said, "it may be boring to you. It is to me, too. But it's a real lifesaver for lonely people."

"I guess," I said. "Let's go back and look at some more of Ellen's favorite hangouts."

"Coming up."

Her fingers flew, and we were able to look at the other listings. "Are there any more chat rooms in there?"

"Doesn't look like it," she said.

"Let's take a gander at the rest of them."

Ellen apparently "hung out" in several places that had to do with the World Wide Web itself, devoted to Web-site design and maintenance. That made sense, I thought; it was how she made her living.

There was another that was a pretty complete catalog of clothing designed especially for "Big Beautiful Women," illustrated. I wondered if Ellen had made any online purchases.

"Next," I said.

This one was to a site called "TOPSTOXXX," and seemed to be all about buying stocks online. "For the serious and sophisticated investor," one line of the copy said, highlighted in red. "Whether you're an experienced and knowledge-able player, or just want to bring your current portfolio up to snuff, you've come to the right place." "Hmm," I said, and noted the URL.

"What?"

"I just think that's a strange site for someone like Ellen to — what's the term again?"

"Hang out?"

"No, the other — bookmark."

"Why?"

"She was a businesswoman, very sophisticated and successful. If she were into the stock market, she'd certainly have her own broker and not be buying stocks over the Internet. Besides, her roommate is a stockbroker."

"Maybe she's not into the market at all," Taffy offered.

"Then why is this site a hangout?"

She tossed her hair. "You're the detective. Maybe it's the Web site of one of her clients."

"You might be right," I said.

We played on the computer for a while longer, and I noted that one of Ellen's other hangouts was Bronwyn Rhys's BeAttitude Web site. Understandable, I guess, because it was Ellen Carnine's own design. Finally I said, "Taffy, I think I've got the hang of it now. I don't see why I should waste any more of your time."

"It hasn't been a waste," she said. "This was fun. Milan tells me you get into some pretty exciting stuff sometimes."

"I do, to my sorrow. But this isn't very exciting; just a sad young woman who decided she didn't want to live anymore and I have to figure out why."

Sobered, she nodded.

"I'll take the laptop with me and fool around with it on my own time," I said. "Can I pick up Ellen's e-mail on this computer from my office?"

"Sure," Taffy said. "Just don't forget her password."

"Taffy, I can't tell you how much help you've been."

"Glad to do it," she grinned. "Any father of Milan's is a friend of mine."

I had a lot to carry when we left: my briefcase, Ellen's suitcase, and the laptop computer. I was glad it wasn't a full-sized desktop computer — that really would have been unwieldy. I wondered for a moment why a computer expert like Ellen would have a laptop rather than a more powerful and sophisticated desktop job, but I figured she'd spent all her working days on a big one and just used this one for play.

I asked Taffy if she was hungry, and when she said yes I drove her up to Little Italy and bought her dinner at La Dolce Vita, one of my favorite little places, on the corner of Mayfield and Murray Hill Roads. Terry Tarantino, the genial owner/chef, seated us at a small table next to the window so we could people-watch as we ate, and sent over a bruschetta appetizer while we scanned the menu.

"Let me write you a check for your time, Taffy," I said. "Unless you'd prefer cash?"

"Um . . ." she said.

"What?"

"I'd rather you didn't write me a check at all, actually. I'd feel funny taking money from Milan's father."

"That's just too bad about you. A deal is a deal. Besides, I'm sure you had better things to do this evening than drive all the way up here and teach me how to play chat room."

"I know, but Milan and I are very close friends, you know? It just doesn't feel right. I mean, you're buying me dinner and everything."

"Give the money to charity if you don't need it, then."

"Whoa! Who said anything about not needing it?"

She finally capitulated and I wrote her a check, and as we progressed through our dinners, the sky darkened and Mayfield Road became nighttime.

Afterward I drove her back to my office where she picked up her car. She hugged me before she got in it; her hair smelled of apricot shampoo.

"It was great meeting you," she said. "Milan talks about you all the time; it's good to get the real thing."

It pleased me more than I could imagine that my son talked about me to his girlfriend. "Let's see more of you, then, Taffy. Maybe the next time I come down to Kent to see Milan we can all have dinner together."

"I'd like that a lot, Mr. Jacovich."

I handed her into her car. "Straight home now," I said. "Drive carefully."

"I'm always careful," she said.

Chapter Ten

I connected the laptop to my own printer and made myself hard copies of all Ellen's e-mails that weren't spam, of her letters and all of her "hangouts" as well. I made a special file folder for them, and put it in the top drawer of my desk rather than into the filing cabinet; for the time being I wanted them where I could easily get my hands on them.

Then it occurred to me that I could get some information without ever leaving my office. I was a cybervirgin, otherwise I would have thought of it earlier. Using Ellen's screen name, "CHUBETTE," I sent a return e-mail to her correspondent, "BREAMBOAT."

Dear Stan,
No, I'm not mad at you. Just been a really busy time for me. Have LOTS to tell you. Write me back, OK?
                    Love, Ellen********

The hook having been baited, I sent another e-mail, to the man who had invited her to the movies while Taffy and I were in the chat room: "OhioCity." If his screen name bespoke the truth, as I imagine few do online, he lives right across the river from Ellen in the near-west-side neighborhood known as Ohio City, very close to where she'd gone off the bridge.

"Hi there," I typed, since I didn't know this one's name.

"I've been working so hard lately that a movie sounds pretty good! (Didn't want to respond in the chat room to-night, it's nobody's business but ours.) Write me back, okay? — Ellen *********

Then I went back to Ellen's file of personal letters and gave the command to print all of them. My printer is notoriously slow, so I knew it would take a while. As I waited, I walked over to the open window and lit a cigarette as I watched the lights of the city across the river. Terminal Tower and Key Tower were both illuminated, soaring brightly into the night. There had been an Indians game that evening, and although it was all over now, Jacobs Field was still lit up like a giant birthday cake against the sky.

I'm a hometown boy. Maybe it's because I've never lived anywhere else — if you don't count the college years at Kent State, just down the road, and nearly a year in Vietnam when I was hardly in a position to do any sightseeing or learn the city — but Cleveland has always been for me a homey, welcoming, warm kind of place, winter weather notwithstanding. Yet for Ellen Carnine that had obviously not been the case; her life here had contained such elements of unhappiness and discontent that in the end she had chosen not to go on with it.

It occurred to me then that it doesn't really matter where you live; you bring your own baggage along with you, and how you deal with it determines your level of contentment.

I went back and scooped up the printouts and put them in the folder with the rest of Ellen's stuff. Then I had an idea.

I went back into the chat area, and clicked on the icon that read, "READ A MEMBER'S PROFILE." I looked up "BREAM-BOAT" first.

Member Name: Stan
Residence: Parma OH near CLEVE-LAND. GO BROWNS! GO TRIBE!

Age: Noneyabizniss
Sex: Male
Marital Status: Single and Looking
Hobbies: CANDLES,   VIDOES,
    POETRY, DANCING, HAVING A
    DRINK W; MY PEEPS
Occupation: Yes I have one
Quote: STAY WITH ME FOR A WHILE,
    IN THIS BENEATH THE GROUND
    SEARCHING FOR MY INNER-SELF
    AND THIS ISM WHAT I FOUND: A
    CHANCE TO LOVE SOMEBODY, A
    TREAT SO HARD TO FIND, I
    HATE TO BE THAT MAN WHO
    CHOOSE TO WALK IT BLIND

None of it made a damn bit of sense to me, grammatically or any other way. *"Vidoes."* I shook my head, but I printed it out, then went on to check out the member known as "OhioCity."

Member Name: THE BIG GUN!
    (Boom Boom)
Residence: Ohio City, Cleveland
    Ohio, surrounded by the beauty of
    the Cuyahoga River and Lake Erie
Age: 1960-something
Marital Status: You don't see a ring,
    do ya?

Hobbies: Insatiable flirt; having fun with my pals on-line, Hi Traci, Ellen, Jan, Kel, BabaWawa . . . geez, there's lots! If I have forgotten someone, I apologize and pleeze lemme know

Occupation: Coffee shop owner

Quote: Without a sence of humor you got nothing. If the conversation is not interesting and enjoyable, you got even less

I printed that one out, too. Then I switched off the laptop and opened up the suitcase from under Ellen Carnine's bed. I wanted to take another look at her diaries from her four years at Bryarly.

I sat down at my desk, the gooseneck lamp switched on, and slipped a pair of reading glasses from the drugstore over my nose. I've reached that age where I need them for close work, and it's often embarrassing when I take a date out to dinner and discover I've forgotten them so she has to read the menu to me.

Either Ellen had kept a lot from her diary or her college years had been pretty dull. She had not written every day; the entries indicated only two or three times a week. Most of them had to do with classes, academics, some extracurricular stuff like the Glee Club. Few names were mentioned; she'd mostly used initials as shorthand. She roomed with *"B"* the first year and with *"S.W."* her final three, *"B"* having apparently transferred to Bowling Green State University.

It was in the second year that she first mentioned *"Prof. Goodman,"* and I remembered her letter to a Professor Richard Goodman. She told her diary that he was a really inspiring teacher — apparently he taught English and American Literature — and that she was learning more from him than all her other professors combined. His name was to appear many more times in the subsequent diaries, first with his title and last name, then as *"Prof. G,"* and finally as *"R.G."* or just plain *"R."* She'd had dinner with him on several occasions during her college years, accompanied him to the theater a few times, had lots of coffee meetings.

Other than her frequent references to Goodman, there was absolutely nothing in the four years' worth of careful, tight, cursive writing that could be remotely described as personal. No thoughts, feelings, fears, joys. Ellen Carnine either had not experienced any, or had chosen to keep the diaries as a record of what she did in college, and not what she felt.

I checked her Day Planner next. Most of her appointments the month before she died looked business-oriented and were scheduled for during the day. One entry got my attention, however: She had planned to have dinner with Richard Goodman on a Thursday evening; she'd killed herself on Monday before she could keep the date.

I made out another three-by-five card for Richard Goodman, and circled his name.

Finally, at about twenty past eleven, I rubbed my tired eyes, replaced the diaries in the suitcase and locked it in the utility room, closed up the office, and went home. I stretched out in front of the TV to watch *Politically Incorrect*, and was asleep before it was half over and the Stroh's half gone.

I slept in until almost eight the next morning, unusual for me. I made a pot of coffee, popped a bagel in the toaster, and retrieved the newspaper from the hall outside my apartment door. A schmear of cream cheese later and I was ensconced at my kitchen table, having my breakfast and catching up on the news of the moment.

I knew I was in for another endless day, so I waited until about nine-thirty before getting dressed. Then I called Professor Richard Goodman at Bryarly College, told him who I was, and asked if he could see me that afternoon.

"Uhhh," he said, clearly discomfited. "I was naturally devastated when I heard about Ellen. She was, after all, a personal friend as well as the daughter of a colleague, and I've known her since she was very young. But she hasn't been my student for many years now. I don't know what I could possibly tell you that might help."

"I don't, either, Professor Goodman, but we won't know until we talk, will we?"

He cleared his throat. "I could see you at about three o'clock. In my office. Would that be convenient?"

I preferred that William Carnine didn't know I was talking to Goodman just yet, so I said, "I'd rather meet with you someplace off campus, if that's all right."

I couldn't miss his sudden intake of breath. "What's this all about, Mr. Jacovich?"

"I told you what it was about, Professor. Ellen Carnine."

I'm not sure, but I think I heard him gulp. When he spoke again there was distinct hostility in his tone. And something else, too, that might have been fear. "You've got the wrong party here."

" 'The wrong party'?"

"You're wasting your time with me."

"I'm beginning to think that isn't so at all," I said.

"Well, I'm not meeting with you, all right? You can make anything of that you like."

I took a deep breath. Every so often in my business I have to play hardball; I don't usually like it, but I do what's needed. "And what will Dr. Carnine make of it when I tell him you refused to see me?"

He thought it over. For almost thirty seconds. Then he said, "You seem to have the upper hand here."

My shot in the dark had apparently struck its target. I waited.

"Do you know the Bob Evans restaurant at the Mansfield exit off I-71?"

"I can find it," I said.

"At three-thirty, then."

"That will be fine, Professor."

"How will I know you?"

"I'll be wearing a light tan corduroy jacket. And I'm big and tall."

"I have the feeling you're not a very nice man, Mr. Jacovich."

"My dog loves me," I said, and after I hung up I wondered what it would be like to even have a dog. I had never owned one in my life. I couldn't imagine having to leave either a surveillance or a date to go running home to walk it.

The fifteen-minute drive to my office gave me some time to think. Professor Goodman seemed awfully nervous and reluctant to meet with me to talk about Ellen. He acted like a man with a secret.

The breeze coming down the channel of the river from Lake Erie carried with it the scent of spring, so I opened all the windows in the office, even though it was warm enough for an air conditioner. My windows are very tall, almost floor-to-ceiling, and arched at the top; the building is ninety years old, but back then they made them with some thought to aesthetics and not simply utility as they do today. I had seen the building many times when I used to go to Jim's Steak House next door for lunch, and it went on the market at just about the time I inherited a nice chunk of money from my last living relative, my Aunt Branka, my beloved *tetka*, who'd been married to my father's brother and had worn her widow's weeds every day for eleven years after Uncle Anton died.

My wiser friends convinced me that I should let the bequest work for me, so I invested in the old building, rehabbed it slightly, and moved my office from my apartment down to Collision Bend.

Now I stood at the windows and filled my lungs with spring air and watched the gulls have breakfast for a while until the realization that I had a lot of work to do took me to my desk. Sometimes reality gets in the way.

I went over the rest of the things Ellen had kept in her suitcase. All Bryarly College. Since she'd practically grown up on campus before matriculating there, she obviously was sentimental about it. I hadn't kept many souvenirs from my Kent State years, although I'd recently bought a sweatshirt and a jacket bearing the school logo. Maybe that kind of memento-cherishing was a "girl thing." I didn't know.

There were a few photographs of Ellen with a slightly older man, skinny and crewcut and very serious looking. The body language in the pictures seemed to say they were being careful to keep some distance between them, although that was only my interpretation. I wondered if it might be

Professor Goodman.

I booted up Ellen's laptop, and went first to her *"ECARNINE"* screen name; she had received no personal e-mail since she died. There were a few spam messages, but I didn't even open them to read.

Switching to "CHUBETTE," I noticed that there were two new electronic missives waiting, both sent early this morning. One was from "OhioCity," the second from *"BREAMBOAT."* Maybe my little phony letters into cyberspace had paid off.

Ellen [OhioCity said].

Wow! You'd REALLY go to a movie with me? I can't believe it! That would be so great. Will you let me take you to dinner first? Anyplace you want. There are some great places here in Ohio City — Kosta's, Lola's, the Great Lakes Brewing Company. You pick, it will be my pleasure. After all this time it'd be fantastic to meet you.

Call me anytime, okay. My number is 555-7874, from eight in the morning until seven at night. Can't WAIT to hear from you.

Don.

I smiled, jotting down the number and

the name, Don. If only all investigative work was this easy.

I pulled out my reverse directory and looked up the number. It belonged to something called "The Kawfee Klub" with an address on West Twenty-fifth Street, sure enough in the neighborhood near the West Side Market known as Ohio City. And Don's e-mail said he was there all day.

Then I opened up Ellen's second e-mail.

Dear Ellen:

Whew! SOOO glad you're not mad at me! I've missed you a LOT!!! I apologize again for my boorish behavior the last time we chatted. I've just been talking to you for so long, I felt very close to you and I just got carried away. And then when I didn't hear from you or see you in chat for so long, I thought maybe I'd frightened you away, and I would HATE to think that was so. I wouldn't want anything to ruin our friendship.

So I hope you can forget about what happened; God knows I'll try to. Write me back and tell me the next time you're going to be in the room so we can chat again.

As ever, Stan*********

While it was certainly more intriguing than Don's e-mail, it didn't give me the same kind of information. I stared at it on the laptop screen for a while. I tried to figure out what "Breamboat" meant. Probably some variant of "Dreamboat." Breamboat's profile didn't give an occupation, and I doubted somehow that the connotation was sexual. So why "Breamboat"?

I switched to the Ameritech White Pages and turned to the *B*'s. It didn't take me long to find a Stanley Bream in Parma.

It wasn't much to go on, I had to admit. From what they had written, it was obvious that neither Stan Bream nor Don from The Kawfee Klub had ever met Ellen Carnine face-to-face. But they seemed to have had some sort of ongoing relationship via the chat rooms and e-mails, so perhaps they could be helpful, at that.

I checked my watch. It was just past noon. I had to leave for my meeting with Richard Goodman a little before one-thirty, Mansfield being some ninety miles down an Interstate 71 chewed up by endless construction. But I certainly had time, I thought, for a quick cup of Kawfee.

Chapter Eleven

The Kawfee Klub was a pretentious little storefront espresso bar that wasn't going to give Starbucks or our own local Arabica coffeehouse any nightmares of competition. There were a couple of small tables with wrought-iron chairs that might just have been made on the first floor of my office building. High ceilings were supported by naked brick, a look that has become popular since Cleveland began renovating and restoring old buildings instead of tearing them down. On one side of the room there were several bins of loose coffee beans in varying strengths and flavors, including raspberry almond and chocolate hazelnut, along with the usual array of thermoses, mugs, and other indispensable coffee paraphernalia. On the other side was the counter, behind which stood several brewing machines and coffee dispensers, trays of biscotti and other pastries, and a cash register. Huge burlap coffee sacks were scattered around for a peculiar decorative touch.

The clientele was mostly under thirty,

and many of them had their laptops open on the table and were busily pecking away at whatever it is they do for a living or for fun — hoping to beat a deadline, finish an assignment, or at the very least impress some other customer with their intelligence and diligence. The coffee shop has come a long way from the little hole-in-the-wall joints with wisecracking waitresses and the smell of grease sizzling on the grill.

The young black woman behind the counter wore thick glasses and a put-upon expression, and my guess was that she was working her way through college at a job she hated. When she asked me what I wanted, I ordered a cup of French roast; after I'd paid for it and had it in my hand, I inquired whether I could see Don.

She glanced over her shoulder toward the back. "He's having his lunch right now," she said.

"That's okay, I'll just go back there and have my coffee with him." I took one sip of the hot beverage so it wouldn't spill as I moved, and started toward the back of the store, ignoring her protests of "Sir? Sir! You can't go back there . . ."

Don was indeed having his lunch at a table in the back room, surrounded by cardboard packing crates and sacks of coffee that made the storage area resemble a warehouse in a Brazilian harbor town. He was eating a giant cheeseburger with everything and fries, and most of the "everything" was oozing out the sides of the bun. As accompaniment there was a chocolate milkshake from the nearest Mickey-D's, with a slab of his own rich biscotti laid by as dessert.

He didn't look as though he'd missed many lunches in his life. He couldn't have been more than five foot seven and he weighed at least two hundred and eighty pounds. Not much of it was muscle. He was probably close to forty, but the excess weight might have made him look younger, stretching the skin of his cheeks smooth. He had a very small face on a very large head, and just beneath his nose was a tiny sprouting of stubble his razor had obviously missed that morning. He was wearing a white short-sleeved shirt with a navy-blue tie that showed traces of a few meals he might have consumed early in the Clinton administration.

"Sorry," he said through a mouthful of fries, waving me away, "I only see vendors first thing in the morning."

"Vendor" was one of those business-speak words that still sounded funny to me. A vendor, in my mind, wandered through the crowd during a ball game hawking beer or hot dogs. But then I have been told many times in the past how retro I am.

"I'm not a vendor," I said. "I'm — a friend of Ellen's."

He looked puzzled. "Ellen?"

"From the chat room. 'Chubette.' "

He stopped chewing, and his face, already pale, turned a few shades lighter. He batted his eyes as if he'd grown suddenly dizzy. Apparently he'd thought he was safe in the anonymity of his chat-room screen name. Finally he swallowed what was in his mouth, licked the special sauce from his fingers, and then wiped them relatively clean with a paper napkin.

"Hey, look," he said, and his voice quavered a little. "I don't know what this is all about, but I've never even met Ellen face-to-face." He made no effort to rise, instead seeming to shrink in his chair, a good trick for someone his size. In the animal world it would have been a classic sign of submission.

"I'm sorry if I stepped on anybody's toes," he burbled. "Your toes. I mean, I didn't even know you were in the picture. Ellen never mentioned you." He laughed almost wildly. "I mean, why would she mention you? We didn't even know each other . . ." He trailed off, having spent his reserve of excuses, and seemed to be waiting for me to fall upon him like an avenging sword.

"It's not like that, Don."

He spent another fifteen seconds processing that piece of information along with his french fries, and then some of his color returned. "Oh," he said, relieved he wasn't going to have to deal with a jealous boyfriend who was much bigger than he was. "Oh, well, good. I mean . . ."

Then the peculiarity of the situation hit him, and his brows lowered into a puzzled frown. He got slowly to his feet and walked toward me. He was so heavy that his entire body rolled from side to side as he walked. "I don't understand. If you're not Ellen's boyfriend, then what — I mean, who are you?"

I took out one of my business cards and handed it to him. He fumbled in the pocket of his short-sleeved white shirt for a pair of reading glasses and propped them up on the end of his nose to look at it.

"Private investigator," he said softly.

"That's right."

He licked his lips again, and his tongue

197

probed inside his mouth for any stray morsels of french fries he hadn't already consumed, and looked back up at me, terrified and probably a little intrigued by my occupation. "I'm sorry. What do you want with me?"

"What's your last name, Don?"

He became guarded again. "What's the difference?"

"Let's not play games, all right? You have any idea how easy it'd be for me to find out? Save me some time, and save yourself some trouble."

"It's Cannon," he said. "Like the big gun. *Boom boom.*"

"Thanks," I said, jotting it down in my notebook as I remembered the "big gun" reference in his online profile. "How well did you know Ellen?"

His huge shoulders rose and fell. "Like I said, I never even met her personally. We were just . . ." He took his glasses off and peered at me. His eyes were a watery blue, and bloodshot. "Hey look, this is my place of business. You can't just come in here and . . . What's this all about?"

"I asked you first, Don."

"I think I have a right to know why you're asking." He was getting a bit snarky now that he knew I wasn't a jealous lover come to pound him into the floor, his chin pointing aggressively at me through the jowls. "I don't have to talk to you at all, you know."

"I know," I said, "but I think it would be a good idea."

"Is that a threat?"

"Not at all. Do you know Ellen's last name or where she lived?"

He thought it over for a minute — not the answer, but whether he was going to respond at all. Then he said, "No. Ellen and I are chat-room buddies. You know, on the Internet. There are no last names and addresses in chat rooms. Like I told you, we've never laid eyes on each other."

"And you never spoke on the phone?"

"No," he said. "Look, how did you know to come here?"

"I'll get to that in a minute. What was your relationship to Ellen?"

"We were . . ." He stopped and drew himself up to his full height and wiped at his mouth again, and somewhere found a wellspring of backbone. "Hey, listen, fuck you. You've got no right to come busting into my place and asking a lot of personal questions. I don't know how you found me, but I'll give you ten seconds to *lose* me again before I call the cops." He looked at the watch strapped around his thick wrist with a cheap leather band and began ticking off the seconds. "One . . . two . . ."

"Ellen has committed suicide."

He stopped counting, and his shoulders sagged. His face didn't really change expression, but the lights went out behind his eyes as if someone had twisted a dimmer switch. After a few moments he said, "Oh, Jesus Christ."

"Her full name was Ellen Carnine," I said, "and last week she jumped off the Lorain-Carnegie Bridge."

His whole body jerked. The Lorain-Carnegie Bridge was walking distance from where we now stood.

"You might have read about it in the newspapers," I said, "or heard it on the television."

"I did," he stammered, "but I didn't know that it was . . ." He gulped and shook his head hard as if that would dislodge the ugly pictures and make them go away. "It can't be! I talked to her in the chat room just yesterday. She sent me an e-mail last night."

"That was me, I'm afraid," I admitted. "Using her computer."

He moved backwards, one arm groping blindly for the chair, and sat down with a *whoosh.* "My god," he said, shaking with betrayal. "Why did you do that?"

"What I'm trying to find out is why she wanted to take her own life, Don. So I'm looking up all the people who might have known her."

He nodded.

"That's why I want to know what your relationship was with her."

He put down the milkshake and gripped the edge of the table with both hands, hard. "We chatted. We flirted. That's what you do in those romance chat rooms. It didn't mean anything." He laughed nervously. "Look at me, for God's sake. I'm not exactly God's gift to women. Being in that room with people who are like me, flirting, teasing . . ." He took a deep breath. "That room, the 'Plain Jane/Cleveland' room, that was my entire sex life, okay?"

"But you wanted to take it out of the chat room, didn't you? You asked her if she wanted to see a movie. Or at least you thought you were asking her."

His mouth was dry, and he reached for the milkshake, sucking hard on the straw. "So what?" He patted at his mouth again, this time with his fingers. "I've been chatting with Ellen for almost a year now. She seemed so nice, so kind. And very intelligent. And she hadn't been in the room for several days and I realized that I really, really missed her. You know? It surprised me, but I'd kind of gotten used to talking with her — chatting with her online, I mean — every night. And that got me thinking that, yes, maybe I'd like to take the relationship out of the chat room, to take it one step further." He looked away from me and down, embarrassed, studying the ruins of his burger. "So when she came back on, or when I *thought* it was her, I said what I said about the movie. Is that a crime?"

"You'd never even talked to her on the phone before?"

He shook his head resolutely. "What do you think I e-mailed her my phone number for?"

He had a point there. "Who else in that chat room was pals with Ellen?"

He put his hands on either side of his face. "Just about everyone. She was funny, and always upbeat. We were all regulars in there, we didn't get many newbies."

" 'Newbies'?"

"Newcomers," he explained. "Look, the name of the room is 'Plain Jane,' so by definition no one would go looking in there for hotties." He glared up at me resentfully.

"You're making it sound like it was something dirty, something to be ashamed of. Well, it isn't. It's just a place where ordinary-looking people like me can connect, talk, have a little fun together."

"I'm sure it is," I said.

"You probably wouldn't understand."

"And you say Ellen was always upbeat? Cheerful?"

He nodded sadly. "She was funny. She kept us all laughing."

"LOL," I thought but did not say. "One more question, Don. In the past few weeks or months, did Ellen seem particularly upset about anything?"

"Upset? Ellen? No, not that I could tell."

"She didn't seem unhappy?"

His face changed, as if it had been liquid before and was now settling into permanence. "Mr. . . . ?" He put his glasses back on and looked at my card again, taking a few seconds to figure out how to pronounce my name properly. "Mr. Jacovich," he said, not getting it right and pronouncing the *J* like a *J* instead of a *Y*, "really happy people don't spend every night of their lives hanging out in chat rooms."

The drive from Cleveland to Mansfield

down Interstate 71 is relatively boring. Construction on the freeway that has been in progress for years slows things down a lot, and there isn't much in the way of scenic distraction except the Ford plant. Once out of the metropolitan area the terrain levels out into flat farmland, so I was free to think about what Don had told me.

It was possible, of course, that he was lying about never having met Ellen Carnine face-to-face, but I didn't think so. He hadn't even known her last name, hadn't recognized it when he heard the news reports of her death. And even if he wasn't telling me the whole truth, he still didn't seem the type of man over whom a woman might kill herself.

You never know, though.

Ellen Carnine had been successful, cheerful, career-driven, and from what everyone I'd spoken to so far had told me, not a likely candidate for suicide. But then Don's final remark rang true: Really happy people don't spend every night of their lives hanging out in chat rooms.

I was still troubled. And I didn't know why.

I got to the Bob Evans restaurant a few minutes before Richard Goodman did. When he came in, I recognized him at once from the photographs in Ellen's suitcase. He was older now, of course, and the crew cut was grown out to a more up-to-date style, although he had a lot less hair in front than he had had ten years before.

I knew the feeling; Slovenian men tend to thin out early in the hair department, and I had been battling it for years. I'm not bald, but a lot more scalp shows through my light brown hair than I'd like. And a couple of strands of silver, too. I don't even look at my college pictures anymore. Too depressing.

In his middle forties now, Richard Goodman was wearing a gray houndstooth-check suit and a muted maroon tie, and glasses I hadn't noticed in the old photos. He stood near the cash register looking around, and I waved at him to catch his eye. He approached me with the air of a man climbing the steps of a gibbet.

"You're Mr. Jacovich?" he said when he arrived at the table. He didn't put out his hand for a shake.

"Yes, Professor Goodman. Please sit down. Would you like something? Coffee?"

He shook his head, then realized it might seem peculiar if he sat there in the restaurant and didn't order anything. So he nodded reluctantly and I told the waitress to bring him a cup.

"All right," he said, his weak chin pointing aggressively and his eyes blinking nervously behind his eyeglasses, "what is it you want?" He drummed his fingers nervously, perhaps playing one of the more complex Mozart pieces on the tabletop. I noticed the hammered gold wedding band. "If this is some sort of ill-conceived extortion plot, it's not going to work. I have nothing."

"Extortion?" I said.

"Isn't that why you've contacted me? With some dirty little shit you think you know?"

"Dr. Goodman, your colleague Dr. Carnine has hired me to find a reason for Ellen's taking her own life. He said the family needed to know. That's why I called you, and it's the only reason."

Now he was really nervous. His hands fluttered everywhere: on his face, at the knot of his tie, pushing up his glasses, patting at his hair. He was afraid he'd revealed something he shouldn't have.

He was right.

I just watched him go through his guilty tics and twitches, waiting to see how he'd get out of it. Finally he said, "What makes you think *I* would know anything about Ellen's death?"

"A hunch," I said. "You were friends when she was in school. She had several photographs of you among her mementos, and she mentioned you frequently in her diaries."

"You read her diaries?" His already pale face drained of whatever color resides there, and then angry red spots appeared on both cheeks like artlessly applied rouge. He looked like a painted puppet. "How dare you read her diaries when she's not even cold yet?"

"It seemed a logical place to look," I said. "And I had her father's permission. And blessing."

He wriggled a little lower in his seat, sitting on the end of his tailbone on the uncomfortable booth cushion. "As it happens, I haven't even seen Ellen in over three years. We'd talk on the phone perhaps every six months or so. And Christmas cards. And e-mails. And that's it."

"Maybe it is. But that was about to change. Ellen had written down a dinner date with you for three days after she died."

Goodman seemed not to know what to

do with his hands. They patted at his hair, dithered at the knot of his tie, pulled at his ear. "Yes," he said finally. "Although I wouldn't characterize it as a date. It was old friends meeting for dinner."

"Did you suggest the dinner or did she?"

"She did."

"Did she say why?"

He looked wildly around for an escape route. "She said she was very upset about something and wanted my advice."

I nodded, thinking of her last e-mail to him. "She didn't specify?"

"No," he said, shaking his head emphatically. "I don't give a damn if you believe me or not, but it happens to be the truth."

The man may have held more degrees than a centigrade thermometer, but in the ways of the world he was as clueless as they come. "Why would I have reason not to believe you?"

He sighed, and then compressed his lips into a thin razor-slash of a line. "Very well," he said. "I'm tired of fencing with you. You understand? I'm just — tired. So let's get right to it. Exactly why did you contact me?"

"I've already answered that, Dr. Goodman."

"I'm a schoolteacher," he said. He was

obviously not listening to me but searching the inside of his skull for an exit. "I haven't got much."

I was beginning to get the picture. I waited some more.

He wasn't ready for the climax yet; he needed to express his contempt first. "Don't you feel like a grave-robber doing this?" he said. "I think you're disgusting."

"Dr. Goodman, we seem to be having a misunderstanding."

"Oh, I understand you perfectly, Jacovich." His face twisted into a sad and bitter scowl. "You're a bottom-feeder. The world is full of them. All right, I'm a married man and you have me by the balls, I admit it. Now what do you want?"

I took a sip of my coffee. It wasn't as rich as the kind Don Cannon brewed up at the Kawfee Klub. "You're not very good at this, are you, Professor?"

"What?"

"You think I'm here to blackmail you?"

He looked puzzled.

"You're way off base. I told you the truth. I'm trying to find out why Ellen killed herself, and I'm talking to all her friends. I assumed you were one of them. And that's all."

The bones inside his face seemed to

melt, and all at once he looked soft and vulnerable, and very frightened.

"Jesus," he said. He took off his glasses and rubbed his fingers in his eyes. I thought for a moment he was going to cry.

"You and Ellen were having an affair."

The word made him jump in his seat as though an electrical charge had gone through him. "No!"

"Professor," I prodded gently, "I've been doing this kind of work for a long time now. Please don't insult my intelligence."

He shook his head almost violently. "No — not now," he said. "Not for a long time."

"When she was in school?"

He closed his eyes and nodded.

"How long did it go on?"

His chin was on his bony chest, showing me his bald spot. "Two years," he mumbled.

"Who broke it off? You or her?"

His intake of breath was ragged and shuddering. "I don't know as how either of us 'broke it off.' It was a youthful indiscretion for her, and not quite so youthful for me. She finished school and moved off campus and out of town, that's all. We remained good friends."

"No bitterness? No recriminations?"

He shook his head.

"She wasn't expecting you to leave your wife for her?"

"Certainly not," he huffed, but there wasn't any heat behind it. Richard Goodman wasn't a man who generated much heat on his warmest days, and there was none at all left now.

"You make a habit of sleeping with your students?"

His head shot up and he glared at me.

"I can understand the temptation," I said. "All those fresh young faces looking up at you and thinking how wonderful, how smart, how wise you are."

"It wasn't like that!"

"Tell me how it was, then."

He dropped his chin again.

"Professor, I couldn't care less about your extracurricular sex life," I said. "All I'm trying to find out is what Ellen Carnine's state of mind was when she died. And if her state of mind included you, then that's what I want to hear."

He looked up again, frightened. "It couldn't have included me," he said. "Our relationship — at least that particular phase of it — ended when she left college. That was seven years ago."

"You don't think she was pining away for

you all that time?"

He put his glasses back on. "Do I look like a woman would pine away for me for seven years, Mr. Jacovich?"

"You don't look like coeds would be rolling over for you all the time, either," I told him, and that one made his eyes flash almost dangerously. "Looks can be deceiving."

"You make it sound as if I sleep with all my students!"

"Don't you?"

"I've only . . ." He stopped, teetering on the edge of another indiscretion. I was right, he *wasn't* very good at this. The muscles at the hinges of his jaw bulged and then receded as he gritted his teeth. "That has nothing to do with Ellen," he said firmly.

"No, it doesn't," I said. "So tell me what does. You scheduled a dinner date with her, and you've exchanged phone calls and e-mails with her." His eyes widened. "Yes, I have access to her computer as well. Was something bothering her? Was she unhappy? Her job? Maybe a love affair?"

He touched the knot in his tie with trembling fingers. "I told you, she'd called me to have dinner because *was* something bothering her. But I didn't know about it.

Didn't know anything specific, that is. If she was involved romantically with anyone, she never mentioned it to me. But then, she probably wouldn't." The red spots appeared again. "All things considered."

"And she never mentioned anything else that troubled her or made her unhappy?"

He sighed. "She had her problems, just like the rest of us. Job problems, mostly. But I think she was working through them all right. There was nothing that I know of that might make her — do what she did."

"Would you say she was a happy person these last few years?"

The despair on his face made me cold. "I don't know what happiness is anymore, Mr. Jacovich. We all have dreams when we're young; I suppose whatever happiness accrues to any of us is in accepting and adjusting to the realization that most of them will not come true."

"That's pretty grim, isn't it?"

"Reality is often grim," he said. He played with his coffee cup, wrapping his fingers around it as if to warm them. Then he sat up straight. "And now I have to excuse myself. There really isn't anything more I can help you with."

"Thanks for talking to me," I said.

"There is something you can help me with, however . . ."

I raised one eyebrow, waiting for what I knew I was going to hear.

"Dr. Carnine is an old and dear friend of mine," he said. "He doesn't know about me and Ellen, and I'd like to keep it that way."

I nodded.

"And of course, my wife . . ."

"Professor Goodman, if you've been telling me the truth today, if there hasn't been anything between you and Ellen for seven years, I have no reason to broadcast a lot of old, tired news."

Breath rushed out of him like the air from an old sofa cushion when someone sits on it. "Thanks for that, anyway."

"But if I find out you've been lying to me . . ."

"No!" he said, louder than he might have intended, and sharply enough so that the few diners who were in the restaurant in midafternoon glanced over at us. Goodman was all at once terrified again, perspiration breaking out on his forehead and his upper lip. "I swear on my children!"

I threw two dollars on the table for the waitress and stood up, preparing to leave. "It's a little late to be thinking about your children now, isn't it?" I said.

Chapter Twelve

I wasn't ready to go home just yet. I wanted to pay a visit to Mr. Breamboat, and since he lived somewhat south of the city, going all the way back to the office or my apartment would have meant doubling my tracks. So I spent some time just driving around out in the country, away from traffic and street crime and people jumping off bridges, just watching the farms turn green and fecund.

I am a city boy born and raised; the closest my existence ever got to rural was certain areas of Southeast Asia which were, at the time, far from bucolic. I don't think I'd ever want to live out in the country. But yet when I am there, when I can smell the lettuce and the kale and the corn in the ground and watch the play of light and shadow on a rolling hillside when a cloud scuds across the sun, when the sky above is the color blue it's supposed to be, like a nineteenth-century landscape — when I can see real cows and horses and sheep in the fields or corrals along the side of the road, the simple little cemeteries in which all the families buried there had known each other personally, and the proud faded old barns whose sides advertise Red Man Chewing Tobacco — something almost primal inside me is aroused. A yearning for a little Norman Rockwell, I suppose. For a little peace.

I wasn't getting much of that from the suicide of Ellen Carnine. Each of the people I'd spoken to seemed to have a different impression of her, like the four blind men with the elephant. I couldn't solve her suicide until I had a solid place to stand, and so far my footing was slippery at best.

And the nagging suspicion that I was missing something was still with me, too. I'd known it when I'd gone through the dossier that her father had provided me. I couldn't tell what it was, but something was definitely wrong.

After driving down rustic roads for almost an hour, I wound up in Medina, which used to be "the country," too, until exurbanite Clevelanders had discovered it, thrown up high-income housing tracts and the other trappings of city life and turned a bucolic small town into just another suburb. I spent another half hour browsing through antique stores and the Village

Booksmith, and eventually enjoyed a too-early dinner at the Grand Market Café, an elegant little restaurant in sight of one of the quaint rustic gazebos that mark so many small-town village squares in Ohio.

I got back up I-71 to Parma at about six-thirty. Parma is a mostly working-class bedroom community west and south of downtown, and despite its being on the other side of town from where I grew up, I feel at home there. Not many Slovenians, but plenty of Serbs, Ukrainians, Lithuanians, and others descended from the immigrants of Eastern Europe make Parma their home, and even though their countries are constantly squabbling with one another, deep down under the politics they are all cut from the same tribal cloth — hardworking, honest, fiercely independent, and home- and family-loving.

Breamboat's home was only about five minutes from the freeway exit, five houses down from the busy thoroughfare of Ridge Road. It was modest, well kept, and not at all out-of-the-ordinary — one of the many cookie-cutter houses that were built in inner-ring suburbs all over America after World War Two with maximum haste and a minimum of imagination.

I rang the bell, and after about fifteen

seconds the door was opened by a thin, tired-looking woman in her middle forties. I was as startled to see her as she was to see me; it had never occurred to me that there might have been a Mrs. Breamboat.

"Yes?" she said, suspicion bristling from her like porcupine quills. I didn't blame her. Door-to-door peddlers and Jehovah's Witnesses are all too familiar in the residential 'burbs.

"Hello. I'm looking for a Mr. Stanley Bream."

She hunched her shoulders slightly, almost as if she was expecting a blow, and I wondered how many other hard-looking men had knocked on her door asking for her husband. "What about?"

"It's a personal matter," I said, and handed her one of my business cards.

She looked at it carefully, then gave a resigned sigh. "Investigator? What's he done now?"

"Nothing that I know of," I said. "I'm not a policeman, Mrs. Bream, I'm private. Is he here?"

She didn't answer right away, and I could tell by the rapid movement of her eyes that she was preparing to lie to me, to tell me he wasn't home. But then he appeared behind her in the small vestibule, dressed in a black denim shirt turning gray from too many washings, and brown corduroy pants.

"Who is it, Pat?" Whiskey voice. Three-pack-a-day voice.

"Mr. Bream? My name is Milan Jacovich." And I reached past the woman, Pat, to give the man another of my cards.

He read it. "So?"

"I wonder if I could talk to you privately for a few minutes."

He looked at me, his chest rising and falling with his too-deep breaths, and the woman glanced at him almost fearfully.

"I'll take care of this," he said, and walked past her onto the small porch, closing the door behind him, shutting her in. I found it interesting that he hadn't asked why I wanted to talk to him where she could hear. Now I was sure I was not the first authority figure who had knocked on that particular door at dinnertime.

He was about ten years older than his wife. Stan Bream was a short man, no more than five foot seven, with a shock of 1950s country-rock-star black hair worn in a silly pompadour and a face that once must have been quite handsome but was now lined and rendered the consistency of saddle leather by forty years of exposure, cheap booze, cigarette smoke, probably a variety of recreational drugs, and waking up on too many weekday mornings next to strangers.

He lowered his voice so his wife couldn't hear, even if she had been listening from the other side of the door. "What do you want?"

"That depends," I said.

"On what?"

"On whether you're 'Breamboat.' "

His eyes widened and his entire face changed as if he'd just been goosed with a cattle prod, and I knew I had my man. "Who the fuck are you, anyway?"

"You have my card, so you know who I am. I'd like to ask you a few questions, if you don't mind."

"And what if I do mind?"

"I'm not a police officer, so you don't have to talk to me. But I think you probably should."

"Why?"

"It's about Ellen Carnine."

His slightly bloodshot eyes remained blank.

" 'Chubette,' " I said.

He lowered his brows, and his cheeks turned a few shades darker; the deep horizontal lines fanning out from the corners of his eyes grew more pronounced. "Jesus Christ," he said. He cast a nervous glance over his shoulder toward the door, and although unlike Richard Goodman he didn't seem to be the kind of man who was afraid of his wife, still there was no sense in starting trouble if it could be avoided.

"Is there someplace we could talk?"

He considered it. "Not here in the house. You mind buying me a drink?"

"Not at all," I said.

"Wait, okay?" He turned and went back in, and I could hear the two of them talking on the other side of the door. He seemed to be doing most of it. After about a minute he emerged again, his face flushed.

"Come on, let's take a walk."

I looked at him.

"It's just around the corner, for Christ's sake."

We marched wordlessly down to the corner; I noticed that Bream had a loose-limbed, aggressive, almost simian gait. At Ridge, we turned left for half a block, and went into a tavern I hadn't noticed when I'd been looking for his street, identified by the large gold-leaf sign on the window as Flooky's Bar and Grill.

If indeed there was a grill anywhere in

221

the place, Flooky managed to camouflage it nicely. It was a typical neighborhood tavern, the bottles on the back bar lighted from behind by colored neon, canned music consisting of bad instrumental versions of older pop tunes, and a silent TV showing those ESPN sporting events like windsurfing and Rollerblading that nobody seemed to care about. Most of the clientele was male and over fifty, and none of them was drinking anything more exotic than whiskey and water. The place smelled of beer and smoke and disinfectant.

A few of the men looked up when we came in, and some of them called out Bream's name or waved. He acknowledged them glumly and led me to a booth near the back. At a table opposite us was a woman in her seventies, wearing billowy black-and-white lounging pajamas, chain-smoking Virginia Slims and drinking martinis straight-up. She was talking loudly in a croaky voice to her male companion, who was large and dumb-looking, wearing a short-sleeved striped dress shirt, an ugly tie, glasses, and a buzz cut. He was about fifteen years younger than she, but still close to sixty. Whether he was her son or her lover or something else altogether, I didn't know.

The woman gave Bream a thousand-yard stare and croaked "Stan" in a voice from deep inside an underground cavern. He nodded recognition and sat down facing away from the door. I slid in opposite him.

"Set me up over here," he yelled to the bartender. "And . . ." He looked a question at me.

"A Stroh's, no glass," I said.

He repeated my request loudly and pulled a crumpled pack of Camels from his shirt. We waited until the bartender brought our drinks; I put a twenty on the table and it disappeared quickly. I never did get any change.

His choice — habitual, I supposed, because the bartender (Flooky?) had brought it without him asking, was some sort of dark whiskey, a double without ice, and a Bud Light. In what was obviously a ritual, he lit a cigarette and sucked the smoke down deep, took a short sip of the whiskey, another of the beer, and then he shot the whiskey down in one prodigious gulp.

Exhaling noisily, he said, "Okay, what's the deal here?" Truculent. Antagonistic. Stan Bream must have fancied himself a bad boy. Maybe at one time he had been, I don't know. Right now he didn't seem very tough; he was just a tired, aging man who drank too much.

"You sent an e-mail to Ellen Carnine," I said.

"Who? Oh. Yeah. Look, I never even knew her last name until you said it."

"To Chubette."

He chewed on that one for a while. "How do you know I sent her an e-mail, anyway?"

"I found it on her computer."

"How did you find *me?*"

"You signed the e-mail 'Stan,' and I thought that from your screen name, your last name might be 'Bream'-something. Your profile says you live in Parma, so I looked you up in the phone book. It also says that you're single, which you're obviously not. It's not nice to fool Mother Nature, Mr. Bream."

He stared at me, awestruck. "You found me *that* easy?"

"It wasn't exactly rocket science."

"Okay," he said, "so I'm stupid. I'll change my screen name and profile as soon as I get back home." The permanent rasp in his voice made me want to clear my own throat. "The question is, why did you come looking for me? You her boyfriend or something? Is this a jealousy trip?"

"No. I'm a private investigator. You have my card."

"So what? Anybody can have a card made up."

"You want to see more ID? My business license?"

He waved the suggestion away. "So okay. What do you want to talk about?"

"You obviously don't know this because you sent the e-mail, but Ellen Carnine committed suicide last week."

His cheeks, which were that peculiarly lusterless texture of the habitual drinker, sagged. "Aw," he said. "Aw, shit."

I watched him carefully. He was genuinely surprised and shocked — either that, or he was a damn good actor.

"She really offed herself?"

I nodded.

"How?"

"She jumped off the Lorain-Carnegie Bridge."

"Aw," he said again. Shaken, he ran his hand over his face, gulped at his beer, and turned and yelled to the bartender. "Tommy! Again here!"

Tommy. Not Flooky — Tommy. That disappointed me; I've never met anyone named Flooky, and I was hoping my luck had changed.

"What I'm trying to find out, for her family, is *why*," I told him. "Okay?"

"Yeah," he said. "Yeah, sure, that makes sense."

I was thrilled to get his approval. "You said you didn't know her last name."

"Nobody knows last names online." He glowered at me. "You give your last name, some asshole sure as hell comes knocking on your door."

I magnanimously chose to ignore the insult. I would not do so a second time. "But you give first names."

"Sure. There must be about a billion guys named Stan online. A billion broads named Ellen."

"You never met her, face-to-face?"

"No, I never met her in real time. We just talked in the chat rooms. And sometimes on IMs. I never laid eyes on her."

"But you said in your e-mail that you were glad she wasn't mad at you, and you apologized for something you did. And you also put a string of kisses after your name at the end."

He colored. "Jesus."

"What was that about?"

"That's about non-eya-fuckin'-business, asshole," he said.

His hand was curled around the beer

bottle. I leaned across the table and grasped his wrist, hard, holding it against the sticky surface of the table. "You call me that again, Mr. Bream, and I'm going to break your hand right off your wrist. Right here. And if you holler too loudly when I do it, I'll break the other one, too." I squeezed harder, and saw his eyes tighten and his lips go white with the pain. "We understand each other?"

Our eyes locked, and for a moment there was a glimmer of understanding between us. In his mind, I was predator and he was prey, because he'd done something bad to Ellen and I knew a little about it.

"Yeah," he whispered.

Not proud of myself for picking on a man more than ten years older and eight inches shorter than myself, I loosened the grip on his wrist as Tommy, the bartender, arrived with a fresh round of drinks. He set them on the table and looked at me expectantly. "Take it out of the twenty," I said.

He shrugged and walked away, disappointed but not very — he'd still pocket more than the usual tip in a place like this.

"Okay, Mr. Bream, I'm going to tell you why it is my business," I said. "A woman is dead, and I'm trying to find out the reason for it. You knew her, at least from over the computer. And you said or did something that you felt you had to apologize for. Something you obviously don't want your wife to know about, or else we'd be standing on your front porch talking, or sitting in your living room. I want to know what that was, and I want to know some other things, too. So, I can talk to you or I can talk to Mrs. Bream. And maybe I can even talk to the police, and after that everybody talks to everybody. Your call."

His look grew more incredulous with every word. When I finished he shook his head so hard that the sprayed pompadour was threatened with demolition. "Police? Jesus, man, you're a real . . ."

"Don't," I warned, leaning forward again. He pulled his hands away, off the table, and let them sit in his lap. He was eyeing his fresh drink with longing, but at the moment he didn't have the guts to reach for it.

"Let's start," I said, leaning back in the booth, and his shoulders released their tension. "How long had you and Ellen Carnine been chatting in the rooms?"

"Maybe a year or so. And it was just the one room," he corrected me. " 'Plain Jane/ Cleveland.' " He took a sip of beer. "Plain fucking Jane."

"What makes you hang out in there?"

"Look at me," he said. "I'm fifty-eight years old and I look like I've been around the corner too many times. Maybe I have. But my days of getting good-looking young beaver are over. I settle for the Plain Janes now." His eyes flickered involuntarily toward the old woman in the black-and-white pajamas. She was batting her eyes at him like Lillian Gish in *Blossoms in the Dust*.

"You spend a lot of time online?"

"Couple hours a night," he said, as if wasting two hours out of one's day attempting to talk dirty with strangers was not so unusual.

"And you would meet with these women you connected with in the room."

He looked down. "Once or twice, yeah."

"And you'd have sex with them?"

He flushed almost purple, not meeting my eyes. "Nobody held a gun to anybody's head," he said. "Nothing wrong with tearing off a piece of strange once in a while, is there? People do it all the time. Ya know, there was a sexual revolution about forty years ago."

"I know," I said, "I read about it in the paper that day. Did you ever meet with Ellen Carnine? With 'Chubette'?" I steeled myself for an answer that I didn't really want to hear.

But Bream reaffirmed my faith in human nature, or at least my own judging of it. He gave me a very small shake of the head. "She wouldn't go for it."

"So if you never met her, what were you apologizing for in your e-mail?"

His fingernail picked at the label of the sweating beer bottle.

I leaned forward with my elbows on the table, causing him to jump, but he didn't say anything for a while. I let him stew.

Finally he said, "I tried to cyber with her."

"Cyber?"

He mumbled something I couldn't hear.

"What?"

"Cyber sex," he said, raising his voice enough so that one of the men at the bar glanced over at him.

"I don't know what that is, Mr. Bream."

"Jesus, where do you live, at the bottom of a mine shaft or something?" He squashed out his cigarette and lit another one. "You have sex over the computer. It's like phone sex, except you type instead of talk."

"Sex over the computer?"

He lowered his voice again, deeply

humiliated. "You know, I say what I'm doing to her, she says what she's doing to me. . . ." He shook himself all over, like a wet dog.

I didn't blame him.

"And you jerk off?"

He nodded glumly.

"With one hand while you type with the other?"

"Hey, come on! This is fucking embarrassing enough!"

"I can understand how it might be," I said. "So you tried to — have cybersex with Ellen?"

He murmured an affirmative.

"When was this?"

He rubbed at the corner of one eye. "I dunno. Two, maybe three weeks ago."

"And she wouldn't go for it?"

"She got very offended and said she never wanted to chat with me again."

"And that's what the apology was for?"

He shrugged. "Hey, listen, I liked her. I mean, I didn't really know her, but she had a good sense of humor. And she was chubby, at least from her screen name, and I like chubby women, maybe because my old lady is skinny as a rail. I was hoping maybe sometime we could get together face-to-face. You know? Maybe do the nasty. So I apologized."

"And this was about two weeks ago? Did you have any contact with her after that?"

"Well, the next night she was in the room again, but she wouldn't talk to me, wouldn't answer my IMs. And then she wasn't on for a long while and I thought it was because she was pissed off at me. So then she was on last night and I talked to her a little and she said she wasn't mad, so I sent her the e-mail. And somebody answered me, too. I don't know who it was, though, if she's . . ."

"I hate to be the one to burst your little bubble, Mr. Bream, but that was me who accepted your apology."

He took a slug from the Bud bottle and lowered his head onto his shoulders so that his neck disappeared altogether. He didn't say anything for a while; he was mentally chewing the hell out of something, and from the look on his face it didn't taste very good. Then finally he looked up at me from under beetling brows.

"Listen," he said, "you don't think . . . ?"

"What?"

He stubbed out his second cigarette and lit a third one. "You don't think she jumped off that bridge because of me, do you? Because I upset her? Because I tried to — you know."

"I don't know, Mr. Bream. That's what I'm trying to find out."

He shrank again. Much more of this and he'd disappear completely. Then he reached for the whiskey. No ritual this time, no sip of beer first, no taste. He threw it back and swallowed the double in one gulp, grimacing as it hit bottom.

"Shit," he said.

Chapter Thirteen

The next morning was Saturday, but in my business there's never any nine-to-five, and when I'm deeply involved in an investigation or project there are frequently no weekends, no way to leave the job at the office and do something else to forget.

So after awakening a little later than usual and taking a bit more time to read the newspaper, I decided that I still had a great deal to think about in the matter of Ellen Carnine's suicide, and it would be more productive to do it at the office where I had access to the file her father had given me, to her own personal memorabilia, and to her computer.

I stopped off at a little deli on Carnegie Avenue called Ella Wee's and got a large coffee and a bear claw, figuring the caffeine would get my heart started and the sugar rush would keep it going strong. Driving down Cedar Hill, pleasantly devoid of all but the lightest weekend traffic, I was still troubled by the gnawing suspicion that I had missed something, left a *t* uncrossed or an *i* undotted. I determined to find it that day. Or evening, if it came to that.

It wasn't as if I had anywhere to go on a Saturday night.

That didn't even bother me anymore. Maybe it was age, or maybe I had just burned out in the romance department. I hadn't really dated anyone since my relationship with Connie Haley had ended a few months earlier. I had met a woman on a case at about that time, one Catherine McTighe — "Cat," to her friends — and we had seen each other on a few occasions. But Cat had made it clear that any sort of a relationship was the last thing she wanted. We were simply, in the parlance of the millennium, "fuck buddies."

I don't do well in relationships. Maybe it's because of my work; more than one woman had balked at accepting the sometime hazards that I accepted as a matter of course. Maybe I'm just too rigid, too set in my ways, to allow anyone into my life on a more than casual basis. I guess I'm just a low-maintenance guy who is strangely and disastrously attracted to high-maintenance women.

For whatever reason, I had pretty much resigned the rest of my life to serial monogamy — dating someone exclusively for a while and then, when it inevitably crashed and burned as it always did, crawling back into my hidey-hole for a while until the next one came along and raised my hopes yet again.

I wasn't all that anxious to be married, truth be told. But I had to admit it would have felt better if I had something fun to do and someone loving and exciting to do it with on that particular Saturday night.

When I got to the office, Tony Radek's wrought-iron works on the first floor was clanking away; they were a small business struggling to keep afloat even after thirty years in the same location, and they couldn't afford the luxury of five-day weeks, either. I opened the windows, drank my take-out coffee and made myself another pot, and sat down at my desk to go over the Ellen Carnine dossier.

I filled out two more index cards with the names of Don Cannon, and Stan Bream. I laid all the cards out on the desk, Ellen's in the middle, and shuffled them around, first putting all the males together on one side and all the females on the other, then mixing the two groups in various combinations, but I couldn't discern any particular pattern.

Maybe there was none.

I stacked the cards and put them together with a giant paper clip, and then opened the leather folder that William Carnine had left with me and started to read the coroner's report again. I had barely gotten past the second page when two unexpected visitors arrived.

Since it was a Saturday, it was a bit of a surprise when the two men came in. My office is not exactly on the beaten path, and I get virtually no "walk-in" business. From the rough-hewn look of the shorter of them I thought maybe they'd been looking for Tony Radek's wrought-iron works and had come up the stairs by mistake.

But then the other one spoke. "Milan Jacovich?" he said pleasantly, and I admitted that I was.

He was in his late thirties, perhaps Hispanic, well dressed in a tweed jacket, dark brown turtleneck shirt, and brown slacks, but he had a mean little slit of a mouth surrounded by a complexion like cottage cheese. He was just under six feet tall and had his hair slicked straight back from his forehead with enough grease on it to make me wonder whether they were still manufacturing Wildroot Cream Oil. He moved and spoke with the confidence of a man who knew how to take care of himself. From one hand a canvas tote bag swung easily; it looked like the kind of thing one might pick up at a convention, because it had the name and logo of a well-known brand of television set imprinted on it.

His companion's physique reminded me a bit of Stan Bream. He was short, solid, about fifty-five, and wore work jeans slung low on his hips and a black sweatshirt with the sleeves cut off at the shoulders to show a set of muscles that must have come from many hours in a weight room. His belly looked as if he'd recently swallowed a volleyball. On his hands were leather half-gloves, covering his palms and knuckles but with his fingers bare. The hair on his arms and body was plentiful and gray, as was his mustache, perhaps compensating for the total lack of hair on his bullet-shaped head. I wondered what possessed a man of his age to actually want to walk around looking like that. His expression was that of a glassy-eyed, slack-jawed baby about to fall asleep in his mother's arms. My first guess was that he was the child of first cousins.

"You do private investigations, is that right?" the taller man said.

"That's right," I said.

"For money?"

I laughed.

"I said something amusing?"

"No," I said, trying to wipe the smile off my face. "Forgive me. Yes, this is a business office. I work for money. Mr. . . . ?"

He shrugged, as if his name didn't matter. It was beginning to, very much, but he wasn't going to tell me. He swung the tote bag up onto my desk with a quick, fluid motion. "Money, then," he said.

I looked at the bag.

"Go ahead, open it."

I didn't have to. The bag hadn't been closed to begin with, and its lips gaped open to reveal several packets of what appeared to be fifty-dollar bills, the newer kind with the off-center blown-up portrait of a dour Ulysses S. Grant.

"You can count it if you want," the man said, "but there's ten thousand dollars in there. Trust me."

Curious choice of phrase, I thought. "For me?"

"That's right," he said. "All yours. In cash, tax-free, and no paper trail unless you put it in a bank. You can stuff it under your mattress and use it every time you go to the grocery store for the next twenty years."

I didn't touch the bag. I knew the money was nowhere near "all mine" yet, and I doubted somehow that it ever would be. "Very nice," I said. "Just what do I have to do for it?"

He smiled pleasantly. "Nothing."

"Nothing?"

"Not a damn thing."

"Well, thank you very much."

"As a matter of fact, we'd like you to take a vacation for a couple of weeks. Go to Florida if you want. Just sit on your ass on the beach, watch the girlies in their thong bikinis, and don't do nothing."

I didn't say anything.

Neither did he, for almost a minute. It was a staring contest, although out of the corner of my eye I kept track of the other one, the older guy in the muscle shirt. He was standing behind and to the side of his companion, massive arms crossed across his barrel chest like a eunuch guarding the sultan's harem.

Then the taller one said, "One thing, though. You drop William Carnine as a client. Today. Call him up and tell him you can't work for him anymore, and then forget you ever met him. Forget you ever met *us*, too."

I leaned forward in my chair. "I haven't

officially met you yet," I said. "What's your name?"

"My name isn't important. Just call me the party who works for the party who wants you to drop the Carnine investigation."

"Why would I want to do that?"

The pleasant smile turned into something completely different. "Because we asked you to."

"That's not much of a reason."

"I know," he said. "That's why the ten thousand."

"I see," I said.

"Yes."

"Can't you even give me a little hint?"

"A hint." He looked at me and shook his head. Then he sighed. "Lloyd," he said to his companion, "give him a hint."

Lloyd stepped forward, lifted my computer monitor off the desk as easily as if it were an empty cigar box, and spiked it onto the hardwood floor like a running back when he crosses the goal line and slams the ball into the ground. It smashed to pieces. The electrical current arced and smoked, sparks flew.

I didn't move. Partly from surprise and partly because I knew I was outnumbered.

"That's your hint," the one who was not

Lloyd said. "It could have been your head. I'd hate to see that happen."

"That's not a hint," I said. "It's a threat, isn't it?"

"You can call it a plate of linguini if you want. It is what it is."

"I don't like threats much."

"Uh-huh." He looked at Lloyd. "Maybe you think we're just kidding. He thinks we're kidding, Lloyd."

Lloyd nodded, delighted with the opportunity to convince me further of their sincerity. I think he was like a little kid who enjoys smashing things, because this time he reached for my hard drive with both hands, apparently to send it to join the monitor on the floor. Before he could grasp it I clamped both his wrists and yanked him forward across my desk, scattering my papers all over the place. As he passed by I caught the strong scent of mints on his breath. I kept pulling, and he slithered over my desk until he was almost upside down at my feet, landing on his head with a grunt. With my left hand I twisted his arm up behind him and rammed my knee into his shoulder blade. Just to make sure I had his attention.

Then I put my size twelve-and-a-half shoe onto his face. Not hard enough to break anything, but applying enough pressure to keep him where he was. With my other hand I pulled open my top desk drawer and extracted the .357 Magnum I always keep there just in case. It's a good thing I did, because he who was not Lloyd was reaching inside his jacket for whatever he was carrying strapped under his arm.

"Don't!" I said, leveling the gun at the widest part of his body, the chest.

He froze for a moment, his eyes focused on the muzzle, and then relaxed, although he took his hand out of his jacket and showed it to me so I knew it was empty. "Won't," he said.

A fully loaded .357 Magnum turneth away wrath.

"I'm not kidding, either."

"A man with heat in his hand is never kidding."

Lloyd was struggling upside down under my foot, his legs flailing. I applied more pressure on his arm, forcing it closer to the back of his neck, and he moaned and stopped wiggling. I could see his ears turning bright crimson as the flow of blood rushed to his head.

"Now, suppose you tell me what this is all about?" I asked the taller one.

He shrugged. "I told you what I wanted

to tell you. That's all you're gonna know from me."

I moved the barrel of the Magnum from his chest to his face, but he smiled and shook his head. "Come on, Jacovich. You aren't going to do me right here, with my hands empty," he said. "That's murder. Not your style."

"Open the left side of your jacket with your left hand," I said. "In slow motion, just like an instant replay."

He pulled his jacket aside, revealing the butt of what looked like a Sig Sauer nestled in a complicated black canvas shoulder harness.

"Take it out with two fingers and toss it into the corner," I said. "You put a third finger on it and I'll shoot it off."

He complied. The weapon made a loud clatter on the floor, and he winced at the sound of it.

"Hike up your pants legs and let me have a look at your ankles."

"Not necessary," he said. "That one is all there is." Nevertheless he obliged. He was wearing burgundy-colored over-the-calf socks with little animal figures on them. He had no ankle gun.

"You have another one someplace?"

"Where do you think I keep it, in my ass?"

"What about Lloyd?" I said with a quick glance down at the topsy-turvy man beneath my foot.

"Lloyd isn't carrying. If he was, he'd probably shoot himself in the dick."

Lloyd's sweatshirt had ridden up over his belly, and I could see he wasn't packing a weapon either at his waist nor on his ankle. "That right, Lloyd?"

Lloyd's eyes, what I could see of them on either side of my shoe, were wide and bloodshot, although I couldn't really say they looked frightened. He blinked a few times and said, "Mmpphh." With my encyclopedic knowledge of languages I took that as a yes.

I let go of his arm, took my foot off his face, and pushed on his feet so that he fell flat on the floor facedown beneath my desk. I stepped back, out of range of anything he might have in mind. "Get up slowly, Lloyd," I said, "like you're just waking up from a two-day drunk."

Lloyd scrambled around so that his knees were beneath him, butt high in the air, and then pushed up with his arms and got slowly to his feet, managing to retain a scrap of dignity. A bright red trickle of blood issued from his nose, and my heel had left a raw-looking scrape on his chin.

He didn't seem angry or even perturbed, although he took a deep, ragged breath as the bright red flush left his face and his blood redistributed itself away from his head. He made no effort to wipe his bloody nose, but sniffed prodigiously instead.

"Go stand over there," I said, "so your buddy doesn't get lonesome."

When the two men were side by side, like little boys called to the vice principal's office for discipline, I said, "I'm calling the police. Since you won't tell me what's going on, you can explain to them."

"We won't be here," the tall one said. He was evidently the designated spokesperson of the two; except for a muffled grunt I wasn't even sure Lloyd spoke English.

"Oh?" My hand lingered on the telephone receiver.

"Nope," he said. "We're leaving. Because like I said before, you're not going to shoot us. Especially not in the back." He lifted an eyebrow, maddeningly sure of himself. "Are you, Jacovich?"

He glanced down at the Sig Sauer over in the corner and then at the remains of my computer monitor. "Keep the piece," he said. "We'll call it an even trade."

"Fair enough. But take your shopping

bag with you," I reminded him. "The monitor didn't cost ten thousand dollars."

"Don't worry," he said, "I was planning on it." He took a step forward, reaching for the bag, but then stopped in suspended animation, suddenly remembering he was under a gun. "Is it okay?"

I nodded.

"Good. I don't want to make you nervous."

"On your best day you wouldn't make me nervous," I said.

He picked up the bag by its handles and backed away to the center of the room again. Then he nudged Lloyd, the two of them turned around, and they walked easily out of my office without a backward glance while I watched, impotent, the Magnum waving foolishly in the air in front of me. He'd been right; I was not going to shoot them in the back.

I got to the window in time to see them climb into a late-model tan Camry two-door and burn rubber getting out of the parking lot, but I couldn't make out a license-plate number. And there were only about seven hundred thousand tan Camrys in greater Cleveland.

All I had to go on was the name Lloyd.

I took a pencil from my Cleveland

Indians cup and went over to the Sig Sauer. I slipped the pencil through the trigger guard, and lifted it. I carried it over to my desk and from the trash basket I fished a small paper sack I had used to transport my Arabica coffee and pastry. I put the automatic inside, fairly certain the serial numbers were either missing or it had been stolen a long time ago. The police might be able to pick up No-name's fingerprints, though — if they didn't get too sticky from the bear claw's sugar glaze.

I decided to wait until Monday to call Bob Matusen and tell him about my visitors, since it was a Saturday and by the time he got over here they could be several counties away. So I locked up the little sticky paper bag in my utility room for safekeeping, and then began picking up the pieces of my monitor.

Someone had sent muscle to warn me off the Carnine investigation. Whoever it was had made a bad mistake. It made everything different. And personal.

I cleaned up the pieces of my monitor, thinking hard. I knew quite a few of the Cleveland bonebreakers, but my recent visitors were not familiar to me. I could think of only one person who might know who they were and why they might have dropped by.

I picked up all my papers from the floor behind my desk and straightened them as best I could. Then I sat down, and called Victor Gaimari at home.

"Milan," he said in his surprisingly high-pitched tone. "How wonderful to hear your voice."

Victor Gaimari and I had history.

Victor was a stockbroker with offices in Terminal Tower — had he been at his desk on this Saturday afternoon he could have glanced out his window down at my own office building. But that was not the only lofty position he occupied; Victor was the nephew of Giancarlo D'Allessandro, the aging head of Cleveland's number one organized-crime family. I'd known him for longer than I cared to remember. I had broken his nose once, and he'd had me roughed up by his uncle's goons. Our paths had crossed many times since, and although I hate everything he stands for and he doesn't really understand the way I think and live, we have become almost friends.

And if anyone would know about two freelance bagmen who went around smashing up people's offices in our town, it would be Victor.

"How are you, Victor?" I said.

"I'm fine, Milan. Thanks. I haven't seen much of you lately. Keeping out of trouble? — as if I didn't know."

"I'm wondering if you do know, Victor. I had two hard guys come in here and try to bust up my office a few minutes ago."

"Hmm," he said. "May I take it that from your use of the word try, they didn't succeed?"

"Only partway."

"And you're wondering if I know anything about it? I'm disappointed, Milan. You know you and I aren't on that kind of basis."

"I know that, Victor. I just thought you might be able to give me a line on who they are."

"I might," he said. "You never know. Why don't we have dinner tonight and talk about it?"

I hesitated. That was Victor's way; he was usually forthcoming with any assistance I might ask for, but he enjoyed making me dance to his tune first.

"My uncle will be there," he said. "He'd love to see you, you know how fond he is of you."

"I'm fond of him too, Victor." And I was. Don Giancarlo had once been a holy terror; you don't get to be the head of a crime syndicate by being a Mother Teresa clone. But he was old now, and not well, and had always shown me courtesy and respect. I couldn't help my fondness for him.

"It's settled, then: Moxie, at eight o'clock. I already have a table booked."

Of course it was settled; no one ever says no to Victor Gaimari.

I hung up the phone and lit another cigarette. I wasn't exactly shaken up by Lloyd and not-Lloyd's visit — I've had too much experience with so-called hard guys. But I was wondering if my refusal to cooperate might bring further trouble. And very bothered by why they wanted me off the Carnine investigation in the first place.

That same unsettling feeling that I was missing something ran up my spine and prickled the hairs at the back of my neck. I took out the Carnine file and read it through again, thoroughly.

It was while I was perusing the medical examiner's report that it struck me like a fist between my shoulder blades.

I called Bob Matusen at home.

"Milan, it's the weekend, for God's sake," he said. "Give me a little peace, okay?"

251

"Bob, I was just going over the autopsy report on Ellen Carnine, and there's something missing you might be able to clear up for me."

He just sighed.

"You saw the body, right?"

"What was left of it." His tone was grim.

"Did you happen to look at her feet?"

"Her feet?"

"Yes."

He paused, and I knew he was lighting a cigarette. "I looked at all of her, sure. What about her feet?"

"Were they dirty?"

"Dirty? No, I don't think so. Not so's you could notice. She wasn't the kind of woman who went without bathing. Why do you ask?"

I felt the thrill of an adrenaline rush. "She wasn't wearing shoes, Bob. And from where her car was parked, she would have had to walk clear across the Lorain-Carnegie bridge before she jumped off. Unless the Cleveland maintenance crews go around hosing down sidewalks at four o'clock in the morning, the soles of her feet would have been pretty dirty from walking all that way."

Another long pause, then an exhale of breath. "Yessss," he almost whispered.

"So she didn't walk across the bridge to do the Dutch, Bob. Someone drove her out there and dropped her over. Ellen Carnine was murdered."

Chapter Fourteen

Less than an hour later I was back at police headquarters on Payne Avenue, sitting uncomfortably across the desk from Lieutenant Florence McHargue, number two on the Homicide Division depth chart. The dreaded Loo, Her Looness herself, the formidable PMSsence of good, tough cop. And she wasn't any happier about being there on a late Saturday afternoon than was Bob Matusen, who leaned against the wall as though it might collapse if he moved away from it.

I always feel morose when I'm in this particular room, and it had nothing — or very little, anyway — to do with Florence McHargue. This used to be Marko Meglich's office. Marko's death was never going to leave me, but when I was sitting across from where he'd always sat I remembered him, remembered our more than thirty-year history together, and I felt the pain that much more keenly.

McHargue probably misinterpreted my discomfort as a manifestation of my dislike for her, and now she was peering intently at me through her trademark blue-tinted glasses; if I didn't know better, I would have thought she was trying to make me disintegrate with a look. Her fingers danced impatiently on the top of her desk.

"Jacovich," she said, "I've got a nice, tidy, cut-and-dried suicide here that's almost two weeks old. Give me one good reason, besides a too-earnest P.I. with a wild hair, why I should open it up again and call it a homicide just because the stiff had clean feet."

"I'd be happy to, Lieutenant. Two hard-asses came to my office this afternoon and offered me ten thousand dollars to quit working for Dr. William Carnine. When that didn't work they started busting up my computer. Under those circumstances, I think it's reasonable to assume that there's something more to Ellen Carnine's death than an unhappy young woman who wants to end it all."

Her look became more intense, but not quite as impatient. She leaned forward across her desk, picking up a pencil and pulling a yellow pad close to her. "Ten thousand, huh? Did you take it?"

I just looked at her.

"Okay, okay, forget I asked. What hard-asses, then? You know everybody in this town — did you ever see them before?"

"No," I said. "But I have a faint, cold feeling that I'll see them again." I shifted in the uncomfortable chair; police stations didn't buy their furniture from Ethan Allen. "One of them was named Lloyd, that's all I know."

"Lloyd, huh? Lloyd Somebody, or Somebody Lloyd?"

"You got me."

The pencil wavered above the paper for a second or two before she put it down. "That's nothing, for God's sake."

I took the paper bag containing the captured Sig Sauer from my lap and placed it on her desk. "Here's more."

She opened the bag gingerly with two fingers. "What's this?"

"The piece I took off one of them. You can run it for prints."

"Lloyd?"

"No, his buddy."

She rubbed her fingers together, feeling the sugary stickiness from the pastry.

"Am I supposed to lick it off first?"

"Sorry about that," I grinned. "It was a field expedient."

"Guns with frosting now. Jesus." She pushed the bag toward Matusen. "See what you can get."

He nodded and picked up the bag.

"All right," McHargue said. "So two bad boys braced you in your office and smashed up your computer. That is a crime, I admit. But this is the Homicide Division, Jacovich, we specialize in murders here. You have a vandalism or an assault, you'll have to take it down the hall."

"What about Ellen Carnine's feet?"

"Ever think that she might have showered before doing the swan dive off the bridge?"

"Yes, I did. First of all, if it was suicide, she must have known that her body would be in pretty deplorable condition after it hit from that height, so showering would be kind of beside the point, wouldn't it? And secondly, even if she did shower, her feet would have gotten filthy walking barefoot from the parking lot to the place on the bridge where she went over. Hell, they would have gotten dirty just walking to the garage next to her apartment building."

McHargue scratched her ear. "That is something to think about, I suppose. But frankly, it isn't enough for us to open a full-scale murder investigation. You're going to have to bring me more."

"More what?"

The angry look came back, stronger this time. "If I knew that, I wouldn't have to ask, would I?"

I chose my words carefully; McHargue didn't like it when I played in her yard. "So I take it that, since this isn't an open murder case on your books, you have no problem with me continuing my work regarding Ellen Carnine's suicide?"

She sighed impatiently. "I have a problem with damn near everything you do. But I don't suppose I can stop you."

"No," I said. "You can't. For one thing, this doesn't smell right to me — it hasn't from the beginning. And at the very least, I don't like guys coming into my office packing heat and trying to muscle me around. So I just want you to know I'm still in this one. For the duration."

"Aw, jeez, Milan . . ." Matusen said.

McHargue glanced at him as though he had just belched in church, and then leveled a red-nailed finger at me like it was an artillery piece. "Just remember one thing, Jacovich."

"What's that?"

"I have no use for vigilante cowboys running around my town causing trouble. If you find anything out — *anything* — I want to hear about it before the ink is dry. You understand me? No going off on your own and being a hero like you usually do. You keep me in the loop at all times, or that loop is going to wind up tightened around your balls. Do I make myself clear?"

I almost replied "Yes, ma'am," but remembered in time that being called "ma'am" made Florence McHargue go postal. "Perfectly clear," I said.

"Good. Now get the hell out of here and let me enjoy what's left of my weekend. You'd think a single guy like you would have something better to do on a Saturday night anyway."

"Oh, I do," I said, wondering how she'd take it to learn that this particular Saturday night would consist of having dinner with Giancarlo D'Allessandro and Victor Gaimari.

Or rather, I wasn't wondering at all.

Moxie is a big, cavernous, casually elegant restaurant on Richmond Road in Beachwood, carved out of what used to be a high-ceilinged space in an industrial park. The place is packed with well-dressed diners every night, the male and female servers are all black-clad and attractive, there is a bustling open kitchen, the food is cutting-edge and terrific, and the murals on the wall are interesting enough to keep your attention should you happen to get bored with your dinner companions.

There would be little chance of that on this particular evening. Say what you will about Don Giancarlo D'Allessandro, he was never, ever boring.

Somewhere past eighty, small and frail and given to fits of coughing, one would never know to look at him that he had once run the premier organized-crime family in Cleveland with an iron hand and survived the experience. Except for his eyes; they were bright and fierce as a falcon's, and missed nothing. While he has lately ceded much of the business responsibility to his nephew Victor, he still has plenty to say about the way things run and is consulted on virtually all the major decisions.

And for some reason that I've never been able to understand, he likes me very much. Even so, I hadn't hesitated for a moment when Victor had asked me to dinner. There was no question that an invitation to dine with the don is tantamount to a command appearance.

They were all there when I arrived a few minutes late; I knew it before I walked in because I saw the don's driver, John Terranova, lounging against the fender of the old man's Cadillac, parked right outside the door in a handicap-designated spot. I had some history with Terranova, too, dating back to when I'd first met D'Allessandro and Victor Gaimari. Terranova was one of three hitters Victor had sent over to teach me a lesson. We said a brief hello now, and shook hands; it had been nothing personal with Terranova, and over the years we've gotten past it.

The story of my relationship with Victor and his uncle seemed to be a long string of getting-past-its. He was a charmer, Victor, educated at Ohio State, and one of Cleveland's glittering sophisticates. Philanthropic, relentlessly social, a culture vulture, and a smooth-talking womanizer, he was never less than enjoyable to be with, and I had to admit he'd always been there for me when the chips were down. Rather, we had been there for each other.

Marko Meglich had ragged on me loudly and often about my association with Victor and his uncle. He didn't think I could trust them. I have to disagree with that a little. I would no more automatically trust a clergyman than I would automatically *dis*trust a mob boss; there are good and bad apples in both professions. And trust, whether it's trust of your word or your wallet or your heart, is something that has to be earned.

But I never let myself forget who Victor Gaimari is and where he's coming from, and he never really overlooks my past as a policeman and my somewhat rigid sense of what is right and what is wrong. So our friendship is cordially cautious, and probably never will be anything else.

From the condition of the table when I got inside the restaurant, the Gaimari party was well into their second round of drinks. I was not surprised to see that the don was with his constant companion of the last twenty years, Regina Sordetto, a handsome sixtyish woman who watched over D'Allessandro's diet and health with the vigilance of a Secret Service agent. Someone had once told me, with a great rolling of the eyes, that she was the widow of one of his past associates, who had perished in a car bombing on the near west side.

Victor sat on the old man's right, of course, dapper as ever with his Cesar Romero mustache and health-club tan and wearing a gray cashmere suit that looked soft enough to disappear in, and a discreet gray silk tie. He made me look like a retired cruiserweight in my blue suit, blue shirt, and aggressively flowered tie. It wasn't exactly loud, the tie, but it wasn't subdued, either. Life is too short to wear dull ties.

The big surprise of the evening was sitting next to Victor. Her name was Cathleen Hartigan, a pretty blonde woman I had met several years earlier on a visit to his house. In her late thirties, she was an attorney, the daughter of a very political family in northeast Ohio.

She was also a knockout. There had been a few sparks jumping the gap between us at that initial meeting, but I had opted not to see where they might lead because she had once been Victor's girlfriend. Of course, that might be said for half the beautiful women in greater Cleveland, but for some reason it had bothered me enough to walk away from her before we could get anything started.

I had regretted it ever since, even after I read she'd gotten married a few years ago. The marriage hadn't lasted. So I wasn't surprised by the little flip-flop my stomach performed when I saw her. I was, however, startled that she was there at all; Victor hadn't mentioned she'd be joining us for dinner.

The fact is, I don't do very well in relationships, and so I've pretty much learned to avoid them. My marriage had slowly disintegrated, and the three major love affairs I'd had since had all turned sour. And I'd rather stick pins in my eyes than submit myself to the many tortures and tribulations of the dating scene.

We all can recount our "dates from hell." I've had a few, but the one that lingers in memory was a young woman I had met at a party given by my high-school friend Sonja Kokol, several years earlier. Her name was Audrey, and I had collected her telephone number, called, and asked her to dinner the following weekend. Before and during the meal she had consumed, as close as I could guess, approximately two and a half bottles of chardonnay all by herself. Midway through the salad course she had loudly declaimed that our waiter, who was only a few steps away and surely heard her, was a fag, and then proceeded to eat her meal, and mine too when I couldn't gulp it down fast enough to suit her, and all of the pats of butter that accompanied the basket of rolls, which she speared with her fork and popped into her mouth like french fries.

After dinner she'd insisted on sitting at the piano bar, where she drank several more glasses of wine. When she learned that the song being played was "Bess, You Is My Woman Now," she had bemoaned the title's grammar, insisting that it should be "Bess, You *Are* My Woman Now."

I had wearily explained that the song was from *Porgy and Bess*, a 1935 folk opera that depicted a settlement of poor blacks in South Carolina, at which time she had reared back and ringingly proclaimed, "A *nigger* song!" My teeth on edge and my nerves by now raw, I had told her in no uncertain terms that that was my least favorite word, and then hastened to advise her that it had been written by two white men, George and Ira Gershwin.

"Jews?" she had said, by now speaking so loudly that we were of a lot more interest to the other patrons of the bar than the music. "A nigger song written by Jews!"

When I recounted this story later, my friends, including Sonja, had all agreed I should have left her sitting there, but she had been very drunk by that time and without someone to look out for her welfare she surely would have been either raped or murdered. Or both.

So when I saw Cathleen Hartigan sitting at Victor Gaimari's table, my heart sank even as it fluttered. Dating was simply not my strong suit.

As I approached I smiled and nodded at everyone, but the first thing I did was to give the don the obligatory kiss on the cheek, his whiskery stubble harsh against my lips. I put my hand on his bony shoulder and he reached up and squeezed it affectionately.

"Milan Jacovich," he said. His lips always pulled back from his teeth when he attempted to say my name. More often than not he called me by both names, taking a certain pride in being able to pronounce them properly, his Sicilian tongue handling the Slavic syllables with care. "You been hiding from us? Or just busy?"

"Busy, I'm afraid. I'd never try to hide from you, Don Giancarlo. It's a pleasure to see you again." And it was the truth, I had to admit. Despite my misgivings about who he was and how he'd made his living for sixty years, I found myself liking him as much as he did me. But like him or lump him, I always spoke respectfully and almost formally to him. Not that he demanded or even expected it, but it just felt right for me to do so.

I said my hellos to everyone else, and took my seat next to Cathleen.

"Have you been hiding from *me*, then?" she said, blue eyes sparkling.

I didn't rise to the bait. "Cathleen, this is such a pleasant surprise. Victor didn't tell me you were coming tonight."

"If he had, would you have come?"

"Hell, I would have gotten here an hour ago." I leaned over to kiss the cheek she proffered to me. It was soft and sweet-smelling.

"We were shamelessly picking Cathleen's brain on a legal matter," Victor said in that surprisingly high-pitched, almost feminine voice of his, "so we got here a little bit early to take care of it. I hope you don't mind."

"I never mind, Victor," I said.

I ordered a drink, and the small talk buzzed and burbled for a few minutes, the almost obligatory time-wasting that attends upon a business meeting in a social setting. Then the don put down his red wine — which he had doubtless brought with him in a paper bag because Moxie probably didn't include a homemade dago red in its cellars — and slowly and deliberately cleared his throat. It wasn't a symbolic gesture; the don often fought an old man's struggle for speech. I have never really known what ails D'Allessandro, but he has been coughing and wheezing and sometimes choking in the ten-odd years that I've known him.

"So," he said, his eyes burning clear and strong amid the pockets of wrinkled flesh. "Victor tells me some men have been bothering you. I want to hear about that, Milan Jacovich."

"Well, they bothered me this afternoon," I said. "First they tossed ten thousand dollars in cash on my desk to bribe me, and then they smashed up some computer equipment."

"Computer equipment," he said, the words tasting sour on his tongue, his nose wrinkling as he contemplated something beyond his ken. "Who knows from that crap? You want to write somebody a letter, you pick up a fountain pen like a gentleman and you write it. Personally. So it means something. What do they call it, the geeks? E-mail? Computers. *Tsk*."

"Ah, Don Giancarlo, everybody has computers now, especially for business," Cathleen said. "The world is changing."

"Don't I know it? Look at you — a lady lawyer. Whoever heard of a lady lawyer? What next?" The don was obviously not a devotee of *Ally McBeal*, but he was fooling no one. He was still living squarely in the middle of the twentieth century just past, but not the nineteenth. He frowned, but he said it merrily.

Then he turned back to me. "Ten thousand dollars is some serious money to offer," he said. "What did they want you to do for it?"

I looked first at Cathleen, then at Mrs. Sordetto. The don said, "You can talk here, you're among friends."

Cathleen nodded, and Regina Sordetto kind of puffed up her chest and looked stern. I had never seen her looking otherwise. And although I was not anxious to broadcast my business to anyone who did not have an absolute need to know, I understood the don meant I was to speak now or forever hold my peace.

"Well," I said, "a few weeks ago a young woman committed suicide off the Lorain-Carnegie Bridge."

"I remember hearing about that," Victor said.

"Her father hired me to find out why." And I told them the story, or at least the bare bones of it. I didn't mention my suspicions of murder, because that might get them exercised and further into it than I

269

wanted them to be, and I didn't name any names or go into much detail, though, until I got to the events of that afternoon, the invasion of my office by Lloyd and his Hispanic friend, the bribe offer to back off the case, the rough stuff, my confiscating the slick one's gun.

D'Allessandro bobbed his head occasionally while he listened, two fingers on his cheek, beaming in approval when I told him about taking away the mug's weapon. When I finished, he took a deep breath and it rattled in his chest. "They weren't any of our people," he said. "Were they, Victor? Nobody would dare; our people all know that Milan Jacovich enjoys our friendship and respect. Besides, whoever heard of an Italian named Lloyd? I never did."

"I was sure it wasn't your people, Don Giancarlo. I respect you too much for that. And I would never have been able to take a piece away from your guys. But when I called Victor, I was hoping he might know who they were."

The old man looked at Victor. "They don't sound like nobody we know."

"No," Victor said.

"That distresses me very much, Victor. I don't like it when freelance guys think they can go around rousting our friends. It makes us look like dog crap — pardon me, ladies."

Mrs. Sordetto made a stiff little from-the-neck-up bow, excusing him.

The loose flesh beneath his jawline wobbled as he shook his head. "Victor, find out who they are."

A nerve in my cheek jumped. I didn't want anyone getting hurt on my account. Besides, I was uneasy about the old man doing any favors for me. In Giancarlo D'Allessandro's world, if you ask a favor, you owe a favor. I had gone through that ritual with Victor a few times, and once it almost got me killed. "That's not necessary, Don Giancarlo," I said. "I just thought they were people you might know about."

"Necessary!" he scoffed. "You're our friend. What the hell has necessary got to do with it?"

He hacked a few times from deep inside his chest, which prompted Mrs. Sordetto to reach for a glass of water and offer it to him, but he shook her away. A look of panic came across his face for a moment as he thought it might turn into a marathon coughing spell, but he fought it down with the strength of his will, and it passed. He smacked his lips a few times and swallowed hard, face flushed and eyes teary. "Allow me to decide what's necessary and what's not. You been a friend to us, we'll be a friend to you," he said. "Someone will call you by Monday evening with names." He reached across the table and squeezed my hand again.

"*Just* the names, please, sir," I said. "Nothing else. I'd prefer dealing with them myself."

He thought about that one for about fifteen seconds, frowning. He wasn't a man who liked doing things halfway. Finally he lowered and raised his head once, which I took to be a nod of acquiescence. "That will be your end of it, then. If that's what you want." He tucked his napkin beneath his chin and patted it smooth against his chest. "You must be stepping on somebody's toes again, like you always do. And somebody like this Lloyd guy, and the other one, the spic, they sound to me like bad paper. You know, Milan Jacovich, you'd probably stay a lot healthier not putting your nose in other people's business."

"That *is* my business, Don Giancarlo," I said.

"I s'pose. But you ought to study your whaddayacallit, your biology a little more, and learn something."

"Biology?"

"Sure." He leaned back in his chair and cleared his throat again, and I knew I was in for one of his philosophical discourses. "Take the bee, for instance. Bees have business to take care of, too, important business. Going from one flower to the other, spreading their stuff, their pollen, making more flowers, making honey, doing good works for everyone."

"Yes . . ." I said.

He raised a cautionary finger. " 'Yes,' sure. But what happens when the bee gets to be a nuisance, and gets into our house, where we live, where we do *our* business, and maybe tries to sting us?"

I waited.

"Then," he said, "we have to kill it."

His eyes were dark and cold, and I had to wonder how many bees had perished during his glory days.

We ordered dinner. Mrs. Sordetto ordered off-the-menu items for Don Giancarlo, a plain plate of bow-tie pasta with olive oil and garlic. He only picked at his salad. Like me, the don was a carnivore by choice and inclination, and I knew he chafed at his enforced low-fat diet. He endured salads, didn't enjoy them. And neither he nor his companion indulged in an after-dinner brandy like the rest of us. "Not good for me," he said, punching softly at his sternum with a gnarled fist.

He was an old lion now, feeble, missing a few teeth, and well past his prime as undisputed head of the pride. But he still had his claws, and the set of his head on his shoulders and the fierce hawk's-gleam in his eyes told of the power and resolve of old, and still demanded respect and, in my case, a strange sort of admiration.

Dinner went smoothly — despite the old man's chilling cautionary tale about the bee — and, to Moxie's credit, deliciously. Don Giancarlo didn't say much, he was too busy eating; I'm sure he was missing the meatballs and the spicy sausages that had sustained him for fourscore years, but he enjoyed what he was allowed, sopping up the garlic-laced olive oil with his bread. I don't know where on his frail old frame he put all of it.

Mrs. Sordetto *never* said much, even at the best of times, and I tried to remember if I had ever had more of a conversation with her beyond "hello." Victor chatted about trivia in his usual charming way; he had social skills to spare. Cathleen and I kept it light, as light as two people can be who have unfinished business between them. She told me that since our last meeting she had been made a partner in her mega–law firm in an East Ninth Street high-rise, complete with her name on the door, and I imagined that her annual income was probably three times mine.

When Victor, Cathleen, and I had been served our cognacs, D'Allessandro looked at his watch, which, in contrast to his off-the-rack brown tweed sports jacket, was a gold Rolex, and said, "Almost ten o'clock." He shook his head sadly from side to side. "I can't stay out late the way I used to. Remember, Victor, they used to keep the restaurants open for me after-hours on Murray Hill? Ah, that was a long time ago. Now it's time for us to be getting back. Getting old stinks, Milan Jacovich, you have to go to bed early like a little kid. Nighttime is for the young, like you."

"Thanks for the 'young' part, Don Giancarlo," I said.

He pushed back his chair and Victor hurried to help him up without seeming to. Cathleen and I stood up, too, and both hugged him good-bye.

"Don Giancarlo, I want you to know I appreciate your help and your kindness," I said. "I treasure your friendship."

His eyes glittered and he looked between Cathleen and me. "Show your appreciation, then, by taking this pretty woman home. We brought her, but she'd rather go with you, I'm sure."

Both of us had the decency to blush. Victor said he'd be back, and he and Mrs. Sordetto flanked the don and led him through the long room, past the bar and out the door. A few of the diners, who probably knew who he was, watched him with awed respect and even a little fear, which was ridiculous. For all Giancarlo D'Allessandro's sins, real and imagined, I was sure he'd never hurt anyone who wasn't threatening to hurt him or his people. He had a code of honor, the don. It wasn't my code and I didn't agree with it, but I had to respect it.

There are lots of people more respectable than he who don't even know the meaning of the word *honor.*

Cathleen and I smiled at each other and sat back down.

"He's something," I said. "This is probably the first time he's eaten in a non-Italian restaurant in forty years," I said.

Cathleen Hartigan laughed. "You'd be surprised, Milan. As he's grown older, he's been getting out a lot more, enjoying the time he has left. Victor and I even got him to the opera last fall."

"An Italian opera, I'll bet."

She nodded. "Of course. Verdi. He was almost crying at the end. It was beautiful to see. That frail, tough old man, moved by the power and beauty of the opera."

"It helps that he knows the language," I said. "I'll start going to the opera when they sing them in English."

"That's because you're a Philistine," she laughed, "and Don Giancarlo is a man of exquisite taste and sensitivity."

"You've known him a long time," I said.

"Ever since I can remember. Our families were very close. We visited him at his house on Murray Hill once, my father and I, when I was about seven. I remember his wife made the most amazing cannoli; I must have had three. And Victor was there, too. He was about ten or eleven — we went out in the front yard and played while the grown-ups talked business and politics."

"What did you play? Doctor?"

She grinned. "That came years later."

I told myself I wasn't going to ask it, but I did anyway. "Are you and Victor an item again?"

"Oh, no. We dated very briefly for about three months — eight, maybe nine years ago. We decided that we were lousy as lovers but great as friends, and that's the way it's stayed."

I took a careful sip of my cognac.

"That still bothers you about me, doesn't it?" she said. "That Victor and I used to go out."

"No, not anymore."

"But it did."

"Yes," I said. "I was young and foolish."

"Is it because Victor is a friend of yours, or because he's — who he is?"

"A little of both, Cathleen. And back when I first met you, Victor and I had a different sort of relationship than we do now, much more — well, adversarial. It just seemed the wisest course to say good-bye."

"So soon after hello, though."

I was saved answering when Victor came back in and sat down again. "You two catching up on old times?"

"We didn't have many old times to catch up on," Cathleen said. "We only met that once. At your house."

"I remember," Victor said, coloring slightly. He had invited me to that particular party to help him acquire a work of art that had turned out to be rather embarrassing for him, and I don't imagine he likes to think about it. Victor had been one-upping me for several years, and that was the first time I'd been able to catch him looking silly.

Of course, that was when he'd tried to pair me up with Cathleen Hartigan, and I was the one who wound up with egg on my face.

"My uncle is really disturbed about those two men, Milan. So am I. Loose cannons running around here aren't good for anybody. But don't worry about it, we'll take care of it."

"I told you I don't want you to 'take care of it,' Victor. I'll do that myself. I just want to know who they are."

"All the things you've told me about Milan were right, Victor," Cathleen said. "He's about as flexible as an iron pipe."

"Slovenians can be stubborn," Victor agreed. "And Milan here is their poster boy."

"Not fair, Victor."

"Check your contract and see where it says it's got to be fair. Look at the things they say about Italians. Because of the damn movies, the world thinks all of us walk around with our knuckles dragging on the ground and saying, 'You talkin' to me?' "

"You mean you don't bite your fist when you get mad?" Cathleen said.

"I never get mad, Cathleen," he said, with a calmness that was more terrifying than a tantrum, "I get even." He flicked his eyes at me and smiled good-naturedly in remembrance before picking up his brandy glass and swirling the thick brown liquid around. "My uncle is right about you, you know. You buzz around and threaten to sting people. One of these days it's going to get you swatted."

"It's been tried before," I said. "I don't swat that easily."

He looked at Cathleen. "I told you he was a tough guy, too, didn't I?"

"You told me that years ago," she said.

"But he's getting older now, just like my uncle. Just like the rest of us. It's not as easy as it once was to walk the walk."

I tried to keep the irritation out of my voice. "I love it when people talk about me like I'm not here."

"That's what I'm afraid of," Victor said, and finished what remained of his drink. "That one of these days you won't be. I'd miss you, my friend."

He let that hang in the air for a few seconds and then pushed away from the table slightly. "Well, children, I should probably call it a night, too. I have an eight-o'clock tee-off time in the morning. And the older

I get, the more sleep I need."

We both stood up and shook hands. "Fantastic seeing you, Milan, it's been too long."

"Thanks for dinner, Victor," I said. "And for — everything."

He glanced from me to Cathleen and then back again. "Everything," he said silkily. He leaned down and gave her cheek a brotherly kiss and then he was gone, a big, handsome man in an expensive suit and a well-trimmed mustache, with enough presence and charisma to suck all the oxygen out of a room just by entering it, moving with the ease of the supremely confident through the tables of late diners. Not a woman in the place failed to watch his progress.

None of this, of course, had brought me any closer to finding out what had happened to Ellen Carnine, but if I could find out who Lloyd and his friend were, I might get some answers. At the very least, it would give me a place to stand should they decide to come back and finish off the rest of my office equipment.

Either or both of them had looked perfectly capable of dropping a woman off a bridge. What I wanted to know about was the motive. Ellen didn't seem the type to hang out with hard guys like that, so I had to assume they were hired guns working for someone else. I wondered who. She had been a quiet, home-hugging, harmless woman who had been carving a pretty good life out of a bad deal — who would be mad enough at her to kill her?

Whoever it was had probably knocked her out first and then driven her out to the bridge, somebody else driving her car to make it look like a suicide. They must have figured that by the time she hit bottom, one bruise more or less wasn't going to make any difference.

"Where are you, Milan?" Cathleen said, jolting me out of my reverie. "Still in the state of Ohio, or somewhere out in the spheres?"

"I'm sorry," I said. "Just thinking about this afternoon's visitors. Can I get you another drink?"

"I don't think so. I need to be clear-headed tonight."

"Am I that threatening?"

She tossed her head back on the slender stem of her neck when she laughed. "You're not threatening *enough* with me, Milan. That's the trouble."

I desperately wanted a cigarette, but Moxie, like so many other fine restaurants, had declared dining-room smoking a no-no. Instead I said, "Can I ask you something, Cathleen?"

"Whoa, that sounds heavy. Is it?"

"Not exactly." I chose my words with the utmost care. "When did Victor invite you to this dinner?"

"Late this afternoon. Why?"

"Did he happen to mention that I was going to be here too?"

"As a matter of fact, he did. It's what decided me to come. I wanted to see you again, it's been too long a time."

"There was no 'legal matter' so important that he needed to discuss it with you on a Saturday evening?"

She shrugged. "We talked a little bit about some corporate stuff, but I imagine it could have waited until Monday morning."

"So he's really trying to get the two of us together again, just like he did four years ago."

"Would that be so terrible?"

"Of course not. What I'm wondering is, why? Victor always has a reason for everything."

"You hang around with a bad element too much, you know that? Everybody doesn't have deep, dark motives for what

283

they do. Not even Victor. I think he likes you a lot, and I know he likes me. Maybe he just figures we'd be good together and he wanted to do something nice."

"Would it be nice, Cathleen?"

"I don't know," she said. "I left my crystal ball in my other purse."

"We live in different worlds."

"That's not necessarily a bad thing, you know. Haven't you ever heard that opposites attract?"

"Sure I have. And I am attracted to you, I always have been. But I don't do relationships very well. That's my history. I've been a bachelor for a long time now, living alone and doing what I damn well please. And I guess I'm used to getting my own way."

"So am I," she said.

"So we'd be banging our heads together all the time."

"That would be my second choice."

I laughed. "Mine too."

"Really?" she said.

"Really."

"You're not going to try and tell me you've opted for the monastic life, are you? Don't even try. I didn't just fall off the turnip truck."

"Hardly monastic. I'm having enough

284

trouble keeping my hair without shaving a tonsure in the middle of it," I said, laughing. "I've tried relationships a few times, but it never seems to work out. Maybe I'm just too focused on my work."

"That could be," she said. "Or maybe you're just scared."

"That, too."

"And you think my being related to half the politicians in the county might compromise you someday."

"It might."

"To say nothing of the fact that I used to sleep with Victor Gaimari."

I shrugged. "I stopped looking for virgins when I was sixteen."

"And a damn good thing. But I meant because of who Victor is. And what he is."

"I've had too many dealings with Victor and his uncle in the past ten years to cast myself as an innocent, Cathleen. That's not a factor anymore. It might have been, once. But not now."

"And you're intimidated by the fact that I make more money than you do."

"Everybody makes more money than I do. Including your ex-husband."

"That was then. This is now."

She played with her coffee spoon. "That could be a problem, I suppose. Are you really going to keep after this suicide thing? Even though it might be dangerous?"

"I took the man's money; I owe him what he paid for," I said, again not mentioning the possibility of murder. You see murders in the movies and on television and you read about them in books, but when it comes to the real thing, people freak out. It was like walking too close to the edge of the fiery pit.

"You might get hurt."

"I might get hurt going up the stairs to my apartment, Cathleen. Besides, I don't like people thinking they can just waltz into my office and push me around. It rubs me the wrong way."

She shook her head a little; then her eyes sparkled. "What is the right way to rub you?"

"How bad do you want to find out?"

She thought about that for a while and then looked at her watch. "It's getting close to pumpkin time for me, too," she said. "You sure you don't mind taking me home?"

"Of course not."

"I'm not going to ask you in, you know."

"It never occurred to me. Well, it did occur to me, but I wasn't expecting it."

She nodded, and we both stood up. When we got to the door she said, "Are you going to kiss me good night, though?"

"I was thinking about it."

"Good," she said. "There just might be hope for you yet."

Chapter Fifteen

The kiss was good.

Not all kisses are, you know. Depending on your personal preferences, some kisses are too wet, too dry, too passionless, too passionate, too hard, too soft, involve the painful bumping of front teeth, or are simply artless and unskilled. Cathleen Hartigan's, delivered in my car at the head of her driveway when I dropped her off after dinner, was like Baby Bear's porridge — just right.

It was our first kiss ever. Hell, it was only the second time in my life that I'd even seen her, with several years between.

I went to sleep thinking about the kiss and smiling. I didn't know whether I wanted to walk down that particular path right now, though.

There was no question that Cathleen, with her new partnership and her famous and politically well-connected relatives, would be high-maintenance too, as well as high-profile, and I had to face the possibility that I'm just not constituted that way. I don't send flowers — not because I don't want to, but because frankly I never think of it. I don't dance attendance. And — this sounds *really* retro, I know — I happen to need a good bit of personal space.

For all my education, I'm really a working-class kind of guy who's not really comfortable wearing a tuxedo to a political fund-raiser and getting my name in the newspaper. And I'm pretty driven in my work, committed to my sons, and, if the truth be known, after more than ten years of living by myself I am very set in my single ways. There are some people who simply are not meant for the joys and rigors of marriage, and while I've spent many lonely nights longing for someone special and warm and wonderful in my life since Lila and I dissolved our union, I fear I might be one of those people.

But I didn't wake up that Sunday morning thinking about kisses — my eyes snapped open to thoughts of Ellen Carnine. To reflections on the pretty good life she had managed to build despite her unattractiveness. To whether she had jumped off the Lorain-Carnegie Bridge or if someone had deliberately pushed her. And to her father and mother, sitting in their nice, well-ordered academic home just off the Bryarly campus, grief-stricken and confused and wondering why.

The more I thought about it, the more unlikely it seemed that Ellen would take her own life. She'd managed to overcome what our society persists in considering a curse, being overweight and homely, and made a success of her life by the skillful and courageous playing of the cards she'd been dealt. She'd been tough and strong and brave, and more the type to come out swinging than to do the Dutch.

I was thinking that somebody owed her the debt of discovering the truth about her demise, and that somehow I had been elected.

If Victor Gaimari was successful in finding out who my two Saturday invaders were working for, that would be a shortcut, certainly. But it was entirely possible that Lloyd and his pal were out-of-towners and even Victor wouldn't be able to get a handle on them.

My uneasiness about involving him and the don grew. What had started out as a simple question had turned into a full-scale favor I would be loath to repay, especially in the kind of currency D'Allessandro might demand. The Cleveland family had always been violently anti-drug, so I knew I wouldn't be flying back from Colombia with a condom full of cocaine secreted inside my butt; they knew me too well to ask me to do anything illegal. But my code of ethics doesn't stretch quite as far as theirs does, and it worried me.

I had to keep working on my own. I had contacted just about everyone on William Carnine's list of friends and associates, and if I could assume they were not lying to me, I was almost certain the secret, if indeed there was one, was locked in Ellen's laptop computer. And I was just too unsophisticated about such things to access it effectively.

So I made a pot of coffee, toasted a couple of sesame-seed bagels, the remains of half a dozen I'd picked up two days before from Bialy's on Warrensville Center Road (the fact that they were no longer fresh wouldn't matter after a session in the toaster), and then called Taffy Kiser down in Kent.

"Taffy, I think I need some more of your expertise," I said. "What does your Sunday look like?"

"I've been studying for finals since seven o'clock this morning, Mr. Jacovich. I started early because Milan and I were going to go do something this afternoon."

"Anything special?"

"No," she said, "we just wanted to get off campus for a little bit, and clear our heads for next week's finals."

"I'd hate to cut into either your study or leisure time, but how would you like to come up to Cleveland and play computer genius for a while? I'll pay for your time again, of course, and take the two of you out to dinner."

"Sounds okay to me. Let me check with him, though, and get back to you."

"Great," I said.

I was doubly pleased; it would give me a chance to steal some time with my son, whose schedule made our time together as rare as the perfect pearl. I dug into the Sunday *Plain Dealer*, and was almost finished with it when Taffy called back to say they would meet me at my office at three o'clock.

I spent the rest of the morning giving my apartment a cursory cleaning. While I am not as stereotypically messy as many bachelors — not an empty beer can or pizza box or dirty sock in sight — my priorities do not include housework when I'm busy with other projects. But this morning I even hauled out the vacuum cleaner, and not only was I forced to admit that the place looked a lot better clean than untidy, I felt a certain amount of pride in the accomplishment.

At about one I drove over to Jack's Deli in University Heights, and after a ten-minute wait was led to a small booth against the wall where reproductions of Al Hirschfeld's famous caricatures of Broadway and Hollywood celebrities stretched the length of the place, and had myself a brunch of chicken soup with rice and matzo brie, a delicious combination of scrambled eggs and fried matzos, washed down with a Dr. Brown's cream soda. Thoughts of cholesterol were banished; I have learned that there are only two things in the world that really taste good — sugar and fat.

Since the Indians were spending the weekend on the road in Oakland, downtown was its usual Sunday-afternoon quiet, and I arrived at my office at about one-thirty. The wrought-iron shop downstairs was closed and the silence in my office made me realize how noisy they usually are.

I put Ellen Carnine's laptop on my desk

and booted it up, noting how strange my own computer looked without its monitor, made a pot of coffee, and waited. Taffy and Milan Junior came in about five minutes early.

As it frequently does these days, it struck me that my son had grown into a man while I wasn't looking. Almost as tall as I, he had filled out and solidified considerably in his year at college, partly from his inheritance of my own genes and partly from the football program at Kent that kept him in shape. He had the dark Serbian good looks of his mother, though, and the dark Serbian temperament to go with it, a direct contrast from my younger son Stephen, who was blond, Slovenian-looking, and relentlessly cheery. I suppose that because Lila was his custodial parent, Milan was closer to her than to me, but since he'd moved to campus we had developed a closer bond than before, close enough that he even allowed me to hug him when they walked in. He was probably the most decent human being I knew.

They were both dressed very collegiate. Taffy was wearing a plaid skirt, black knee socks, and a sweater over a white-collared blouse. Milan was in khakis and a loud print Hawaiian shirt and tan suede shoes, with a white sweater over his shoulders, the arms looped dashingly around his neck. He needed a haircut. He had a canvas Kent State book bag with him, and dragged one of my client chairs over to the open window so he could enjoy the fresh air and the view of the river and the city skyline while he studied for his finals.

I installed Taffy behind my desk at Ellen's laptop.

"What are we looking for today?" she said.

"I still don't know, Taffy, but I want to take a closer look at a few things."

She fished a CD-ROM disk from her fanny-pack and put it next to the laptop on the desk. "I got hold of a password-detecting program," she said, "like I told you about yesterday. I borrowed it from the computer lab at school. Just in case we might need it."

"Taffy, you're a marvel."

"I could have told you that," Milan called.

"How does it work?" I said.

"It can search for and determine a password when you don't know it. Like, if we'd had it when we were trying to guess Ellen's password, it would have saved us a hell of a lot of time."

"What's the sense of having a secret password if just anyone can find out what it is?"

"Just anyone," Taffy said, "doesn't usually have this software. It's the same one federal agencies like the FBI use. It's expensive — pretty doubtful the ordinary computer user would own it."

"Let's hope we don't need it," I said.

"So, what's on the agenda for today? Want to go back into the chat room?"

"Maybe later. First, let's see if she has any new e-mail."

Taffy's fingers flew over the keyboard, getting herself online with Ellen Carnine's password, and I could hear the guts of the computer humming and clicking. After a few moments a list of Ellen Carnine's new e-mails appeared. But it was a fruitless exercise. There was no new personal mail, only spam.

"Nothing interesting here," I said. "Let's try one of Ellen's clients, a Web site she helped design. See if you can find www. beattitude.com."

"Spell it," she said.

I did.

"You could have accessed that on your own computer," she said.

"I know, but as you can see, I don't have

a monitor at the moment."

She noticed the bare space atop my hard drive where the monitor had sat, and looked at me quizzically.

I didn't want to tell her the truth, especially in front of Milan. "I dropped it," I said.

Across the room, Milan laughed. "How can you drop a monitor? Why were you carrying it around in the first place?"

"It needed cuddling. And you're supposed to be studying."

"Whatever," he shrugged, and went back to his book. The new all-purpose answer among the under-thirty set: Whatever.

After a few minutes Taffy said, "I've got it. It's a clothing store."

"I know." I came around the desk and peered over her shoulder. The Web site was indeed handsome-looking, as Bronwyn Rhys had boasted. The text was reminiscent of some of the more flowery passages that used to adorn the J. Peterman catalog, and unashamedly targeted the snobbish and well-heeled, and the more than seven additional pages of graphics consisted of photographs of beautiful models wearing subtly elegant clothes. Bronwyn Rhys was featured in three of the photos, and her patrician good looks made the other models seem ordinary by comparison.

"What are those sites highlighted at the bottom?" I asked, pointing to three lines of bright blue type.

"Those are links. Maybe the designers or the manufacturers. Shall we take a look?"

"Might as well, as long as we're here."

Using the keyboard lever, she moved the pointer to the first link and clicked. In about a minute another site came up; it was indeed the home page of one of the designers of the clothing BeAttitude sold. More attractive models, more beautiful dresses. I wondered why it was that high-fashion models always looked as if they were incensed about something.

"Think you'll ever be able to afford clothes like this?" I said, jotting down the manufacturer's name just for the hell of it.

"Sure," Taffy replied. "I'm going to marry rich."

Milan looked up from his book. "I don't know if I can handle that kind of pressure."

"If you snooze, you lose," Taffy said merrily.

I gulped away the sudden lump in my throat. My son was eighteen years old; talk of his marrying, no matter how jocular, unnerved me. I fought down my fears by taking a deep whiff of common sense. Both Taffy and Milan had miles to go before they'd be thinking in terms of a permanent liaison, so I chose to regard what I had just heard as idle banter.

Taffy clicked on the second link, which yielded more of the same, only from a different manufacturer. "We don't have to look at all the pictures on this one," I said, "unless you're thinking about spending eight hundred dollars for a party dress."

"Maybe if somebody took me to a party once in a while," she said, glancing over to the window, "I would."

"Bitch, bitch, bitch," Milan said, his nose still in his book.

"Want to look at the other site, too? It's probably more clothes I can't afford."

"Not really," I said, "but let's."

She did some more of her magic, and the third site appeared. It wasn't a women's-clothing manufacturer, however, but a home page for an online stockbroker that looked familiar.

"For the serious investor," it began, and as I read on I realized it was the same site that I had seen before as one of Ellen Carnine's "hangouts."

"This is odd, coming off a designer-dresses link," I said. "What do stocks have to do with high fashion?"

"It doesn't seem to fit," Taffy said, "but it really isn't so unusual. This stockbroker is probably paying BeAttitude a fee for the referral on the site, which helps with the cost of their own home page. It happens all the time on the Web. That's how people make their money. Look, there's even a link on this page that probably leads to another referral."

"It still doesn't explain why Ellen had it bookmarked in the first place."

Taffy shrugged. "Maybe the stockbroker was one of her clients, too."

"That makes sense," I said.

We went into the chat room again — PLAIN JANE/CLEVELAND — but there were only seven people this time, and none of the screen names I had seen on my earlier visit; maybe Sunday afternoon is not the optimum time to talk with strangers. The talk was even more boring than before, and we only stayed around for a few minutes.

Then Taffy accessed Ellen Carnine's saved online files, messages she had either sent or received by e-mail. There weren't many of them. One, though, was one she had sent to Richard Goodman about two weeks before she died.

Richard, she had written.

You once told me that if work was fun, I'd have to pay them instead of the other way around. I understand that. I also understand that frequently we are forced to do things that go against our grain just to make a living, and I've accepted it.

But I absolutely loathe some of the things I have to do for this company and some of the people I have to deal with. It now has gone beyond unpleasant; it is immoral. Evil, even. I think you know what I mean, Richard, we have spoken of it before.

For a long while I was able to ignore it, although I see now that I was simply burying my head in the sand. On paper, my job is stimulating and exciting and meaningful. In practice, it is rapidly becoming something else. I've worked hard to get to where I am in my profession, and I don't want to throw it all away because of something over which I have no control. I also don't want to be perceived in the workplace as some sort of a Goody Two-Shoes — you of all people know that is not the truth.

But some of the things I am being

forced to do are making me lose sleep, and ruining my appetite (which, I suppose is not all bad). I have spoken about it to Barney Landenberger on several occasions, and if things don't get better really quickly, I may be forced to do something that will probably change my entire life. That bothers me, Richard.

Tell me I'm wrong. Tell me I'm being a tight-ass. Tell me to grow up and live in the real world. I trust your judgment, you know that. I always have.

Love, Ellen

I stared at the screen for a long time. Too long probably, because Taffy said, "See something that bothers you?"

"I'm not sure. Can you print this out?"

"I'll have to connect the laptop to your printer."

"Okay," I said. While she worked, I wandered over to where Milan was studying, and lit a Winston, taking care to blow the smoke out the window because I knew my son, a dedicated athlete, disapproved of smoking.

He glanced up from his book. "Creepy, huh?"

"What's creepy?"

"Poking around the personal stuff of a

woman who's dead."

"I suppose it is, Milan."

He shook his head. "I don't know how you do some of the stuff you have to do. Must be depressing."

"It is, sometimes."

"To say nothing of how many times you get hurt."

"When you go up to catch a pass and the defender tries to take your head off, you could get hurt, too."

"That's true," he observed, "but the guys in the secondary aren't usually carrying guns."

"This is a suicide," I said. "No guns." I decided not to mention Lloyd and his friend. My son affected a macho jock attitude sometimes, but I knew that he worried about me. I never discussed my work with my kids, but there was no way I could have kept secret the fact that I have been slashed with a knife, beaten up several times, and shot. I think I was safer when I was a cop; at least then I had some backup.

"Still," he announced, "I think I'm going to go in for a safer line of work."

"I'm glad to hear it," I said, with some relief and only a twinge of disappointment. I would have been proud if my son wanted to follow in my footsteps, but I would have worried a thousand times more about him than he did about me. "Are you leaning toward anything specific?" Milan had not yet decided on a career path, and it had been an ongoing discussion between us ever since he'd started college.

"I don't know, Dad. I've still got time to think about it."

There was truth in that. When I was a kid, most of us had a career goal, whether or not we ever turned it into reality. But it seems that at the turn of the twenty-first century a lot of young people have no definite ideas about what they want to do with their lives. Some of them don't even get on track until they're well into their thirties. So I didn't bug Milan about it. God deliver me from being the kind of parent who begins most sentences with, "When *I* was your age . . ."

Taffy had the printer set up and connected within minutes; it probably would have taken me an hour. I finished my cigarette, resisting the urge to flip it out the window into the river, and got back to my desk in time for her to hand me a printout of Ellen's e-mail to Richard Goodman.

It bothered me that Goodman hadn't mentioned the letter to me when we'd talked on Friday. It certainly indicated the frame of mind Ellen was in just before she died. I wondered what else he had kept from me, and made a mental note to find out.

Taffy and I visited several more sites Ellen Carnine had bookmarked; they all seemed to be the Web pages of Wheetek's clients, probably the ones Ellen had worked on, and yielded little in the way of information or insight.

All except the last one, which frankly knocked me for a loop, and made Taffy gasp audibly.

It was, she informed me, a "fetish" site, one of many available on the Web. This particular one was called "OTK" and featured about two dozen thumbnail photographs of women, mostly young and attractive, being spanked or whipped on their bare asses, most often by men but sometimes by other women. The pictures could be enlarged by clicking on the thumbnails, and although half of them looked as if they had been staged for the camera, others of them were, I am sure, very real. In those, the women seemed to be in genuine pain, and their buttocks were reddened or bruised purple, and in a few cases were bleeding. It was pretty grisly stuff at its worst, and about as sexy and erotic as intestinal flu.

Perhaps the most astonishing thing about the page was that at the bottom there were several links to other sites, and one of them was to beattitude.com.

"What's 'OTK'?" I asked.

Taffy didn't answer for a moment; her eyes were fixed on the screen, wide and frightened, and she was holding her breath. Then she said quietly, "I think it stands for 'over the knee.' "

"My God," I said, "the sick way some people get their kicks."

That brought Milan Junior out of his chair and over to the computer screen to look. I thought about telling him not to, but then felt silly about it. He was a grown man, after all, and Taffy was looking at them, too.

"There are other sites like this on the Web, Taffy?"

"There is damn near everything on the Web, Mr. Jacovich. Every sexual fetish and perversion you can think of, and quite a few that you couldn't." Her lips looked thin and white. "Of course, those are harder to access, but they're there if you're dedicated enough to look for them."

"Why do you suppose Ellen Carnine would have bookmarked this one on her personal computer?"

"Maybe she got off on being spanked," Milan said. Taffy looked up at him sharply.

I thought about that. There had been nothing in her personal effects to indicate that bondage and discipline was one of Ellen's interests — no books, papers, magazines, fetish clothing. No chat room or "hangout" that dealt with the topic. And from what I could figure out, she hadn't been in any sort of a sexual relationship, sadomasochistic or not, for a long time.

It didn't sit right with me.

"I don't think so," I said. "From what I know of her, she suffered a lot of rejection and even unkindness from men in her life. If she was involved in a real-time love affair, it would probably have been a nurturing, gentle one. Not like . . ." I glanced at the screen, which now displayed a photo of a young brunette bent over a chair, being flogged by an ugly-looking middle-aged man with a long, thin cane that left ugly welts across her buttocks, and winced. "Not like this."

Taffy had pushed herself back from the laptop screen. "Can we get out of this site now, Mr. Jacovich?" she said. "I don't particularly want to look at this anymore."

"I'm so sorry I got you involved in this,

Taffy," I said, meaning it. "You too, Milan. I'm sorry you had to see that."

"Come on, Dad, it's not like we haven't seen stuff like this before."

"You have?"

Taffy was busy exiting the spanking site and logging off.

"Dad," Milan said, "everybody on campus has a personal computer. And you'd be surprised what they do with them in between studying. Stuff you couldn't even imagine. Pictures of people peeing on each other. Torture chambers. Obese people, dwarfs, lesbians, children . . ."

"And an awful lot of the Web pornography has to do with abusing women," Taffy said, her voice tight and strained. "I know it takes all kinds, but there are some kinds that ought to be institutionalized for life." She took a deep breath and then let it out slowly. "Of course, that's just my opinion."

"Mine too," I said.

"Surfing the Web can give you quite an education."

"Not exactly the kind of education most parents have in mind when they send their kids off to college."

"Don't worry, Dad," Milan said, "I don't spend my time downloading porno. Neither does my roommate. But some of the other guys in the dorm — well, like Taffy said, it takes all kinds."

I nodded. I'm an avowed and vocal foe of censorship of any kind — but sometimes that pesky First Amendment can be a double-edged sword.

Chapter Sixteen

When I asked them where they wanted to eat dinner, Milan and Taffy opted for Shooters, a popular hangout in the Nautica complex on the west bank of the Flats with a great view of the river and the railroad bridge that was the gateway to Lake Erie. When we got there and were seated near the window, I found I was at least twenty years older than anyone else in the place.

The kids both ordered burgers and pop — not my idea of a Sunday dinner, but then I'm not nineteen. I had a steak sandwich smothered with onions, french fries, and coffee. I really wanted a beer — I felt I needed one after my trip through the world of cyber-spanking — but I was with minors and didn't want to set a bad example. Despite the noisy and somewhat festive atmosphere of Shooters, there seemed to be a dark cloud of tension hanging over our particular table. Milan was being his usual taciturn self, and Taffy wasn't saying much, either. I tried to get the conversation going.

"Is Taffy a nickname?"

"On my birth certificate it says Tiffany," Taffy answered, but talking seemed to be an effort for her.

"Oh my god," Milan said. "I never knew that."

"You've been dating her all this time and you didn't know what her real name is until now? You're a real romantic, Milan."

"I think it's kind of a gross name," Taffy said. "I suppose it was trendy nineteen years ago, and my parents are always trendy." She paused for a moment, her eyes going dead, and then she shook her head and went on. "The kids in school started calling me Taffy in the first grade or so — because of my hair, I guess, and it was pretty close to my real name — so it stuck. I much prefer it, anyway."

"How are your grandkids going to feel about having a grandma named Taffy?" Milan said.

"They'll just have to live with it!" she snapped, wheeling around to face him, her face red.

His eyes widened, startled by her vehemence, and then his mouth became a thin line and his jaw hardened in that way he had when he got stubborn and withdrawn, and he turned his attention to the boats on

311

the river outside, returning to their berths from a Sunday afternoon on the lake.

At first I wasn't going to open my mouth, not wanting to get in the middle of a lover's quarrel. But Taffy was breathing heavily, her pretty face graveyard-pale and pinched, and my son looked grim and wounded. "Taffy," I finally said, "is something wrong?"

She lowered her head and bit her lip, fighting tears that were welling up in her eyes and looked ready to roll down her cheeks at any moment. "It was that damned Web site," she said.

I waited.

"I'm sorry, it has nothing to do with either of you." She shook her head hard, then turned toward my son, taking his hand. "I never told you this, Milan — I never wanted to talk about it . . ."

She dropped her head for a second or two, seemingly staring down at her fingers intertwined in Milan's. Then she raised her chin, and the waning light from the window caught the glittering wetness of her eyes. "My father used to spank me all the time — a couple of times a week — until I was fifteen years old and my mother threatened to leave him if he didn't stop."

I tried to swallow but found my throat

blocked by a large, immovable object. Being the only child of old-world parents, I had been whacked the usual number of times during my boyhood, like every other kid from the old neighborhood, but infrequently. Never did it approach anything ritual, and it was certainly without any pleasure on the part of my father, whose discipline most often consisted of looking sad and disappointed in me for my infractions.

Milan Junior winced visibly at what Taffy said. Nobody dared speak, and even the noisy ambiance of the restaurant seemed to go away for a moment. There are some things that are unanswerable, and both Milan and I were smart enough to know it and keep very quiet, letting her say whatever it was she wanted to get off her chest and not pressing her for more.

"Up until I was about twelve I thought he was just strict," she said, almost too softly for the human ear. "Then I began to realize he was actually enjoying it. Really getting off on it."

"Hey," Milan whispered. He reached over and covered their interlocked hands with his other one. She allowed him to, but didn't look at either of us.

"So when we stumbled on that OTK Web

page today by accident, I just found myself having a flashback. And getting pretty angry that there were so many sickos out there who enjoy the pain of other people." She sniffed, although she still wasn't crying. My guess was that she'd taught herself not to cry, that crying would have meant defeat and capitulation and she was too strong for that. "Just give me a few minutes," she whispered. "I'll be okay."

A large powerboat drifted by the window. A middle-aged guy with a jaunty yachting cap not quite covering his silver hair and wearing a loud shirt was up on the flying bridge piloting the thing; his passengers, two women in halter tops and shorts, were at the stern, looking almost blue from the cold. It doesn't do to rush the season in northeast Ohio; in May the temperature drops quickly out on the lake when the sun gets low.

It had nothing on the deep-freeze at that table, though. The kids' burgers and fries were getting cold because we'd all lost our appetites. The pop was going flat and watery from the melting ice, and nobody was saying anything. Nobody even moved, as if the slightest change in the molecular structure of the air would shatter and destroy something fragile.

Finally Taffy drew in a deep breath and let it out slowly, then looked up and attempted a small smile. "Sorry."

"Nothing for you to be sorry about, honey," I said.

"Every party needs a pooper, and I guess I was elected tonight."

"Not at all. You've managed to overcome a lot; some people can't."

And I couldn't help thinking again of Ellen Carnine and what she'd had to overcome. For Taffy, at least the abuse had stopped; for Ellen, her looks had haunted her for her entire life. I found myself wondering whether the same had held true for my childhood schoolmate, Eunice Bostic.

I guess Taffy was thinking about Ellen, too, because she said, "Do you suppose the woman you're trying to find out about, the one who killed herself, came from a background like mine, and that's why she'd bookmarked that Web site?"

My heart thumped in my chest; that hadn't even occurred to me. "I don't know, Taffy. Maybe that's something I should find out." I smiled at her. "You have the makings of a first-rate detective."

She waved a hand in front of her face. "No thanks. I've dug through enough dirt in the last few days to last me a lifetime."

Then her eyes widened and softened. "I'm sorry, Mr. Jacovich, that was pretty rude. I didn't mean to say anything bad about the way you make your living."

"I didn't take it in a negative way," I said, "because that's exactly what I do. I dig through the secrets and the dirt of other people's lives, and sometimes it can get downright unpleasant. But the good part is that if you dig through enough of it, you eventually get things clean."

My son looked at me with astonished admiration and a jolt of enlightenment, as if I'd just delivered the Sermon on the Mount. "Wow, Dad," he said, "I never thought about it that way."

Whoever said childhood is the best and most carefree time of our lives must have had a lousy memory. Childhood is traumatic for the best of us. We're younger and smaller than almost everyone else, and virtually helpless. We have no power to make even the most minor decisions, we have to do what we're told, the law makes us go to school whether we want to or not, and all too frequently we're hit or punished in some other way whenever we displease our masters. Anybody who considers that carefree has either been brainwashed by the new psychobabble or else is in deep denial.

And yet, most of us survive it. We're all walking around with the memories of that traumatic and helpless time. And some of us, like Taffy Kiser, have worse memories than others.

Taffy was a hero. The hurt and humiliation she had suffered at the hands of a father who was abusive at best and perverted at worst had been put behind her. Not forgotten — not ever, I was certain — but tucked away in a bottom drawer in the corner of her mind, and she was going on with her life and not laying off blame or finding reasons why she couldn't succeed. She was simply succeeding.

And Ellen Carnine had been a hero, too. If she'd been given a choice she probably would not have opted to be overweight and homely, but since she was, she'd forged ahead with her life and studied and learned and become a success without bewailing her unlucky appearance, without thinking of herself as oppressed, even though there were times she surely must have been.

Times when she was insulted or overlooked or rejected because of her looks. Times when good things she might have deserved were instead bestowed upon more comely women. Times when she cried alone in her room over a situation that was not of her own making.

But she kept going. She excelled in her work and worked hard at her friendships. She didn't moan about getting a bad deal. She persevered.

That was what made her the best kind of hero, and why the idea of her committing suicide off a high bridge was so ludicrous. Someone had to have deliberately murdered her.

Why?

When I got back to my apartment it was not yet nine o'clock, so I phoned Dr. William Carnine at his home in Bryarly and made an appointment for eleven the next morning. I wanted to meet with Richard Goodman as well, to ask him about the e-mail Ellen had sent him two weeks before she died, but I had promised him that if he cooperated with me I'd make every effort to keep his wife from finding out about his long-ago affair with Ellen Carnine, so I decided to wait and contact him at the college in the morning.

I went to bed at about eleven, but I found myself staring at the ceiling, with its strange little crack in the plaster that looks like an outline of Brazil. Finally I got out of bed and watched an old James Bond movie on television in the den. It was a Roger Moore. Moore is a great-looking guy and a competent actor, but for my money there's only one Bond, and his name is Connery — *Sean* Connery. There's only one Sherlock Holmes, too — Basil Rathbone. And don't even talk to me about any Tarzan other than Johnny Weissmuller.

Something else was bothering me about the Ellen Carnine case, too — enough so that my mind wandered away from *For Your Eyes Only.* Why did a woman like Bronwyn Rhys, who sold overpriced designer clothing to very rich women, have a link on her Web page that displayed photographs of naked young women being physically abused?

I had no answer for that one, but it was my last thought before I nodded off in front of the TV in my big leather armchair. Roger Moore was going to have to save the world all by himself.

I woke up before seven, stiff in the neck and back from sleeping in an armchair all night, and hauled myself into the shower, letting the water pound on my sore places as hot as I could stand it. Then I shaved, threw on a bathrobe, and went out in the hallway to get the morning's *Plain Dealer*. My longtime neighbor from across the hall, Mr. Maltz, had died a few months earlier at the age of ninety-four, and I missed those occasional mornings when we'd fetch our newspapers at the same time and exchange pleasantries about the weather. He always made me feel like a bum; I could count on the fingers of one hand the times I had seen him when he wasn't wearing a tie.

I made a pot of coffee and shook some Cheerios into a bowl to consume while I read the paper. Then I got dressed — a light blue sweater over a white shirt, navy slacks and black loafers — and headed down the freeway toward Bryarly. The Cleveland sky was overcast, gray clouds drifting in from the lake, but the farther south I got, the brighter it became, until I finally came to the Bryarly exit and found myself driving in bright sunlight.

Carnine's wood-paneled office was on the third floor of the biology building, a roomy and airy space made stuffy by several hundred books, boxes of files, magazines, and framed diplomas and posters. Yet there was a terrible, almost compulsive kind of order about it all; I was certain that if I had asked him for the April 1967 issue of *Scientific American*, he could have located it within fifteen seconds.

He was wearing his usual bow tie, today a red one, with a stiff white shirt and a brown vest and pants; the jacket to the suit was neatly hung up behind the door. The only photograph visible was one of Ellen, atop a credenza behind Carnine's desk — right next to a microscope that seemed to be there more for decorative purposes than practical ones.

I gave Carnine an up-to-date progress report, or as up-to-date as I dared. I left out a few things, such as my suspicion that his daughter had been murdered. To have opened up that particular can of worms in front of him without any proof would have been cruel and useless.

But he wasn't happy.

"You started on this investigation a week ago, Mr. Jacovich. I was hoping for results by now."

"It's pretty hard to find out about twenty-eight whole years in just a week, Dr. Carnine."

"I frankly don't care a damn about the first twenty-eight years," he said, getting louder and edgier. "I'm paying you to find out what happened within the last few months. I want to know what drove Ellen to want to end her life."

"It isn't that simple."

"I don't see why not."

He wouldn't see, of course, and I suppose I was foolish to have expected him to. He was a scientist, and scientists deal in hard facts. It's either a bullfrog or a bull moose, and there's no dispute about it. But the motives people have for doing whatever it is they do are not that cut-and-dried.

"Because biology is very different from psychology," I said, trying not to sound pedantic. "What happened to us many years ago can easily imprint us and affect what we do today. That's the direction I'm going."

He harrumphed a bit, stirring uneasily behind his desk, and shuffled some papers around.

"What can you tell me about Ellen's childhood and adolescence?"

He looked nonplussed for a moment. "I don't see where that's germane, Mr. Jacovich. Ellen's childhood was unremarkable in every way. After she reached puberty and started to gain weight, it wasn't easy for her. Socially, I mean. You know how cruel a high school caste system can be to outsiders. And I'm sure you also know how hard adolescents can be on themselves. You can walk away from the jeers and the rejection, but you can't escape the way you feel about yourself."

I nodded my agreement, but what he said gave me a queer feeling. It was almost as if he were talking himself into accepting his daughter's suicide. Or trying to talk me into accepting it.

I shook off the creepy-crawlies for the moment. "I was wondering more about her home life."

He frowned.

"Was she a difficult child?"

"Difficult? I don't understand."

"You know, around the house. Did she misbehave much?"

"What on earth would that have to do with anything?"

"I don't know, Dr. Carnine. You tell me."

"I'm not sure I can. No, Ellen was a very good child most of the time."

"Most of the time?"

He shifted impatiently. "Yes. Every child has his or her moments, I suppose, but on the whole . . ."

"What happened when Ellen had 'moments'?"

Now he looked angry. "What do you

mean, what happened? Like any other kid, she had to learn right from wrong."

"So you were strict parents?"

"I didn't say that, and I wouldn't say it, no. We were probably more on the permissive side, actually."

"So, when you punished her . . . ?"

"When she was smaller, she'd be sent to her room. After she'd grown up a little, there would be no television for the evening. Later, when she was in her teens, she'd be grounded for the weekend. What's all this about?"

"You never spanked her?"

His breath hissed as he drew it in between his teeth. "Never. Not once. Neither my wife nor I believe in hitting children."

He said it so firmly and sincerely that I had no choice but to believe him.

He stared at me, shocked. "What in *hell* are you inferring, Mr. Jacovich? And for God's sake, why?"

I didn't want to tell him about the spanking Web site I'd found on Ellen's computer. Not yet. "Just curious," I told him.

Chapter Seventeen

When I got back down to the parking lot, I used my cell phone to call Richard Goodman's office. I lucked out; he was between classes and I reached him on the first try. He wasn't happy to hear from me, though — in fact he sounded downright annoyed. But I told him I had to talk with him, and after some initial resistance he grumblingly agreed to rendezvous with me in an hour, back at the Bob Evans restaurant where I'd first met him.

With what I had on him, I think he was afraid not to.

I was glad it was lunch time so I wouldn't have to sit there again without ordering anything. I had to wait ten minutes for a table to become vacant, but Goodman was almost half an hour late, and I was halfway through my cheeseburger when he came in and looked around until he spotted me. He walked toward my table, dragging his feet as if fettered with an old-fashioned ball and chain. Under his brown suit jacket his shoulders, narrow at the best of times, had almost disappeared now, and his head was hanging low.

He didn't bother starting with a hello or an apology for his tardiness, but slid into the booth opposite me and slumped there like a new toy that had been discarded the morning after Christmas. "So is this the way it's going to be from now on, Mr. Jacovich?" he said without preamble, his tone an irritating and self-pitying whine. "My having to jump every time you say so? I don't want to live like this."

"You're here on your own volition, Professor."

"What is it you want from me, then? I don't like this. I don't like having to talk to you all the time."

"You're not going to like this any better, I'm afraid."

He took off his glasses and rubbed the bridge of his nose. "What?"

"I apologize up front for having to ask this," I said. "When you and Ellen were intimate, back when she was attending school . . ."

He twitched involuntarily, a violent jerking of his head and shoulders, like one of those myoclonic spasms that almost throws you out of bed at night while you're sleeping. "Be very careful, Mr. Jacovich," he murmured.

"I don't know how to do this and be careful, too, Professor. When you and Ellen were sleeping together, was she — Well, would you characterize her sexual preferences as at all, uh, kinky?"

His face reddened to the color of raw beef, all except for his lips, which were bloodless white. " 'Kinky'? I don't know what you . . ."

"Come on, Professor Goodman, you teach at a college, you've surely heard the word before."

He swallowed hard, several times, and then he got huffy. "I am deeply offended. *Deeply* offended! You have no right, Mr. Jacovich. Poor Ellen is still warm in her grave, and you . . ."

"That's why I'm asking, Professor. Don't press me for details as to why, just answer my question."

He fought for composure. Then he got arrogant and pissy again. "I have no intention of answering your question. What Ellen and I had was private, personal. I don't discuss intimate things like that with strangers."

I pushed my plate away and took out my notebook and a pen. I clicked the ballpoint open deliberately. "I'll take that as a yes, then."

"No!" he said. "I mean, she wasn't . . . We didn't . . ." He stopped, clamping his lips shut.

I just stared at him coldly, waiting.

His eyes closed to mere slits, but I could still see the rage glittering deep inside them. "My God, Jacovich, you're a loathsome human being!"

"I'm not making any judgments. I just need to know."

"Why?"

"Let's just say it's very important, and let it go at that."

He gnawed at the skin on the side of his thumb, looking around as if the truck drivers and travelers who had stopped for lunch at Bob Evans could somehow liberate him from having this conversation. Then the air went out of him and his chin sank even lower onto his chest, and his white scalp showed through the thinning hair. He looked very small and defenseless, and I had to lean forward to hear what he said.

"There was nothing like that," he mumbled. "I was Ellen's first lover. She didn't even know the basics, much less anything arcane."

"Always the teacher, hmm?"

His eyes met mine for the first time in a while, and again there was some fire behind them. "That is a singularly lousy thing to say."

It had been, but I pressed on. "And did you teach her some of the more esoteric aspects of lovemaking? Like bondage, perhaps, or S and M, or spanking?"

He looked truly shocked. "My God, no!"

"You sure?"

"Of course I'm . . . What in the *hell* are you talking about? Are you trying to tell me Ellen was into perverted stuff like that?"

"If I knew that, I wouldn't be asking."

"Well, that's ridiculous. And I repeat, the question insults me."

"I didn't mean to insult you," I said. I wasn't yet sure whether or not I believed him, but being a private investigator and not a badge-toting minion of the law, I couldn't really press him further. Besides, he wore the look of a man who'd been pushed to the edge; one more question on his sexual experience with Ellen Carnine and he'd either go over, or turn on me in fury.

A change of subject seemed in order. "There's something else I want to ask you about."

He looked almost relieved at that.

I took a printout of the e-mail Ellen Carnine had sent him from my pocket and put it on the table in front of him.

"What's this?" he said.

"Take a look, I'm sure you'll recognize it."

He read it without touching it. "Where did you get this?"

"That doesn't matter. What's important is why you didn't tell me about it when we talked the last time. You said you wanted to help, and I asked you whether you knew of anything that was bothering Ellen. You didn't mention it."

He didn't look at me.

"She's not very specific about her problem in this e-mail, but she says here that you've spoken of it before."

He started to say something, then sputtered, thinking better of it.

"Let me get you some coffee," I said, looking around for a waitress.

He shook his head. "Coffee won't help."

I had the idea that a good slug of bourbon would, but Bob Evans doesn't serve liquor. I waited.

"Look," he said, "the company Ellen worked for — Wheetek?"

I nodded.

"They're into all sorts of bad stuff. Porno stuff."

"I know," I said. "Her former bosses were very open about that. They also told me that it disturbed her."

"Disturbed? Ellen hated it. Really hated it. She wasn't what you might call a radical feminist, but like most women she could go crazy on the subject of pornography. I mean, I suppose she thought it had its place for those who wanted it, but she was very uncomfortable about having to handle it herself. You understand what I mean?"

I nodded.

"So much so that she was almost ready to quit."

"Is that what she meant when she said" — and here I turned the printout of her letter around so I could read it — " 'I may be forced to do something that will change my entire life'?"

"I think so," he said.

"Why didn't you mention the letter to me when we first talked?"

He hung his head again. "I guess I didn't want you to know that Ellen was involved in the pornography industry in the first place," he said softly. "Even as indirectly as she was. I didn't want anyone to know. I wanted to protect her. Her memory. I didn't want anyone thinking ill of her." He lifted his chin toward me and his voice got stronger. "And I certainly didn't want her father finding out."

That made sense. Not a lot of sense, but some. I decided to let it go for the time being. I thought Richard Goodman was a jerk, but I couldn't quite cast him in the role of murderer. As far as I could see, he had no motive. Nevertheless, I've been wrong before. "Your understanding was that she wanted to meet with you so you could give her some advice?"

"I think so, yes. I've always been sort of a mentor to Ellen."

Right, I thought, especially horizontally. I didn't say it, though. Instead I asked, "Was she at all specific about what was bothering her?"

"You read the e-mail," he said with some bitterness.

"Before that. In your discussions on the telephone."

He shook his head. "No, she wasn't specific. Other than the fact that it had something to do with her work."

"With Wheetek?"

"I would assume so."

Maybe it was the OTK site with its graphic spanking photos that had gotten to her, I thought, even though there didn't seem to be any history of that kind of abuse in her past. Then again, in her letter to Goodman she had spoken of something that might be illegal, and while spanking pictures are admittedly execrable, they are certainly within the law, at least as far as the Internet goes.

What is illegal, online or anywhere else, is child pornography. And Landenberger and Munch had assured me that they kept their hands off that particular money-maker.

Of course they were telling the truth; no one has ever lied to me before.

"That's all my questions for today, Professor," I said, "but I might have some more at another time." His face froze at that one, so I added, "I'll try my best not to bother you, though."

The tightness in his jaw relaxed a little; I hadn't realized that for most of the conversation he'd been gritting his teeth. He shook his head sadly. "I wish you'd just leave it alone," he said. "All these questions, raking up all this ugliness — it's not going to bring Ellen back, is it?"

Of course it wouldn't. But what I didn't tell him was that it might help to catch a murderer.

★ ★ ★

Just about everyone is compulsive about something. Some people put their kitchen spices in alphabetical order, some have the same breakfast every day for forty years, some keep their homes immaculate enough so that brain surgery could be performed on the living-room carpet without fear of infection.

My obsession, I guess, is that whenever I go anywhere, I always like to accomplish more than one task. For instance, when I pick up my dry cleaning, I often feel compelled to stop at the bakery or the delicatessen and buy something, too, even if I don't particularly want or need it.

And now here I was, coming back from Bryarly, driving through the west side, the freeway within five minutes of BeAttitude, and it seemed an egregious waste of time and gasoline not to stop there and ask Bronwyn Rhys about the interesting link to her Internet Web site. I couldn't exactly make any connection between spanking for fun and who might have killed Ellen Carnine, but I've learned that the more questions you ask, the more you learn. And it was in the neighborhood anyway.

Once more she was alone when I walked into BeAttitude, and I wondered whether anyone else ever worked in the shop and, if not, who watched over things when Bronwyn Rhys went to lunch. Then I remembered that the doors were only open from noon on. Besides, Bronwyn Rhys probably never ate lunch. My guess was that she never ate anything during daylight hours besides an occasional Ultra SlimFast shake, and at night she lived on caviar, and Dom Perignon sipped from a crystal flute.

Her dress today was buttercup yellow, falling in soft drapes and folds that managed to call attention to her body while covering most of it. There aren't many women who could successfully wear that color and still look classy and sexy. She seemed only mildly irritated by my presence, and although she looked up and nodded when I walked in, she didn't even stop folding a collection of dazzling silk scarves atop one of the counters.

"I hope you're here to buy some clothes for your girlfriend," she said, "because I really don't have the time to spend with you about anything else."

"Just one more question, Ms. Rhys."

"I'm sure I can't add anything to what I've already told you about Ellen Carnine."

"Humor me a little," I said, and her put-upon sigh crackled with annoyance. "I accessed your Web site, just out of curiosity. You were right, Ellen did a great job with it. Very elegant."

"Thanks," she said. It was perfunctory; Bronwyn Rhys was probably so used to getting compliments that they didn't faze her anymore.

"That spanking site is very elegant, too."

Her cheeks colored for a moment, then she met my gaze directly. "Oh?"

"Life is just full of surprises, isn't it?"

The perfect arches of her eyebrows lifted a quarter of an inch.

I nodded. "Seems a little unusual, having a Web site devoted to fine clothing linked to something that sordid. Specially since the OTK people seemed not to be wearing very many."

She put the scarves aside then, and allowed herself a nasty little smile. "Why did you find that site so interesting, Mr. Jacovich?" she said, as breathy and faux erotic as a phone-sex operator. "Does it excite you? Does it turn you on?"

She came around to my side of the counter, standing a little too close to me, her perfume making me slightly giddy; if I hadn't known better, I would have thought she was being deliberately seductive. But I know when I'm being goaded, and I didn't care much for it.

"Did you start thinking maybe that's something you'd like to get into?" she continued. "Maybe you discovered that you're a little bit kinky yourself. Is that why you're here, to find out more about the bondage and discipline scene? Maybe you'd like to know where in the Cleveland area you can connect with some people who share your interests."

"Hardly," I said. "But Ellen Carnine designed your site, and at the moment I'm walking down every path to see if I can make sense of what happened to her."

Disappointed she hadn't gotten a rise out of me, Bronwyn Rhys moved away. "It has nothing to do with Ellen," she said. "Go back to your computer and do your homework again, Mr. Jacovich. At the bottom of the OTK site's last page you'll find several other links. One of them is to a company that designs and distributes fetish clothing."

" 'Fetish clothing'?"

"My, you *are* a naïf, aren't you?" she said, her condescension stinging. "Yes, fetish clothing. Leather. Rubber. Latex. There are those who get turned on by that sort of thing, you know. In fact, some people absolutely can't become aroused, can't — perform — without it."

"And so BeAttitude designs fetish clothing, too?"

"Not BeAttitude, no. But I have a minority interest in a company that does. The spanking site is linked to my page, and mine to theirs. And their link leads to another company of mine that manufactures fetish clothing. It's cross-plugging, I suppose you'd call it. It's all strictly business, Mr. Jacovich, that's how the Internet works. It's all about money." She tossed her head dismissively. "And it has nothing to do with Ellen Carnine."

"She didn't design the OTK site, then?"

Rhys laughed, with another toss of her head, this one seeming forced and artificial. "My God, no! She would have been mortified to death!" Then she sobered instantly, the inappropriateness of her remark sinking in. "Sorry, I guess that wasn't in the best of taste — it just popped out. But I'm sure she would have disapproved heartily if she'd been asked. There are more things in heaven and earth, Horatio, than were dreamed of in Ellen Carnine's philosophy."

Bronwyn Rhys was certainly fair to look upon, but I can't remember ever meeting a woman I had disliked more intensely. I decided to give her a little of her own back, and moved closer to her, my voice dropping to as close as I ever come to a seductive purr. "What about you, Ms. Rhys?" I said. "Is erotic spanking dreamed of in *your* philosophy?"

She sucked in a startled breath.

"Does it turn *you* on?" I pressed. "Are you into 'the scene'?"

Her eyes flashed dangerously and her sensual mouth turned hard. "Don't even think about it," she hissed.

In a life that's been peppered with more violence than I care to think about, I have never hit a woman. But I had to admit that at that moment I was itching to deck Bronwyn Rhys. I shoved my hands into my pockets instead. "Pity," I said.

Chapter Eighteen

When I got back to my office later that afternoon and pulled out the Carnine file to input my notes from the day, I noticed on the desk the password-detecting disk Taffy had borrowed from school. She had probably forgotten to take it with her the day before because of her emotional upset over the spanking Web site. I put it in the drawer carefully, hoping she wouldn't get in trouble when her professor found it missing.

I was interrupted by the ringing of the telephone.

"Have a drink with me tonight, Milan," Victor Gaimari said. From the hollow quality of the connection I gathered he was in his car. I hate using those damn things except in case of an emergency, and when I do I almost always pull off to the side of the road. There is a Cleveland suburb, Brooklyn, where pressing a phone to your ear while driving will result in a traffic citation; I wish every place had a similar ordinance. I always worry that while chatting on the car phone, someone is going to drive into a utility pole.

Or into *me.*

"Victor," I said, not feeling much like socializing, "I've had a long day . . ."

"I have that information you were asking about."

I guess the one dinner on Saturday night had whetted his appetite to be my best friend again. Or maybe he was just doing another one of his famous power plays. "Wouldn't it be easier to just tell me?"

"Not on the telephone," he said. "We can even have the drink on your patch. Shall we say Nighttown, at six o'clock?"

I looked at my watch; that gave me two hours. Nighttown was only two short blocks from my apartment, right at the top of Cedar Hill. I do a lot of my drinking there, but never before with so visible a Cleveland personality as Victor Gaimari, and I wondered if he'd be recognized by the regulars. Whether that would enhance my reputation at my neighborhood bar or blacken it, I didn't know.

Either way, he and Don Giancarlo had gone to no little trouble for me, and I supposed that having a drink with him was only the gracious thing to do. So I agreed to meet him at six o'clock. The prospect of killing half an hour in the warm, convivial atmosphere of my favorite local saloon was not exactly unpleasant anyway.

I jotted down all my remembrances from the conversations with William Carnine and Richard Goodman in my notebook and then stuck the pages into the Ellen Carnine file. I didn't put them into my computer's hard drive because I still didn't have a monitor. I made myself a note to go pick one up that evening after my meeting with Victor.

Nighttown was hopping by the time I got there, the bar jammed elbow to elbow with a mixture of middle-aged Cleveland Heights intellectuals, homeward-bound boomers, dedicated afternoon drinkers, and a few young guys wearing their baseball caps backwards who looked like they should have been drinking down in the Flats where the under-thirty crowd hangs out. Brendan, the good-natured tavern-keeper, greeted me in his lilting Irish brogue and rushed off; the man is a perpetual motion machine.

Victor had found himself a spot in the corner of the room just behind the bar under a bright lamp at one of the round tables whose tops were hand-painted with the long, sad visage of some artist's idea of Leopold Bloom. Nighttown is relentlessly

Irish, the name itself taken from one of the wilder neighborhoods of Dublin.

Victor was wearing an almost-black suit today, over a sparkling white shirt and a plain gold silk tie, and he had already ordered a martini — Bombay Sapphire gin, he explained, straight up, with the barest splash of vermouth and a lemon twist. I felt like a bum ordering a Stroh's with no glass — in the presence of Victor's glittering elegance I often felt that way — but Nighttown, as he had pointed out, is my turf and not his, and I was damn well going to drink what I wanted.

"So," he said after I'd been served, "did you and Cathleen have a nice talk after everyone left the other night?"

"I'm sure you've already heard all about it. As you once told me, you know everything that goes on in this town."

"When it comes to my friends, I do." He looked too smug to bear.

"You invited Cathleen Saturday night especially for me, didn't you?"

He ducked his head, grinning. "Yes, I did. I hope you didn't mind too much. You certainly didn't look like you minded."

"I didn't mind," I said, "I just wish you'd told me first."

"I would have, but it was a last-minute

343

inspiration," he said, his dark eyes shining wickedly. "I knew you two hit it off the first time you met, so many years ago, but I think you backed away because she had dated me once upon a time, and you couldn't handle it. I just wondered if time hadn't mellowed you a little." He lifted his martini in a toast. "Well, has it?"

"This is about as mellow as I get, Victor. And please don't do that again, all right? I felt like a high school kid being fixed up."

He pointed a finger at me. "Cathleen is a great lady, believe me. You could do a lot worse." And then he leaned forward toward me and added in a near-whisper, "You *have* done a lot worse."

"I appreciate your help in finding out about those two guys; I'm less appreciative of your concern for my love life."

"Somebody ought to be concerned about it," he said.

"What are you, a relationships expert now?"

"Hardly. I don't really believe in committed relationships — not for myself, anyway. I play the field, and I admit it. I have fun. That isn't your way, Milan, I know that. But sitting alone in your living room night after night isn't good for you. Use it or lose it, as they say."

"Who's they?"

"They is me."

"I'll keep it in mind."

He showed no signs of letting go. "So are you going to call her again?"

"No disrespect intended, Victor," I said, fully aware of his own views and those of his uncle on the subject of respect, "but that's none of your business."

He shook his head sadly. "Hard-ass to the end, aren't you?"

"Is this the end? I hope not. But I suppose that all depends on what you've got to tell me."

"Well, none of it is good," he said. He changed directions as easily as an NFL running back. On the empty chair next to him was a leather attaché case that probably cost as much as his suit. He reached for it, unzipped it, and took out several sheets of paper. He removed a pair of glasses from his breast pocket and slipped them over his nose. I tried not to smile; I'd never seen him wearing glasses before. We're none of us getting any younger.

"According to the best information my sources have," he said, his eyes moving quickly across the page, "your friend Lloyd's last name is Severson. Fifty-four years old. He was born in Durango, Colorado, and spent much of his life in Denver — that is, when he wasn't serving two terms as a guest of the state in the Cañon City lockup, which is probably where he picked up the tattoos you mentioned. All told, he served thirteen years for various offenses, including assault, armed robbery, and extortion. And he was the prison middleweight boxing champion, too. Of course, that was several years ago, when he was in much better shape."

"What's he doing in Cleveland?" I said.

"This and that, from what we've been able to find out. He's only been here about six months, which is why we weren't able to get a real line on him. From his previous record, I imagine he's probably been dabbling in petty street stuff since he got here, except . . ."

"Except?"

"Except he seems to be hanging around with a fellow name of John Vargas, who doesn't do petty stuff at all. He's not big-time, not national, but he doesn't peddle dime bags on street corners, either."

"Vargas. I wonder if that's the other guy he was with."

"Vargas is thirty-nine, Milan, and half

Mexican, if that fits."

"It does. He peddles drugs?"

"No, not that we know of. But John Vargas is a bad actor. At one time, he was a cop."

"That fits, too. He had that cop confidence, that quiet arrogance about him." It explained how well he kept his cool when he was looking down the barrel of my Magnum. It also made me sick. I have a lot of respect for cops, having been one myself; it saddens and angers me when one of them goes bad and tars all the others with a dirty brush. "The name doesn't sound familiar to me. Was he with the department in Cleveland?"

Victor shook his head, scanning the paper in his hand. "Detroit, which is where he's from originally. He was with the vice squad, as a matter of fact. He was pretty good at his job, made detective in four years, but then he got greedy. They first nailed him for shakedowns — he'd cut his own deal with a few of the local bookmakers, and was squeezing them so tight that one of them rolled over on him. And after the Internal Affairs Division looked a little closer they found out he was running a string of hookers out on Woodward Avenue, too."

I took a long pull on the Stroh's. Apparently this John Vargas was even more formidable than he looked — they play hardball on Detroit's Woodward Avenue. "Did he do any time for it?"

Victor shuffled the papers. "A little over a year in the penitentiary at Jackson. They kept him mostly isolated from the other inmates, of course, because a dirty cop wouldn't have lasted two weeks in there. Apparently he was well connected in the D.A.'s office, or perhaps he had something incriminating on a judge or something — pimps usually have all sorts of dirt on some pretty-high-up people, as you might imagine. In any case, he served some pretty easy time, and then they gave him shock probation after fourteen months."

"He was a former cop taking bribes and pimping, and they gave him shock probation?"

"Yes, but only on the condition that he get out of Dodge for good. It's not that far from Detroit to here; he showed up in Cleveland about two years ago, right after he checked out of jail."

"You didn't know he was here until now?"

He looked deep into the ash-blonde depths of his martini. "We knew about

348

John Vargas, yes. And we know he has some girls on the stroll out on Lorain Avenue, too. But that was just general information. As you know, Milan, we're not in the flesh business, so a west side pimp is none of our concern. The only reason I'm bringing him up is because my guess is he was the one in your office with Lloyd Severson."

I took out my notebook, but Victor pushed the papers across the table at me. "Here, don't bother. I made copies for you. Vargas's last-known Cleveland address is in there, too. It's about eight months old so it might not be valid anymore, but it's a beginning."

I riffled through the papers without really looking at them. "Victor, this is a big help," I said.

"Why don't you let us help you more, then?" he urged. "It would be a relatively simple matter. We'll just send some of our people to visit these two guys and get them off your back."

"No," I said, more sharply than I'd intended. "I know all about your visits."

"I'm not sure you have a choice," he said. "We don't like freelance talent walking around town intimidating our friends — or anyone else, for that matter. Because

349

if they screw up and do something really wrong, the first place the police always look is our family. It causes us time and trouble and it's expensive, lawyerwise. That's not good business, and my uncle and I are businessmen."

I shook a cigarette out of my pack and dug a book of matches out of my pocket; I noted it had been collected on an earlier visit to Nighttown, which told me that I was perhaps drinking too much and that my single and unattached status was making me spend too many nights in bars. My hand trembled slightly as I held the flame to the tobacco. There hadn't been a mob hit in Cleveland since Shondor Birns got blown to pieces in a car bombing on the corner of Detroit Road and West Twenty-fifth Street more than twenty years ago, and I wanted to keep it that way. I didn't want the responsibility, even indirectly, of the deaths of two men I hardly knew. I didn't even want them roughed up — at least not by anyone but me.

"Victor," I said, trying to keep my voice as level as his, "am I correct that if it wasn't for me, you wouldn't be all atwitter about Lloyd Severson and John Vargas?"

He nodded.

"That you got this information solely to help me?"

"Of course."

"Then help me all the way. If you run them out of town — or whatever you're thinking about doing with them — I might not ever be able to find out what their connection was to the case I'm working on. And it could be key. So I'm asking another favor — to let it alone. Let it go this time. I'll take care of it myself."

"Vargas is not a nice man, Milan," Victor said. "He's mean as a snake. Word is that one of his girls back in Detroit held out forty bucks from him one week to buy herself a down parka to keep herself warm on the street and he took a linoleum knife to her face."

"Don't worry about me, Victor," I said, filling my lungs with poisonous smoke and letting it out slowly on a long sigh. "I'm not one of his girls."

Even though Nighttown was thirty seconds from my apartment by car, I first drove over to OfficeMax in the Severance Town Center and bought another monitor for my computer. It wasn't that much money, but I was still mightily annoyed at John Vargas and Lloyd Severson.

It was the principle of the thing. In that, Victor and I were uncomfortably alike; if I allowed just anyone to walk into my office, vandalize it, and lay their hands on me, pretty soon everyone would be doing it and I'd be the town doormat. And I didn't want the word getting around that every time I had troubles I ran to Victor and the don to get me out of it. That would be bad for business, and worse for my self-esteem.

I hoped like hell Victor would back off. He'd promised he would, and whatever else could be said about and against Victor Gaimari, he had never gone back on his word to me.

When I got home I tossed some pasta into a pot of water, set it to boiling, and sat down at the kitchen table to carefully read the dossiers Victor had obtained for me. I didn't choose to dwell upon where he might have gotten them.

Lloyd Severson must be a tough guy, for sure, just to have survived two trips to Cañon City. He'd probably lost a step or two due to age, which is why I had been able to take him in my office so easily. Being a middleweight boxing champion, even in a prison, was impressive. But although I'd never boxed formally, I'd had some training when I was a kid, and boxed a little bit in the army before they shipped me off to Southeast Asia where there was no time or inclination for such extracurricular frivolity, and where the Vietcong had not followed the Marquis of Queensbury rules.

I'd been a heavyweight, too. And there was an old boxing axiom that had been coined back in the forties when the then-unbeatable Joe Louis was fighting a classy light-heavyweight named Billy Conn. I was too young to have been around for that one, but my father had passed it along to me: A good big man can beat a good little man.

So I wasn't much worried about Lloyd Severson.

John Vargas was another story. Any guy who disfigures hookers with a linoleum knife bears watching. I'd been around long enough to know that there was nothing as mean or sneaky or unpredictable as a pimp.

I wouldn't take Vargas lightly again.

I drained the pasta and then tossed it in olive oil, garlic powder, oregano, and fresh-ground Romano cheese from Alesci's Italian Deli on Mayfield Road, and warmed up a loaf of Orlando's Ciabatta Bread in the oven. Then I took my plate into my den along with a bottle of Stroh's, and ate on a TV table while watching reruns of *The Drew Carey Show*. He's a pretty funny guy, Drew Carey. A Cleveland guy. He's from the west side, though.

I finished my dinner and read once more the papers Victor had delivered to me. I was intrigued, to say the least. I was certain that Vargas and Severson were simply "the help," that someone had commissioned them to first try to bribe and then to intimidate me. Until I found out who that someone was, Ellen Carnine's death would go unexplained and unpunished.

Victor Gaimari and I have vast differences. We operate on opposite sides of the law, for one thing. For another, our codes of ethics seemed to have come from two different galaxies. But we both disliked being muscled, being pushed around. Whoever was behind Vargas and Severson had payback coming from me. And I always pay my debts.

I rinsed off the dishes and left them in the sink, strapped a holsterful of a Glock 9mm automatic under my arm, put on a leather jacket, and went downstairs to fire up my car.

I got to the address Victor had given me for John Vargas, a few minutes after nine o'clock. It was on the west side in an old but fairly upscale neighborhood, and it turned out to be a huge stone four-story apartment building just off Clifton Avenue, built blocky and solid before World War Two, with a name engraved between two chubby cherubs on the stone archway over the front door: THE SENTINEL. The building looked well cared for, although the rhododendron bushes on either side of the entry were fading fast and the stone facade had been weathered by too many savage Ohio winters. I looked around for the two-door tan Camry but didn't see it, and then I figured they might have come to my office on Saturday in Severson's car. My guess was that Vargas had a much fancier set of wheels than that; pimps don't usually drive two-door Camrys.

I parked a quarter of a block away and walked back, my jacket open despite the wind so I could easily get to the holster, all the while hoping I wouldn't have to. Checking the names over the doorbells in the vestibule I saw that a *J. Vargas* lived in apartment 2A.

I went back out onto the sidewalk and looked up; one of the apartments on the second floor was dark, the other's lights were blazing. I had no way of knowing which one belonged to Vargas, but in any event I wasn't about to go charging in there waving my Glock. That way madness lies.

Instead I went back to my car and prepared myself for a long vigil, wondering whether Vargas's apartment was the lighted one or the one whose windows were shrouded in darkness.

Did pimps stay home at night? Certainly the ones who ruled the black ghetto near East Fifty-fifth Street and Central Avenue did not; they were ever-present and highly visible on the streets in their gussied-up, custom-detailed pimpmobiles, cruising, watching, vaguely menacing, protecting their interests, flashing their pinkie rings, and yoked with neck chains with gold links the size of candy bars, collecting and counting their cash and enjoying an occasional toke.

Somehow I couldn't picture John Vargas that way. He had a little more class, if indeed that word could be applied to someone who lives off the proceeds of women selling their bodies. Staying at home and waiting for his stable to come to him to deliver their earnings seemed more his style. He'd been a cool one in my office

Saturday, even looking down the barrel of a Magnum. A capable, self-assured, almost cocky son of a bitch.

Not unlike Victor Gaimari.

Although Clifton is a very busy east-west thoroughfare, there was hardly any traffic at all on the side street where Vargas lived, so at twenty minutes to ten I couldn't miss the big white Mercedes that cruised slowly by, the driver obviously female from what I could see of her head in silhouette through the window, craning and straining as if looking for a house number. When she found it, she parked as close to Vargas's building as possible, and slid out of the car with a flash of stockinged thigh. And even though it was dark, when she stood erect and straightened her skirt, there was no mistaking the long black hair and elegant carriage of Anna Zarafonitos.

She crossed the sidewalk with a furtive look over her shoulder, which didn't do her much good because she didn't notice me scrunched down behind my steering wheel. Through the closed car windows I heard the tap-tap of her high heels on the walk-way as she made her way to the apartment doorway and went into the vestibule. I couldn't see her after that, but whoever she was visiting must have been home to buzz her in, because she didn't come right back out.

Now why, I wondered, was a beautiful and obviously successful young woman visiting a sleazy pimp in his apartment at ten o'clock in the evening? Especially a sleazy pimp who had leaned pretty heavily on me not to investigate the death of one of her close friends, who also had worked for her lover, Red Munch.

Maybe this was a professional visit, then; maybe Anna Zarafonitos was hooking on the side. I never had asked her what her occupation was.

But I didn't really think she was part of John Vargas's stable. She wasn't the type to stroll the streets, or even go out on calls to entertain visiting firemen from Pittsburgh or Indianapolis. I could more than believe she was somebody's mistress — a kept woman living languidly and high. But not an ordinary prostitute, no way. And even if she had been, she would have been operating on the penthouse circuit; being as beautiful and classy as she was put her way out of the league of a man like Vargas, running a string of streetwalkers on Lorain Avenue.

After about twenty minutes Zarafonitos came out of the building. I suppose that was enough time for them to have had sex, although allowing five minutes each for getting undressed and then dressed again, it hardly would have been worth the effort. She didn't look at all rumpled, either.

So what had she gone to his apartment for? To tell him something? She could have done that over the telephone. To deliver something? Perhaps — although all she had carried both going in and coming out was her small clutch purse.

And did it have some connection with Ellen? That conclusion seemed inescapable. As far as I knew, Ellen Carnine was the only thing these two very disparate people had in common.

She pushed her hair back away from her face the way she always did, got back into her Mercedes and started the engine. I scooted down in my seat as she drove slowly by me. Glancing in my rearview mirror after she passed, I could tell that when she got to Clifton she turned and headed east, back toward downtown. I made a note of her license-plate number, just for the hell of it, just for something to do besides sit. Then I lit a Winston, dug a palm-sized portable radio out of the console and switched it on so as not to run down the battery in my car, listening to jazz on the public radio station, WCPN, waiting for something else to happen.

A stakeout isn't like you see in the movies or on TV. It's uncomfortable and cramped and mind-numbing and hell on the kidneys, and only rarely does one learn anything pertinent to the case. It's damned hard work, made even more difficult because it's frequently boring. Remember that, the next time you see some blow-dried television private eye swimming his way through martinis and beautiful women.

There was nothing more to look at until a few minutes after eleven-thirty.

That's when a blue Pontiac Grand Am that had seen better days pulled up in front of the apartment building and idled there. A young woman got out, her hair styled the way they used to wear it in Texas in 1968 — big and bouffant and sprayed stiff. She was wearing a leather miniskirt, just inches from being illegal, and a pink bandeau top wrapped tightly around her skimpy breasts. She must have been chilly. A lit cigarette hung from her mouth. I couldn't see her face very well, but her body seemed young. Over her shoulder was a faux leather purse the size of a saddlebag. She ran quickly up the walkway and into the vestibule. In the car, which was still running, another woman sat behind the wheel, also smoking a cigarette, listening to hip-hop played too loud, her bare elbow extending out the opened window. It was too dark to tell, but from what I could make out by the illumination of the streetlight half a block away, her skin looked cocoa-brown.

After less than ten minutes the first girl came out again, walking rapidly, and this time I could see her face a little better. She was probably twenty years old or so, but it was twenty the hard way. Her eyes were as huge as a fawn's, her hair dyed a dark, phony-looking red. She hopped into the Grand Am. She and the driver conferred for a few minutes and then they drove off, heading southward.

It fit the scenario I'd created in my mind earlier; Vargas stayed home and his stable of "girls" stopped by periodically to drop off the money. The good thing about being a pimp, I guessed, was that it was a strictly-cash business. I imagined he had a cute, secure little safe up there in the apartment. No paper trail, and a virtual license to cheat on your income tax.

After another half hour the scene was repeated, this time with two different women, both black, and driving a ten-year-old Ford Taurus, although the one who went upstairs stayed a few minutes longer.

Maybe Anna Zarafonitos *was* turning tricks for John Vargas. But I still didn't think so.

I waited for ten minutes until after the Taurus went away, and then decided to call it a night, figuring I had seen all I needed to. I got onto Detroit Road heading east, and then cut across West Sixty-fifth Street to Lorain Avenue, driving slowly in the direction of downtown until I spotted her.

It was the young hooker who'd gone up to Vargas's apartment shortly after Anna Zarafonitos had left. She was standing in a doorway on the south side of the street, near a streetlight so that the shiny pink of her bandeau top beamed like a beacon. Her shoulders were hunched against the chill night air. Getting a better look at her now, I realized I had overestimated her age. She was closer to sixteen than to twenty, but it was still the hard way. We made eye contact and she smiled at me and licked her lips in a grotesque parody of sensuality, looking both hopeful and frightened. After I passed her I glanced in my rearview mirror and saw she was gazing after me forlornly; I imagine she'd thought

I was a live one and was disappointed to see me drive off with my money still in my pocket.

With one hand I fumbled for another cigarette and shook my head. Children peddling their asses on the street. Web sites for spanking devotees. What in hell had I gotten myself into? And what did it all have to do with Ellen Carnine?

I was heading for the Lorain-Carnegie Bridge where she had died, and decided I couldn't face crossing it without some fortification. I turned off Lorain just past the West Side Market and dropped into one of my favorite haunts, the Velvet Tango Room, for a drink. Linda and Maribeth, the bartenders, greeted me warmly, and together we discussed the movie playing silently in black-and-white on the TV set at the front end of the bar. It was *Imitation of Life*, with Lana Turner. Paulius, the boniface of the Velvet Tango, favored the American Movie Classics channel, and the TV was always toned down to black-and-white hues as a fond salute to the good old days, even during Indians games. The Tango itself was a throwback to the era of great saloons and great conversation, and at their long, warm bar one was as likely to be sitting next to a billionaire as next to a bum.

I needed more than beer this night to wash away the ugly pictures the Ellen Carnine case had imprinted on my brain. I had three Absolut vodkas on the rocks, and they must have done the job all right, because I sat there until the Tango was ready to close.

I have very little memory of getting home.

Chapter Nineteen

Florence McHargue held the six sheets of paper in her hand, considering them, but her eyes were focused on me, glaring at me through those blue-tinted glasses. It was her hardest look, although I rarely saw any other kind from her. She'd be an attractive woman if she didn't spend her entire life scowling.

The window behind her, which probably hadn't been washed in several years, was begrimed and vaguely beige from air pollution. It faced eastward, and here at nine o'clock in the morning the sun was streaming in through the dirt, creating a nimbus around her shiny black hair. The seating arrangement caused it to glare directly into my eyes.

"John Vargas and Lloyd Severson," she said, hefting the papers in her hand as if she were weighing them, and chanting the names like a mantra.

"They're the ones."

"I never heard of Severson before, but I know about John Vargas from when I worked Sex Crimes." She wrinkled her nose in distaste. "I know every pimp in the Cleveland area, more's my sorrow. Ex-cop from Detroit, as I recall. He's some piece of work — a real scumbolina."

"That was my impression, too."

"These are just names on a piece of paper," she said. "You don't even have any real proof that these are the two guys who rousted you."

"I don't have any real proof that the world is round, either, Lieutenant. I just know."

She looked skeptical.

"In any event, last night I saw this Anna Zarafonitos going into John Vargas's apartment."

"How'd you happen to be there to see that?" She crossed her arms across her chest. "Staking out Vargas? That's illegal, you know. It's called stalking."

"Not when you have a P.I. license," I said. "Zarafonitos was a friend of Ellen Carnine's and she's sleeping with Ellen's boss. And John Vargas is one of the guys who tried to scare me off the Ellen Carnine investigation. Probably." I leaned into the word too hard.

She was obviously thinking it over, so she didn't say anything right away. That's a page out of my book; I like to remain silent until the other guy feels he *has* to talk. But I fell for it from her, by shooting my big mouth off without thinking: "You might want to call it a coincidence, Lieutenant, but I'm damned if I'm going to."

She slammed her hand down flat on the top of her desk, so sharply that it brought Bob Matusen upright from where he'd been lounging in his accustomed spot against the wall of her office. "You're damned if you're not!"

Florence McHargue pushed away from the desk and got to her feet. She wasn't a big or heavy woman, but she was no sylph, either, and she had a formidable presence and the power of the law's majesty behind her, so when she leaned across her desk, looming over me like a wolf about to take its first bite of a fresh throat dinner, I actually shrank in my chair.

"We had Ellen Carnine's death all neatly buttoned up as a Dutch act, Jacovich, until you came in here making all that noise about dirty feet and made us reopen it as a homicide. Okay, fine. But you've stepped on your own dick." She straightened up as though she were reciting in class. "Private investigators aren't licensed to go anywhere near open capital cases, and in fact are pro-

hibited by law from doing so. As you goddamn well know. So that means if any of
my people are out in the field on this one
and they happen to stumble over you getting in their way, you're going to be using
that P.I. license of yours for a spitball."

"Ellen Carnine's father . . ."

"Is a suspect," she said. "But I don't
want him to know that just yet, so I don't
want you telling him. So are her bosses
and friends and roommates. And Vargas
and Severson, if that's really who your two
buddies were. Everybody is a suspect until
they're cleared — that's how it works, and
you were a cop long enough to know it."
She seemed to relax a little — but with
Florence McHargue that wasn't saying
much. "I'm sorry to fuck up your bottom
line, but if you've accepted a retainer from
Dr. Carnine, you're just going to have to
give it back."

Yeah, right.

"Do you have any problem with my
trying to find out whether Severson and
Vargas are the two guys who threatened
me and vandalized my office?" I said carefully. "Or am I just supposed to retire to a
rocking chair and eat chocolates all day?"

"I don't give a goddamn what you do as
long as you keep out of my way," she said.

"No more staking out suspects on your own in the middle of the night. And keep the hell away from Vargas, and the Zarafonitos woman, and from all the rest of our witnesses as well. You are officially off the Carnine case." She looked at her wristwatch to make her point. "As of right this minute. I don't want to catch you anywhere near a homicide investigation."

"Is it okay if I watch *Law and Order* on TV?"

"Don't get funny with me, Jacovich. You know the rules, and I expect you to follow them — if you have any ideas of continuing to function as a private investigator in this state."

I stood up and stretched. "Oh well," I said. "I can always fall back on my second career."

She narrowed her eyes at me. "And what's that?"

"A ballet dancer," I said.

I felt her glare on my back as I walked out; it nearly set my jacket on fire.

Bob Matusen accompanied me downstairs, I think because he needed a cigarette. Or maybe he just wanted to make sure I was really leaving. We hit the front steps and he pulled his Camels from his shirt pocket.

"Damn, Milan, why do you deliberately irritate her all the time?"

"Why does she always treat me like I'm a typhoid carrier?" I said. "I have a friendlier relationship with my ex-wife's live-in lover."

He stuck a cigarette into the corner of his mouth and cupped his hands against the breeze to put a match to it. "McHargue is strictly by-the-book. Hell, she's got the book memorized, chapter and verse. And there's nothing in the book about ex-cop P.I. types telling her how to do her job. She gets her knickers in a twist every time she sees you. And then when you mouth off at her it only makes things worse."

"Okay, mea culpa, so I'm a smart-ass. Does that mean she's not going to follow up on Severson and Vargas just because it came from me?"

He shrugged. "I'll talk to her, Milan. However much a pain in the ass she is, she's a good cop. And she'll do the right thing. Hell, if it pans out for the Ellen Carnine thing, she might even thank you."

"Sure, Bob. I have a big oil painting of *that*."

"But like she said, you're not even sure it's Vargas who's the bagman. You can't expect her to go crashing into his place like the gestapo just because this Anna Whatever-her-name-is came to see him last night."

"There's a regulation against the police asking questions?"

He dug into his ear with a finger. "Trust McHargue, Milan. She knows her job. And as for you, just keep a low profile on this one, all right? For my sake."

"Your sake?"

He ducked his head and sucked in some smoke. "The Loo has the idea that you and I are buddies."

"Aren't we?"

He looked studiously down at his shoes as if he'd have to answer questions about them later; they needed polishing. "Well, I think you're a good guy and all that, you know? Your being so tight with Meglich and all makes you okay on my list. But friends? Cops don't have many friends outside the department, Milan. Hey, you know what they say, don't you? To a cop, there's only two kinds of people — cops and assholes."

"I'm an ex-cop," I said. "Does that count for anything?"

He finally met my eyes. "Sure it does," he said. "It kind of puts you in the middle."

I didn't expect Bronwyn Rhys to be glad to see me, but she didn't even bother to pretend politeness when I walked through the door of BeAttitude. "Mr. Jacovich," she said from behind the glass counter, "you're starting to bore the hell out of me."

"I wish I could say the same, Ms. Rhys, but frankly you get more and more interesting with every passing day."

"Why is that?" she said.

"You're friends with Anna Zarafonitos, aren't you?"

"Not best friends," she said, "but friends, yes."

"You got together with her through Ellen Carnine?"

She had to think about that for a bit. "I'm not really certain how I met her. Do you remember where you met all your friends?"

"You have a lot in common?" I said, meaning more than I was saying.

"We're both single," Rhys said. "And around the same age." She batted her eyes at me in a parody of flirtation. "Don't ask what that age is, Mr. Jacovich, it's impolite for a gentleman to ask a lady."

"Can we knock off the Blanche DuBois act, please? Your friend Ellen is dead, Ms.

Rhys. And it looks a lot like she didn't jump off that bridge but was pushed."

She gasped involuntarily, and all the natural color in her face fled, leaving just her makeup glowing hotly on chalk-white skin. Against her natural pigment it looked elegant and understated, but with her skin pale from shock, the cosmetics appeared clownish. "My God," she said, appearing truly shocked. "I had no idea."

"So stop treating me like a pest, and stop putting on your various come-fuck-me acts, because all I want from you are some answers here. And if I don't get them from you, maybe I'll call up my pal Lieutenant McHargue from the Homicide Division and *she* can come over and ask them. How will that look to your ritzy customers, Ms. Rhys? A store full of uniforms asking questions about a murder."

She groped blindly behind her until her hand found a stool; then she almost collapsed on it. "You don't believe I had anything to do with . . ."

"I don't believe anything. Why would you think I did?"

She raised her head to look at me, and this time she wasn't acting; shock and fear were written all over her face. I wondered why I'd ever thought her attractive. "Ask me anything," she said. "I have nothing to hide."

"All right, then. What's your relationship with Anna Zarafonitos?"

"What has that to do with Ellen?"

"I'll let you know when you answer me and I've figured it out."

She took a deep breath, sucking at the air as if it gave her sustenance. Then she said, "Anna helped me with my Web site."

"I thought Ellen did that."

"The other site," she said. "The — fetish site."

"The spanking one?"

She nodded.

"What does Anna know about Web sites?"

Her eyes opened wide. "I thought you knew," she said.

"What?"

"Anna is a computer-graphics designer. Like Ellen, except that she worked freelance. She's one of the most sought-after designers in the Midwest."

I got back to my office hot, having worked up a good head of steam on the drive from the cop shop to BeAttitude and back to the Flats. McHargue was right, I had no business involving myself in an unsolved murder case. On the other hand, I knew in my gut the two guys with the bribe money had been Vargas and Severson — if Victor said it, you could carve it on the cornerstone of a cathedral. And Anna Zarafonitos's visit to the Vargas apartment the previous night had not been any sort of coincidence. I hoped like hell the police would follow up.

I made some coffee, my fingers itching to get to the phone and confront Zarafonitos. But McHargue had very specifically warned me not to, and I was feeling impotent and frustrated.

And madder than hell.

I wasn't about to let Florence McHargue tell me who I could and could not work for. And I certainly wasn't going to return William Carnine's retainer simply on her say-so. That's no way to run a business.

But for me, it wasn't about money anymore; it was about Ellen Carnine. And it was about two guys muscling their way into my office with threats and a bag full of currency. I wasn't about to let it go.

Still, I had been specifically shooed away from Vargas and Severson and Zarafonitos, and from the rest of Ellen's inner circle, too, and while I didn't think McHargue really had the clout to get my license pulled by the state if I went against her orders, she could certainly cause me a lot of time, trouble, and most probably, attorney's fees. And there's nothing I hate worse than giving money to a lawyer.

That didn't leave me with much, except Ellen Carnine's laptop. I opened the lid and booted it up. I wasn't looking for anything specific; I didn't really *know* what I was looking for. I just felt that the activity, going through the motions, was better than sitting and doing nothing.

First I checked in the PLAIN JANE/CLEVELAND chat room, but apparently none of the regulars were in attendance, because nobody greeted me with a "Hi, Ellen" when I entered. I didn't type in any sort of message; instead I watched quietly, or "lurked," for about five minutes, but nothing happened except that my eyes began to glaze from boredom. I once again marveled that anyone of Ellen Carnine's intelligence could find any sort of intellectual or emotional nourishment from such a banal activity, but loneliness makes us do strange and sometimes desperate things.

Then again, it was only eleven o'clock in the morning; perhaps the discourse in PLAIN JANE/CLEVELAND was more interesting in the evening when Ellen had usually spent time there.

I revisited Ellen's other bookmarked sites, the Web-site design and maintenance pages, and the site selling clothing for oversized women. I searched on that one for a hyperlink that might send me to another site for fetish clothing or any other sort of kinkiness, but there was none.

Then I moved again to the online stockbroker's page. I still couldn't figure out why that one was among Ellen's most often visited. The design of the Web site was pedestrian, even boring, and when I thought about the creativity that had gone into some of her other work, I couldn't imagine that Ellen had designed it, or, if she had, that she was proud enough of it to want to look at it at home.

I noted the name of the company, TOPSTOXXX, and looked them up in the Cleveland phone book. They weren't there. Not suprising — physically, they might have been located in Katmandu, for all I knew.

For lack of anything else to do, I called Victor Gaimari. He was, after all, a stockbroker himself, and I thought perhaps he had heard of them.

"No," he said when I got him on the line, "I haven't. But that doesn't mean anything. They're probably some fly-by-night outfit that does most of their business with penny-ante day traders who are, frankly, fucking up the market for serious investors. There are probably a thousand sites like that on the Internet, and my guess is that they weren't there a year ago and won't be there next year, either. It's the invasion of the dot-coms."

"What are day traders?"

"They're a pain in the ass," Victor said. "They're people who take advantage of the momentum in a given stock. They may be in and out of the same stock several times in one day. With the advent of online brokerages like this TOPSTOXXX you're talking about, who charge very small commissions, and with the skyrocketing gains in high-tech and e-commerce stocks, day traders are growing in numbers by leaps and bounds. I understand that in New York, even the cab drivers have computers and cell phones in their cabs, and do their trading from the front seat. It really adds to the volatility of the market. To say nothing of raising the traffic-accident rate in Manhattan." He sighed. "Bastards."

"Okay, good," I said. "Now, how likely would it be for someone like that, a day trader who plays the market online, to also have an account with a more established brokerage firm like yours?"

"It's highly unlikely, Milan. They're basically two different animals, two completely different types of investors. I suppose it could happen, but it would be very unusual."

I scribbled notes on a yellow pad. "Thanks Victor, that's all I wanted to know."

"May I ask why? Is John Vargas playing the market?"

"Yeah, that's it, Victor. He and I trade stock tips every morning."

He laughed. "All right, don't tell me."

"I can't tell you right now, because there's nothing to tell. It may or may not be related to Vargas. I'm just following down every lead, that's all."

"Well, good luck. By the way," he said, his tone shifting. "Have you called Cathleen yet?"

I guess I waited too long to reply, because he went on. "You can be so goddamned pigheaded, Milan."

"Victor, right now I can either do my job right or else I can work on my love life. Not both."

"Why not both? Everybody else does. You think that everyone who falls in love is either independently wealthy or unemployed?"

"Point taken," I said.

I thought about it for a little while after I hung up, and came to the conclusion that maybe I just didn't *want* to be in love right at that moment. As it is, I fall in love far too often for someone who's as bad at it as I am.

My next call was to Duane Starrett at her brokerage firm. She was distinctly annoyed when she found out it was me, and sounded rushed.

"Mr. Jacovich, you've called at a really bad time," she said. In the background I could hear the murmur of other voices, probably all talking on the phone.

"I'll be quick, then," I said. "Did Ellen Carnine invest in the market?"

"Yes, she did. I handled her account."

"Was she what you'd call a day trader?"

She almost laughed. "Careful, conservative Ellen? My God, no. She had mostly mutual funds, and a few high-tech stocks like Quaalcom and Microsoft. And she bought herself five shares of the Cleveland Indians when they went public a few years ago, which is about as reckless as she ever got. She was way too cautious an investor — and too smart — to play funny games like day traders do."

"Thanks," I said. "One more question. Have you ever heard of an online trading company called TOPSTOXXX?" I spelled it for her.

"No," she said. "I ignore dot-com brokers, and I hope to hell they'll return the favor and ignore me, too. Now, I've really gotta go."

And go she did, before I even had a chance to say good-bye.

I had some more coffee, unpacked my new monitor and connected it to my own computer. I played with it for a while to make sure it was in working order. Then I found my way onto the Internet and typed in the URL for the TOPSTOXXX Web page.

It hadn't changed.

I clicked on the "SIGN-UP" link and was taken to a page where I was to fill in my vital information and a credit-card number in order to open a trading account.

I went back to the home page and noticed again that some of the copy, the line that read, "Whether you're an experienced and knowledgeable player, or just want to bring your portfolio up to snuff, you've come to the right place," was highlighted in red. I wondered if that, too, might be a link to somewhere else. I moved the cursor beneath the text and clicked.

A tiny hourglass appeared and I waited for nearly a minute. Then I got a screen that told me, "Enter your password for admission to this site," and a boxed space in which to do it.

Of course, I didn't have a password. But I did have a severe case of curiosity.

I shut down my computer and went back to Ellen's laptop, and repeated the process. When I got back to the TOPSTOXXX password page, I tried entering Ellen's, "BRYARLY84." I got a message telling me I'd screwed up and entered an invalid password.

Okay, I thought, I'll play your silly game. I typed in "CHUBETTE," with the same negative results. And then "ECARNINE." Still no soap.

I lit a cigarette and puffed at it recklessly, sending Indian war signals up toward my ceiling while I sat there, stymied and growing angrier by the minute. *"How all occasions do inform against me,"* I remembered Hamlet saying, and all at once I knew how he felt.

Passwords, for God's sake. Very cloak-and-dagger, very black-and-white movie, very World War Two, and here in the twenty-first century in front of technology that no one could have even dreamed of fifty years ago, pretty childish, it seemed.

And people tell me *I'm* retro.

I didn't want to call Taffy Kiser for help again; I'd done enough the last time, thank you. I knew that almost any high-school kid was more computer-literate than I, but after guiding Taffy into that grotesque spanking site, I was pretty leery of looking for help in that area.

I tried to think of anyone else I knew who was a computer maven, who could walk in and stroke a few keys and open up the world for me. Most of my friends were my age or older, and probably as lost on the Internet as I was.

I lit another Winston with the lighted end of my previous one; the goddamned "ENTER PASSWORD" prompt blinked mockingly, taunting me from the laptop screen. The clock was ticking — the moments of my life were tumbling by and I was at a complete standstill.

It was getting toward lunchtime; I'd been in such a hurry to get down to police head-quarters that morning to tell McHargue what I'd learned about John Vargas that I hadn't eaten anything except two pieces of toast, and my innards were gurgling omi-nously.

For probably the two-hundredth time in the last three years, I wished that Jim's

Steak House, the old Cleveland landmark right next door to my office, had not closed its doors forever. It had always been perfect for that quick lunch and a beer sitting at the bar, and during the day there were always people in there that I knew slightly and could talk to. But tastes had changed, diners had become more health-conscious, and the steak sandwich and oily, crispy hash browns that had been Jim's signature lunch dish were now considered dangerously old-fashioned.

Like passwords.

And all at once I remembered Taffy's password detector.

I suppose the aforementioned high-school tech genius would have known what to do right away, but it took me about half an hour to read the directions for the password detector, follow the onscreen prompts, and get it fully installed and running on Ellen's laptop.

It took me two more cigarettes and the mysterious software another seven minutes before it could detect her secret password to sign on to the TOPSTOXXX link.

And then it came up highlighted on the screen, the cursor pulsating on it almost obscenely.

"NAWTYGRL84," it was.

I typed the password into the white box, clicked, and waited. It took almost ninety seconds for the search engine to find the page it was looking for. When it came up, the word WARNING was in bright red 42-point letters.

Beneath it, in passionate purple and in a slightly smaller font, I was advised: "This site is not for the faint of heart. You've never seen anything like this in your life." In bright green italics then, I was advised that "content is updated every two weeks." And beneath that, in big red letters again, it said, "CLICK HERE AT YOUR OWN RISK."

I clicked.

Why not? I thought. What's the worst thing that could happen?

Chapter Twenty

One of the reasons I don't spend very much time surfing around on the Internet, other than that it goes against the grain of my normal Luddite proclivities, is that everything takes so damned long. The smart-guy techies would simply tell me it was my own fault, that I needed a faster modem or more RAM or that I needed to get rid of some of my gigabytes or some such — I never know what they're talking about anyway. My answer is, it's too much trouble and not worth it — I'll just read.

So it was with the TOPSTOXXX site. Once I found Ellen's password, entered it, and clicked at my own risk, I still wasn't where I wanted to be. The computer burped and buzzed and made a funny sound like a tambourine at a Hungarian wedding, and then another message popped up to entreat me to be patient because the movie was downloading and would take about twenty-four minutes to do so. This had the attention-grabbing effect of a news bulletin breaking into a regularly scheduled sitcom, because up until that moment I'd had no idea I was going to see a movie in the first place.

So I relaxed a bit, emptied my brimming ashtray into the wastebasket with some distaste — smoking really is a foul and disgusting habit and I wish I could quit — and got myself some more coffee while the machine beeped and buzzed through its solemn *brachas*. The Internet, I mused, was a lot like the way I remembered the army. They shared a common malaise: Hurry up and wait.

Finally — it felt as if it had taken a lot longer than twenty-four minutes — the computer decided to let me have a look. A square inset appeared on the screen with several highlighted buttons below it and the instructions to "CLICK HERE TO START." Inside the square, frozen in a state of suspended animation, was what looked to be a wooded, leafy glade. The quality of light indicated that it was midafternoon.

I moved the cursor to "START," and clicked.

Immediately the leaves of the trees began rustling on the screen, silently because there was no soundtrack, blowing slightly as the camera pulled back to reveal a rough dirt path through the woods. Along one side of the cleared walkway was a large colony of beautiful, delicate little pink flowers, a variety I didn't remember ever seeing before, and they swayed and nodded in the breeze like the graceful arms of dancers in a *corps de ballet*.

After a few seconds a couple came walking up the path, from behind the camera. The man was carrying a blanket. When they got to a small clearing, he unfolded the blanket, flapping it like a sheet, and spread it out on the ground. Then he turned to the woman, pulled her to him with one hand and roughly clasped her breast with the other, and shoved his tongue deep into her mouth.

Okay, I thought, it's going to be a porno movie. But then I knew that some of Wheetek's clients were porn purveyors and I wasn't terribly surprised.

What I was wondering, however, is what a porno movie was doing on a link to an online stockbroker's Web page, and why Ellen Carnine had bookmarked this particular site and gone to all the trouble of setting up a password for herself.

The man looked young, perhaps in his early twenties, and was heavy-jawed, tall and ropy in blue jeans, workboots, and a sleeveless muscle shirt. He had a funny haircut, his light brown hair shaved close at the sides and thatched on the top, giving him what I'd always considered a sort of doofus look. His face was scarred with pustules of acne, and he wore a silver earring in his left ear. His eyes were dull brown and squinty and his mouth was slack, looking as though he might have been the offspring of first cousins. He was one ugly-looking son of a bitch.

The woman was even younger, certainly no more than eighteen, and skinny and pale. Her hair was straight black, long and unkempt, and it flowed down almost to her waist. She was wearing a black miniskirt and a maroon sleeveless blouse, and her bony bare legs culminated in flat-heeled black ballerina-style shoes that were scuffed and ratty-looking. As the camera zoomed in for a tight close-up of their mouths and tongues working together I saw that her face was blotchy and also bore a few pimples; her eyes were wide and her pupils dilated and there was a redness around her nostrils that could have meant she had a cold. But I didn't think so. Really little more than a child, and stoned out of her mind.

I fired up another cigarette and leaned forward in my chair. I suppose I'm as horny as the next guy, but watching other people having sex has never done much for me. I was about to view this film only out of a curiosity as to why Ellen had bookmarked it.

The man started undressing the girl, popping the buttons from her blouse and pulling it off. Beneath it she was wearing a dark red bra that seemed none too clean, and he tore that off, too. A black stubble darkened her underarms. Her breasts were small and flaccid, and she winced as he bit one of them. Then he yanked her skirt up to her waist and literally ripped off her black cotton panties, tossing them away into the colony of wildflowers. He took her hair in his fist and forced her to her knees in front of him, unbuttoning his fly with his other hand.

For the next ten minutes or so it proceeded as one might expect. It wasn't that much different from any other sleazy porn movie I'd ever seen, except that the guy probably should have been penalized several times for unnecessary roughness. He didn't even bother stripping, instead pulling down his jeans and a pair of once-white boxers that were now a dull tattletale gray. When he was naked from the waist down I saw why such a homely young man had been hired for a porno film.

However, there was no doubt in my mind that the girl was a willing participant, or as willing as one can be while that thoroughly zonked, and I was certain that the harsh way her partner was using her sexually had been decided upon from the beginning.

It ended up with the girl on her hands and knees and the guy taking her anally from behind, and while she seemed to be in real discomfort and not very happy about it, she still did not appear unwilling; rather she looked resigned, as if thinking that this was a tough way to make a buck. When he was finished, he pulled out of her and stood up, moving out of camera range.

And then as I watched, a second man, stocky and potbellied and visible only from the chest down, entered the frame and came up behind the girl. His forearms and wrists were thick and his belly round, and in his hands he carried about three feet of what appeared to be piano wire. Bending at the knees, he quickly looped it around the girl's neck and began to twist it.

Startled and then frightened and in obvious pain, the girl tried to turn her head to see what was happening to her. Her mouth opened in a terrified O and she began to struggle; this obviously had not been part of the script. Her hands clawed at the wire around her throat as it tightened with each twist, and her face began to redden as she fought for breath, her feet kicking and thrashing spasmodically.

I wanted to look away, to run, to smash the laptop against the wall, but I was riveted to my seat, paralyzed and sickened.

I knew this was not staged. This was the real thing. No one was that good an actress. The scene was even more horrifying in dumbshow than if there had been a soundtrack, and I was sitting at my office desk and watching it, watching a real murder being committed — a senseless murder without motive, for fun. And not even fun for the killer, but for the twisted perverts who obviously paid good money to this Internet site to watch it.

The straining victim suddenly lost control of her bladder, urine spraying onto her legs and the blanket beneath her. The hands holding the piano wire shook her like a rag. Then she relaxed and went limp, hanging by her neck from the wire, her head at an impossible angle. After a few more seconds, the man let go of the garrote and walked out of the frame, and she slumped onto the now-stained blanket like a broken and discarded puppet. The camera zoomed in mercilessly for an extreme close-up on her purple face; her eyes were bulging and filled with blood, and her blackened tongue protruded grotesquely from one corner of her mouth. Strings of drool ran down her chin and streaks of blood striped her breasts and shoulders where the sharp wire had cut cruelly into the flesh of her neck. In the background the delicate pink flowers bobbed and swayed.

Then the nightmare image faded out and the monitor went blank, but I didn't even notice. I was too busy registering the fact that the man who had wielded the piano wire, at least as much of him as I could see, looked awfully familiar to me.

I was also too busy crying.

Chapter Twenty-one

So much for the basic decency of the human animal. I was going to have to revise my estimate.

Florence McHargue had never been in my office before. She'd dropped in at my apartment unexpectedly about a year earlier, but that was because it was on her way home and she hadn't wanted to end that particular workday without giving me a bad time. But when I'd called and invited her to watch a movie, giving her a rundown of the plot, she and Matusen made it from the Roaring Third to the Flats in record time.

When they finished watching it on the screen of Ellen's laptop, McHargue made a sound of disgust. Her coffee-brown face had gone gray. Bob Matusen, on the other hand, was looking green. I hadn't watched it again while it played for them; I had walked over to the window, smoked a cigarette (being careful to blow the smoke out into the air) and watched the gulls gather over Collision Bend for lunch. Some movies simply don't bear a second viewing.

I came back and sat down behind my desk; McHargue and Matusen were in the two client chairs. McHargue was staring dully at the now-blank screen.

"That's the worst thing I've ever seen in my life," she said. "I was in Sex Crimes for six years and I've been in Homicide for two, and I never really saw anything that would give me nightmares for the rest of my life before. Jesus." She took off her glasses and put them on the desk in front of her.

"The link on the TOPSTOXXX Web site said it all," I observed. "Triple-X and 'Bring your portfolio up to *snuff.*' I should have figured it out earlier."

"No way you could, Milan," Matusen said. "I mean, who in their wildest fucking dreams — Excuse me, Lieutenant."

McHargue waved a dismissive hand and drew a ragged breath. "I've heard about snuff films, of course, but I'd never seen one before. I've seen kiddie porn, I've seen sadomasochistic films that would make you puke. But nothing like this."

"Imagine anyone actually getting a sexual kick out of watching something like that," Matusen said.

"Imagine enough people getting a kick out of it to have a Web site devoted to it," the Loo said. "Shit. I've been a cop too long. Finally I can say it — I've been a cop too goddamned long."

"What now?" I said.

She ran her hands through the hair on either side of her head. "I don't know, I'll have to think about it."

"I think Ellen Carnine stumbled on this site by accident, and she was killed before she could blow the whistle on it."

"You're probably right, Jacovich, but we have no proof of that yet. I'll call the FBI and run it by them. Meantime, Matusen, get somebody to check out TOPSTOXXX and see where they operate from. And then put a crew together — six officers at least, whoever's free right now. I want to move in and fall on this Landenberger guy like the avenging sword of God."

Matusen nodded, pulled a cell phone from his pocket, and got up and went over to the windows to talk.

"Having a Web site like that can get him a lot of years in the slammer," I said, "but unless he produced the film itself, it's not murder. Ellen Carnine's death *was* — and so was that young woman's in the movie."

"One thing at a time, all right?" McHargue snapped.

"There's something else you can do. I think."

She glanced wearily over at me.

"The actual snuff — the killing you just saw — I think it was filmed locally."

"It could have been anywhere," she said. "The woods in Nebraska look just like the ones in Ohio. So do the woods in Austria, for that matter. What makes you think it happened around here?"

"Because I think I recognized the guy holding the piano wire. I couldn't swear to it, of course, because his face wasn't showing, but it sure as hell looked like the guy I think is Lloyd Severson."

She put her glasses back on. "You have a fucking obsession with this Lloyd Severson, you know that? You're seeing him in your dreams."

"And now," I said, "I'll see him in my nightmares."

She stood up and began pacing. My office is eight times the size of hers and she was taking advantage of the space. "I suppose we could pick Severson up, if we could find him," she said, "although it'd be pretty hard to identify him from that video. You have an address on him?"

I shook my head. "No, just on John Vargas."

"That kid on the video, that wasn't Vargas, was it?"

"Not hardly."

"Then I've got no excuse to bring him in."

"You've got an excuse to ask him questions," I said. "He's a known associate of Severson's."

"Known by whom? The source that gave you all that crap you laid on me?"

"By me," I said. "They visited my office together. I'll even press charges against Vargas for vandalism and attempted assault if that'll help you out."

"If you do that," she warned, "you'll probably have to roll over on whoever gave you the information on them in the first place. Are you ready to do that?"

Roll over on Victor Gaimari and Don Giancarlo D'Allessandro after they went out of their way to do me a favor? I didn't even consider it. It would not only be hazardous to my health, but it would be a betrayal of confidence. And friendship. "No," I said, shaking my head, "I'm not."

"No matter," she said. "We'll just send some people over to give Vargas a minor tune-up and see if we can get him to play nice."

She turned off the power on the laptop, closed the lid, and deftly disconnected it from my phone line. "We're taking this with us, of course, as evidence. Unless you wanted to watch the video again."

I didn't even answer her.

"I thank you for bringing this in," she said, hefting the laptop by its handle. She didn't even say it reluctantly. "For doing your duty as a citizen."

"God bless America," I said.

Matusen put his cell phone away and came back over, giving her a nod.

"There's one more thing, Jacovich."

I sighed, waiting. There was always one more thing.

"You might think it redundant, but I mean to emphasize." She put her glasses back on; the blue tint of the lenses masked her eyes effectively. "Consider this little talk our come-to-Jesus meeting. You are as of this moment, gone. I accept your conjecture as to why Ellen Carnine was killed, even. But it's going to be federal now — Carnine, the little whore in the video, the Web site, everything. And I have enough problems with the FBI throwing their weight around here without having to

399

make pathetic mewling sounds to them explaining why every time they turn around, a rogue private eye keeps running up the crack of their ass. So you make amends with your client, or whatever else you have to do, but get out and stay out. I'll have the goddamn mayor write you a letter of commendation if that's what you want, but consider yourself officially notified that I don't want to see your face again."

"Does this mean I can't come to the Homicide Division Christmas party?"

"Crack wise," she said. "You won't be laughing when you lose your license and start working night security in a shopping mall." She spun around and stalked out on her sensible heels, swinging the laptop from one hand.

Matusen scowled and shook his head. "Why do you aggravate her all the time? She was thanking you, for Christ's sake."

"Is that what it was, Bob? A thank you? It felt more like a mugging."

He started to say something else and then realized she must be downstairs waiting for him, and hustled his butt out the door fast. Matusen was never anyone's idea of a Dirty Harry, but he was a capable and honest cop and Meglich had liked and respected him, which was good enough for me, and I hated it that Florence McHargue was turning him into a lapdog.

The next day was an interesting one. I called William Carnine, who by now had been informed by the police that what he'd thought was a suicide was indeed a murder, and severed my business connection with him. Of course he was shattered all over again, but I think that buried deep within his grief for a lost daughter was a relief, too, that she had not taken her own life. I could understand that.

He wanted me to stay on the case, to find Ellen's killer, but I explained to him that I was forbidden by law to do so. So I didn't have a client anymore, and I busied myself with the nuts and bolts of my business — writing reports, filling out insurance forms, sending out invoices, and returning telephone messages from some people who wanted to hire me as a security consultant for their businesses, which is my real line of work anyway.

Busting pornographers is a sideline.

It was a stressful day for Barnard Landenberger, too. Two Cleveland cops accompanied four FBI agents to his office to arrest him on a federal warrant for complicity to commit murder and he was taken to a holding cell in the Justice Center to await arraignment. The Cleveland police were figuring that they could eventually nail him for Ellen Carnine, too, as well as for the unfortunate young woman in the video if that murder had happened to take place within city limits.

Redmond Munch was invited down to the Third District for a little talk as well. He expressed shock and disbelief that Barnard Landenberger, a longtime friend and colleague, could be capable of such a heinous act. He told Bob Matusen that he was in charge of sales, that he had no idea of the contents of any of Wheetek's Web sites, and that he was unaware of any client of theirs named TOPSTOXX. He also repeated what he'd told me — that he was more or less computer-illiterate except for the most basic word-processing and e-mail functions. While he said that he would use all his resources to prove Landenberger innocent, he promised to cooperate with the police investigation in any way he could.

In the meantime, Bob Matusen told me on the phone later that evening, a team of detectives had dropped in on John Vargas, awakening him at eleven o'clock in the morning, and all their threats and cajoling, and even taking him downtown for questioning still in his silk pajamas, had garnered nothing. He denied knowing Lloyd Severson, and even when two detectives from the Sex Crimes Unit threatened to put a padlock on his prostitution business unless he cooperated, they got nowhere. They mulled over the idea of charging him for vandalism and attempted assault at my office, but the fact was that he hadn't done much more than talk; even the bribe offer wasn't illegal. And it was Lloyd Severson who had busted up my computer. They didn't have a damn thing on John Vargas and he knew it. So did his lawyer. The detectives couldn't think of anything solid to book him for, so they had to let him skate.

Even without Vargas's help the cops finally tracked down where Severson was living — in a little two-room apartment over an Arab-owned mini-market on St. Clair Avenue, about thirty blocks east of where I'd grown up; but when they got there he had disappeared, taking everything with him but a well-thumbed copy of *Hustler* and an empty tin of Altoids. I remember the smell of mint on his breath when I'd turned him upside down behind my desk. I guess he mainlined Altoids —

still not a felony.

So I was out of it, except perhaps as a witness for the prosecution, although I wasn't sure what testimony I could give that might help. And I suppose I should have felt pretty good about how things had turned out, since I was the one who had discovered the snuff site and turned it over to McHargue.

But I didn't.

It seemed unfinished somehow, not quite right. I'd talked to a lot of people about Ellen Carnine, and in the end they had all turned out to be nothing more than satellites who had orbited around her briefly and in very limited ways. False friends like Bronwyn Rhys and Anna Zarafonitos, past seducer Richard Goodman, and would-be users like Stanley Bream and Don Cannon all fell into the category of bottom-feeders, but as far as I could tell, none of them were killers.

I shrugged it off. It wasn't my concern, really. Except for a smashed computer monitor, I had no complaints. And, wonder of wonders, Bob Matusen called to tell me that Florence McHargue had confided in him that she thought I'd done a hell of a job and that I wasn't such a bad guy after all — for a private ticket.

And then, two days later, Victor Gaimari was on the phone to congratulate me on breaking the back of the snuff-film Web site. I didn't ask how he'd found out about it, because frankly, I didn't want to know.

"I hope the information I got for you was helpful in some way," he said.

"If the cops can ever track down Lloyd Severson it will be," I said. "But whether or no, I appreciate the favor."

He paused, a half second too long. "Would you be interested in returning it, Milan? The favor, I mean?"

Ice crystals formed in the pit of my stomach. I knew about Victor's favors; I had repaid them before. And the way he'd just put it left me little doubt that he considered it a duty.

"If I can," I said.

"Actually, it's a job," he said. "You'll be paid well. And don't worry, it's all legal. As a matter of fact, you'd be working for my attorney. Tom Vangelis. He asked for you specifically. You know Tom, don't you?"

I knew Tom, all right, but not to talk to. Thomas Vangelis was one of the most successful criminal attorneys in the Midwest, on retainer not only to Victor and his uncle, but to half of the mob guys in the state. I'd seen him in action in a courtroom once, flamboyant and theatrical and mean as a snake when he had a prosecution witness backed into a corner. He was something of a Cleveland legend, one of the last of the Jake Erlich/F. Lee Bailey courtroom superstars.

Private investigators, the real ones who do it full-time, get most of their work from attorneys. I've worked with lawyers rarely because my main business is security consulting and I deal directly with the client. But I know that when a P.I. is hired by a lawyer he is automatically wrapped in the cloak of the attorney-client privilege and can't get leaned on by the authorities to blab information that might be damaging to the client. I imagined that Tom Vangelis had a whole list of investigators he'd used before, so I wondered why he wanted to hire me.

I asked Victor.

"I don't know all the details, but Tom will explain everything to you," he said. "I've taken the liberty of setting up an appointment for tomorrow morning at nine. Hoping, of course, that you'd be amenable."

Right — like I really had a choice. He's some piece of work, Victor. "I guess I'm amenable," I said. "As you knew damn

406

well I would be."

"Ha-ha," he said. Victor Gaimari never really laughed; his trademark "ha-ha" was as close as he ever came.

And so it was that at ten minutes to nine the next morning I found myself in the elevator of the Bond Court office building on East Ninth Street. There had been a particularly brutal murder-robbery in that building a few years earlier, but it's still one of the city's more glittering office venues, a fitting setting for a high-ticket law firm like Vangelis and Partners.

A stunning African-American receptionist whose expensive clothing and gold jewelry told me she either had a very rich husband or a second income, brought me coffee in a delicate Wedgwood cup and gave me the morning paper to read while I waited. I read Ed Stahl, of course, and hadn't even gotten through Dick Feagler's column before Vangelis came out into the enormous reception room to greet me at two minutes after nine. I had to like him for that. No head games, no power trips, no making the hired help cool their heels.

"Milan, hi — Tom Vangelis," he said. He shook my hand as though he was really glad to see me. He was probably seventy years old, but he looked at least fifteen years younger than that, and his energy was that of a thirty-year-old. He wore a dark gray suit, and against his white-on-white shirt was a luxuriously wide, gray silk necktie, knotted thick, that somehow looked as if it were a cravat someone might have worn a hundred years earlier. His hair was full and black and curly; if it was artificially colored, it was a damn good dye job.

He took me down a long corridor and into his office. It was everything you'd think a hotshot lawyer's office would be, including a big picture window overlooking the lakefront, but although the furniture and accessories were expensive and tasteful, it didn't seem as if Vangelis were trying to impress anybody. It was just a nice office, and he sat opposite me on one of the twin sofas in front of the window so I could enjoy the view; not behind his desk so he could intimidate.

And when he offered me more coffee, he didn't buzz for it, he poured it himself out of one of three silver carafes and into another lovely Wedgwood cup and saucer on a table which was apparently used for nothing else. One narrow-mouthed decanter was regular Colombian, he informed me, one was decaf, and one was vanilla-almond. It was too early in my morning for anything but plain.

"I suppose you're wondering what this is about?" Vangelis said.

"Naturally."

"What would you say if I told you I've been retained to defend Barnard Landenberger in the snuff-film thing?"

The coffee suddenly tasted rotten, but I tried not to let him know it. "I wouldn't be surprised, Mr. Vangelis. Landenberger is rich enough to afford the best, and you're one of the best defense attorneys in the country."

He inclined his head and smiled slightly to accept the accolade. "You have no feelings about it one way or the other?"

"About your representing him?" I shrugged. "No, sir."

"About his guilt or innocence, I mean."

"According to my sources, the Web site is traceable to Wheetek. And he's the head honcho at Wheetek."

"So you'd like to see him swing?"

I nodded. "From the tallest tree."

"You think he's capable of something like what was on that video?"

"I don't think he was the guy with the piano wire," I said. "I don't even know if he was the money behind the video or

409

whether he bought it from an outside source. In any case, the charge isn't homicide, it's complicity to commit."

"That's now," he said. "But the police have reclassified Ellen Carnine's death from suicide to homicide. Thanks to you, I understand." There was no malice in it; it was said almost admiringly, and I nodded. "I believe the prosecutor is going to make the posit that Ellen Carnine found out about the snuff site and was killed before she could tell anyone about it," he continued.

"That's the only thing that makes sense to me, too."

That didn't seem to ruffle him. "The old saw about innocent until proven guilty doesn't fly with you?"

"Sure it does, Mr. Vangelis, but I saw that video."

He frowned with distaste. "I did too, and I can assure you I was as appalled and revolted as you were. And call me Tom, please."

"All right, Tom."

"Barney Landenberger swears he doesn't know a damn thing about that snuff site."

"I imagine he does. I'm sure you're aware that prisons are full of people swearing they're innocent."

"I happen to believe him."

"You're his attorney. You should."

"Not necessarily," he said easily. "I represent lots of people who aren't innocent. That's my job, and I happen to be pretty good at it. I also happen to be proud of it, because before lawyer jokes and frivolous lawsuits and attorneys hawking their wares on television like car salesmen, it was a pretty noble profession. I'm not going to give you that old speech about everyone being entitled to a defense — you've probably heard it before."

"Just last week, I think, on some television show."

"Ah, television lawyers. Talk about fiction! I wish I got half the nookie some of those guys . . . Well, what the hell. I think Landenberger is telling the truth. He's the only one at Wheetek with the technical expertise to set up a sophisticated operation like that one, and he never heard of it. And apparently he wasn't making a nickel from it. There's nothing in the books, either, the accounts."

"He'd be a damn fool if there was," I said. "He didn't get to be a multimillionaire by being dumb. Putting snuff-film revenue into your books for the IRS and anyone else to see would strike me as being egregiously stupid."

"You've closed your mind, then?"

"I try never to do that."

"Because," he went on, "Barney was very impressed with you when he met you last week, and you're familiar with the Ellen Carnine case, so I won't have to spend time getting another investigator up to speed. The county prosecutor is determined to attach Carnine's murder to the snuff-film beef if he can, so Barney would be most appreciative if you'd help."

"How?"

"Help to prove his innocence."

I tried not to blink in surprise, so I took some more coffee. I wanted a cigarette but it didn't even occur to me to look around for an ashtray because I was sure there wouldn't be one. Sitting on a cushy leather sofa or no, I was getting the sense of my back being against the wall.

"That bothers you?"

I set my cup down on its saucer. "Mr. Vangelis — Tom — you and I both know it doesn't matter a damn if it bothers me or not. You're Victor Gaimari's attorney, and Victor did me a favor recently and he asked me to repay the favor to you. So we both know I'm going to say yes."

He smiled, not unkindly, and nodded an

acknowledgment. "But you won't like it."

"No, I won't."

"I'll pay double your rate. Plus all your expenses, of course." Which meant, of course, that Landenberger would be paying me double. Lawyers like Tom Vangelis are always very generous with other people's money. I was sure he was billing his client for the time it was taking to talk to me.

"Thanks," I said, "I'll take it. But throwing money at it won't make me like it any better."

"Will your not liking it get in the way?"

"Of giving it my all? No. If I only worked for people I liked, I'd be sleeping in a cardboard box under a bridge."

"Technically speaking, you'll be working for me. Do you like me, Milan?"

I pondered the question. He was a power broker, a Cleveland superstar, a flamboyant courtroom actor, and a mouthpiece for the mob. But he had pizzazz. Flare. Panache. And at what he did for a living, he was the best. So I told him the truth.

"Yes, Tom. I think I do."

Chapter Twenty-two

They were holding Barnard Landenberger for arraignment at the Justice Center. After arraigning he'd probably be a guest of the sheriff over at the county lockup, but for now he was the Cleveland PD's problem, and could be for some time. Don't believe what you hear on the TV cop shows about holding a suspect for only seventy-two hours and then having to release them; the cops could hold Landenberger for just as long as they could convince a judge that they had a good reason, such as further investigation.

When I visited him in an interrogation room that afternoon, Barnard Landenberger didn't look like a smug, confident rich guy anymore. They'd allowed him to wear his own clothes for the nonce, and from their condition it was obvious he'd slept in them. The wrinkled slacks and shirt, combined with a look in his eyes, like a rabbit caught in the headlights of an onrushing truck, gave him the appearance of a young, confused guy who was damn scared because for the first time in his life he was faced with a situation that neither his charm nor his money could control. He still talked adenoidally and through his teeth, only not with the prep-school intonation anymore, because those teeth were clenched with tension. The gold bracelet and Rolex were gone, and the tinted lenses of his glasses were no longer cool-looking, but just emphasized the ghostly paleness of his face. He hadn't been inside long enough to develop prison pallor, only two days; his ashen color came, I was sure, from the knowledge that he was in trouble like he'd never been in before.

He shook my hand and then gave it an aftersqueeze as if I were a long-lost lover. Then he sat down across from me at an old, scarred wooden table. We both heard the loud *click* of the lock as his jailers made sure he wasn't going on any unauthorized trips. "I appreciate your coming, Milan," he said in a way that convinced me he meant it. Back in his office a few days before, I'd been "Mr. Jacovich," and I wondered whether the sudden familiarity was because he was now indirectly paying my salary or if he just needed a friend — any friend. In any case, he looked almost ready to cry.

He leaned forward with his forearms on the table and swore to me that he was innocent, which was just what I expected him to say. He said he was shocked all over again to learn that Ellen's death had not been self-inflicted. And he raised his hand as if taking an oath when he said he hadn't known about the snuff site until the police had barged into his office and arrested him for it.

"That's going to be pretty hard to make anyone believe, Mr. Landenberger," I told him.

His chin quivered a little. "Why? It's the truth."

"Maybe so, but it defies logic. You're a successful businessman, the president of your company, and you don't even know you're the Webmaster for a snuff-video operation? If they go after you for Ellen's death, it's strictly local. But the Web site thing, that's interstate, even international. And that makes it a federal beef, and that means it's FBI business. The federal prosecutors don't fuck around, Mr. Landenberger. They're going to try to make you out as either a liar or a moron."

That brought the first flush of color to his otherwise pallid features, but he was hardly in a position to take offense. "Naturally I knew that TOPSTOXXX was a client, but I had no reason to believe that the site was for anything besides securities trading. There are lots of online brokers these days, and I know some of them might not be around next year, but that wasn't any of my business. So I simply assumed they were what they said they were." He looked up to heaven for help and succor, but the stamped-tin ceiling of the interrogation room got in his way. "I even designed the site."

"When was that?"

He scrunched up his face. "Six months ago, seven. I'm not sure. It's easy to check, though."

"Who is behind TOPSTOXXX, anyway?"

"A woman named Rita Sadwith. I never actually met her," he said. "We only talked over the phone."

"Isn't that a little unusual?"

He shook his head. "Not really. She lives in Michigan — Grosse Pointe. She said she used to be a stockbroker with a big firm in Detroit. I guess she made a lot of money at it and decided she wanted to work for herself. So she quit her job a year ago to develop the idea for TOPSTOXXX."

"You have an address for her in Michigan?"

"I'm not sure. That was Red's end of it. I know we had her e-mail address, because she and I corresponded several times that way. As I told you, Red Munch is the businessman in Wheetek. I'm just the nuts-and-bolts guy."

"And Ellen Carnine was the creative one."

"Creative, yes. But she was fantastic with people. That's why all our clients loved her."

"Did this Rita Sadwith from TOPSTOXXX love her, too?"

He looked blank . . . lost. "I don't even know if they spoke. Again, Red was the one who was mostly in contact with her."

"Yeah — Red," I said. "The police are questioning him, and they'll undoubtedly check your story out, you know."

"I know."

"The three X's didn't give you a clue?"

He shrugged. "I didn't think much about it one way or the other. For all I know, 'T-O-P-S-T-O-X' or 'T-O-P-S-T-O-C-K-S' was already taken as a domain name. You know there are sharpies out there buying up domain names like crazy and then selling them for a profit, don't you?"

"Uh-huh. What about the link to the snuff page?"

"I never saw it or heard of it," he said. "It must have been added to the TOPSTOXXX home page later."

"By whom?"

"I don't know. That's what I want you to find out."

"Could it have been your partner?"

He gave me the closest approximation of a laugh he could manage under the circumstances. "Red is technologically challenged and he admits it. He's the sales guy, the marketing guy. He doesn't know the first thing about how the Internet works. He couldn't have set that site up if he'd wanted to."

"Who else could have, then?" I said. "Who at Wheetek had the technical know-how?"

"Nobody else. Well, some of them had the know-how, but nobody else had the passwords to access the pages." Then a thought dawned on him. "Nobody but Ellen, that is."

"Red Munch didn't have the passwords?"

"He wouldn't have known what to do with them," Landenberger said.

"And where were these passwords kept?"

"In my office safe. It's in the floor, covered by the rug under my desk."

"Ellen had the combination to the safe?"

"Nobody else did, no. She had her own set of passwords. I don't even know where she kept them."

"Red didn't have the combination, either?"

He shook his head.

The next question was a tough one, but I had to ask it. "Do you think Ellen might have been the one who added the snuff link?"

He looked appalled. "I'd bet my life she didn't."

"You *are* betting your life, Mr. Landenberger."

A tremor shook his body and wobbled his chin, and I couldn't help feeling a stab of sympathy for him. I'd done a little research on him after my talk with Vangelis. He'd been born to privilege, gone to a tony prep school out in the eastern suburbs and then on to Brown University. He'd probably never been in any worse trouble before than getting called on the dean's carpet for drinking in the dorm or getting a speeding ticket for roaring down Chagrin River Road in his Porsche. And now he was in custody and perhaps looking at spending the rest of his life there, or worse — a final date with a lethal needle on Death Row. It would be a daunting spot to be in, even for the hardest of street rats, and Barnard Landenberger, although smart and savvy and aggressive and talented, was nowhere near being a tough guy.

But he was a greedy guy, too, and when I'd spoken to him in his office, he'd seemed to have had few compunctions about being a high-class, high-tech pornographer. I wondered now whether he'd changed his mind.

"You know what your attorney might say?"

"What?"

"That you should try to switch all the blame to Ellen to get yourself cleared. That she's dead, and it really wouldn't matter."

His head jerked back as if I'd slapped him, and his mouth actually dropped open a full half-inch. "That's insane. I'm sure Ellen had nothing to do with it."

"It's a defense," I said. "And a good one at that. That's what defense attorneys get paid for."

"Well, it's out of the question," he said, and clamped his teeth firmly together again with an audible *click*. Flashes of the confident rich kid he'd been until two days ago appeared in his eyes and put some iron in his spine.

I waited for further amplification, and he looked a bit incredulous to think that I needed any.

"I wouldn't do that to Ellen, even if she is dead," he continued awkwardly. "That's disgusting."

"Even if it keeps you out of prison?"

His lungs filled with air and he drew himself up tall in his chair. "Even if it keeps me out of the death chamber," he said. "But it's not going to come to that, because I'm innocent."

I sighed. Barnard Landenberger may have been a computer genius, and he might have been hell on wheels on a polo field, but he wasn't nearly streetwise enough to know that innocence and purity and wealth doesn't always keep people out of the slammer.

But his absolute refusal to shift the blame to the deceased Ellen Carnine in order to save his own ass made me want to believe him.

It took until almost six o'clock that evening to learn that the TOPSTOXXX Web site had been constructed out of pure fantasy. Turns out that Rita Sadwith had been a wealthy maiden lady, the only daughter of a highly placed and well-paid executive from the early days at General Motors. She had died seven months earlier, at the age of eighty-one, from a fall down the cellar stairs of her home in Grosse Pointe, Michigan, which had been ruled accidental just three weeks before her American Express platinum card had paid $3,261.90 to Wheetek, Inc. for the TOPSTOXXX Web site. In a pleasant, cooperative conversation with her attorney, one of the senior partners in a big, conservative Detroit law firm, I learned that she had indeed dabbled in the stock market herself, but had maintained an account at Merrill Lynch for more than fifty years, and her portfolio was stuffed with conservative old-line blue-chip stocks, including a hefty block of GM. No high-techs, no dot-coms. All her securities were traded on the New York Stock Exchange and none on the technology-heavy NASDAQ.

The will specified the disposition of her estate, which was valued at a few bucks more than three million dollars. Rita Sadwith had left a hundred thousand to a niece in West Palm Beach, Florida, and another fifty grand to one Parker Pidcock of Houston who, apparently unbeknownst to her, had predeceased her by eleven years; her lawyer thought perhaps Mr. Pidcock might have been an old, long-lost flame. After deducting burial expenses and various assorted legal and real-estate fees (which ran to six figures), the rest had been bequeathed to various charities, the bulk to an Episcopal church in Grosse Pointe.

Not exactly the profile one might expect for a hardcore pornographer.

And when I went to my computer and accessed an Internet reference site that was a virtual Yellow Pages for just about every business in the United States, I discovered that there was no such company as TOPSTOXXX. Whoever had set up the account with Wheetek had done so with a credit card stolen from the late Rita Sadwith. The thought occurred to me that Ms. Sadwith's unfortunate tumble down the cellar stairs might not have been accidental, after all — how does a rich elderly woman, who must have held several credit cards, report the loss of one of them if she's dead? And with no immediate family or even a close friend, who would notice it missing until long after the fact?

The FBI, in their infinite wisdom and with more sophisticated databases from which to choose, would surely discover what I had; but it wouldn't get Barnard Landenberger off the hook for the Web site, and at first glance it had virtually nothing to do with Ellen Carnine's taking a header off the Lorain-Carnegie Bridge.

The FBI probably wouldn't care about it anyway. Like a busy waiter in a crowded restaurant, they would simply announce that it wasn't their table.

Which meant, I guess, that it was mine. Because the surest way to prove anyone innocent of committing a crime was to find out who actually did it. And that would put me smack in the middle of Florence McHargue's homicide investigation once more. A losing proposition.

But not nearly as deleterious as turning down Victor Gaimari's request to return a favor.

Not that I'd wind up with broken knee-caps, or at the bottom of Lake Erie with my feet in cement — Victor and his people haven't operated that way in decades. Besides, it was really no skin off Victor's ass personally whether Barnard Landenberger had a fatal chemical pumped into his veins courtesy of the state of Ohio or walked out of the Justice Center the next morning to renew his season subscription to the Cleveland Orchestra.

But Tom Vangelis was the mob's lawyer and Victor was simply trying to help him. And it seemed more prudent for me to keep the D'Allessandro-Gaimari family as friends than set them up as enemies.

So I was in. Working on a case the Cleveland police had warned me away from, and which two hoodlums had tried to muscle me into dropping. New client, but same deal.

It was going to be a long evening.

Just as I was getting ready to lock the door on my workday, the phone rang. I was surprised to hear the voice of Sarah Donnem on the other end.

"I'm glad I caught you, Mr. Jocovich," she said. "I was just wondering how your — investigation was coming along."

"You were?" I said.

"Well, Ellen *was* my friend. Naturally this whole thing is bothering me. How she died, I mean. I keep wondering whether I was a good enough friend to her; whether I might have made a difference."

With a start I realized that Sarah Donnem had no way of knowing that Ellen Carnine had not committed suicide. I tried to find something noncommittal to say. "I can just about guarantee you that Ellen's death wasn't your fault, Ms. Donnem."

"Are you sure? I mean, there might have been a question I should have asked. I could have been more sensitive to the fact that she was hurting, and maybe said or done something to help her."

"I really wish you'd put that out of your mind," I said. "You're torturing yourself for nothing."

Her tone changed, became sharper. "Why? You've found something out?"

"No, not really. But I know enough that none of Ellen's friends could have made a difference one way or the other."

She didn't seem convinced. "You're sure?"

An unsettling chill ran through me. "Ms. Donnem," I said, "I have a paying client; I can't really discuss this with you any further. I'm sure you understand."

She sighed. "All right," she said. "As long as you're sure there's nothing I could have done to save her."

I hung up, shaking my head. Why do some people insist on believing that everything that happens in the world is about *them?* I wouldn't have imagined that Sarah Donnem was so self-involved as to think a friend's suicide was her fault — unless, of course, there was something she wasn't telling me.

I drove home joylessly, feeling unaccountably tired. I peeled off my clothes as soon as I walked in the door; I'm sure it was my imagination, but they seemed to smell like the jailhouse. Places where prisoners are incarcerated all have the same sour, hopeless stink — stale sweat, old smokes, fresh fear.

Dressed in a bathrobe and rubber thong sandals, I went into the kitchen and smeared butter on half a loaf of Ciabatta, and while it heated in the oven I boiled some pasta until it was al dente, then tossed it with olive oil, a chopped-up clove of garlic, and some Romano cheese. I opened a Stroh's and took the whole business into the den to consume it while I watched the Indians game; they were playing the Baltimore Orioles, who were now led by our former manager, Mike Hargrove, lending an extra fillip of emotional interest to an early-season tussle.

The pasta was kind of bland and so was the ball game, which the Tribe wound up losing by two runs. But I kept glued to the set anyway because the only time I ever watch television is when someone is doing something with a ball, and I was too keyed-up to read. Besides, baseball is slow enough that it left me plenty of time to think between swings of the bat.

The game was over a few minutes after ten o'clock. By eleven, I was dressed again, blue jeans, heavy workboots, and a sweatshirt, with my gun snug in its holster beneath a satiny Cleveland Indians warm-up jacket, and ready to set out on the first sojourn of my newest commission — to save Barnard Landenberger from spending the rest of his life in prison.

Lorain Avenue, which begins its life at the western end of the bridge where Ellen Carnine had died and ends up in the far reaches of the western suburbs, has many facets and faces. The hundred-year-old West Side Market is an anchor on the corner of West Twenty-fifth Street. A few blocks beyond is the recently remodeled St. Ignatius High School, a perennial regional football power. Tired-looking antique shops dot either side of the street, interspersed with discount stores and hole-in-the-wall diners that serve the best hot dogs in town. Past West Forty-fourth begins a string of neighborhood taverns. And at night, usually around eleven o'clock, Lorain is one of Cleveland's premier strolls for hookers.

Detroit Road, several blocks nearer the lake, has its share of practitioners of the world's oldest profession, too, but Detroit is brighter, gaudier, and heavily trafficked. Lorain in the wee hours seems narrower, darker, more dusty. And Lorain was where I had seen the skinny young woman who'd made a quick stop at John Vargas's apartment, standing in a doorway and looking at me with a mixture of hope and resigned despair as I drove slowly by.

I cruised up and down the street for more than an hour, listening to Dan Poletta's nightly jazz program on the public radio station, WCPN, and checking out every solitary female who walked slowly on the narrow sidewalks with her head turned toward the traffic, on the lookout for business. After the third or fourth pass, the street people of the night were beginning to recognize my car and ignore it, probably figuring I was a police officer since I was obviously not in the market for the various commodities they might be selling — marijuana, uppers and downers, coke, crystal meth, or quick, commercial sex. I doubted whether there was much crack cocaine for sale or barter over here west of the Cuyahoga; crack is an east-side ghetto specialty.

Finally, at about a quarter to one, I spotted the skinny young prostitute, about a block east of where she had been standing the first night I'd seen her, walking very slowly toward downtown. Tonight she tottered on high stiletto heels, wearing very brief black shorts, a tiny fake fur jacket, and a silvery top against which the nipples of her small breasts poked like bullets.

I slowed my car to a stop, rolled down the passenger-side window and called out a hello.

She turned her head and looked at me, her face lighting with a fake, desperate smile. "Hey, what up?" she said, and moved over to the car, bending from the waist and sticking her head through the open window so I could see down the front of her shirt. There wasn't much to see. "Looking for a date?"

"I thought maybe we could spend some time together," I said. "I'll make it worth your while."

"Cool." She gave the word two syllables. She opened the door and slid in beside me. There was a small scab on her right knee, as if she'd skinned it in a playground. In the greenish light from the dashboard I

could see she was wearing very dark, pur-
plish lipstick and a grotesque amount of
plum-colored eyeshadow that made her
eyes, which were small and a little too
close together, seem even tinier. She
would have looked like a little girl who'd
gotten into her mother's makeup case if
not for the telltale redness around her nostrils.

"What's your name?" she said, too
brightly.

"Milan."

"Milan? What kinda name is that? I
never heard that name before."

"It's Slovenian."

She was not impressed. "Whatever," she
said, obviously not having the slightest
idea of what a Slovenian was. "My name's
Snowy."

I doubt if that's what her parents had
christened her. A street name — probably
derived from the cocaine habit that had
reddened her nose. "Nice to meet you," I
said, because it seemed like the thing to
say.

"You ain't no cop, are you?" Her accent
was pure West Virginia.

"No," I said. I didn't think telling her
that I used to be one would have started
our relationship on the right note.

She stuck out her hand for a quick shake, keeping it very businesslike. Her hand was scrawny, long fingers with bitten-down nails. "Well, nice to meet you, too, Milan. What ya looking for? It's twenny bucks for straight head, forty for a half-and-half." No nonsense here, no small talk. Time is money. "I don't got a room we could use," she said, "but I know a nice quiet place where we can go in the car — ain't nobody gonna mess with us there."

"How much just to talk?"

Her little eyes got smaller with suspicion. "What kinda talk? You want me to talk dirty to you?"

"No."

"You wanna talk dirty ta *me?*" She drew away from me a little, as if the very thought was appalling to her.

"Nope. I'd just like to ask you a few questions."

"What kinda questions?"

I took five folded-up twenties from my jacket pocket and showed them to her. "The kind that are worth a hundred bucks," I said.

Her mouth opened in astonishment. "A *hundred?*"

"That's right, Snowy. You don't have to do anything, just talk to me a little, while

433

we drive around. And as soon as you want me to, I'll bring you back here. What do you say?"

She seemed to get a little smaller. "I never knew no guy wantin' ta shoot a C-note just for talking."

"Let's just say I'm a generous guy," I said.

She was as suspicious as hell, and a little scared too, and confused. In Snowy's world, oral sex with a stranger for a twenty-dollar bill was a lot more understandable than conversation. But her eyes stayed glued on the money in my hand. Finally the money won out; it usually does.

She was still uneasy about it. "Okay, then, but I don't wanna drive around. There's too many cops out. We'll go ta that place I told you about. Okay?"

"Okay," I said, and she snatched the money from my hand as if she was afraid I'd change my mind. With the speed and efficiency of a Las Vegas cashier she counted the bills to make sure there were five, then stuffed them into the waistband of her tight little shorts.

She directed me to a dark street and told me to park as far as I could from the nearest streetlight, in front of an old brick factory shuttered for the night, and across

the street from the looming cement structure that supported the Shoreway.
Although cars whizzed by above our heads,
it was a secluded place indeed, albeit not
very atmospheric for an amorous assigna-
tion. I guess men who pick up hookers on
the street aren't too fussy about ambiance
with their blow jobs.

"Kill the lights and turn the engine off,
okay?" she ordered with the authority of
experience. I followed her instructions.

"So what you wanna talk about?"
Despite her unusually high pay for this
particular job, she was anxious to be done
with it and get back out on the street to
earn some more.

"You're new to Cleveland?"

She bobbed her head once in what I took
to be an affirmative nod. "About two
months." She pronounced it "muntz."

"West Virginia?"

"Jeez, yeah. How'd ya know?"

"Have you been out here on the streets
all that time?"

"Yeah. I mean, I got a place to live! Me
and this other girl."

"Do you and your roommate both work
for the same guy?"

A flicker of fear widened her eyes, and
she sucked her lower lip between her teeth

and chewed off some of her purple lipstick; most of it stuck to her incisors. She didn't answer right away, but finally offered a begrudging nod.

"Snowy, since you've been in Cleveland, has anybody ever asked you to do a movie?"

Her eyes lit up. "You in the movies?"

"No," I said. "Just wondering."

She seemed a trifle disappointed that I wasn't a producer or a talent scout, and she crossed her arms across her chest protectively. "Whaddaya mean by 'movie'? You mean a porno?"

I nodded.

"I ain't done one yet, but this guy I know, he said he wanted me ta do a fuck flick sometime. Said it'd be good money, too, like seven hunderd bucks." She breathed the amount with wonder.

"They make movies like that around here? Pornos?"

Her bony shoulders shrugged under the fake fur jacket. She was breathing through her mouth. "I guess."

"Do you happen to know any of the working girls here on the street who've made one?"

"Nuh-uh," she said. "There was one girl who said she was gonna do one, but I don't know if she did or not."

The flesh on the back of my neck tingled. "How come you don't know? Didn't she say?"

"Naw — 'cause I ain' seen her for about five weeks now. Maybe she got sick of the life, I dunno."

I tried unsuccessfully to swallow, but my throat was beginning to close. Maybe she got sick of the life, or maybe life got sick of her.

"What was her name? Do you remember?"

She shrugged again. "Whattaya, nuts? None-a the girls use their real names. But on the street they called her 'Razorblades.'"

Razorblades, I thought. Along with the edge of a credit card, the favored tool for making nice, neat little lines of cocaine.

"What did Razorblades look like, Snowy?"

She rubbed violently at her nose and sniffled. "I dunno. Young, skinny like me, long black hair." All at once her shoulders grew rigid and she sat up straight. "Hey, what's the deal here? Why you axin' all these questions an' shit? Are you sure you ain' no cop?"

"I ain't no cop."

She started looking around nervously.

"Hey, that's it now. Take me back out ta Lorain, okay? I gotta make some more money."

I hesitated, wondering if I could pry a few more facts out of her before she clammed up on me completely.

"You promised you'd take me back whenever I wanned," she reminded me petulantly. "You said."

I had said. And I'm a man of my word, even though I had lots more questions to ask her. "Sure, Snowy. No problem."

I lit a cigarette, turned the key in the ignition, flicked on my lights, and pulled out of the parking space.

"Hey, how 'bout lettin' me bum a coupla smokes?" she said plaintively. "For later."

I gave her the rest of the pack, about half-full. There was another late-model sedan up at the end of the block; two heads were silhouetted in the front seat, one seemingly male and one definitely female. I imagine he was paying far less than a hundred dollars, but I couldn't believe he'd gotten any more for his money than I had.

I pulled up to the curb close to where I'd picked her up. She started to get out of the car. I leaned over to her before she closed the door and said, "Snowy, if anyone asks you to do a movie again, don't."

"Huh?"

"Just say no."

She shook her head in wonder. "Whattaya, nuts?" she asked again. "Say no to seven hunderd bucks?"

"I wish you would say no, Snowy." I said. "Otherwise you might not live to spend it."

Her face showed terror again and then closed up tight. She slammed the door and began walking away rapidly. I sighed, put the car in gear, and drove off.

I was sorry I'd frightened her, especially since I doubted very much that she'd heed my warning. So, I thought, it was up to me to see that her movie offer never came.

Chapter Twenty-three

I couldn't sleep. All the things I'd learned that day kept bouncing around inside my head, shouldering their way into the forefront of my consciousness. Finally I invoked my forty-five-minute rule — I refuse to lie sleepless in bed staring at the ceiling for any longer than that — and got up and went out into the kitchen. I sat at the butcher-block table with a beer and considered everything I knew, and what else I needed to know.

Here's what I had: Rita Sadwith, a rich, elderly woman in Grosse Pointe, Michigan, had died from a fall down the stairs. One of her credit cards had been stolen, and that card had been used to pay Wheetek, Inc., for an Internet Web site devoted to snuff films — films in which someone was actually killed on camera. A young prostitute named Razorblades had been offered big money to make a porno movie and had then suddenly disappeared off the streets of Cleveland. Snowy knew her, and since she was one of John Vargas's string of hookers, it wasn't such a leap of logic to think that Razorblades had been, too.

I wondered if anyone had filed a missing-persons report on the girl. Poor little Razorblades had been an ideal victim. Probably a teenage runaway, so no one would really notice that she was missing. Anonymous. Untraceable. Disposable.

That made me believe that the disgusting film had been made somewhere in the Cleveland area and had been put up on the Wheetek system. Both the FBI and Florence McHargue seemed satisfied that Barnard Landenberger, my new client, was responsible. In order to prove he wasn't, I needed to find out who had produced the film and who had added the computer link that Ellen Carnine somehow had discovered.

And probably had been killed because of it.

Bronwyn Rhys, one of Ellen's friends and clients, had a spanking fetish link on her upscale clothing site on the Web, which Ellen might or might not have known about. Another of Ellen's gal pals, Anna Zarafonitos, knew John Vargas, the pimp, who had come to my office to bribe me and to scare me away from the Carnine case. Furthermore, Anna was sleeping with Ellen's boss, Red Munch, who supposedly did not have the passwords to have put up the snuff link. Barnard Landenberger and Ellen Carnine were the only ones who did have the passwords, and now Ellen was dead and Landenberger was facing federal charges for complicity to commit murder, the murder of one of Vargas's hookers which had been graphically photographed for the edification and enjoyment of the worst kind of pervert.

After two beers and five Winstons, I got an idea. It was a long shot at best, but if I could make sure that the film had been made in the Cleveland area, I might be able to save some other young woman's life — maybe even Snowy's.

I went back to bed, managing to fall asleep at last at about three-thirty in the morning. But it was a fitful rest, interrupted several times when I woke up drenched in my own sweat. Finally I threw off the blanket and dozed beneath the top sheet, but even in May it was still too chilly in northeastern Ohio for that to be very comfortable. When the clock radio blasted on with Lanigan and Malone at seven-thirty, I felt worse than if I hadn't gone to sleep at all.

The sound of rain took me to the window to check the skies. Rain was falling, a light, steady rain, nowhere near some of the gully-washers that often visited us in the spring, and the sky, although dark, wasn't at all ominous, so I figured things would clear up by noon. I ground some French-roast coffee beans from the freezer, turned on my Mr. Coffee, and showered while it perked. Then, wrapped in a green-and-yellow terrycloth robe my son Stephen had given me several Christmases before, I sat at my kitchen table and gulped down three cups while I scanned the morning paper.

For the third straight day Barnard Landenberger's arrest had made the front page, which is usually reserved for national or international items. But a rich young entrepreneur suspected of making snuff films was far too juicy and prurient for the inside pages of the Metro section. I'd learned long ago, sometimes to my sorrow, that in the wonderful world of journalism, "If it bleeds — it leads."

I didn't read the story all the way through; I already knew about it. Now everyone else in northeast Ohio did, too, and for all I knew, the rest of the country. Guilty or innocent, Landenberger's reputation was shot, and I imagined that even if he walked away from the charge, his days as a mover and shaker in Cleveland were numbered. It was too early in the morning to tell, but my guess was that by eleven o'clock the price of Wheetek stock would drop right off the NASDAQ.

I dressed in gray slacks, a blue corduroy jacket, a brightly colored shirt of a shade that some fashion designer would undoubtedly have called "cantaloupe," and a blue-and-yellow tie, and went downstairs to my car. I headed down Cedar Hill, but instead of taking Carnegie, which was the quickest way to my office, I veered off onto Chester Avenue toward downtown, and when I hit East Ninth Street I cut over to Superior and parked in the high-priced garage across from the massive Cleveland Public Library.

The library had built a brand-new wing a few years ago, dedicated to longtime but now-retired congressman Louis Stokes, and a beautiful garden. Then they restored the old library building into the architectural jewel it had once been. I crossed the street admiring both of them.

The young man at the reference desk was wearing a Bugs Bunny tie over a denim shirt, and had earrings in both ears. I remember the days when librarians all looked like Jessica Tandy, in her later, old-lady roles. The times, they are a-changin'.

"I'm interested in finding a book on wildflowers," I told him.

He gave me the look. Finally he directed me to the proper section, and within a few minutes I was loaded down with books and heading for a library table half occupied by an earnest-looking young woman who was poring over a volume on electrical engineering. She made brief eye contact when I approached, then put her nose back in her own book. She didn't nod or smile.

Since I had no idea what I was supposed to be looking for, I started turning pages. After a while my tablemate glanced over at me with some amusement; I must have seemed to her like a small child who couldn't really read but just wanted to look at the pictures.

I think I blushed a little. "I'm looking for a flower," I explained.

She nodded gravely. "Aren't we all," she said. Then she went back to her own business.

I didn't know anything about flowers, wild or otherwise. I could recognize a tulip or a pansy by sight, and I knew how a sunflower looked smiling prettily at the side of the road. I'd given my high-school senior-prom date a gardenia corsage and my ex-wife Lila roses on an occasional anniversary, but that's the extent of my botanical knowledge. I guess we only tend to learn things that we care about, and while I can enjoy the beauty of a field of wildflowers with the best of them, I have little interest in what their names might be.

So it took me two hours and several books before I found it, but there it was, in full color, in a slim volume about wild orchids. It was called pink lady's slipper, or pink moccasin flower. Latin name: *Cyprepedium acaule.*

The same little pink flower I had seen in the snuff film.

This particular lady's slipper attracted bees with its bright color and scent, to trap them in its pouch, and only let them out through a small opening which makes sure the bee deposits its load of pollen and picks up a fresh one. And that's all the bee gets out of it. No nectar for honey. Pretty soon the bees get wise and avoid the flower until a new and more easily fooled bee comes along to repeat the process.

Maybe that's what had happened to the young woman in the snuff film; she got trapped by the lure of easy money and couldn't get out again, with or without nectar. Mother Nature is a mistress of irony.

This particular pink lady's slipper, I read, was found mostly in the Midwest, and grew naturally in acidic soil, usually on steep slopes, or in something called "sphagnum bogs." A little more research, this time in the dictionary, told me what "sphagnum" is — a soft moss.

I took the book to the copying machine and made as many copies of the *Cyprepedium acaule* page as I had quarters, which turned out to be five. Then I went back to the table, closed all the botany books and picked them up, cradling them in my arms. "Have a nice day," I told my companion with the electrical engineering text, and went back up to the reference desk and the kid with the earrings and the Bugs Bunny tie.

I deposited the books in front of him. "Is there anyone on the staff here who could give me some information about a particular flower?"

"More information than you could find in those?" he said, looking balefully at the pile.

"I need to know where in the local area a particular wildflower might be growing."

He fingered one of his earrings. "That's

pretty specific information," he said. "I'm not sure anyone here has that kind of expertise."

"Where could I go to find someone who does?"

"It's a local flower?"

"I think so, yes."

"Hmmm," he said, and thought it over for half a minute. "You could go over to the botany department at Case and see if you could scare someone up. Or Cleveland State. But I think your best bet would be to try one of the tree-huggers out at the Holden Arboretum."

I was glad the rain had finally stopped, because it was a long haul out to Kirtland where America's largest arboretum sprawls over more than three thousand acres. I suppose the remoteness is to be expected — an arboretum, or open-air tree museum, is by its very nature, rural. Even the drive from the entrance to the Holden Arboretum Visitor's Center is more than a mile and a half. A pretty drive, but a long one nonetheless.

The inside of the Visitor's Center looks a lot like a cafeteria in a middle school. The young woman at the front desk smiled professionally as I approached. When I got closer I saw that her brass name tag identified her as Lori Punkar. She was a slim, shortish blonde, cute and pert. Just my type, if she hadn't been several decades too young for me.

"Hi there," she said. "Welcome to the Holden Arboretum."

"Thanks, Lori." My use of her name widened her smile.

She began collecting a handful of brochures that would tell me all about where I was and what I was about to see when I stopped her. "I'm not going to be taking a tour today," I said. "Actually I'm just looking for some information."

She looked almost disappointed and put the brochures back where they belonged. "I'll help if I can."

"Do you know a lot about flowers?" I asked.

She shrugged. "That's why I'm here. I'm majoring in botany at Kent. I work here two days a week for credit." She dimpled. "I want to be a horticulturist when I grow up."

I tried not to smile as I remembered how Dorothy Parker, the legendary wit, had replied when asked to use the word *horticulture* in a sentence: "You can lead a horticulture but you can't make her think." I didn't think Lori would appreciate the wordplay, though, so I just said, "I went to Kent too," a bit of information that seemed to please her.

She looked me up and down. "Football?"

"Good guess," I said. From my jacket pocket I took one of the pages I'd photocopied at the library, unfolded it, and spread it out in front of her.

She looked at it and smiled in recognition. "Ah, the pink lady's slipper. Sure. What would you like to know about it?"

"Where in this area does it grow, specifically?"

"Well, as it says on this page, it's pretty rare because believe it or not, the bees catch on quickly that they aren't going to get anything for their trouble, and go after other flowers instead. So although there are colonies all over, there aren't as many as for other flowers."

"Colonies?" I said.

She smiled patiently. "That's what they call them, yes. I mean, you won't find huge fields of them anywhere like you would poppies, for instance. Just in rare little clumps."

"Are there any rare little clumps in the Cleveland area?"

"Now that you mention it," she said, "the largest known colony in Ohio is just a few miles away, right here in Lake County."

"Where?" I said, my heart hammering against my rib cage.

I guess I must have appeared overeager, because she frowned a little bit. "You're not planning on picking any, are you? They're not only protected by law, but they're on private property."

"No, I'm not going to pick them." I held up my hand in an oath. "Scout's honor. Whose property are they on?"

"It's quite a well-known farm," she said. "The original owner was a rich shipping magnate, and the farm was kind of a weekend retreat for him. He used to call it 'Eagle's Gate.'"

"He doesn't own it anymore?"

"Oh Lord, no. He's been dead fifty years or so. His family inherited it when he died, and they held on to it for a long while. But you know, times change, and I guess the young grandkids or great-grandkids thought it was kind of a drag going out to this little country house every weekend — more fun stuff to do in town. So they sold it a few years back. Two or three, anyway. But I'm sure there must have been some sort of rider or covenant in the sales contract that required the new owner to keep and maintain the colony of lady's slippers. It's so rare around here, it's almost like an endangered species."

"Do you remember who they sold it to?"

"I don't," she said. "But it would be easy enough to find out." She cleared her throat and tried to be tactful, but she was obviously bursting with curiosity. "You don't seem like one of the serious flower-lovers we get in here all the time. Do you mind if I ask why you're so interested in the slippers, anyway?"

I folded up the photocopy and put it back in my pocket. "I've got a shoe fetish," I said. She giggled at me — but since I'd been surfing the Internet on Ellen's computer, I knew all about fetishes.

Lake County is north and east of Cleveland, and in the wintertime when the lake-effect snow and storms roaring out of western Canada turn northeast Ohio into a winter wonderland, the county usually bears the brunt. The county seat is in Painesville Township, once a small town and now, with a population of 225,000, experiencing growing pains. Its courthouse, a spectacular building erected in the middle of the nineteenth century with a pedimented Doric portico, Italianate details on the windows and cornices, and a double dome soaring high atop its tower, is on the Register of Historic Places, and deserves to be.

I went to the local library first, and it took me another forty-five minutes of browsing through the special Lake County section to find anything about the farm known as Eagle's Gate. It was in the village of Concord, and had been purchased in 1921 by a shipping tycoon named Walter Shandy, who built a modest house on the crest of the hill and used it as a weekend and vacation retreat. There was no indication in the books of who the Shandy family had sold it to.

So that sent me to the courthouse, to the subterranean office where real-estate records were kept. After almost an hour, and after being warned by the attendant that it was after five o'clock and they were closing, I found what I was looking for.

The Shandy property, known since 1921 as Eagle's Gate, was a sixty-two-acre parcel in the village of Concord. According to the records, upon Walter Shandy's death, ownership of the property had passed on to his grown children, Walter Shandy Jr. and

Althea Shandy Eccles, in February of 1949. In 1958, on the occasion of Junior's passing, full proprietorship had reverted to Mrs. Eccles and remained that way until 1975 when she died, and as part of her own estate it had passed to her only son, Walter S. Eccles.

In 1997 Mr. Eccles had sold the property for $780,000. When I saw the new and current owner's name, my heart pounded and did a balletic leap inside my chest.

It was Herman D. Munch. The father of Redmond Munch, the junior partner in Wheetek.

I felt as if a great yoke had been lifted from my shoulders, because now I knew I wasn't working for the bad guy, or at least not for the bad guy's attorney. Barney Landenberger, while an admitted pornographer, was as innocent of murder as he claimed.

It was Munch all along. Red Munch, who was nearly as computer-illiterate as I was. I felt it in my gut. But my gut wasn't enough to take to the police just yet. I had to check it out myself.

I scribbled down the exact location of the farm, but couldn't do much else before the attendant crept up behind me, looking pointedly at her wristwatch and saying, "Sir . . ."

When I got out to my car, much to the relief of the Lake County civil servants who wanted to go home, I pulled out my cell phone and dialed Third District police headquarters and asked for Florence McHargue, only to be told she'd already left for the day, as had Bob Matusen. I tried Matusen at home but his wife told me he hadn't arrived yet and asked if I'd like to leave a message.

I thought about it and said no.

After all, what did I have to tell him? That Red Munch's family owned a farm in Lake County that was the site of a colony of lady's slippers, the same kind of flower that was visible in a snuff film? It wasn't the only place in the world where they grew, and Munch being their caretaker was hardly enough for the Cleveland PD — which was more than happy to blame Landenberger for everything since he was already in custody anyway — to come roaring in with a search warrant that far out of their jurisdiction just because of the coincidence. And I imagined that with such flimsy evidence, especially since I didn't have a copy of the film anymore, even the Lake County Sheriff's Department would chortle me right out of their office.

I needed proof. And from where I sat, cell phone in hand in the front seat of my Sunbird, there seemed to be only one place I could get it.

Chapter Twenty-four

It was about a twenty-minute drive from Painesville to Concord and the rural farm site of the sphagnum bog that was home to the largest colony of pink moccasin flowers, or lady's slippers, in Ohio. I hadn't made a copy of the plat map at the hall of records, but I struggled manfully to remember the way as I turned off State Route 44 and started up a hilly country road, passing several houses on either side that, from their style, probably were built back in the 1950s when ranch homes had been all the rage.

About a mile and a half up, the road ended abruptly at a smaller one that ran at a right angle to it. Deep drainage ditches on either side took the place of curbs. I swung the wheel to the right, and within two hundred yards I saw the wooden sign hanging from a crossbeam. It was carved and woodburned and painted with a swooping bald eagle, and it proclaimed that I had found Eagle's Gate Farm.

I turned into the driveway, which gave up all pretense of being anything but a dirt-and-gravel access road, deeply rutted and uneven, and the Sunbird's suspension bounced and groaned. After another fifty yards I came face-to-face with a swinging gate. It was wide and rickety and wooden, made of unfinished logs with a diagonal strip of heavy board like the gate on a corral in an old western movie. Looped around it was a thick leather-covered chain and a padlock it would take an industrial chainsaw to cut through. While it couldn't live up to its name and deny entrance to an eagle — what *was* an eagle's gate, anyway? — it effectively brought my journey to a temporary halt.

I backed up, did a 180 turn, and switched off my engine, deciding to leave the Sunbird there and explore on foot. I realized the car would be conspicuous parked right outside the gate, but less so than if I left it out on the road, which wasn't heavily traveled and had no real room for parking. I did want the nose facing outward, however, in case I would need to beat a hasty retreat.

I collected all the things I thought I would need from the glove compartment and the little storage well in the console — my cell phone, a little 35mm snapshot camera, a microcassette tape recorder so I could make notes hands-free, a pen-sized flashlight, and my Glock 9mm automatic. The camera went around my neck, the recorder into my shirt pocket next to the pen light, the cell phone in the pocket of my jacket, and since I had no shoulder harness with me, I stuck the weapon in the waistband of my slacks, just to the center of my left hipbone.

The gate had been built across the driveway to keep cars out, but there was nothing stopping a pedestrian from simply walking around it. I did so, the ground still wet from the earlier rain and sucking at my shoes. As I moved, I mumbled a running description into the tape recorder in my pocket. I'm not sure why, except that I get a little compulsive when it comes to details.

The road led to a kind of clearing which was obviously used as a parking area, since the tracks of many cars had permanently flattened the vegetation, although there was no vehicle parked anywhere in sight at the moment. From there the roadway narrowed into a gravel path; to the left was a wide meadow of tall wild grasses that hadn't been mowed in a year. In the aftermath of that morning's rain it looked almost silver beneath a sky the color of a pewter plate.

Ahead of me was a barn that must have been new at about the time Archduke Ferdinand was assassinated in Sarajevo to kick off World War One. The wood was rotted and gaping with holes, but there was a lone window that was miraculously intact, though too dirty to look through. I cupped my hands around my eyes and peered through one of the many gaps in the siding; in the waning light of the afternoon I could see a new-looking tractor inside, covered with dust.

Past the barn and up on the side of a hill were several antique hand-harrows, strictly for atmosphere, leaning against four wooden wagon wheels that had become a permanent part of the scenery since shrubs and vines had grown up and curled around their spokes to anchor them to the land.

Carved into the hillside to my right was a concrete bunker that postdated the barn by at least fifty years. I stuck my head inside briefly; picks and shovels and several coils of rope were propped against cement walls glistening with dampness and smelling vaguely of mildew.

Some seventy feet away, a large wooden A-frame cabin had been built into the side of the hill. "Cabin" is probably a misleading description, since it was larger than the houses most Americans live in. I waited, ineffectually hiding behind a tree, but saw no sign of life inside. Then I began approaching it carefully, and described it audibly for my tape recorder as I went.

Almost the entire front wall of the first floor was glass, providing a sweeping vista of a sloping meadow that obviously had been cleared of trees decades earlier but had not been mowed within recent memory; the grass was thigh-high in places. At the bottom of the slope was a large and seemingly impenetrable stand of woods right out of a Robert Frost poem — lovely, dark, and deep.

Looking through the front windows of the house I could see that the first floor was all one huge room — on one side a living space with comfortable, overstuffed couches and chairs, and a small bar in the corner, the other side a sleeping area with a queen-sized bed against a wall that was otherwise all bookcases. Toward the back of the house the room widened out to become a roomy kitchen, in the middle of which was a butcher-block table big enough to play billiards on. A lime-green dimestore coffee mug sat on the table next to a paper napkin; from where I stood I couldn't tell if there was any coffee in it. The refrigerator was stainless steel and industrial-sized, and next to it an opened door revealed a main-floor bathroom.

On the right side of the main floor a wide stairway of dark, rough-hewn oak led up to what appeared to be a spacious loft bedroom. There was no one visible on the first floor, and I couldn't see if anyone was upstairs.

I didn't try the door.

Instead I headed down the slope across the unmowed meadow of high, damp grass. My pant legs were soaked by the time I got to the trees. I moved into the forest along a pathway that had been cleared many years ago, and worn down by the depredations of many shod feet over the past three-quarters of a century. It seemed the logical place to go.

Thirty seconds into the woods and I might just as well have been in some uncharted wilderness. Even if I craned my neck, I could barely see the sky through the thick branches of tall pines, oak trees, and silver maples which in some places were almost a hundred and fifty feet high. Cinnamon ferns waved at me from either side of the crude pathway, which had been covered over in places by rough-hewn wooden planking. It was as quiet as a cathedral in there, save for the ambient rustling of leaves, the buzz of insects, the chirping of frogs, and the occasional swish of underbrush as some tiny unseen wild creature, startled from its sylvan peace by my approach, made haste to get out of the way of my big feet.

Every few seconds I had to stop and fan at my face as gnats and midges dive-bombed my nose, mouth, and ears. Their assault was so relentless that it was almost frightening. I hoped the insects weren't the biting kind, or my face was going to resemble that of a chicken-pox victim by the time I got out of there.

A modest little creek wound along and across the path, meandering into the trees and then reappearing suddenly. In some places the stream was spanned with more wood planks and in others I just had to jump across. Even after the morning's rain the water was only a trickle and barely moving, only deep enough to sustain the mosquitoes and the frogs who love them.

As I moved slowly into the deeper part of the woods, I noticed that at intervals some of the tree trunks had been splashed with bright blue paint, and where the trees were too far from the path, wooden grape stakes similarly painted with blue had been driven into the ground — the modern-day equivalent, I suppose, of Hansel and Gretel's breadcrumbs.

It would be terrifyingly easy to become disoriented, to lose one's sense of direction among those towering trees and never be able to find the way out again. I tried never to stray out of the sight of one of those blue smears. I whispered my notes into my tape recorder now, reluctant to violate the stillness.

Spring that year had been a windy one, and the weather had taken its toll on tree limbs; there were enough of them lying on the ground to start a bonfire that could have kept all of Akron warm for the winter. They were brown-to-black, dead-looking, with jagged edges where they'd broken off their trunks, the heart of the wood shockingly pinkish brown like barely healed wounds.

I pushed farther in along the makeshift path. It was muddy in spots, and I was leaving distinct footprints. I could smell the musty dampness of the moss, the freshness of the wet leaves and pine needles, the sweet decay of felled tree limbs and dead chipmunks and the trickling, nearly still water of the little creek. The wind moaned above me in the tall pines and the insects buzzed in my ears, but otherwise the silence was palpable, a living presence to remind me that I was indeed deep in the woods.

I glanced over my shoulder nervously. I was feeling claustrophobic, as if the forest had closed in around me. The hair on the back of my neck bristled.

I'm not much for psychic, mystical stuff. I have friends who burn green candles for prosperity with every new moon, who live by their astrological charts and their tarot cards and have their auras cleansed regularly. I don't exactly believe in it, but I'm not going to pooh-pooh it, either. And I knew I was very close to something here. I could sense it.

I was in a place of death.

I didn't share that particular feeling with my tape recorder, though; it would have made me feel foolish if I'd listened to it the next day.

After another ten minutes or so, always keeping the blue markers within view, the path took me across the creek again and up around a curve and over a ridge. When I got to the top, I stopped and had to catch my breath. Not from exertion but from the shock of familiarity.

It was the colony of wild lady's slippers, with the wide, spoon-shaped clearing in front of it. Exactly the way I'd seen it in the snuff film on the Web. This was where they'd filmed it, I had no doubt about that. This is where the young woman whose street name might have been Razorblades had given her last performance.

The colony was really a patch rising up out of a mossy bog about forty feet by thirty feet, just off the footpath, with a little printed sign I hadn't noticed in the film, explaining what the flowers were. They were tiny and delicate, ranging in hue from magenta to whitish pink. Their little heads bowed and nodded in the slight breeze, as if they knew it all. They had seen a lot, these little moccasin flowers. Perhaps that was why they blushed pink — in shame and sorrow.

I walked around the little clearing for a while, talking rapidly into the tape recorder. I was trying to get just the right vantage point — bending here, squatting there, searching for the proper perspective. Then, when I thought I was more or less at the same angle from which the murder had been filmed, I uncapped the lens of my camera, raised it to eye level, and snapped off about a dozen different shots.

I found what I thought was the precise spot where Razorblades had died, and squatted down in front of it, trying to avoid either standing on it or touching it. I'd been a cop long enough to know about preserving the integrity of a crime scene. But there was no sign of anything here, although perhaps a police forensic team could find something, some trace, even after a rainstorm and God-only-knew how many days or weeks. I took a few more photographs.

I decided to explore further, with no real idea of what I was looking for. I went past the lady's-slipper colony and headed deeper into the woods, still battling the tiny insects that seemed so drawn to the orifices of my face. About a quarter mile later, I came across a large pond, its surface covered with a greenish algae. Almost in the middle was a natural island on which a few scrub oaks grew. Not much sunlight found its way down here through the nearly solid canopy of trees overhead. I picked up a small stick and tossed it into the water to ascertain its depth. From the splash it made, the pond appeared to be only a few feet deep. Along the edge the grasses were trampled down, as if someone had walked there recently.

Taking a firm sighting on the nearest blue-marked tree, I left the regular path and started walking around the perimeter of the pond. The brackish water hosted a veritable mosquito air force, and they rose up in righteous wrath against me for disturbing their early evening tranquility. After a while I simply stopped swatting at them.

At the far end, the broken stalks of grass seemed to head deeper into a copse of pines. I followed beside it carefully.

About a hundred feet in I found something. The earth had been seriously disturbed here, obviously dug up and then filled in again, with some sticks and old leaves strewn over its top in a halfhearted attempt to make it look like the rest of the forest floor. Scraggly wildflowers grew sparsely in the new dirt, struggling to survive.

A large bird flew overhead with blazing speed, so fast that I almost didn't see it at all. It could have been a hawk on the lookout for an early dinner. It startled me for a moment, and then I relaxed again.

I squatted down, feeling the damp grass hit the back of my thighs, and pushed my fingers into the newly turned dirt, only a little way at first, and then up to the knuckles. The soil was soft, loose.

It could have been a freshly dug grave.

With a timpani banging away inside my chest, I stood up and took some more pictures from every angle until the roll of film was used up. I rewound it quickly, opened the camera's back, removed the canister, and put it in my pocket. Then I started heading back around the edge of the pond, trying not to step on the grasses that had already been mashed down in case they might contain some evidence of the crime the police could find helpful, like shreds of fabric from a woman's clothing, or perhaps even a strand or two of hair.

When I got back to the path I panicked momentarily when I wasn't able to locate a tree trunk with blue paint. Then I spotted one, and experienced another moment of terror when I couldn't remember which way I had come; the side trip around the water's edge had disoriented me a little bit, and I knew if I turned the wrong way I'd only be heading deeper into the wilderness.

The sun was well hidden behind gray clouds, so there was no way to navigate by its position. Even if it had been visible, the chances of much direct sunlight filtering through the heavy canopy of tree branches overhead to the forest floor would have been next to nil.

Then it occurred to me that the footpath, probably blazed many years before by someone in the Shandy family or in their employ, might actually be circular in nature and end up exactly where it started, coming together at the entrance to the meadow below the house. There was no reason, after all, for someone from the farmhouse to want to walk clear to the other side of the woods and whatever might be out there. That made me feel a little better as I made my decision and turned to my right.

As it happened, my sense of direction wasn't as shaky as I thought it might be; in a few minutes I reached the colony of lady's slippers again. I breathed a short sigh of relief and climbed up the curving pathway to the ridge, deadfall tree branches crunching under my shoes. I was heading back to the meadow, the farmhouse, and on to where I'd left my car.

I didn't quite make it.

The slug whizzed past my face close enough to smell it, almost before I heard the report of the revolver. The mind does funny things at times like that, and for a few seconds I didn't even realize I'd been shot at until the bullet tore a big bite out of the silver maple standing just off the pathway and the splinters flew into my cheek. All around me startled birds leapt skyward from their nests, and after the initial flurry of their wings there was dead silence.

I'm not sure whether it was my long-ago military training kicking in or just gut instinct, but I dropped to the ground, taking the impact of the fall on one shoulder and one hip, and rolled off the path and into the trees where I wasn't quite as visible a target. When I stopped rolling, behind a slender sapling that offered virtually no protection, I clawed the Glock out of my waistband and thumbed off the safety.

The shooter was nowhere in sight from where I was lying, but I could see the bluish gray gunsmoke drifting in the still air, down at the bottom of the ridge just off the pathway. Whoever he was, he must have fired once and then taken cover himself. Which told me that he probably knew what he was doing.

My cheek smarted from the splinters, and an uncomfortable thought struck me as I inched forward over the muddy ground, trying to get a look at whoever was trying to wipe me off the board. Property owners don't usually try and kill random trespassers in the middle of the woods — even property owners who might have a body buried somewhere. There are just too many questions that would have to be answered later. So I had to assume that my friend down there in the brush knew exactly at whom he was shooting.

Me.

I inched my way forward along the damp ground in the accepted infantry crawl, fully aware that everything I was wearing would be ruined, and that the camera hanging around my neck was dragging in the mud. Getting killed, however, did not seem an acceptable alternative, so I wriggled my way across six feet of open space, hugging the mud, and positioned myself behind a bigger, thicker tree that would at least stop a bullet. My slacks were torn where my right knee was skinned, and a trickle of warm blood ran down my left cheek. I pulled a few of the larger splinters out of my face with my fingers.

Cautiously I raised myself onto one elbow and stuck my head around the trunk for a peek. The light was beginning to fade quickly in the early moments of the evening, and I still couldn't see anyone. But I could hear him — if indeed it was a male — down at the bottom of the rise, his feet crunching on twigs and branches and the dried leaves of many autumns.

Movement caught my eye, and through the dense forest I could see him now, moving around trying to get into a better position for a shot. He was wearing sensibly dark clothing, pants and shirt and jacket, while I positively glowed in my goddamned cantaloupe shirt.

I raised the Glock, lined up the sights, and squeezed off a shot, and the dark figure hurled himself to one side and down onto the ground. I wasn't sure whether or not I'd hit him, but I didn't think so. He didn't make a sound, and there aren't too many people who can take a bullet silently.

He returned fire in my general direction, too close for comfort, and I tried to make myself small behind the thick tree trunk. The thought struck me that he might not be alone, and I turned around as fast as I could to make sure no one else was sneaking up behind me.

But I realized that didn't make much sense. To my rear was the deepest part of the woods, and someone would have had to make a lot of noise and gone to a lot of trouble to go past me in order to then turn

473

around and box me in. Besides, as I was making my way carefully around the edge of the pond earlier, I would have been a perfect and unknowing target.

I gritted my teeth, determined not to wind up occupying another unmarked grave beyond that pond. I peered around the tree, looking at where I'd last seen the shooter. He was still flat on the ground, but moving, and I was fairly certain he hadn't been hit.

In that case, my staying in one spot was as good as waving a red flag at him. I knew I had to change position and keep him guessing. I gathered my legs under me and lunged, keeping low, sprinting about seven feet to the next tree. He saw me and snapped off two quick shots that whizzed over my head. Good, I thought. I only had what ammo was left in the clip, and I didn't know how much extra he had, but it would be nice and convenient if he were to run out of bullets before I did.

I had one slight advantage over him, and that was that I was on higher ground than he; anyone who's ever been in the military can tell you that it's a lot easier to defend a hill than a gully. I had a better angle to see him, too, and he knew it, because after firing he scrambled away, finding shelter behind his own copse of trees before I could set up for another shot.

The light was going fast — in northeast Ohio, when daytime decides it has finally had enough, it wastes no time on long good-byes — and the thought of dueling him in darkness was unsettling, because he probably knew the terrain far better than I did. And even if I survived him, trying to find my way out of these woods in the dark with only a small flashlight wasn't a prospect I relished, either. It was tough enough walking around in there in the daytime.

Through the spindly trees I could see him dimly. He was moving to his right, and I sent a 9mm bullet in his direction. It missed him again, but I heard it playing havoc with the tree branches. Once more he threw himself flat on the ground and out of my sight.

I decided to move again, taking advantage of his momentarily prone position. I straightened up and began to run. But he recovered more quickly than I'd imagined he could, and the proximity of his next shot — it passed by within inches of the back of my neck — made me stumble involuntarily. My left ankle turned beneath me in the mud, sending white pain shooting clear up to my knee, and I lost my balance completely, hitting the ground and tumbling from the top of the ridge downward, rolling and sliding for a good thirty feet over sharp sticks and rocks and brambles, and finally coming to rest with a bump at the base of a gnarled old oak near the bottom of the hill.

The fall had knocked the breath out of me, and my ankle felt as though it were being microwaved. I was now bleeding from too many minor cuts and scrapes to count. Worst of all, though, was the realization that sometime during the quick trip down the hill, I had lost my weapon. I could see it in the half-light, about fifteen feet away from me, and in order to retrieve it I would have to expose myself to his fire. I wouldn't last half the distance.

I scrambled around behind the tree, which didn't offer much in the way of a shield, and tried to catch my breath. But now I was glad for the waning light; maybe he wouldn't be able to see me.

For several minutes the woods were still and hushed. There was only the wind moaning in the highest branches of the trees. The day creatures had gone home until morning; the night roamers hadn't come out yet; and the in-betweeners were laying low because of the shooting.

Except the bats. They were sending out their advance scouts in the gathering dusk — out of the corners of my eyes I could see them swooping, just a scattered few at first; in five more minutes there would be thousands of them.

And then I heard him. Walking.

Slowly and cautiously — he didn't know exactly where I was, or even if I was still alive. But I'm sure he didn't want any surprises. So the footsteps were measured, careful.

And coming toward my tree.

Blinking my eyelids rapidly to discourage the swarming gnats, I felt around on the ground for some sort of weapon, my fingers finally closing around a stick about three feet long, a medium-sized limb that had broken off, jagged, and fallen from the tree directly above me. It wasn't much, only a little thicker than the skinny end of a baseball bat. If I hit him right in the head with it, it would serve only to seriously annoy him. But it was all I had.

His footsteps were growing a little more bold, whoever he was. He must have thought his last shot had nailed me. He was getting very close now — just on the other side of the tree. I could even hear his breathing.

I got to one knee carefully, trying not to make a sound, my good foot supporting my weight. As he passed by the tree I lunged forward, using my stick as a club, going for the hand in which he held the gun.

The wood cracked onto his wrist, splintering in half from the impact and driving his hand down against the side of his leg. Then I pushed off on my good leg and drove the stick upwards toward his midsection, using the sharp end like a spear.

The revolver slipped through his suddenly numb fingers and landed on the carpeting of fallen leaves on the ground. Instinct made him rear back and lift one leg to protect himself. It probably saved his life, because instead of finding his stomach, the wicked point of the stick drove deep into the inner part of his thigh. He screamed, the sound eerie and hollow in the silent woods. I stood up, yanking the point of the stick upward, and he fell onto his back, his arms crossed over his face.

My sprained ankle protested silently as I jerked the crude spear out of his thigh and poised it over his throat, my foot pushing down on his chest.

That's when I recognized Lloyd Severson.

To give him his due, I have to say that he didn't look particularly frightened with the jagged point just inches from his throat. He simply looked up at me through eyes slitted from pain, his face gray as the sky and losing color just as quickly. He seemed calm, and more than a little disgusted with himself. This was the second time I'd bested him.

"Hello, Lloyd. We meet again."

He didn't answer. I remembered from our first meeting that he wasn't much of a conversationalist, but even the most voluble of souls probably wouldn't be in the mood for small talk with blood pumping out of a jagged hole in his leg.

"Anyone else out here with you?"

He shook his head.

"You sure?"

His breathing was ragged and he tried to croak through it. "I'm sure, okay? You going to put that thing in my neck?"

"I'm thinking about it."

He closed his eyes and then opened them again.

"Unless we can make a deal," I said.

"I got nothing to deal with."

"Sure you do. You can talk to me. It's

lonely out here in the woods — nobody to talk to except you. And the bats." I looked up into the trees, barely able to see the flickering dark shapes as they swooped from their daytime resting places. "It's getting close to their time to go night-clubbing. But they won't talk to me, Lloyd, and I like being talked to."

"Whatever," he said.

I took the stick away from his neck, bent down and picked up his revolver. It was a snub-nosed Smith & Wesson .357 Magnum, not unlike the one I kept in my office, only with a shorter barrel. It had every bit as much stopping power, though. I tossed the stick away, held the gun loosely in my right hand, and knelt to look at the hole in his thigh. It was rhythmically pumping out gouts of blood.

"I'm going to press my finger here, Lloyd," I said. "And it's going to hurt like hell. But if I don't, you're going to bleed to death."

"That bad?"

"Look at the color of the blood. Bright red. Look at how it's spurting. That's an artery, big guy. The femoral artery."

His head lolled to one side. "Jeez," he said softly.

I ripped the hole in his pants open wider

and fumbled around inside, finally pressing my finger just above the wound where it would do the most good, and he arched his back in pain. In another minute he wouldn't feel it anymore.

"So talk to me," I said.

He didn't; he just cocked an eyebrow.

"I know all about the Web-site snuff film, Lloyd. I even recognized you there at the end. I want to know everything. Who set it up, who filmed it, who the girl was — the whole megillah. And you're going to tell me all about who killed Ellen Carnine, too."

"Fuck you," he said. "Shoot me."

"That'd be a waste of a bullet. I don't have to shoot you. All I have to do is take my finger off your leg and leave."

He blinked.

"You'll bleed to death," I said. "Slowly. If you try to walk out of here, which would take you at least ten minutes even on a good leg, it'll make you bleed faster. So you'll have plenty of time to think about it."

His tongue came out to bathe his parched lips.

"And when you finally collapse from loss of blood, you'll be able to talk to the bats while you're dying. They can smell it.

They'll all be down here about five seconds after I walk away. Listen to them," I said, cocking an ear. "Listen to their wings humming, Lloyd. They like the taste of blood."

His body jerked as if from an electric shock. He groaned, his eyes rolling back in his head so I could see the whites.

"Imagine those little teeth in your neck, Lloyd — imagine those sticky wings on your face. They're rodents, did you know that? They're little flying rats."

His mouth hung slack, his eyes were glazing. I could feel his blood pumping against my finger. "Well, I can't stay here all night, Lloyd. So I'll just take off. Okay?"

His fingers closed around my wrist. "Wait," he said, the word squeezing out from the deepest part of wherever his fear lived. "What do you want?"

" 'All the news that's fit to print,' Lloyd. Tell me and I'll keep my finger here so you won't bleed to death, and then afterward I'll use the cell phone in my pocket to call for help. Otherwise, I'll say good-bye right now and you can lie here and wait for the bats. And the rats. And the bugs — flies laying eggs in you that will turn into maggots. Maybe even a lynx or a coyote. But for sure the bats." I smiled benevolently down at him. "Your call."

It should be pointed out here that I have an advanced college degree, and that I'm perfectly aware that bats are helpful little creatures who are the innocent victims of media hype and horror movies. I know they subsist on insects, and that without bats we'd all be dealing with more mosquitoes and flies than we could handle. I also know bats don't drink human blood, they can't be chased away with the wave of a crucifix, nor do they turn into Bela Lugosi when the sun goes down.

I was, however, gambling that Lloyd Severson's only knowledge of the flying mammals of the order *Chiroptera* had come from watching Dracula movies, and that he didn't know what I knew.

My gamble paid off. I switched on my tape recorder again and Severson began spilling his guts. At that point I don't think he cared how much he revealed to me, even that which might incriminate him.

As long as I was there to keep the bats away.

Chapter Twenty-five

After I called both of them on my cell phone — the damn things *are* handy to have around in emergencies, despite my reservations — the ambulance arrived at the same time the Lake County sheriff's deputy did. It's a good thing, too; my hand was getting numb pressing on Lloyd Severson's femoral artery to keep him from bleeding to death.

The deputy sheriff, whose name was Art Chapman, had lots of questions to ask me, of course. It was full dark now, the ghost of a moon trying unsuccessfully to shine through the clouds, and we sat in his cruiser just outside the farmhouse at Eagle's Gate for more than an hour, talking things over, while the paramedics whisked Severson off to the emergency room.

When we first started talking, I'd told Chapman to call Florence McHargue at the Cleveland PD for the background — and for her assurance that I was more or less legitimate, because he wasn't any more fond of private investigators than she was.

She wasn't at the office, of course, but they'd managed to find her at home, and she and Bob Matusen arrived in an unmarked car an hour later, just as Chapman and I had finished our conversation.

When she first saw me, McHargue didn't say anything, but her piercing gaze, even through the blue-tinted glasses, could have carved her initials on my chest in letters of fire. Finally she came over to me, one fist on her hip.

"Hot-looking shirt, Jacovich," she sneered. "What do they call that color? Pumpkin?"

"Cantaloupe."

She closed her eyes in dismay. "Aw. That's cute as a button. Don't go anywhere."

She and Matusen took Chapman off to one side and conferred with him in whispers; occasionally one of them would look over at me. In the rush to get Lloyd Severson to a trauma center, in the excitement of a shooting and a probable murder in the rural area that, despite a high-profile mass killing in nearby Kirtland several years ago, was normally quiet and bucolic, nobody seemed to care that I was bleeding in several places, most notably my cheek, and that I could barely walk on an ankle that had swollen significantly in the last two hours. I asked one of the ambulance cowboys to take a look, and he took the larger wood chips out of my face with tweezers and gave me an ice pack to hold on my ankle. That was all. I guess they figured no one ever died from a sprain or from splinters.

Finally McHargue and Matusen finished with Deputy Chapman and came back over to me. "Give me your keys, Milan," Matusen ordered. "The lieutenant wants me to drive your car back to Cleveland, and you'll ride in with her."

"Am I under arrest?"

McHargue stifled an irritated sigh. "If you were under arrest you'd be cuffed by now, Jacovich. But I want to hear the whole story firsthand. That is, if that's convenient for you."

"I'm feeling kind of beat-up, Lieutenant," I said. "Can't it wait until morning?"

"No it can't," she said ominously. Then she added, " 'Lucy, you got a lot of 'splainin' to do'."

I couldn't decide whether to be annoyed at having to tell the story all over again or to be amazed that, for the first time since I'd met her, Florence McHargue was showing some slight evidence of having a sense of humor.

I limped over to her car and slid into the passenger seat, my ankle pounding and the various scrapes and cuts all over my body feeling like hell. The hour being late, she'd brought her personal car instead of a departmental vehicle, and I was glad of that. The inside of a cop car always smells like tobacco smoke and perspiration; McHargue was a fervent anti-smoker, and I don't think she'd ever broken a sweat in her life.

She put it in gear and we bounced over the access road. "Talk to me," she said. "Tell me why you're out in the boondocks stabbing people with sharp sticks."

I gave it to her from the beginning — how I'd traced the lady's slippers and then found out the farm belonged to Redmond Munch. How I'd gone out there to take a look around, something the Cleveland police would not have legally been able to do on little more than a hunch. How I'd found what I firmly believed to be an unmarked grave near the pond. And how Lloyd Severson had stalked me through the woods.

"He said he was staying out there at the farmhouse," I said. "They'll find his clothes and stuff in the upstairs loft, I imagine. He'd gone out to get some beer, and when he came back he saw my car parked outside the gate."

"Wasn't too swift of you to leave it there."

"Where should I have parked it clear out in the middle of nowhere? In a six-level garage?"

"All right, all right," she said. "So what did you do to him to make him talk? A confession isn't worth a bag of dog dirt if it was obtained through coercion. You know that."

"I didn't coerce him, exactly."

"What did you do, then," she said. *"Exactly."*

"I just told him I was going to leave him bleeding in the woods so the bats would get him."

"Bats?" She threw me a sidelong glance of disgust. "Bats don't eat people, Jacovich. And they don't suck their blood, either."

"Isn't it lucky Severson didn't know that, then?"

She shook her head. "So what did he say?"

"I told Deputy Chapman everything there was to tell."

"Goodie. Now that you've rehearsed it

so nicely, you can tell me."

I took the recorder out of my pocket. "It's all here on tape," I said. "The whole story."

She took one hand off the wheel and plucked it from my hand. "Thanks for the recorder," she said. "It's now official police evidence. But a taped confession isn't admissible in a court of law. And you damn well know it."

"Then ask Severson again when he's feeling better."

She set her mouth in a rainbow arch. "He might not be so cooperative when he isn't scared out of his pants that a vampire's going to suck his neck."

"Maybe not," I said. "But at least you've got a place to start."

She looked at the recorder and then slipped it into the pocket of her jacket. "Just give me the Cliff's Notes, all right?"

"Sure," I said, "if you'll remember that I heard all of this while I was trying to keep a man from bleeding to death with my thumb."

She nodded.

"According to Severson, Red Munch was the driving force behind the snuff Website idea, and the moneyman as well. He got John Vargas to arrange for the actors, if that's what you want to call them."

"When was this?"

"Severson said about six weeks ago. And he said that Munch paid him five hundred bucks to strangle the girl at the end of the film."

"That didn't bother Severson?"

"I asked him that," I said. "He told me it was just a job."

"A real sweetheart. And then they buried her out by the pond?"

"That's what Severson said, yes. I guess the Lake County guys will dig her up in the morning." A chill made me shudder. I had been gingerly massaging my ankle with the ice pack while we talked, but it wasn't the cold that was giving me the shivers.

"Who were the people in the film?"

"Severson didn't know, other than that the boy was some street hustler Vargas found. He said the kid knew he was going to do a porno flick but he didn't know what was going to happen afterwards, and was scared to death. He thinks Vargas cleaned him sometime later, but he's not sure about that."

She slipped a finger under her glasses and rubbed her eye. "Either way, he's probably long gone from the neighborhood. What about the girl?"

"He said she was one of Vargas's hookers, a cokehead. I don't know who she was, really, but I think her street name was Razorblades."

"*You* think?"

I told her about Snowy.

"You have interesting friends, Jacovich." She shook her head. "But you're telling me about two homicides that are Lake County's business. I want to know about Ellen Carnine."

"Severson didn't know much background on that, but he said he thought Ellen had accidentally found out about the Web site, and Munch had wanted her disposed of, too, before she could blow the whistle on all of them."

"Who actually did it? Did Carnine, I mean."

"Severson and Vargas did the hands-on stuff, but Munch went with them to kind of direct the operation — he figured she wouldn't open her door to two strange men in the middle of the night, but she'd let her boss in."

"Even at that hour?"

"If your boss, if the safety director or the mayor, rang your doorbell at four o'clock in the morning, would you tell

491

him to hit the bricks?"

She mulled over that unlikely posit for a few seconds, then nodded. "Point taken," she said. "What happened?"

"Vargas hit her on the head as soon as she opened the door. Then he drove her out onto the bridge, Severson tagged along in her car and parked it in the lot to make it look like a suicide, and the two of them dropped her over the side. They figured she'd be so busted up by the fall that the coroner probably couldn't separate the blunt trauma to her head from the rest of her injuries."

"This is all on the tape?" she said.

"All of it."

"You sure?"

"I just put in new batteries last week, Lieutenant."

"You're a marvel of efficiency. So where was Redmond Munch when all this was going on with Carnine?"

"He went home," I said.

"And what about Landenberger?"

I shook my head. "Severson doesn't even know the name. From what he said, it was Munch's deal from the beginning." She looked as if she didn't believe me. "Why would Severson spill his guts about everything else and lie about that?"

"Why indeed?" For a few minutes we drove silently, now on Interstate 90, heading for downtown. Then McHargue said, "Something else here that doesn't compute, Jacovich."

"What's that?"

"Severson and Vargas coming to your office to try and bribe you off the Carnine investigation, and then rough you up when that didn't work. That was just plain stupid. And Munch didn't strike me as a stupid man."

"I asked Severson about that. He said it was Vargas's idea, that Munch didn't even know about it. And I guess he hit the ceiling when he found out."

She smiled, but there wasn't much mirth in it. "That's what happens when you hang around with small-time crooks. Small-time crooks are all dumb by definition — otherwise they'd be big-time crooks."

"You think this snuff film business was small-time?"

"Hardly. Do the math. Munch was probably charging his subscribers somewhere around ten thousand dollars a pop to be a 'member' of that site. That means all he needed was a hundred members to gross a million bucks. And my guess is that he had a hell of a lot more than a hundred rich sickos." She allowed herself a small but wicked grin. "The nice thing about the Internet is that you can't do a damn thing without leaving tracks. Electronic footprints. The FBI is going to be able to trace every damn one of those perverts once they put their minds to it."

"I'm glad to hear that," I said.

"I learned more in four years in Sex Crimes than I ever wanted to know. And I never got used to the fact that sex, which can be such a beautiful thing, such a spiritual, or just plain *fun* thing — can also turn so dark and so ugly and so evil. I think that anything two consenting adults — or more — want to do in the privacy of their own homes is okay. Whatever floats your boat, I guess, even though I find some of it really disgusting. But consenting and adults are the key words here — and that's where rape and pedophilia and the terrible shit that was on that film crosses over the line. Way over."

I knew what she meant. My excursion into cyberspace had opened my eyes to some things I didn't even want to think about. I decided to change the subject.

"So you think the petty criminals are dumb but the big-time crooks are smart, huh?"

"They're smart, all right," McHargue said. "But eventually they screw up. Everybody makes mistakes, even the smart ones. And that's my job, to catch them when they do." She turned her head and glanced over at me briefly before returning her eyes to the highway. "My job, Jacovich. Not yours."

I squirmed in the seat. "I was kind of hoping that what I did today would earn me a few gold stars in your book, Lieutenant. But I guess not."

"I only give out gold stars for perfect attendance," she snorted. "Here's the thing, now. By tomorrow morning both Red Munch and John Vargas are going to be in custody, and if Severson's story checks out, Barnard Landenberger is going to walk away a free man. So it'd be easy to say that results are what count. But the fact is, I'd like to break your goddamn neck for going out to that farm today. I told you to stay away from this case and you blew me off. I don't like that."

"I'm working for Tom Vangelis," I said, "on behalf of Barnard Landenberger. I had every right to pursue that investigation to the best of my ability."

"And make the police department look like shit in the process."

"I think if you check your messages, you'll find that I called your office before I ever went out to Eagle's Gate Farm, but you'd already left for the day. I even called Bob Matusen at home — you can ask his wife."

"You couldn't have talked to the officer on duty?"

"And told him what? That I found out a certain kind of wildflower was growing on a farm owned by Red Munch that might be connected to the murder of a young hooker who was killed in another county, and to please send out the SWATs and a forensic team? Give me a break, okay?"

She didn't answer me.

"Nobody was trying to do an end run on you," I went on. "And I sure as hell wasn't trying to make your department look bad; I owe Marko Meglich's memory too much to do that."

For about half a minute the only sound was the hiss of the tires on the damp pavement. Then she said, "You and Meglich were tight."

"Since the fifth grade."

"And he bought it because he was doing something that was none of his business — covering your ass on a murder that took place in another country."

I stared out the window; it hadn't started raining again, but there was a heavy mist in the air from the lake just to our right, and McHargue's headlights turned it into little diamond pinpricks. We were on the Bratenahl curve now, heading for downtown. "Lieutenant, do you think I don't remember that every fucking day of my life?"

"Maybe you ought to stop remembering it so often," she said. "I think you know that Meglich had a thing about justice, about what was right and what wasn't. That's why he became a cop. And he was a damn good one, too. A little too slick, maybe. A little too social, a little too much of a politician for my personal taste. And he ran around with women who were too young to know who Sting is, for God's sake. But a righteous cop all the way."

It was as good a summing-up of Marko Meglich as I'd ever heard.

"And he went by the book. Always. That's how it's done. You're not a by-the-book kind of man, Jacovich. You're a by-the-seat-of-your-pants guy. It's a good thing you turned in your service revolver and ankled the department when you did, because eventually you would have stepped knee-deep in dog poop." She took a deep breath and let it out slowly. "That's fine for you, but not for anyone wearing a badge. The first time Meglich forgot about the book, he took a bullet."

The lighted towers of the downtown skyline were visible through the mist now, and I always felt a strange little flip in my stomach when I looked at them. Cleveland was my town, from birth. It had also been Marko's.

McHargue went on. "I'm by-the-book, too. As you might have figured out by now. I believe in the system. I've got to, otherwise I couldn't function. And that's our problem, you and me. It's nothing personal between us, but ever since I took over Homicide after Meglich died, you've been nothing to me but a boil on the ass."

I started to say something, but she put up a hand. "I know, you helped us out on a couple of things this past year, and frankly I'm grateful to you. But that still doesn't make it right. You're a P.I. — you have no official status, and you have no business poking around in capital cases."

"I was just doing what I was hired to do, Lieutenant. What I'm licensed to do. You have your job and I have mine. Sometimes they dovetail, which is great, and sometimes they get us locking horns."

"Uh-huh," she said. "Well, while you're

doing your job, maybe you ought to think about Redmond Munch not having the passwords to Wheetek's Web sites. Now, how do you suppose he got them?"

Chapter Twenty-six

I didn't get out of Florence McHargue's office until two o'clock in the morning. She'd made me listen to the audiotape I'd made with Severson twice, stopping every so often to ask me a direct question. I hate hearing myself on tape; I have a very low, deep voice, and on a recording I sound like an obscene phone call.

She and Bob Matusen grilled me for another hour, after which they invited the local FBI agent who'd been assigned the snuff-film case to grill me some more. In case you were wondering, even after midnight FBI agents never go outside without wearing slim, form-hugging suits and blindingly white and impeccably starched shirts.

By the time they shoved a typed version of my statement under my nose two hours later, I would have signed damn near anything just so I could go home to bed.

Matusen had parked my car in the employee lot behind the main building. I crawled into it like a groundhog returning to his safe warm burrow and sat there for a while, hunched up, aching and exhausted. When I started home, I was glad it was my left ankle that was damaged and not my right, or I wouldn't have been able to drive at all.

Once inside my apartment I stripped off my clothes; there were rents and tears in everything. I wadded the whole mess up and put it in the trash. Slacks were slacks, so I didn't care that much, and the blue corduroy jacket had seen better days so I took only a moment to mourn it. And I was glad to be rid of that damned cantaloupe-colored shirt anyway.

All I wanted to do was to get to sleep, but I was filthy from rolling around in the woods, and although I'd attempted to wash it off at the police station there were still traces of Lloyd Severson's blood on my hands and under my fingernails. So I got into the shower, as hot as I could stand it, and tried to feel better. Both knees and one elbow were skinned like those of a little kid who'd tumbled off his roller skates, and the water made my other various cuts and scrapes sting like hell.

After I toweled off, I regarded my face in the bathroom mirror. The places where the wood splinters had cut my cheek were red and angry-looking, and I was afraid they'd become infected. The antiseptic I splashed on them almost sent me through the ceiling.

I sighed. It would probably be a good idea to see my doctor, Ben Sorkin, sometime during the next day. He'd minister to my cuts and abrasions, do something about my ankle, give me some pain pills, and then lecture me the way he always does. Ben has been my friend since college and my primary-care doctor for the past sixteen years, and he's fond of telling me I'm getting too old to live the kind of lifestyle that puts me in jeopardy so often.

The trouble is, I don't know what else I could do to make a living. I hardly think the hiring bosses in today's corporate world would be impressed with my twenty-year-old business degree. Or with my years of experience in making sure company employees weren't stealing paper clips, spying on insurance cheaters, and occasionally bringing down a killer.

Besides, I like my autonomy, my independence. Except for my football years I never have played well with others.

Of course, that independence had gotten me shot at out at Eagle's Gate Farm. It wasn't the first time. I can't count how many bullets have come close, but I remember both of the ones that hit me — one through the pectoral muscle in a crack house off East 105th Street, and once, embarrassingly enough, right in the buttocks. If I ever run into a bad guy who can shoot straight, I'm in trouble.

I downloaded more Tylenol than I should have and dropped into bed like a redwood falling in the forest. The last thing I remember before sinking into a fitful sleep was dreaming about the stink of cordite in my nostrils.

I didn't set the alarm for morning, so I slept in, figuring I deserved it. When I finally awoke at about nine o'clock, I staggered around the apartment, took some more Tylenol, made a pot of coffee I didn't feel like drinking, and called Ben Sorkin for an appointment. After making the usual mother-hen noises at me for risking my neck again, he said he could take me at noon.

Then I put in a call to Tom Vangelis, who is probably the only big-shot lawyer in America who doesn't put callers on hold for ten minutes. I reported the events of the previous evening, and he sounded so pleased I was sure that in the privacy of his office he was actually licking his chops.

It was ten o'clock, and I didn't see much point in going to work before seeing Ben, so I lurched into the den and switched on the TV set. Not much to look at: Regis without Kathie Lee, talk shows, game shows, cooking shows, and syndicated reruns of *Matlock*, which has become the most inescapable nonprime-time television presence since *M*A*S*H*. Force someone to watch morning television for a month and you've probably created a lifetime book-reader.

I went out to Ben Sorkin's office in Beachwood, got some smaller and heretofore-overlooked splinters and gravel tweezed out of my face and knees, received a tetanus shot, had my temperature and blood pressure taken just for the fun of it, listened to my expected scolding, and walked out of there with a small bandage on my face and laden down with enough physician's samples of antiseptic and infection-killing ointments and salves to minister to a battalion of combat infantrymen.

The rumbling in my stomach made me realize that I had eaten neither dinner the night before nor breakfast that morning, so I stopped and had a late lunch at a place on Bellflower, a carriage house–turned–

504

restaurant in University Circle imaginatively named That Place on Bellflower. It's right in the middle of the Case Western Reserve campus and very close to the Cleveland Museum of Art and to Severance Hall, the home of the Cleveland Orchestra. I was pretty sure I was the only one in the dining room who'd spent the previous evening dodging bullets.

When I finally got to my office, I had to type up two separate reports on the same case, for two different clients. The one that was going to Tom Vangelis on behalf of Barnard Landenberger was going to make both of them happy. The one for Dr. and Mrs. William Carnine was going to bring no joy at all, and I realized that no matter how my investigation had come out, it was no substitute for their lost child. It was a melancholy chore, and so I saved it for last.

Just as I was finishing up the report for Vangelis, the phone trilled at my elbow. It was Bob Matusen.

"You get any sleep, Milan?" he wanted to know.

"Damn little. How about you?"

"Hey, I'm a public servant; losing sleep comes with the job. I just thought you might want to know how things are shaking out around here."

"I'm very anxious to hear, Bob."

"The Lake County guys did find a woman's body buried behind that pond," he said. "They're looking around the entire property to see if they can find any more unmarked graves."

I fumbled for a Winston. "What about Lloyd Severson?"

"Oh, he's gonna make it, thanks to the Red Cross blood bank. You did quite a job on him with that sharp stick."

"I'm a throwback to my Jurassic Age ancestors who used to hunt woolly mammoths with spears," I said.

"They had woolly mammoths in prehistoric Slovenia?"

"Sure, right along with caveman polka bands."

"Well, the docs said you saved his life, anyway. He would've bled to death in fifteen minutes without you."

"If he hadn't been able to tell me what I wanted to know, I would've let him."

"Sure," Matusen said. "Tough guy."

"Exactly."

"Yeah, right." I heard him take a gulp of something, probably bad station-house coffee. "Okay, the other thing is, we picked up both Red Munch and John Vargas in the middle of the night. Vargas was in bed with two of his underage whores when we broke down his apartment door."

"Was one of them called Snowy?"

"They both could've been called Snowy, I guess. Both of them cokeheads. But the names they gave us were Lanetta Atkins and Simone . . ." I heard him rattling papers. "Simone Thorne."

I wondered if Snowy used to be Simone Thorne. When she was a little girl. Before her compelling addiction to white powder had turned her into the casual and paid-for bride of a thousand strangers. "Where are they now, Bob?"

"We had nothing to hold them on, so we cut them loose." He chuckled mean-spiritedly. "The FBI guy who was with us was actually shocked. At the three-way sex act, I mean."

"Fibbies shock easily, I guess."

"Munch is fessing up to running the Web site but he says he didn't know anything about producing the snuff film. He swears he thought he was buying them from South America somewhere."

"My ass," I said.

"That's what the FBI agent said, too. Actually he said, 'Like Hell.' I don't think they like FBI people to cuss."

"What about John Vargas?"

"Nothing but name, rank, and serial number. He's stonewalling all the way until he can get hooked up with a good lawyer. Hey, he knows better than to run his mouth off. He's a career criminal, don't forget."

"I'll bet if you lean on the Grosse Pointe cops hard enough you'll find he knew Rita Sadwith, and probably killed her for her credit card."

"We're on that, Milan. Severson doesn't know anything about that one, but he's lying there in that hospital bed, handcuffed to the rail and singing like Whitney Houston about everything else, including Ellen Carnine. I think even without the Sadwith thing we've got a righteous case against Vargas. And Munch, too."

"That'll help in the final reports I'm writing for my clients," I said. "I appreciate your letting me know."

"Lieutenant McHargue told me not to tell you."

"It's our secret, then, Bob."

He sounded more than a little relieved. "Uh, I don't know how this is all gonna end up, but I imagine the feds and both Lake and Cuyahoga Counties are gonna want a piece of it. It's gonna be pretty high profile once the newspapers and TV get their hands on it, and there are three young prosecutors out there probably thinking this one is gonna make their political bones. Are you willing to testify in court if they want you to?"

"Sure."

"It may be more than once or even twice."

"That's okay," I said, puffing angrily on the cigarette. "I just want all three of those bastards either fried or put away for good."

"Yeah." He paused long enough for me to grow several years older. "Hey, listen, Milan, just between us — thanks. Okay?"

"For what?"

"If it wasn't for you and that clean-feet business, we would've marked Ellen Carnine a Dutch act and put the file in a drawer. And then we never would've known about Eagle's Gate Farm."

"So now McHargue and I are best buds, huh?"

"You would be if you was still a cop," he said.

"Bob, I heard that song at least once a month for eighteen years from Marko Meglich. Don't you start in on me now. Besides, I'm in my forties. I'm a little bit too old to start over again, going through the academy and then spending the rest of my life chasing bad guys on the street. My doctor told me that this morning. 'Act your age,' is what he said."

"Yeah, well. You should always listen to your doctor."

There wasn't much more to talk about after that. As soon as I hung up, I revised the report to Vangelis, finished it up, and printed out four hard copies of it — two for my files and two for Vangelis, one of which I was sure he'd give to Landenberger. The report I'd send to William Carnine would be essentially the same but without the grisly details of his daughter's death. It was depressing enough a task as it was, and while I was sure it would give him the answer he had so desperately sought, it would bring him only cold comfort.

I thought of all the people I'd met, who had been directly or indirectly involved with Ellen Carnine and touched by Redmond Munch's greed. Ellen's family, of course. Her friends — Anna Zarafonitos, Bronwyn Rhys, Sarah Donnem, and Karen Conley. Her first lover, the coed-fancying Richard Goodman. Her roommate, Duane Starrett. Vargas and Severson, who had dropped her off a bridge. Barnard Landenberger, of course, and all her other co-workers. And even those two sad little men who had fantasized about her over their computers, Stanley Bream and Don Cannon. Not to mention Snowy. And Razorblades. And whoever the young man in the video was — wherever he was.

This had been an ugly case, right from the beginning. A case in which human life was deemed less valuable than a couple of bucks and the perverse entertainment of a bunch of computer-geek sickos. A case in which nobody's moral compass seemed to point to true north. I was glad to be seeing the end of it.

I opened my drawer to get my little magnetic plastic cube of paper clips for the reports. When I looked down, I happened to notice the CD-ROM disk Taffy Kiser had left with me — the one that could find secret passwords on computers.

And I realized with a start that the Ellen Carnine murder case wasn't quite finished after all.

Chapter Twenty-seven

The apartment building was in the farthest corner of the Warehouse District. It was the last one before the lake, but that didn't mean it had a lake view. A sprawling gated parking lot, the concrete sides of the Shoreway, and the new Cleveland Browns Stadium were in the way. It was also the last one before the topography of the level downtown area fell off abruptly down a steep hill and into the Flats. Not the gritty, industrial part of the Flats where my office was, but the section where side by side chain restaurants, self-consciously sleazy saloons and dance clubs for the young and not-very-discerning hugged both banks of the Cuyahoga River until it snaked its way under the railroad trestle and widened out to drain Lake Erie.

It probably hadn't always been an apartment building, but was rehabbed from some sort of industrial use about ten years ago like so many other old structures in the neighborhood. Of late, Cleveland has taken the high road and preserved and converted its nearly century-old edifices instead of simply tearing them down to build glass boxes, as so many other cities have.

Not that this building was architecturally distinguished. Probably even more off the beaten path when it had been built in the 1920s than it was now, it had simply been thrown up for its utilitarian value. I doubt the original builders had ever envisioned it as a warrenlike multiple dwelling for up-scale Gen-Xers with Volvos.

The car I was looking for wasn't in the lot when I drove up in the seven-o'clock twilight of a spring evening. I parked at the curb — this must be the only street down-town where free curbside parking is readily available — and then walked a block to a little bar that looked and smelled like a sailor's tavern on the Marseilles water-front, where I smoked three cigarettes, had a beer, and ate a hot turkey sandwich with french fries.

When I got back to my car, night had fully arrived and was settled in. But the gated parking lot next to the apartment building was brightly lit for safety's sake — in that remote neighborhood there was probably no such thing as too much secu-rity — but the car I sought was still among the missing.

I settled into my front seat and rolled the windows down. It was chilly there so close to the lake, but I thought I might be in for a long haul and I needed the fresh air, especially if I was going to smoke. And I certainly was. I always did when on a surveillance; it was the only thing that alleviated the almost excruciating boredom of hunkering down in a car seat to wait God-knows-how-long for something that might or might not happen.

This particular stakeout was creeping toward its third hour when finally, mercifully, I saw a white Mercedes-Benz roll up to the parking lot entrance, positively glowing under the arc lights. The driver slipped a card-key into the slot, the gate opened, and the big car rolled slowly down a wide aisle until it found its assigned berth against the side wall of the building.

I waited until Anna Zarafonitos had come out the wrought-iron gate and was tapping her high heels over the sidewalk toward the front door before I got out of my car, tossed what must have been my tenth cigarette of the evening away and crossed the street to intercept her.

"Milan," she said, and treated me to one of her patented seductive smiles. She showed no surprise, playing it with her

514

usual cool, smiling and flirting. But I had caught the momentary flicker of panic in those big green eyes when she'd first caught sight of me. It could have been the startled reaction of a lone woman being quickly approached by a large man on such a quiet street, but I didn't think so.

"Hello, Anna," I said.

"I imagine you didn't just happen to be passing by in this neighborhood," she said, "so I assume you're here to see me."

"Bingo."

"Well, look," she said, and she put her long-nailed hand on my arm. "I'm sure you've heard what's happening with Red. The arrest and all. As you can imagine, I'm very upset. This is not a particularly good time."

"There's never going to be a good time, Anna. Let's get it over with, shall we?"

The practiced smile flickered and faltered before it came back again full-strength, looking strangely pathetic in the orange-yellow glow of the arc lights. Zarafonitos was good, all right — but she wasn't that good.

"Well," she said. "I suppose so. Did you want to come up?"

"I think that would be a good idea."

We went into the vestibule of the

building and she opened the inner door with her key. We went down a long corridor, uncarpeted but covered with expensive-looking tile, and got into the elevator. It was one of those elevators that was too small to avoid invading anyone's personal space, and we rode up to the fifth floor in uncomfortable proximity, both staring fixedly at the floor indicator over the door.

Her apartment was 5G, at the end of the corridor. Inside, the living room was expensively and coldly furnished with sleek modern furniture — blonde Scandinavian woods, white and black leather, lots of glass and crystal. The carpet was white, the same glaring white as the walls. A large picture window afforded a stunning view of the stadium, lighted up even though it was another four months until football season. Stunning, that is, if you consider a football stadium scenic.

Zarafonitos took off her long white duster, revealing a wide-pocketed black minidress that showed almost all of her long, slim legs. She didn't hang the coat up anywhere, but tossed it languidly over the chair that matched a small writing table against the wall. "Would you like a drink, Milan?" she said.

"No, thanks."

"Do you mind if I have one?"

"It's your house."

She blinked once. "Sit down, then, I'll just be a minute," she said, and disappeared into what must have been the kitchen. I didn't sit, however, but wandered over to the window and looked out at the brand-new stadium, opened in 1999 on the site of the old Municipal Stadium. Personally, I'd preferred the old one, with all its crumbling facades and inadequate bathrooms and some seats directly behind a pillar. But then I'd preferred the old Browns, too, the Jim Brown–Lou Groza–Frank Ryan Browns of my childhood and the latter-day Bernie Kosar–Clay Matthews–Ozzie Newsome Browns.

But that was in another lifetime. Back when Ellen Carnine was still alive and I had never seen a snuff film.

When Zarafonitos reappeared, quite a bit more than a minute later, she was carrying a tall, cloudy, colorless drink I imagined was vodka and lime juice. She took quite a healthy bite out of it. "Whew!" she said, exhaling noisily. "I needed that. It's been a difficult day, as you can imagine. I mean, the man I've been dating for the past seven months has been arrested for murder. My God!" She seemed to quiver all over, and took another deep slug of the vodka.

"It must have been very upsetting to you."

She rolled her green eyes back in her head and consulted the ceiling. "You have no idea." She collapsed gracefully onto the white leather sofa and gave me the scenic tour as she crossed her legs. "So, what brings you here, Milan?"

"I wanted to talk about computers, Anna. I understand you're something of an expert at it."

She inclined her head and batted her eyelashes at me. "I guess you might say that. It's what I do for a living, after all."

"Just like Ellen Carnine did."

"In a way, yes." She pushed her luxuriant hair back over her ears in what I had come to think of as her signature gesture. "I freelance, of course, and she worked for a company. And she was a lot more — well, artistic, I guess you might say. I'm more of a nuts-and-bolts kind of gal." Even she couldn't keep a straight face at that one.

"Enough nuts and bolts to crack the Wheetek company's passwords?"

The eyes went from emerald green to the

cold, murky color of Lake Erie on a cloudy spring day, and she tossed her head arrogantly. "I'm not exactly sure what you're getting at."

"Sure you are," I said. "Your boyfriend Red was a salesman. The money guy. He didn't know the first thing about computers or the Internet, and that's why he didn't have the passwords to Wheetek's Web sites. But you're an Internet maven, Anna. It wouldn't surprise me at all if you had the same software somebody loaned me — which can decipher passwords and crack codes."

Her mouth was turned down at the corners now, angry and contemptuous. "And your point is?"

"That it was you who helped him get into the TOPSTOXXX Web site, and you who set up the link for the snuff films."

She raised one perfectly sculpted eyebrow. "You think so, do you?"

"I know so. And the other night you went over to John Vargas's apartment, probably to warn him that I was getting close and that he should lay low for a while until the heat was off. Because the whole snuff site wasn't Red's idea after all. It was yours. Red had the means and the company, you had the inspiration and the expertise."

She simply nodded, admitting nothing but not denying, either. She didn't seem very upset about my accusations, but by now her voluptuous lips had almost disappeared into a tight, grim slash.

"You're right about one thing, Anna," I continued. "Your work isn't nearly as artistic as Ellen Carnine's was. But then I suppose that to a twisted pervert who can only get off by watching a young woman get raped and murdered on film, style and art aren't really that important."

"I suppose you have proof of all this?"

"No, but it won't be that difficult to get it. Not for me, not for the police, and certainly not for the FBI."

"I see," she said. She took another sip of her drink, more delicate and ladylike this time, and set it on the glass-topped table next to the sofa. Her calm was more frightening than if she'd started screaming. "So what's the next step here? Am I supposed to put my hands up?"

"I think the best idea would be for you to come with me and talk to Lieutenant McHargue at police headquarters," I said. "At the moment, you're looking at accessory to murder. But I think that if you cooperate with her and roll over on

Munch, you'll probably be able to plea-bargain that down to something else that would only carry a few years inside."

"A few years inside?" she said. She uncrossed her legs and sat casually, her knees too far apart for the minidress she wore. "And suppose I say no, that I won't come with you to talk to this lieutenant. What then?"

"It'll just go harder on you. The feds probably won't try to nail you for Ellen's death, just for the Web site. So it's not murder one. You're lucky."

"Lucky's my middle name," she told me. "It always has been."

"The police are aware of your part in this already, Anna."

She laughed. She actually laughed. Grace under pressure? Or had she simply lost her senses. "Milan, you're a very silly man. Of course the police aren't 'aware.' If they were, they'd be here instead of you."

"Come with me anyway. It's best."

She shook her head. "Not best. Let me suggest something better. You're smart and you're tough. Come with me. We can work together on this. It's made me rich. You can get rich too, Milan. Eventually richer than you'd ever imagined." Her knees parted even more so I could see up her skirt to the white flesh above the tops of her thigh-high dark stockings and the black panties she was wearing. "And I'd make you happy in other ways, too. Red's out of the picture, now. I'm available. How does that sound, baby? A couple of million bucks and me, too."

I took a deep breath. "I'd rather stay celibate the rest of my life, Anna."

She didn't even seem disappointed. I don't think she'd really expected it to work, anyway. "Oh, well," she said. "That won't be so bad, actually. Because the rest of your life just got much, much shorter." Casually, without any urgency whatsoever, she reached into the side pocket of her dress and extracted a small black gun. She raised it, pointed at the widest part of my body.

"Were you carrying that around with you all evening?" I said. "Or did you get it when you went into the kitchen?"

"The kitchen," she said. "I keep it in a cupboard out there. Just in case."

"So you're going to shoot me right here?"

"Something like that."

"The blood will ruin your pretty white carpet."

"That's all right," she said. "I'm

insured." She levered herself up out of the deep sofa cushions, but the gun never wavered. It was a snub-nosed .22 revolver that could have fit into an evening purse — the stereotypical "lady's gun."

"And how are you going to explain a dead body in your living room?"

"That part's easy," she said. "As soon as you're dead I'm going to unzip your fly and then rip the buttons off the front of my dress and tear my panties. After that, I'm going to scream the walls down, and when the police come, I'll tell them you were going to rape me."

"You have it all figured out."

"I didn't have it figured out until a few minutes ago. But I improvise well — it's one of my strong points."

"Figure it out to the end, then, Anna. If you shoot me from across the room, you'll have a hell of a time convincing anyone I was trying to rip your clothes off when you did it. There need to be powder burns. You'll have to get close."

"I'll get close." She cocked the pistol with her thumb and started moving toward me. "And because of your stupidity, or your stubbornness, or some convoluted sense of honor, it's as close as you're ever going to get to me. Bad judgment on your part, Milan. You could have had me, and instead you're going to die. You poor, sad, *sorry* son of a bitch."

Maybe she wasn't as cool and in control as she was letting on. Or maybe it was just that people shouldn't go around waving guns at other people unless they're comfortable enough with them to do it right. In any case, when she reached out and tried to stick the gun into my belly, it was pretty easy for me to slap it right out of her grasp; it bounced slightly on the thick white carpet. Then I brought my arm up quick and hard and backhanded her right across the face. The impact sent her flying backwards, tottering off her high heels and finally landing hard on her back, the breath momentarily knocked out of her, her legs sprawled and blood welling from her mouth.

I bent over and snatched up the gun like Omar Viszquel scooping up an easy ground ball to shortstop. She raised up onto one elbow and shook her head groggily as she tried to focus her eyes at me. They were wide with pain and shock.

And fear.

I leveled the gun at her. "Pull your dress down, Anna," I said.